Dr Tafili L P Utumapu
8 Chelburn Crescent
Mangere Auckland 1701
NZ (09) 2756257

Xmas 2003 gift from Tim.

Forever in Paradise

Forever in Paradise

APELU TIELU

PANDANUS BOOKS
Research School of Pacific and Asian Studies
THE AUSTRALIAN NATIONAL UNIVERSITY

Cover: *The White Frangipani*, by Ernesto Coter

© Apelu Tielu 2003

This book is copyright in all countries subscribing to the Berne convention. Apart from any fair dealing for the purpose of private study, research, criticism or review, as permitted under the *Copyright Act*, no part may be reproduced by any process without written permission.

Typeset in Weiss 11pt on 13.5pt and printed by Pirion, Canberra

National Library of Australia Cataloguing-in-Publication entry

Tielu, Apelu, 1954–
    Forever in paradise.
       ISBN 1 74076 036 0
       1. Samoa — Fiction. I. Title.

A823.4

Editorial inquiries please contact Pandanus Books on 02 6125 3422

www.pandanusbooks.com.au

Published by Pandanus Books, Research School of Pacific and Asian Studies, The Australian National University, Canberra ACT 0200 Australia

Pandanus Books are distributed by UNIREPS, University of New South Wales, Sydney NSW 2052 Telephone 02 9664 0999 Fax 02 9664 5420

Editor: Julie Stokes

Production: Ian Templeman, Duncan Beard, Emily Brissenden

*I dedicate this book to my wife, Grace,
who has been my number one critic and supporter,
and to my parents, Fauo'o and Sera Tielu.*

Acknowledgements

I owe a great debt of gratitude to my former English teacher, Mrs Dorothy Thorpe, whose positive assessment of, and suggestions for improvement in, the first and subsequent drafts maintained the excitement to continue with this project. I am also grateful to my friends Valerie Carter, Jane Spray and William Tibens for their comments on subsequent drafts. My good friend *Afioga* Tanuvasa Isitolo Lemisio was my consultant on certain aspects of Samoan culture, and I would like to thank him for sharing his knowledge with me. The beautiful cover was the work of another former teacher and friend, Mr Ernesto Coter, and I would also like to thank him and his good wife, Maria, for their support and friendship over the years. My thanks to Ian Templeman and the staff of Pandanus Books for their support, and to Julie Stokes for her excellent editing of the manuscript. My brother Fatu inspired many who have been fortunate enough to know him, and he was the inspiration in writing this book; thank you, bro. Finally, I would like to thank my wife, Grace, and daughters, Amabel Sera and Amy Jane, for their support throughout this project; my wife's advice on all the drafts was invaluable in getting this book to its final form.

Apelu Tielu
Canberra

One

Solomona Tuisamoa closed the book he was reading and glanced through the window at the calm waters of the Pacific Ocean below, as his plane began its descent. Ahead lay the beautiful city of Auckland with its yacht-filled harbour and island-dotted gulf beyond. The brilliant mid-morning sunlight accentuated the city's lush green parklands. He had seen this breathtaking view many times before, but each time he felt the same thrill.

He removed his glasses and quickly wiped them, as the plane circled, preparing to land. Putting his glasses back on, he took a closer look out the window. In one direction, he could make out the pine trees, and huge ficus and *Pohutukawa* trees of the Auckland University campus. The university had been the centre of his life in the past four years of his undergraduate studies. He searched for the hostel that had been his home during that time. Always a place of fun and adventure, it would once more be his home while he completed his doctorate in economics. He smiled as he thought about some of the funny characters he had met at the hostel, and the practical jokes that were part and parcel of campus life.

It would be different this time, as he was returning to be the Hostel Master. He felt excited about his new role, but a little anxious about looking after exuberant, sometimes too exuberant, undergraduates. His thoughts drifted to family and friends back in Samoa, and he began to feel homesick. He started to doubt the value of spending another two, or perhaps more, years completing a degree that he might never use. He used to think of it as a final frontier to be conquered in his pursuit of knowledge, but he now wondered if there should be some other purpose in pursuing an education besides meeting a challenge and satisfying one's curiosity.

He looked at Manukau Harbour below, its murky waters dancing in the light morning breeze. A small boat steaming into the harbour left a trail of white foam in its wake. He smiled to himself. He swore he could see a school of fat flounder, near the muddy bottom of the harbour.

'I could eat a couple right now,' he thought to himself, even though he had not long finished the in-flight breakfast.

As the plane descended, he saw the green parklands and brownish sea rising quickly towards the aircraft. Then, a sudden thud and shrieking engines announced the plane's arrival at Auckland airport.

Silently, Solomona said a short prayer to thank God for the safe flight and landing. Grabbing his satchel from the overhead compartment, he joined the steady stream of disembarking passengers. At the door he made a point of thanking the flight's crew — he knew many people in the state-run Polynesian Airlines.

With the usual quarantine, immigration and customs checks completed, Solomona picked up his bag and a box of *umu* from the baggage carousel. Outside in the arrivals lounge, a large crowd awaited the arrival of relatives from Samoa and Tonga. He spotted his cousin Faye Filemu, waving from the back of the noisy crowd. To his surprise, standing beside her was his girlfriend, Helen Ruth Jones, grinning broadly.

Solomona and Helen had known each other for over three years. They met towards the end of Solomona's first year studying undergraduate economics and mathematics. Helen and Faye were then students together at Auckland Girls Grammar School. At the end of the year, they were due to sit for the New Zealand School Certificate examinations, and both had been worried about the mathematics examination.

During the September school holidays, Faye asked Solomona, who had gained a near-perfect result in mathematics in the same exam, and similar results in both pure and applied mathematics in subsequent bursary examinations, whether he would help her and her friend. Always willing to assist any family members, Solomona happily agreed to tutor Faye and Helen during the school break.

Their tutorials were held in Solomona's neat, spacious room at the hostel. From its elevated position in the campus grounds, the hostel overlooked the parklike grounds of Auckland Domain and the bustling harbour beyond, with stately Rangitoto Island at its mouth. A thick growth of native vegetation and pine trees at the rear and side of the hostel gave it a feeling of rural isolation. It was unusually quiet for a place so close to the heart of a busy city.

The first time Solomona and Helen saw each other, there was an instant attraction. Helen was disturbingly beautiful. She was slim and tall, with greenish eyes and beautiful dark eyebrows. Her face was small, and bore a strong likeness to the distinctive features of her mother's Jewish, Greek and Balkan ancestry. Her straight, silky, dark hair, which hung loosely to her waist, shone in the sunlight.

Solomona too was very attractive; his smile and voice were totally captivating. He was very tall, and solidly built, with handsome brown eyes behind gold-rimmed glasses, and his distinctive reddish, wavy hair complemented his perfectly tanned skin.

During that first session, Solomona, despite struggling to exercise discipline and restraint, found it hard to concentrate. He could feel his heart pounding against his chest as if ready to explode. He had never experienced such feelings before. Even though it was a cool spring morning, in no time his T-shirt was soaked with sweat. Helen could not stop grinning. She gazed frequently at Solomona and fiddled with the tip of her pen. She soon learned that, in spite of his charming manner, he had a wicked sense of humour.

The attraction between them grew stronger each day, and quickly developed into love. They increasingly found it impossible to be apart. Despite the hours they spent talking on the telephone, Helen felt the need to see Solomona at least once a day. When classes resumed for the final term, Helen and Faye would spend the afternoons after school studying with him at the university library. Helen confessed she had never studied so seriously, or so well, before.

The girls went on to pass their School Certificate mathematics with excellent grades. Their results amazed their teacher, and thrilled all of them, especially Solomona. Their joy, however, was short-lived. Early the following year, Helen and her family moved to England because of her father's work. Solomona and Helen wrote frequent letters to each other, and it was during that period that they discovered their true feelings for each other.

Now, excited at seeing Helen for the first time in over three years, Solomona's pulse raced. He felt like running, but a characteristic Polynesian shyness restrained him. Instead he quickened his pace.

Greeting Helen and Faye with a big smile, he threw his arms around Helen. They hugged each other for quite a while. 'You didn't say you were coming home, you naughty girl,' he chided, looking intently at her.

'I know,' she replied, smiling broadly. 'I know how much you enjoy surprising people, and I thought we would arrive in time to surprise you before you went home. But our flight was delayed, then we missed our connecting flight...'

'And you didn't even call me in Samoa to let me know you were home?'

'Faye and I felt that we could still spring our surprise when you returned, and I think we did,' she said, winking at Faye.

'Well, you most certainly did,' Solomona said, as he hugged Faye. 'Are you here by yourselves?'

'No,' Faye replied. 'Mum, Dad and the others are over there.' She pointed to the far end of the arrival lounge where her parents were talking with other relatives.

'Well, let's go and meet them.' Solomona started to push the luggage trolley towards where his relatives were waiting. As is customary, he embraced all of them, before returning to Helen's side.

'Did you drive to the airport?' he asked Helen as she took hold of his hand.

'Yes, I did,' she replied, smiling as she played with the palm of his hand.

He smiled back and winked at her. Helen blushed and looked at the ground.

'Well, guys,' he said in Samoan to his aunt Fiasili, uncle Filemu and the many relatives who had come to meet him, even though he was returning after only a three-month holiday in Samoa, 'I have arrived safely, and here is the *umu*. It's the only important thing that I brought with me. Now I'm going over to the hostel, but I'll see you all tonight. Faye, are you going to come with us?'

'No, I will go with Mum and Dad. See you both tonight.'

Solomona grabbed his satchel, hoisted his bag onto his back and started walking towards the car park with Helen holding on to his arm.

'See you tonight, Faye,' Helen called, as she turned and waved to everyone.

'You'd better come to the house tonight, Mona,' Fiasili sang out to Solomona. 'We have something important to discuss.'

Solomona turned to reply to his aunt, 'Yes, I will Aunt Sili,' then continued on towards the car park.

Right at that moment he was not interested in knowing what his aunt wanted to discuss. He did not want to think about anything else. He was too excited at seeing Helen again. It had been three long years since they last saw each other. Helen was not saying much, but was quietly savouring the joy of being close to him again. She studied his face to see if he still looked the same. Smiling affectionately, she leaned her head against his shoulder.

'Oh, I really missed you, Mister Tui,' she whispered, gently squeezing his hand. Solomona's friends often called him Mister Tuisamoa when they wanted to tease him. Helen found shortening it to Mister Tui more convenient and rather endearing.

'I missed you too, HR. I never thought a man's life could be so miserable until you left.'

Helen smiled; she had felt the same despair at being so far away from the man she loved. 'The car is over there,' she said, pointing to a white car several cars away.

'Beautiful, like its owner.' Solomona winked at her.

'Do you like it?'

Then he hesitated. 'Yes, it's beautiful, but it's a… Passat… made by… Volkswagen,' he said haltingly, as if suddenly troubled.

'It's mine. It's ours,' she said excitedly. 'Dad bought it in England as a birthday gift. Here, you drive,' she added as she offered him the keys.

Solomona stood immobile, distracted. He did not take the keys from Helen, nor respond to her invitation. Deep in thought, he looked at the ground, then glanced at people passing by.

'Mona, are you all right?'

'Yes, I'm all right, HR,' he assured her, but still pensive.

'Then why won't you take the keys, or say something? What's the matter?' Helen was totally bewildered.

He hesitated again, as though searching for the right words. 'Helen,' he said finally, 'I'm sorry to disappoint you.'

'What do you mean?'

'I'm sorry, HR,' he replied, trying to smile, 'but I can't ride in or drive a car made by Volkswagen.'

'Why? What's the problem, Mona?'

'Well,' he said, struggling for words, 'I promised myself that I would never knowingly use or own anything made by any company that has exploited, enslaved or killed human beings, either directly or indirectly, at any time in its history.'

'But why Volkswagen?'

'Virtually all German companies during Hitler's time did just that. Volkswagen was among the most notorious of German companies. It was one of Hitler's pet projects. The people who worked for Volkswagen, and other German companies, at that time were virtual slaves. Many were subjected to the most inhumane conditions ever known. Many of them, mostly Jews, and some may have been your relatives, died from the treatment and conditions they were subjected to. I'm sorry, HR, but the small voice inside me will not allow me to renege on that promise.'

'You don't have to apologise for your convictions, Mona,' she assured him as she caressed his back. 'And knowing you, this is certainly a serious matter.'

'I'm sorry, HR,' he said again.

Standing on tiptoes, Helen kissed him on the cheek. 'That's okay, Mister Tui,' she whispered. 'Don't worry about it. But what will we do now?'

'I'll take a taxi and meet you at the hostel.'

Helen did not like the idea. After so long apart, she just wanted to enjoy every possible moment with him. 'I have an idea. We can swap cars with the Filemus, and I'll fetch my car from their house later on. How about that?'

'You're the boss, HR,' Solomona smiled and winked at her.

When Faye and her parents reached the car park Solomona asked his uncle Filemu if they could swap cars.

'What's wrong with Helen's car?' his aunt asked. 'It's nice and much newer than ours.'

Helen gestured that it was something else. Fiasili nodded as Filemu exchanged car keys with Helen.

'Do you still have your car?' Helen asked Solomona, as she directed him to a Ford Falcon parked nearby.

'Oh, it was old and getting costly to run, so I sold it at the end of last year,' he replied. 'It served me well when I was a poor undergraduate student, but I'll need to get some new wheels now.'

'Don't worry about it,' she urged as she slid into the passenger seat. 'I'll exchange the Passat for something else, and you can use it to go to rugby training and to drive us around.'

'Oh, don't do that, HR.'

'Mister Tui, what's the point of me having a car if you can't ride in it? It's important that we are in the same car, you know?'

Solomona glanced at her. He realised that she meant what she said, and smiled, 'As you wish, HR.'

'Great,' she replied as she buckled her seat belt. 'I'll just swap cars with Dad. I'm sure he would like that. He loves the Passat.'

'But how can I use your car when you live on the North Shore?'

'Aha,' she smiled knowingly, 'I have a surprise for you, Mister Tui.'

'What is it?'

'We are going to be neighbours!'

'You've rented a flat in town?'

'Nope. I have enrolled in music to study oboe.'

'And why is that a surprise?'

'I have also moved into the hostel,' she grinned, glancing sideways at him.

'You've got to be kidding, HR.'

'I'm not kidding, Mister Tui. In fact, you might be even more surprised to know that my room is right next to yours.'

Solomona shook his head in disbelief. 'You must be joking, HR.'

'No, Mister Tui. I'm not joking.'

'But how did you manage that?'

'Manage what?'

'I mean, how did you get accepted into the hostel?'

'Well, I will be a student there this year.'

'I know that, but you live on the North Shore, not far from the campus.'

'Oh, I forgot to tell you that Mum and Dad have just bought a new house at Whangaparoa. We haven't moved in yet, but that will be quite some distance from the university.'

'Not quite as far as Samoa… I just have a sneaking suspicion that you must have pulled some strings,' Solomona winked at her.

'No, I went through all the proper channels, Mister Tui. Don't you like me being in the hostel and next door to you?' she pouted.

'Oh, yes I do. It's just that you've taken me completely by surprise. But it's a nice surprise.'

'I thought you'd like it.'

Solomona started the engine and pulled out into the traffic. Helen turned sideways so she could have a good look at his face.

'Well?' he inquired, raising his eyebrows.

'Nothing,' she replied with a smile. 'I'm just enjoying looking at you. It's been so long since I last saw your smiling face.'

'You're making me feel a little nervous, HR.'

'Why should you feel nervous, Mister Tui? Were you a naughty boy while I was away?' she teased.

Solomona hesitated. 'Maybe just a teeny-weeny bit,' he laughed.

'Mister Tuisamoa!' Helen feigned shock as she pinched him playfully.

'We're going to have an accident if you don't stop that, Miss Jones,' he laughed. 'I wonder if there is a law against women harassing men while they're driving?'

'Oh, you're very funny, Mister Tui.' Helen was relieved that nothing had changed in the three years they were away from each other. Solomona was still the same man she felt comfortable with and his sense of humour remained the same. She was anxious that her response to him had not changed, or that he had not become a different person while she was away. However, seeing this carefree man beside her reassured her.

'So you'll be studying oboe, eh?' he asked as the Falcon headed out onto the main road leading into the city.

'Yep, and I'm really looking forward to it.'

'Studying with Doctor Davids?'

'Do you know him?'

'Yes, I do. I've been taking some advanced lessons in piano and organ since you left, and we've been playing together at the university and at the Methodist Church in the city, where we also sing in the church choir.'

'You mean you go to a Methodist Church now?'

'Yes, I do. Why?'

'I thought you were Congregational, Samoan Congregational.'

'I'm a Christian, and it doesn't really matter what the denomination is. So long as its teachings are based on the Bible, and nothing else, I'd feel comfortable with it. And besides, the Methodist Church is only a short walk from the hostel.'

'But weren't you playing the organ for your aunt's Samoan Church?'

'Yes I was, but my brother Albert —'

'Yes, I heard that he's here now.'

'Yes, well, he plays for them now. I still go there on the first Sunday of every month, but on other Sundays I go to the Methodist Church. They have a fantastic pipe organ, a grand piano, a small orchestra and an absolutely divine choir. It provides me with the opportunity to practise on a regular basis, and the Samoan pastor understands that. Anyway, now that you'll be living in the hostel, maybe you can join us in the orchestra and choir. What do you say?'

Solomona burst into a rendition of Cesar Frank's *Panis Angelicus*, which really amused Helen. She always enjoyed listening to his singing, something he had often done spontaneously whenever they were together before. He had a beautiful and powerful tenor voice.

'Your voice sounds even better now, Mister Tui. Perhaps even better than Pavarotti's. Maybe you should consider joining him in the opera.'

Solomona smiled. '*Panis* is one of my favourites. Excellent and powerful melody with beautiful lyrics by one of my favourite philosophers, the Divine Doctor Saint Thomas Aquinas. And Latin must be one of the few languages that God speaks because it's phonetically the same as Samoan,' he laughed. 'My voice has improved as a result of a few voice lessons, but I'll let Mr Pavarotti entertain the world; I'll entertain God and you. That's enough for me... Will you join us? I promise you an experience of a lifetime and the opportunity to practise and perform with some of the best musicians in town, including yours truly,' he laughed again. 'We can also join the Samoan Church on the first Sunday of every month.'

Helen did not answer right away. She turned to face him. 'I'll go wherever you go, Mister Tui. Where you worship, I will worship. Your choir will be my choir, and your orchestra my orchestra.'

'You're starting to sound like Ruth in the Bible... but I'm really pleased that you'll be joining us,' he said. 'But what about your parents? Won't they object to you worshipping in a Protestant church?'

'Mum is a little conservative, but Dad is open-minded. They always let me make my own decisions. Besides, they'll just be pleased that I'm attending church regularly.'

As they reached the top end of the city, Solomona turned left at the street just before the university.

'I thought we were going to the hostel,' said Helen curiously.

Solomona tried to look serious. 'Yes, we are. Well, eventually. I have something more important to do first,' he said, winking at her.

'And what's that?'

'You'll find out very soon, Miss Jones,' he replied, pretending to concentrate on his driving. He turned into upper Queen Street, Auckland's main street, put on the hazard lights, then drove slowly, straddling two lanes heading down the hill towards the harbour, and tooting his horn.

'What are you doing, Mona?' Helen asked, beginning to feel rather uncomfortable.

'Miss Jones,' he replied, trying to sound serious, 'this is Queen Street in downtown Auckland, New Zealand's main street. It's posh, modern and clean. This is where Auckland and New Zealand parade any famous prize they win. Well,' he smiled, gesturing at her, 'there is none better than what I have here, and I am proud to parade her before all. Now, let's see. We have a nice crowd for a Saturday morning, a growing convoy behind us; all we are missing is the tickertape from Queen Street's skyscrapers,' he laughed.

Curious bystanders stopped to watch. Helen was unsure of how to react. She knew Samoan students were renowned for their practical jokes. She herself had experienced it during an end-of-year *fiafia* at the university, which the Samoan Student Association had hosted, not long before she and her family left for England. Near the end of the *fiafia*, some of Solomona's friends invited her onto the dance floor with a promise to teach her the dance they were performing, then quickly left her on stage by herself. Solomona saved her embarrassment by getting up to dance with her. Despite that experience, she always had the impression that Solomona was more reserved than his friends.

The big Ford continued to edge down Queen Street. Managing a smile now and then, Helen just sat and looked at the people who waved back at them, and at Solomona who was grinning and continually pointing at her. At the bottom of Queen Street, they turned at the traffic lights, and headed up the hill to the campus. Stopping the car in front of the Old Arts Building, Solomona ran around to open the passenger door. He lifted Helen in his arms and carried her into the park opposite.

'What are you doing, Mona?' she asked, still bewildered by his behaviour.

Solomona did not respond. He ran, with Helen in his arms, to a bench near a spectacular flower-clock in Albert Park. He sat her down as he tried to catch his breath.

'There you are, Miss Jones,' he said, panting, as he slumped beside her. 'Remember this place?'

'Mona, what's going on? You're behaving a bit weirdly.'

'Ah, weird, HR, is merely your perception,' he replied, still struggling to catch his breath. 'You should know Samoan humour by now. But you haven't answered my question.'

Moving closer to him, Helen held his hand as she rested her head on his shoulder.

'Of course, I remember this place,' she smiled as she gently ran her fingers over his hand. 'The first day we met, we dropped off Faye after our tutorial, then we drove back here, sat on this very bench and chatted for hours. It's where it all began, isn't it?' she whispered as she leant over and kissed him.

Solomona nodded. A light breeze was blowing across the park causing the dangling branches of the enormous ficus trees to sway as if nodding in agreement. The lawns and garden beds were in immaculate condition. Wandering couples savoured the sweet smell of fresh-cut grass and the fragrance of beautiful flowers still glistening with dew. The flower-clock struck 12 noon as the sound of the clock-bell from the tower of the Old Arts Building echoed through the park. Helen turned and leaned back slightly so she could have a good look at Solomona's face. She smiled as she gently stroked his temple with her free hand. She felt comfortable and relaxed. She snuggled in closer as she tightened her grasp of his hand.

'You know,' he said, 'whenever I wanted to feel close to you, I would come here, sit on this bench, close my eyes, and I would be with you. That was always special.'

'No wonder I often found myself missing you so much,' she said, looking fondly at him.

'Must have been ESP,' he smiled, winking at her. 'Come on, you must be hungry.'

He pulled her to her feet. They hugged each other for a long time, then walked, holding hands, to the car. Elated to be together again, they drove on to the university hostel.

Two

The hostel was fairly quiet when they arrived. The only noise was the distant echo of vehicles passing along the motorway at the bottom of the valley. Solomona parked the car, then led Helen to the cafeteria. After a quick lunch, they collected his bags from the car.

As the new Hostel Master, Solomona would be staying in the Master's room. He had moved his things in a few months back, before he left for Samoa. Fastidiously neat and clean, his room, at the northern end of the hostel, was almost three times the size of normal student rooms. It had a telephone and computer and all the supplies he would need for his new administrative role. The walls were bare except for three laminated poems — *Footprints*, *Don't Quit* and *The Impossible Dream* — and a copy of Reinhold Niebuhr's Serenity Prayer above the bed.

Three large bookshelves were crammed full of his books — Solomona's interests ranged widely. Mathematics, computing and economics books filled one bookshelf. Another contained books on literature, science, philosophy, politics, anthropology, sociology, history and religion. The third held works on art and music, and many books and videos on sport, especially rugby. Solomona played for the University Rugby Club.

His library was an impressive collection of works by some of the great scholars and famous authors of western civilisation. Whether it was a book by Plato, Newton, Nostradamus, Shakespeare, Weber or Darwin, chances are that Solomona had it. He had received gifts of money from relatives, an important part of Samoan culture when family members visit each other. He had saved all of the money and, together with his stipend, invested it in books and knowledge rather than banking it, where he knew that inflation would eat it away.

A large desk near the window looked out over the Auckland Domain, the harbour and Rangitoto Island. The desktop was virtually bare except for a study lamp and Bible on one corner, and photographs of Helen and his family on the other side. His computer was set up next to the desk. A hi-fi sound system and a large collection of CDs and cassettes on shelves, near the foot of the bed, reflected his love of music.

Helen made herself comfortable on the bed as Solomona opened the curtains and turned on the sound system. Flicking through his CDs, he found a guitar concerto by John Williams, some classical pieces by Mozart and Vivaldi's *Four Seasons*. He put them all on to play and proceeded to unpack and put things away.

Helen lay on the bed and thought about the time they had spent together before she left for England. Memories came rushing back: the same music, the same emotions. She recalled the long philosophical discussions she had had with him, and how these had changed her perspective on life, as well as often prompting her to question her values. Her focus had definitely shifted from material things to people and, to some extent, more spiritual matters. Their close rapport had helped to convince her that she wanted to spend the rest of her life with him. She was feeling relaxed and happy, and the music was starting to make her feel sleepy.

'Close the curtains and lie down beside me, Mister Tui,' she said, yawning.

Solomona found a CD of Leo Sayer with the song *When I Need You*, and put it on. He changed to a *lavalava* and sleeveless undershirt, then sat down beside her, resting his back against the bedhead.

'I want the curtains closed please, Mona,' she urged, moving closer to him.

'Do you know that the universe would be totally dark if it were not for stars like the sun?' he suggested as he made himself comfortable.

'What do you mean?'

'I mean, let's appreciate the light and energy that the sun provides while it's there.'

'You are a very stubborn man, Mister Tui,' she pouted, knowing she would not win the argument.

Listening to the music, Solomona realised how lonely he had been without her. 'At night before I went to sleep,' he whispered as he stroked her long hair, 'I would play this song, and I always felt closer to you. Anyway, I haven't asked you anything about England yet. How were the English men?'

'The English men? They were stuffy and boring. I can assure you that I'm still a disciple of Mother Mary,' she smiled as she raised her head to look at him. 'You may satisfy yourself of the truth of that, if you wish,' she continued, lowering her voice.

'Oh, I trust you, HR. You know this morning before I left Samoa,' he added, laughing, 'I prayed to God, as I do almost every day, not to lead me into temptation.'

'I'm sure God wouldn't mind a teeny-weeny sin,' she teased as she pinched his side.

'Whatever did those English men do to you, HR?' he asked, still playing with her hair. 'You seem different.'

'The English men? I told you they were uninteresting. I'm just happy to be with you again, that's all.' She toyed with the hair on his chest. 'I was just trying to give you back some of your own brand of humour. I know you're a tough nut to crack.'

'Oh,' he smiled, 'you don't realise how hard it is to resist temptation whenever I'm with you... especially now after not seeing you for so long. It's a good thing the devil doesn't live in the pockets of my *lavalava!*' He laughed loudly.

Helen slid up until she could look directly into his eyes.

'Well, Mona, we made a commitment to each other before I left,' she gently ran her fingers over his lips, 'and my love for you grew so strong while I was in England that it wasn't possible for any man to get close to me... Mind you, some did try, but without luck, because a handsome and charming Samoan man had won my heart,' she added as she kissed his lips.

Solomona blushed. He smiled shyly as he brushed her cheek with the back of his hand.

'Same here, HR. It felt like my world turned upside down after you left.'

'Mona,' she kissed him again, 'you may not realise it, but the qualities I really love and respect about you are your discipline and your principles.'

Forever in Paradise

'Really?' He sounded surprised.

'Absolutely,' she said emphatically, looking straight into his eyes. 'I read somewhere that Samoan men are free lovers, and it appears that most men just want to bed a girl, but you are different; you don't fit the stereotype.'

Solomona smiled. 'Ah, you've read too much of Miss Mead's nonsense. Samoan men are like men anywhere; we are human with the same appetites as anyone else. It's very hard to resist normal urges, but if your focus is God, and you have strong values and convictions, then it's not too hard to stay on track, and, in the end, it's well worth it.'

'You've told me that before,' she said quietly.

'Well, yes, and I have also told you many times before that true love does not equal sex. As Plato suggested, it is possible for a man and a woman to love each other without sex. It's my belief that relationships based on sex, or primarily on sex, do not last because there is such a thing as diminishing marginal returns.'

'Ah, that must be the economics of sex,' she laughed, stroking his temple.

'Come on, be serious. You need other things, especially the more important and lasting ones. If you have only sex, or mainly sex, very soon the additional level of satisfaction from sex diminishes to zero, or even goes into the negative.'

'A brilliant analysis, Mister Tui... Go on.'

He smiled, 'Sex to me is like coffee and biscuits in a five-course meal; it comes last. See, we have been enjoying a good relationship for over three years without sex, just through the intercourse of our minds and hearts, where even distance was irrelevant. And as I've said before, sex should occur only within the context of marriage because, as Christians, that's what we believe is right.'

'That must be the Tuisamoa philosophy of male–female relationships.'

'Well, one cannot have sex all the time. In fact, according to some surveys, twice a week is all the average couple can handle,' he said, grinning broadly.

'That's just like you, giving a statistical analysis of sex,' she teased, lightly kissing his cheek.

'But it's true,' he insisted, 'and if that is so, then what do people do with the rest of their time, let alone their lives? No wonder divorce is at alarming rates. See, we've been enjoying just talking since this morning, and we're still having a good time, I hope — without the trimmings.'

'Oh, Mister Tui, I'm really enjoying being with you. I've missed talking with you so much. But you know what?' she asked with a suggestive smile.

'What?'

'I think I'd like some coffee and biscuits right now,' she laughed.

'Oh, I see,' he said, slowly pushing her away. He sat up and slid to the edge of the bed, removed his shirt and tossed it onto the floor. He sat with his back to her for a moment. Helen turned on her side and watched with a broad smile, wondering what was going through his mind. 'Well,' he said finally, as he turned to look at her with a wry grin, 'I'll change first, then we'll go to the cafeteria.'

Helen burst out laughing. 'Very funny, Mister Tui.'

Solomona retrieved his shirt from the floor, put it back on, and sat down again beside her. They continued talking until late in the day. As the light started to fade, he remembered his aunt's urging that morning at the airport that he visit them tonight for a family discussion.

'I wonder what Aunt Sili wants to talk about,' he mused. 'Do you have any idea?' he asked, as he stood up to change.

Helen hesitated. She said she thought she knew, but she could be wrong. Solomona insisted that she tell him what she knew.

'It's probably about your sister, Ao.'

'Ao?' He recalled that he hadn't seen his sister Fetuao earlier. 'That's right, she wasn't at the airport. What about Ao?'

'Mona, don't get upset, but—'

'But what?' he interrupted, beginning to feel apprehensive.

'She... she's pregnant,' she replied moving closer to console him.

'Pregnant?' he exploded. 'Damn it, I'll kill that Alegi!' Alegi, known by some of his friends as Alan, had been his sister's boyfriend ever since she arrived in Auckland.

'Mona, take it easy,' Helen said, gently rubbing his back.

He brushed past her, sat down on the edge of the bed and covered his face with his hands. Helen noticed his face was turning red. She sat down on the bed beside him, put her arm around his shoulders, and stroked him gently. As he raised his head, Helen noticed tears in his eyes.

'Oh, my sister...' he whispered softly. 'I have failed in my duty.'

'Mona, you can't be responsible for everybody's life —' she said trying to comfort him, but he cut her off.

'Helen,' he said sharply as he turned and held her at arm's length, looking straight into her eyes, 'please, you don't understand. I'm not responsible for everyone's life, but my sister... sh... she *is* my responsibility,' he continued, struggling to overcome his anger and disbelief.

'I'm sorry I upset you, Mona.'

'Oh, HR. I'm sorry too. Come here,' he pulled her toward him. 'I'm sorry. I'm just glad you're with me. I would have gone crazy, perhaps done something stupid, if you hadn't been here.'

'I'm glad too,' she said, hugging him.

'Oh, you don't realise how important this is to me, HR,' he confessed, speaking more calmly. 'You see, in Samoan culture, the brother–sister relationship, which extends to cousins, is governed by what is known as the *feagaiga*. This is an unwritten covenant between brothers and sisters. A sister has a sacred status in the Samoan family, which requires a brother to protect her from anything that may harm or disgrace her. A brother cannot raise his hand against his sister, or any other female, regardless of the situation. The sister's part is to do everything in her power not to disgrace herself, her brother and, of course, her family. The most disgraceful thing that can happen to a Samoan girl is getting pregnant out of wedlock. This guy, Alegi, whom I know very well from university, would have been a goner if it were the old days. My family will feel especially disgraced by this, and I think my aunt could be more worried about that than about my sister's welfare.'

'Your culture is so fascinating, Mona. Anyway, you should also know that your sister is in hospital.'

'Why? What happened?'

'Apparently she has been quite sick. She couldn't keep any food down, she was throwing up all the time and had to be put on a drip. She was really dehydrated and lost a lot of weight. Whenever she stood up, she felt dizzy. And she was starting to get contractions, so the doctors decided to admit her to monitor her condition. Apparently the doctor treating her has recommended that the pregnancy be terminated.'

'I see,' Solomona said thoughtfully. 'I think I should go and see Ao before we go to Aunt Sili's.'

Three

Auckland General Hospital was less than five minutes away by car from the hostel. At the reception desk, Solomona and Helen asked where they would find Fetuao. As they made their way along a corridor, they met up with Felix Fa'aluma, a young Samoan doctor who was also on a government scholarship. He had just completed his medical studies at Auckland after transferring from Otago University for the final three years of his program, and was now undertaking his internship.

A stocky man who smiled continually, Dr Fa'aluma was friendly with everyone. He had darker skin than Solomona, and he loved telling people that he didn't mind being dark since God had already given him the brightest brain. He was one of Solomona's closest friends, their friendship going back to their time at boarding school in Samoa.

'Hey, King, welcome back, man,' he greeted, shaking Solomona's hand. Solomona had been called King by his closest friends ever since school days. 'Well, well, who is the unlucky lady?' he chuckled.

'My friend, this is the young lady who broke my heart, then ran away to England to look for her Prince Charming, not realising she had just left him behind,' smiled Solomona.

'I didn't run away, Mona,' Helen protested.

'Of course not,' he replied. 'Anyway, my friend, this is Helen. Helen Jones, meet the future Nobel Laureate in Medicine, my good friend, Doctor Felix Hubert Fa'aluma.'

'It's a real pleasure to meet you, Helen. I thought Helen of Troy was beautiful, but I know now why Mona almost swam to England one day,' he laughed.

'Now, come on, mate,' smiled Solomona. 'Don't exaggerate.'

'Anyway, Helen, just call me Fili, and forget the rest,' he said with his customary broad smile.

'It's a pleasure to finally meet you, Fili,' she replied as she shook hands with him. 'Mona often talked about you in his letters.'

'I hope he said nice things.'

'Oh, yes,' she confided. 'They were always nice things. By the way, thank you for keeping him happy during the last three years.'

'Well, it was very hard to cheer him up, you know? He always seemed to be somewhere far away, and even talked in his sleep, although I'm not sure if it was your name that he mumbled,' he laughed.

'It probably wasn't my name,' she responded, winking at Solomona.

'Oh, it was sure to be this beautiful angel I met in the library,' Solomona teased.

'Ah, Mister Tui, the truth is coming out now.' Helen squeezed his hand.

Solomona really wanted to chat with his friend, but they hadn't yet seen his sister, and they still had to go to his aunt's house in Greylynn, about ten minutes away. Concerned with the time and the need to move along, he changed the subject.

'Anyway, Fili,' he said, 'we'll have more time to catch up, but we've come to see my sister. Do you —'

'Ah yes, Ao…' Dr Fa'aluma stroked his chin thoughtfully. 'Actually I just finished talking to her. Her condition is pretty good now. Sorry for what happened to her, my friend.'

'Thanks, Fili, but are you the one looking after her?'

'Doctor Fox is, and I'm assisting him. I'm still learning the ropes, you know.'

'My sister's condition… is it serious?'

'Let's put it this way. It may be serious, it may not be. It all depends on how well she copes with everything. But when you're dealing with someone's life, you don't take any unnecessary risks.'

'But there is a chance of her getting through the pregnancy okay?'

'Well, yes, but I have to say she will need to take great care.'

'Thank you, Fili. It's been weighing heavily on my mind. I'm relieved to hear your prognosis. We should go and see her now. I'll talk to you again soon, maybe at rugby practice next week,' said Solomona as he led Helen along the corridor.

'Nice meeting you, Fili,' called Helen as she turned to wave goodbye.

'A pleasure,' he replied, waving back.

Fetuao was lying in bed, her head leaning against the bedhead, reading a book. She paled when she saw her brother. Solomona smiled as he greeted her. He sat down on the bed while Helen went to find a vase for the flowers they had brought with them.

Fetuao was a beautiful, tall young woman with gorgeous brown eyes and a fairer complexion than Solomona. She had the same distinctive reddish hair as her brother, which she wore long. At the moment, however, her normally beautiful eyes were fixed firmly on her brother. She had lost weight and looked quite frail. Feeling nervous and ashamed, she wondered how Solomona would react to her being pregnant. She knew her brother loved her dearly and they had always been very close. At home in Samoa, he had always given her whatever she wanted. Many a time, he had been her confidant, but now she felt she had let him down. She felt faint. This was the moment she had dreaded, and she did not know what to do, or how to react.

Without saying a word, Solomona leaned over to kiss his sister. Fetuao was so surprised and relieved that she threw her arms around his neck, holding him tight.

'Oh, Mona, please forgive me.'

'Shh,' he whispered. 'We don't want to disturb the other patients. They might think somebody has died if you haven't shocked the life out of them already.'

Fetuao sensed immediately the warmth and love in her brother's manner instead of the anger she was expecting. The tone of his voice comforted her. Feeling less afraid, she let go and wiped away tears with the back of her hand.

'Listen, Ao,' Solomona explained, 'I'm not here to judge you or anything, nor to ask you what happened, because nothing is more incriminating than the lump in your tummy,' he said, trying to look serious.

Helen was also trying hard to look serious. Catching a glimpse of Helen struggling not to smile, Solomona started to laugh. Relieved, Fetuao laughed too. All three burst out laughing. The patients nearby looked on, bemused.

Facing his sister, Solomona became serious. 'No, honestly, Ao, I'm not here to judge you,' he repeated. 'We came to see how you are. By the way, you know Helen, don't you?'

'Yes, I do. We met just after you left for Samoa.'

'We had lunch with Faye one afternoon,' added Helen.

'Good. Are you two friends then?'

'Yeah, we are. Right, Ao?' smiled Helen.

'Yes, we get along well together,' agreed Fetuao.

'That's good; that's very important, you know,' he continued with a smirk.

'You're not angry with me?' Fetuao asked.

'Angry with you?' he replied. 'Oh, no! No way! How can I be angry with my only sister. And why should I be?'

'But I have shamed you, and the family.'

'No, Ao, you have not shamed me, and damn the family. No one talks about shaming the family when Dad fathers the children of other women. No one! Nor with our brother Pati living with his girlfriend without being married. So stop talking about shaming me, or anyone else.'

Fetuao was quite taken aback. Helen realised that something else was bothering Solomona. He told her later that it was the inconsistent way Samoan culture treated people, the double standard, that he found annoying.

'Hey, lower your voices a bit,' urged Helen. 'People are listening.'

'Sorry, I got upset,' he whispered, 'but I want you two to listen carefully. You two, and Mum, are the people who matter most to me. Of course I care very much for Dad and Pati too, as well as the rest of the family. But the three of you are really special.' Fetuao and Helen looked at each other and started to laugh. 'Guys, I'm serious,' he continued. 'You three are really special, but just don't behave like Jesus' disciples and ask me which one is more special,' he joked. 'Honest, guys, you see, a young man's love for his mother is different from his love for his sister, which is different again from his love for the woman in his life. See?' In spite of the seriousness of his words, Solomona laughed too.

'I was really scared that you would be angry with me,' confessed Fetuao, looking a lot brighter, knowing that at least her favourite brother supported her.

'Well, I did get very angry, but not at you. It was just an instinctive, selfish response on my part to a circumstance like this. But I did feel like killing your useless boyfriend,' he said, raising his voice slightly to emphasise the point.

'Oh, he's not useless. Maybe not as smart and good at as many things as you are, but he passed all his exams,' Ao said defensively.

'Ah, so you do love Alegi? I suppose it is a little too late to say that you are still a bit too young to know your own mind,' smiled Solomona.

'Of course, I love him!'

'Mona,' interjected Helen. 'I was only 16, and in Fifth Form at school, when I fell in love with you. Ao is almost 18 and has finished high school.'

'Yes, you're right, HR,' he conceded. 'Anyway, let's talk about your condition, Ao. What did the doctor say?'

'He said it may be unlikely that I will carry the pregnancy to full term.'

'So?'

'He said the baby may have to be aborted, but I'm scared. I don't know what to do, Mona.' Fetuao's eyes filled with tears.

Solomona hugged his sister. 'That's okay. Don't cry,' he comforted. 'We'll work something out.'

'I haven't even seen Alegi since I've been here in hospital. He called me to say he's too scared to come,' she said wiping her eyes.

'See! I told you he is a chicken,' chided Solomona, trying to cheer her up.

'Wouldn't you be scared if you were in his situation?' Helen asked him.

'Me, scared? No way! Solomona the brave is scared of no one! Except God! Anyway,' he added, looking at his sister, 'have you thought carefully about this and have you made any decisions yet?'

'Oh, I don't know, Mona. I'm worried about my studies.'

'Well, forget the studies for now — if you were dead, then obviously you couldn't study anymore. There are no universities down there, you know,' he smiled. 'Let's try and get you through this first, then worry about your studies later on. But you have to make the decision yourself. I can't make it for you.'

'Oh, well. I would really like to keep the baby if possible. I don't want to kill my baby so that I can live. I would regret that for the rest of my life,' she cried, tears running down her cheeks again. Solomona gently stroked his sister's hair, trying to comfort her.

'It's okay, don't cry,' he whispered. Helen took out a handkerchief from her handbag and handed it to Fetuao.

'I understand that's what you want, and so it will be. I just had a chat with Fili, and he feels that if you have the resolve, you should be able to pull through this.'

'I think I can do it, Mona, but I'll need your support.'

'Well, you know me better than anyone else. You know you can count on my support.'

'Yes, Ao, we'll be with you all the way. Don't worry,' added Helen.

'Thanks very much, guys. You've certainly given me peace of mind,' smiled Fetuao, relieved. 'Mona, you'll need to make an appointment to see Doctor Fox as soon as possible,' she added.

'We will, but right now we have to go to Aunt Sili's. We'll see you tomorrow.'

Solomona and Helen hugged and kissed Fetuao goodbye. As they passed the administration office, Solomona made an appointment to see Dr Fox.

Four

It was past 6 pm when Solomona and Helen arrived at Fiasili's house. Helen decided to take her Passat home to see if she could exchange it with her father's car. So while she was away, Solomona took the opportunity to spend time with his relatives and catch up on what had happened while he had been in Samoa.

Helen's parents were watching television when she arrived home.

'Hi, everyone!' she called out from the front door. In the living room she kissed her parents and flopped into an armchair. 'Hey, Dad, can we exchange cars?'

'You look happy, dear,' her mother couldn't help noticing the glow in her daughter's cheeks. 'But what's wrong with your car?'

'There's nothing wrong with my car, Mum,' she replied. 'Mona is back and he doesn't have transport at the moment, but he won't ride in a Volkswagen.'

'Why not?' asked Mrs Jones, rather puzzled.

'Because he said it's a company that enslaved and subjected people to inhuman conditions during Hitler's time.

Apparently they killed a lot of people, many of them were Jews — they could even have included some of your relatives, Mum.'

'Did he really say that?'

'Yes, he did, and if you know Mona, he won't change his mind. He will stick to his convictions, no matter what.'

'Hmm, he sounds like a very interesting fellow.'

'I told you he is a fascinating person. He can appear hard to understand at times, but he is really, really nice and funny... and you know how smart and good-looking he is,' she smiled.

'How does he know about all this? I thought he was an economics student.'

'He did an honours science degree, majoring in maths and economics, but he reads very widely, and history, politics and philosophy are his pet subjects.'

'But aren't he and Faye part-German?'

Helen smiled, 'He said he'd counted exactly 25 drops of German blood in his veins, and he's ashamed of each and every one of them, because of the holocaust and what Germany did during the Second World War. He vows his heart and soul are totally Samoan, although he does keep in touch with his German relatives.'

'How interesting... we must invite him over for dinner some time.'

'That would be nice, but it will need to be soon because once varsity and rugby start, it will be difficult for him to find time.'

'What about the second Saturday after lectures start?'

'That sounds fine, Mum.'

'Do you have anything that weekend, darling?' Mrs Jones asked her husband, who was watching television and not paying much attention to the conversation.

'I have no commitments for the whole of March, dear.'

'Good. That settles it.'

'So, is it okay if we exchange cars, Dad?' Helen asked again.

'Yes, sweetheart,' he replied. 'Does that mean the Passat is mine from now on?'

'I guess so, Dad. The Passat is now yours and the Accord is mine.'

'Well, I think that's a fair exchange,' he smiled.

'I thought you might like the idea. Anyway, I've got to go.'

'Are you coming home tonight?' her mother asked.

'No, Mum. I'll sleep at the hostel.'

'Okay,' said Mrs Jones. 'Look after yourself.'

Helen quickly kissed her parents, then left.

She arrived back at the Filemus' place just as they concluded their evening prayers. Solomona's brother Albert and his girlfriend, Andreana Smith, had just arrived too. Faye, her older brother Brandon, and two male cousins, who had recently arrived in Auckland to finish their schooling, were helping to prepare dinner and setting the dinner table.

'Smells nice, Faye,' Helen commented as she removed her shoes near the door.

'We'll see if it also tastes nice,' smiled Faye.

Helen had met everyone except Albert and Andreana. Albert, also known by his Samoan name Alapati (often shortened to Pati), was about to begin his second year of law studies at Auckland University. He looked very much like his older brother but was a little shorter. Like Solomona, he was athletic and an excellent footballer, who also played for the University

Rugby Club. Solomona introduced Helen to Albert and Andreana.

Albert, who had not gone to Samoa for the holidays, wanted to hear all the latest news. 'So how's everything at home, big bro?'

'Well, people are a bit miffed at Samoa not being invited to participate in rugby's first-ever World Cup in a few months time. Yet Fiji and Tonga have both been invited, despite the fact that Samoa is the current Pacific champion. They are particularly disgusted at rumours that it was New Zealand who opposed their inclusion. I can understand their frustration.'

Just then, Faye announced that dinner was ready. Mindful of observing Samoan custom, even though removed from her homeland, Fiasili asked the younger ones to watch television while the adults ate first. Dinner included some of the food Solomona had brought with him from Samoa. The rest of the *umu* had been given away to relatives and friends, with the pastor receiving about half of it.

'You like Samoan food, girls?' Fiasili asked Andreana and Helen as they sat down to eat.

'I'm slowly developing a taste for taro,' smiled Andreana. 'Pati likes his taro, so we try to have it at least once every couple of weeks.'

'Yes, potato has no taste at all — it's good for toothless people,' chuckled Albert.

'I like *palusami*, it's very tasty,' said Helen. 'I like *taro* too, but it can be a bit heavy in my tummy; I always feel sleepy afterwards whenever I eat it.'

'But it will make you strong and your bones as tough as steel,' said Filemu, smiling, as he broke open a whole taro.

'Oh, I'll just stay closer to Mona for my strength,' Helen laughed, nudging Solomona.

'That's good, because there are no potatoes in Samoa,' smiled Fiasili, winking at Helen and Andreana.

After dinner, the older family members retired to the living room for the discussion that had been foreshadowed earlier.

'Well, Mona and Pati,' Fiasili began in a rather serious tone, 'I'm glad you could come tonight. I think you both know why we need to talk. This thing about Ao has been weighing heavily on my mind. I know you three live on your own, but I am a mother, and your father's eldest sister. So, in his absence, I am supposed to be a mother to all of you, not just to my own children. When this happened to Ao, I felt as though I had let my brother down.'

'Man, I could kill that guy Alegi,' interrupted Brandon.

'Don, keep quiet or go into the kitchen and help make the *koko*,' his mother ordered.

Brandon remained in his seat. He knew Faye and his cousins would prepare the *koko* as soon as they finished clearing the dinner plates.

'And the thing is,' continued Fiasili, 'everyone knows about it. And you know what Samoans are like, everyone is gossiping, sniggering at us. Oh, I am so ashamed. I can feel everyone's eyes on me as I walk into church. And you know this is one of the most shameful things a family can suffer. I feel especially sad for you two, because she has disgraced you, too. You are doing well at university and this could affect your studies. Ao is supposed to start university herself next week, but how can she study with a baby? Oh, I don't know. The doctors say she is too weak to carry the child to full term, so they are recommending aborting the child. Now that decision will be up to you, Mona, because you have to sign the papers for the abortion since Ao is still a minor. But if the child is not aborted, then I'd like Ao and Alegi to be married. That way, the shame can be overcome.'

After Fiasili, it was Filemu's turn to speak. As an in-law, he could not make any decision or suggest any solution, but he could offer advice. He spoke mainly in support of what Fiasili had said. Then it was Solomona's turn.

'Thank you Aunt Sili and Uncle Mu,' he began. 'I know Ao's getting pregnant without being married, and while still a student, is weighing heavily on everyone's minds. Perhaps it has also brought shame to the family. I know you are concerned about the family's honour, and that is important to me too. But my main concern now is the welfare of Ao and the child she carries. I'm sorry if I don't share your views, but the child will not be aborted. I am not God, and I have no desire to preside over anyone's death,' he continued, trying to make it sound as though the decision was his and not just what his sister wanted. 'If anyone must die, it must be because of natural causes alone, not because of my signature. May God strike me down if that ever happens.'

'But what if they both die?' queried Fiasili.

'Well, I suppose that should please everyone, shouldn't it?' he replied. 'There will be no more Ao and no illegitimate child to remind us of the shame.'

'You're not serious, Mona?'

'I am deadly serious, Aunt Sili.'

'Your own sister?'

'Yes, my only sister. I love her dearly, but if she dies of natural causes, I have to accept that. I do not know God's purpose in most things, but I always trust His wisdom.'

'But if you have the chance to save one life?'

'I would take it, but not if it means killing another human being,' he replied firmly.

'You can't talk like that to your aunt, Mona,' objected Filemu.

'It's okay, Mu,' said Fiasili, gesturing to Filemu to keep quiet.

'I respect your opinion, Uncle Mu,' said Solomona, 'but it's my sister we are talking about here, and as the eldest in the family, it is my duty to defend her.'

'You're right, man,' murmured Brandon.

Fiasili motioned for Solomona to continue.

'Ao and Alegi shall be married, but only if that is what they want. There will be no marriage simply because we want it. And I warn all of you not to do anything silly; leave Alegi alone. As for Ao's schooling, well, people still go to university even if they are married and have children. There was a 70-year-old man in one of my classes last year. This is New Zealand where anyone who wants to study can, and in their own time.'

'Yeah, Mum,' interrupted Brandon. 'You can even go back and get your degree in "tree felling",' laughed Brandon, using a Samoan slang term for chitchat to refer to his mother's love of gossip.

There was giggling from the kitchen, and even Solomona and Albert had to smile.

'Don, shut up. Go and help Faye with the *koko*,' ordered Fiasili.

Brandon did not move.

'Anyway,' Solomona continued, 'schooling is not a priority right now for Ao. Her health and that of the baby are the most important concerns.'

Albert took his turn to speak after Solomona. Faye, Helen and Andreana were preparing the *koko* and some cakes in the kitchen, with Faye translating what was being said in the next room. Albert sat up straight, leaned forward slightly and clasped his hands in front of him.

'Thank you for the opinions that have been expressed so far,' he said, wringing his hands and looking at the floor. 'I too am very ashamed. I never thought my only sister would do such a thing. I know my opinion will mean nothing in terms of the end result. Mona has spoken, and that is it. But from now on, I consider that I no longer have a sister.'

There was a hush following Albert's announcement. Everyone was shocked at what he had just said. Solomona's face reddened with anger. He looked at the ceiling, trying to calm himself. Helen, realising how upset he must be, came in from the kitchen to see if he was all right. Solomona assured her that he was fine, and she returned to the kitchen. The silence continued. Finally, Fiasili spoke up.

'I'd like to thank all of you for your thoughts,' she said slowly and deliberately, 'but Pati, you cannot say that about your sister. There is a saying that you can choose your friends, but not your family, or something like that. It's your duty as a brother to look after and protect your sister. You know us Samoans, we readily forgive people the bad things they do to us. So —' Fiasili's comments were interrupted by Brandon.

'Ah, Mum's right. First we assassinate them, then we forgive them,' he joked.

Giggling could again be heard from the kitchen.

'Don,' snapped Fiasili, exasperated with her son, 'I told you to keep quiet. You are not even supposed to be here.'

'But I'm as old as Mona,' he objected.

'But Mona has completed a degree and Pati is at university. You are a no-hoper,' his mother countered. 'You can't even be serious when situations call for it!'

'Go and help get the *koko* ready, Don,' ordered Filemu.

Smiling, Brandon got up quietly and went into the kitchen.

'As I said,' continued Fiasili, 'please don't do this to your sister, Pati. Come on, let's have some *koko* before you go. Faye, can you bring in the *koko* please?'

Faye, Helen, Andreana and the boys brought in the hot drinks and cake and handed them around.

'Have you been to the hospital yet, Mona?' asked Fiasili.

'Yes, we actually came here straight from the hospital.'

'How is Ao?'

'Oh, she was looking pretty good by the time we left. I suspect that part of her problem was her fear of our reaction. I reassured her that no one is angry with her.'

'Good, because she didn't look too good when I was there earlier today. When are you going to see her again?'

'On Monday, to consult with Dr Fox.'

'Good. I'll come too.'

When they finished their supper, Solomona, Helen, Albert and Andreana said goodbye and left. Outside, Solomona pulled Albert aside. Andreana and Helen walked ahead and stood chatting together.

'Pati, I know you're hurt, and that's understandable. I was hurt too, but I realised it was just a selfish instinctive reaction on my part. But, man, don't do this to our sister. She needs us now more than ever. She needs your support and the reassurance that you still love her. You should have seen the glow in her eyes when she found out I was not angry with her. So please, don't do this. I know you didn't mean what you said tonight... Please!'

Albert looked nervously at the ground, and did not reply straight away.

'You know, big bro,' he said eventually, 'I was really, really hurt, but what I said in there tonight was stupid... I should never have said it, nor should I even have thought it.'

'I'm really relieved to hear that.'

'I feel really bad about having said it now.'

'Oh, don't worry, Pati,' Solomona assured him. 'We all make mistakes, and say things we later regret. The important thing is to let bygones be bygones, and move on.'

'I'm really sorry, bro.'

'Don't worry, Pati. Look, we are going to the hospital about 10 am on Monday. It would be good if you and Andreana could come, too.'

'We'll be there,' Albert promised.

'Good.'

Solomona and Albert walked over to where the girls were waiting. After saying their goodbyes, they walked to their cars. Helen clung tightly to Solomona's arm.

'Mona, what do you think about us living together like Pati and Andreana?'

Solomona smiled, 'So that's what you two were talking about, eh?'

'One of the things,' she said, squeezing his arm.

Solomona was quiet as they drove back towards the city. 'Mister Tui, I asked you a question,' she reminded him.

'Oh, I'm sorry, HR. I didn't think you really needed a reply.'

'I wouldn't mind one.'

'Well, the answer is simple, HR.' Solomona winked at her. 'We don't have to do what Pati and Andreana do, nor follow what anyone else does. We will do things our own way, the right and proper way. I think the hostel is ideal for us right now. We'll be spending virtually all our waking hours together, and although we'll be sleeping in different rooms, only a brick wall will separate us, not thousands of kilometres. I'm confident we'll have more fun than them.' He glanced towards her waiting for her reaction.

Helen sat quietly, feeling mildly chastised. The streets were fairly empty and quiet as she focused her attention on the city lights.

'I must say that this Honda Accord responds very well,' he said, interrupting her thoughts.

'I quite like it, too. It's mine now,' she responded, allowing him to change the subject.

'Really?'

'Yep. Dad has agreed to a permanent exchange of cars with me.'

'I hope I didn't cause this.'

'Don't worry, Mona. I did it for us. There was no point having a car when you wouldn't ride in it. Besides, Dad really likes the Passat.'

'Well, that's good.'

'By the way, they've invited us to dinner on the second Saturday after lectures start, if that's all right with you.'

'I'm sure that will be okay.'

'I'm glad. Mum is really keen to meet you, especially after I told them why you wouldn't ride in the Passat.'

'I hope she doesn't think I'm some sort of moral crusader.'

'I don't think so. I think she is just intrigued by your stubbornness.'

'It's a matter of principle, Miss Jones, not stubbornness,' he smiled.

'But aren't you incredibly stubborn too?'

'Of course, I'm stubborn, but I'm simply sticking to my principles.'

'That's what I mean.'

Five

It was late when Solomona and Helen reached the hostel. Except for a few students wandering back from a night out in the city, everything was fairly quiet. As they walked down the corridor towards Solomona's room, Helen noticed movement outside his door.

'Looks like there's someone waiting for you, Mr Tui.'

'It's probably some idiot locked out of his room or who's lost his keys at the pub.'

As they approached, the person rose to his feet. Solomona realised it was his sister's boyfriend.

'Oh, no. It's Alegi!' Solomona whispered.

Helen felt uneasy. She didn't really know how Solomona would react, especially after the discussion that had just taken place at the Filemus'.

Alan was not a big man. He was tall, but only slightly built. He was good-looking and had fair skin, with straight, dark shoulder-length hair. Having completed all his secondary education in New Zealand, he was about to begin his second year of undergraduate studies in law.

'Please go easy on him, Mister Tui.'

'Don't worry, HR. I'll just kill him and dump him by the roadside.'

As they came closer, Alan dropped to his knees.

'Alegi, what the hell are you doing here at this time of the night?' Solomona asked.

'Oh, please, Mona,' Alan begged. 'Please, I have come to apologise.'

'Apologise for what?' Solomona pretended to be unaware of what Alan meant. 'Go home and get some sleep.'

He opened the door to his room and led Helen inside, then closed the door behind him.

'Aren't you going to let him in?' Helen asked.

'I told him to go home,' he replied.

'But I don't think he will go home until you hear him out,' she said. Solomona said nothing. He turned on the sound system putting on a Samoan song. Alan knocked and asked again to speak to him.

'Mona, please,' begged Helen. 'Do it for me; do it for your sister. Please, just hear him out.'

Solomona got up slowly, turned down the stereo, and opened the door. Alan was still on his knees in the corridor. 'Alegi, come inside.'

'Thank you, Mona,' said Helen, curling up in an armchair near the bed.

'Okay, Alegi, what do you want?' asked Solomona, pacing the room.

'Please, Mona, I have come to ask for your forgiveness.'

'Forgiveness for what?' Solomona continued to feign ignorance.

'For... for... getting Ao pregnant,' confessed Alan.

'Oh, really?' Solomona pretended to sound surprised. 'You got my sister pregnant, and then... then you have the audacity to come here and ask me to forgive you? You must be a brave man, Alegi. You know what could happen to you, don't you?'

'Yes, I do, but I have come because I love Ao.'

'Ah, so you love her?'

'Yes, I do.'

'And your idea of loving her is to get her pregnant?'

'No, man,' pleaded Alan.

'But you did,' accused Solomona, turning to face him. 'By the way, this is Helen. We have known each other for more than three years, but not once... I repeat, not once, have I touched her. You know why? Because I love and respect her too much. And you... you've only known Ao for one year, and you've already got her pregnant.'

'It was a mistake, Mona.'

'A mistake? You call that a mistake? Man, did it ever occur to you that it could've been a very costly mistake for you?'

'Yes, Mona. I realise that now, and that's why I have come to ask your forgiveness.'

Solomona continued to pace, as though he hadn't heard Alan's plea.

'Please, Mona, I'll gladly marry her.'

Solomona suddenly stopped pacing. His face began to turn red.

'Now, don't make me angry, Alegi,' he said slowly, his voice getting louder. Realising how upset he was, Helen tried to calm him. 'You've made one serious mistake,' he reminded Alan, 'a second one will not be tolerated.'

Alan trembled visibly. He thought he had done the right thing by offering to marry Fetuao, but obviously it had not pleased Solomona. Nervous and unsure of what to expect next, he started to shake. Helen got a blanket and wrapped it around him, but he continued shaking.

'It's all right, Alan,' she assured him. Solomona was standing still, his head bowed slightly. 'Mona was upset, but he's okay now... He calms down very quickly, don't you, Mister Tui?' she said, winking at Solomona.

Alan remained silent so as not to create any further upset. Finally, Solomona broke the silence. 'Look, Alegi, I know you mean well, but you have said some really stupid things. But... I forgive you,' he added grudgingly.

'Oh, thank you, Mona!' Alan sighed with relief.

'But... you shall sin no more,' cautioned Solomona.

'Oh, I've learnt my lesson, Mona. I have been so miserable and so frightened.'

'See,' said Helen. 'I told you Mona gets over his anger quickly. Now it's all over. I'll make some coffee, and get us some biscuits,' she offered as she filled the electric kettle.

'Oh, no thanks —' Alan tried to excuse himself.

'Please, Alegi,' said Solomona firmly, looking straight at him.

'Okay, I'll have some,' he agreed timidly, not wanting to make another error of judgement.

'Good,' said Solomona. 'You won't have many chances to be served coffee and biscuits by such a charming young woman. Make yourself comfortable.'

'Thank you.'

Helen was gone only a couple of minutes before returning from her room with gingernut biscuits, coffee, sugar and milk. She quickly made three cups of coffee, and handed them a cup each with some biscuits. Alan was starting to feel more at ease.

'Okay, Alegi, what are your plans?' asked Solomona.

'Well, with Ao —'

'No, no, no... I mean *your* plans, not you and Ao,' clarified Solomona.

'Mona —' Helen tried to intervene.

'Shh,' he responded, frowning at her.

'Well, I hope to finish my degree, get admitted to the Bar here, then return home and see if I can find a job.'

'No intention of staying here?'

'Well, it all depends on where I can find a job.'

'That's good. Now, do you and Ao have any plans?'

'Well, with things being the way they are, we haven't had much time to talk about our plans.'

'Let's assume that Ao recovers well, with the baby, of course.'

'I hope that we can get married.'

'Do you want to get married?'

'We have talked about it, and now with Ao being pregnant, it's kind of brought everything forward.'

'That's all right if that is what you both want, but you shouldn't consider it if it's only because Ao is pregnant.'

'Oh, yes. We really want to get married.'

'That's good, and it's fine with me, but let's wait and see what happens to Ao. As of now, I suggest that you don't approach any member of our family. They might skin you alive.'

'Thanks. That's why I came to you — I knew it was all up to you.'

'Well, I do have some authority in the family, but only up to a certain level. So what are your plans after you get married?'

'We feel that New Zealand is a good place to bring up children, mainly because it has a better education system. So we'll probably go home to serve Ao's bond, then return here sometime later.'

'Good. Well, it's getting very late,' declared Solomona, checking his watch. 'Whew, it's past 2 am and I've been up for over 24 hours. Now listen, Alegi. You are safe. No one will bother you, but please be careful. We are going to see Ao at 10 am on Monday, where we will discuss whether to abort the child or not. It would be a good idea if you're there too. I suggest that you come with us, so be here about 9.30 am.'

'I'll be here before 9.30,' he promised.

'How did you get here tonight?' asked Solomona.

'Oh, I borrowed my uncle's car.'

'Okay, you'd better go now. We all need to get some sleep.'

Alan shook hands with Solomona and Helen, then left. Solomona closed the door behind him.

'Poor guy,' Helen said as Solomona dropped onto the bed. 'It must have been a living hell for him all this time.'

'Yep, a moment of unsanctioned sexual excitement can land you in hell forever,' he said sarcastically.

'Well, Mister Tui, I'm just glad you were able to offer him some peace, but it seemed like you were enjoying tormenting him at first.'

'I was just playing games with him.'

'But you got quite angry.'

'Just a bit.'

'You seemed to get over it fairly quickly, though.'

'There was no point in allowing the anger to consume me. I knew what he was trying to say and why he wanted to say it. But of course, with you here, it's difficult for anyone to remain angry for long.'

'Oh, I'm really proud of your capacity to forgive, Mister Tui. It must have been difficult to forgive someone in Alan's situation.'

'Forgiveness is a necessary condition for meaningful relationships, and vital for human existence. As a Christian, it was the only option available to me.'

'I know. I'm glad that it's all over with now. Well, Mister Tui, I'm off to bed.'

Helen kissed Solomona good night, then went to her room. It had been a long and involved day for Solomona. He was very tired; too tired to sleep. He dropped onto his bed and tried to relax. Not long afterwards, he heard frantic knocking on his door. Helen was calling out for help.

'Mona, could you please come?'

Solomona jumped to his feet, and flung open the door. 'What is it?'

'There's someone moaning outside, Mona,' she said in a frightened voice. 'Sounds like someone's badly hurt.'

Solomona ran outside, where he found Alan lying in a pool of blood.

'Helen, go and call an ambulance and then get me some towels and sheets,' he instructed.

'What's happened?'

'I don't know. Go on, please hurry,' he urged, concerned that Alan appeared to have lost a lot of blood.

Solomona ran his hands through his hair. 'Will this day never end?' he muttered as he bent down to assist Alan.

In less than ten minutes, an ambulance arrived. The paramedics attended to Alan while Solomona and Helen watched in the misty stillness of the early morning. After a thorough examination of Alan's injury the paramedics staunched the bleeding from Alan's head, cleaned up his face and inserted a drip in his arm. Once bandaged and stabilised, Alan was placed into the back of the ambulance for the short drive to the hospital.

'Are his injuries serious?' inquired Solomona as the paramedics prepared to leave.

'He has a bad cut on his forehead, and he's lost a lot of blood, but I don't think it's too serious,' assured one of the paramedics. 'But we're taking him to the hospital as a precaution. He'll be monitored overnight.'

'Thank you,' said Solomona, as he took Helen's hand and led the way back to their rooms. 'We'd better get some sleep before church.'

'Are you going to call Alan's family?' she asked.

'I don't have their number. Anyway, the police can do that if they need to.'

'I wonder what happened,' she said, curious to know how Alan had been injured.

'I'm sure we'll find out, but it's time now to hit the pillows, Miss Jones. I'm absolutely exhausted. It's been a very long day,' he yawned, as he saw her to her room. 'Let's hope there is no further disturbance tonight! Good night,' he said as he closed Helen's door.

Six

Solomona and Helen drove into the hospital car park just as Albert and Andreana, who had Fiasili with them, arrived.

'You look beautiful, Sili,' Helen commented as she and Solomona joined the others.

'Thank you, Helen,' replied Fiasili straightening her sleeves. 'You've got to look good in places like these.'

They stood and chatted for a while in the sunshine.

'Are we expecting anyone else?' Albert asked Solomona, noticing his brother looking around.

'I don't think so,' Solomona replied slowly. 'Well, Alegi was going to come but —'

'What for?' interrupted Albert.

'Well, he's the father of the child, and he has just as much right to be here as any of us.'

'Did he call you?'

'He was waiting outside my room when we returned from Aunt Sili's the other night. He came to apologise, naturally. I could tell he was genuinely sorry, so we sorted things out.'

'So is he coming?'

'I'm not sure. There was some kind of mishap outside the hostel as he was leaving, and he was brought to the hospital by ambulance.'

'I see.'

'Shall we go inside?' asked Solomona as he started walking towards the foyer.

In the reception area, they met Alan on crutches. His head was still bandaged. Fiasili tried to ignore him. Albert was feeling rather uncomfortable.

'Alegi, you're obviously not in good shape,' said Solomona.

'No, not very good, as you can see,' he replied. 'By the way, thanks for coming to my rescue. I could have died if it were not for you guys.'

'He should have been left to die, the stinking pig!' Fiasili thought to herself.

'What happened, anyway?' inquired Helen. 'Did someone mug you?'

'Oh, it's a bit embarrassing,' replied Alan, smiling weakly.

'Why?'

'Oh, you know, I was so relieved and happy when I left you that I was running and leaping around. But something tripped me, and I just fell and hit my forehead, I think, on the car's bumper bar.'

'Really?'

'Yes. I must have been knocked out for a while because, the next thing I knew, you and Mona and the paramedics were there.'

'Do you feel strong enough to come with us, Alegi?' inquired Solomona. Fiasili was hoping he would say no.

'Yes, I do,' he replied. 'It's not painful anymore.'

'Okay, let's go up then. The doctors must be waiting for us,' Solomona said leading the way to the elevator.

Dr Fox and Dr Fa'aluma were talking to Fetuao when everyone reached her room.

'Oh, poor child,' whispered Fiasili, bending to kiss her on the cheek.

While the women fussed over Ao, the men milled around the door.

'Hey, Legi,' said Dr Fa'aluma, motioning to Alan, 'nice turban you have, man. I didn't know you'd changed your religion. Since when did you become a Sikh?' he laughed.

Alan shrugged, feeling a little embarrassed, while Albert, who had been fairly quiet, joined Solomona and Dr Fa'aluma in loud laughter.

'So, whose workmanship is that?' continued Dr Fa'aluma, still laughing. 'The economist's development model or the law student's sibling defence?'

'He was caught playing peeping-tom by an 80 year old, and she hit him on the head with a broomstick,' laughed Solomona.

Dr Fox was getting a bit impatient with the general hilarity. He was keen to get Solomona to sign the consent forms to have Fetuao's baby aborted, but he could not proceed while Dr Fa'aluma and his patient's brothers were teasing Alan.

Dr Fox cleared his throat. 'Ah, gentlemen,' he prompted, 'we have a serious matter to discuss, and I'd like to proceed once you are ready.'

'Yes, of course,' said Solomona. 'We do, indeed, have some serious matters to discuss.'

'Come on, fellas,' said Dr Fa'aluma, trying to look serious. 'Behave yourselves now.'

'Sorry, doctor,' apologised Albert.

'Yes, doctor, we're sorry,' added Solomona. 'Let's move on to the serious business of the day.'

The two doctors and the two brothers moved outside into the corridor, away from Fetuao and the others.

'Right,' said Dr Fox as he spoke to Solomona and Albert. 'We wanted to talk to both of you because your sister will need to have her pregnancy terminated — we feel she is not well enough to carry it to full term. However, since she is still a minor, and the procedure has to be carried out as soon as possible, one of you will need to sign the consent forms.'

'I see,' said Solomona seriously. 'For your information, Dr Fox, Alan is the father of the child. Does he have any say in this matter?'

'No, he doesn't.'

'But he is the father of the child, while we are only Fetuao's brothers.'

'That is exactly the point, Mr Tuisamoa. The patient is your sister, and the reason why you and your brother are the ones directly involved. We are not dealing with the foetus here.'

'Excuse me, doctor, but can you enlighten me please? Did you say we are not dealing with the child?'

'That's right, Mr Tuisamoa.'

'But doesn't terminating a pregnancy require the killing of the unborn child?'

Helen started to feel nervous hearing Solomona's exchanges with Dr Fox. She excused herself from the ladies and joined the men, standing just behind Solomona. Dr Fox was baffled by the question.

'Naturally, Mr Tuisamoa. It does mean the cessation of the foetus's life.'

'You mean the child's life, Dr Fox?'

'We prefer the term foetus, Mr Tuisamoa.'

'Does it matter what we call it, doctor? It's all semantics, isn't it? Whether we call it a rock or a coconut, it doesn't change one iota the fact that we are dealing with a human life, that obviously you do not seem to have any regard for.'

'We do have regard for human life, Mr Tuisamoa, but we do not consider a foetus a human life, yet.'

Solomona was stunned by Dr Fox's statement. He paused for a moment.

'That's an extraordinary statement, doctor. Being a medical doctor does not qualify you to define when being human begins and ends, as in the case of my sister's unborn child.'

Dr Fox was shocked by Solomona's challenge to his authority. 'In fact,' he continued, 'no one is qualified to define when being human for an unborn child begins. No one! Only God knows! But we have done so for the convenience and selfishness of those who speak loudest, because the unborn child has no voice. Isn't that terrible?' Dr Fox did not reply. 'But you know very well, doctor, that human life begins the moment a human egg is fertilised, and correct me if I'm wrong, by a *human* sperm.'

'That's correct, Mr Tuisamoa.'

'Good. Now, if that fertilised human egg is left to develop, it can only become a human baby. Isn't that correct, doctor?'

'Of course.'

'So you see, doctor, a fertilised human egg, call it a zygote, a foetus, or whatever you like, will always be born a human baby, and that's all that we really need to know to reach the only obvious conclusion that the child in my sister's womb is as human as any of us here.'

'I'm not sure I agree with you there, Mr Tuisamoa.'

'Of course it is, whether you agree or not. It's not a matter of opinion. It doesn't make any sense at all, that today the child is not human, and tomorrow he is. Either he is, or he is not.'

Dr Fox was unsure of how to respond. Alan, listening from a chair next to the bed, clapped quietly and smiled at Fetuao. After a long silence, Dr Fox spoke.

'Thank you for sharing your views with us, Mr Tuisamoa. However, we have a decision to make. Our options are limited to saving one life, and in this case it's the life of your sister.'

'Doctor Fox,' said Solomona, 'what I just shared with you is not a belief, nor an opinion. It's the only possible conclusion one can reach objectively. Can I ask you a question?'

'Of course, you can, Mr Tuisamoa.'

'Is there a chance that my sister could survive the pregnancy without having to abort the child? I want an honest answer, please.'

Dr Fox hesitated. 'Well, I suppose there is always a chance in any case.'

'Dr Fox, I asked you a simple question: is there a chance or is there none?'

Feeling uneasy, Dr Fox started to sweat. 'Yes, there is a chance, but a remote chance,' he replied hesitantly.

'Thank you, doctor. My sister wants to take that chance.'

'But —' Dr Fox began, but Solomona showed no interest in what he had to say. Turning to Albert, who was whispering to Dr Fa'aluma, Dr Fox pleaded, 'Please, Albert, the pregnancy has to be terminated or your sister's life will be at risk.'

'I'm sorry, doctor,' Albert replied, shrugging his shoulders. 'I can't overrule my brother.'

Dr Fox pulled Dr Fa'aluma aside and whispered to him. 'Felix, you've got to help,' he begged.

'What do you want me to do?' asked Dr Fa'aluma.

'You're a good friend of Solomona. I'm sure he'll listen to you.'

'Are you kidding? Solomona listens to no one… people listen to Solomona. That is the order of things, Dr Fox.'

'What is he? A king?'

'Well, we call him King Solomon, and some call him the philosopher, and you have just found out why. But, if you really want to know, he is the eldest son of a Paramount Chief, and you've got to be a Samoan to fully appreciate what that means.'

'I see,' said Dr Fox rather despairingly.

'Yes, Polynesian royals, unlike their European counterparts, tend to be far more intelligent, and the combination of brain and traditional power is almost impossible to overcome.'

Dr Fox decided to try again. He walked over to where Solomona, Helen and Alan were talking and tried to persuade Solomona again. 'Please, Mr Tuisamoa,' he pleaded, 'please be realistic —'

'Dr Fox,' Solomona replied, 'I am not God, nor is my brother. I will not be responsible for anyone's death, young or old, born or not yet born.'

'But you should consider saving at least one life.'

'I would consider saving at least one life, but not if it means killing another.'

'So would you rather they both die?'

'No, I'd rather they both live. That would be ideal. However, if it is God's will that they both die, difficult as that would be, with Ao our only sister, I would have to accept that. Such is life... I don't know what God's purpose is, but I have always learnt to trust His wisdom. You see, Dr Fox, my sister cannot contemplate the thought that her baby has to be killed so she can live. She can't, and she cannot live a life haunted by that knowledge.'

'So you won't sign the consent forms?'

'I'm sorry, Dr Fox, but I am not God,' replied Solomona, spreading his hands wide.

'But that means Fetuao will have to stay in the hospital for the remaining seven months of her pregnancy,' thought Dr Fox, aloud.

'Ah! So that is the problem, eh doctor?' Solomona responded in a slow and purposeful voice.

'What is?'

'It's all about economics, isn't it?'

'Oh, no, it's not,' objected Dr Fox.

'Yes, it is. You just admitted it. It's not about saving lives; it's all about saving the mighty dollar. Well, well, well. Whatever happened to New Zealand's once-proud health system?' he continued, smiling sarcastically.

'It's not about saving money, Mr Tuisamoa. Please believe me.'

'But what you are saying, doctor, points to saving money, and you are even willing to kill my sister's child for it, and, perhaps, gain a promotion by doing so. That's very sad... that's very, very sad, indeed,' he said as he rubbed his chin and looked away. 'I'll say no more about that, Dr Fox, but if it's money that worries you, then we'll pay for my sister's expenses.'

'Oh, no,' objected Dr Fox. 'It's not about money, Mr Tuisamoa.'

'If that's the case, doctor, then I suppose we have concluded the serious business of the day. I'm terribly sorry, but I just can't bring myself to play God. I hope you understand.'

'Yes, I do.'

'Thank you.'

Dr Fox collected his papers and hurried back to his office. Dr Fa'aluma excused himself and followed after him. The others gathered around Fetuao's bed for a chat before they left.

'That was an impressive performance, Mona,' admired Alan.

'Why can't he shut up, the dog!' Fiasili thought to herself.

'All you need is an unexpected visit at midnight and to have to call an ambulance around 3 am to sharpen the mind,' chuckled Solomona. 'By the way, Ao, just in case you don't know yet, the handiwork on Alegi's face was not caused by any of us.'

'I know,' his sister smiled. 'Helen told me.'

'Good. He went a bit crazy early yesterday morning and decided to fight a car that was minding its own business.'

'That was a bit silly,' she replied.

'I did warn you that I wasn't sure whether Alegi was sane or not,' laughed Solomona.

'Come on, Mona, stop picking on Alan,' said Helen.

'Thank you, Helen. I have been the butt of jokes all morning,' complained Alan.

'It appears these guys enjoy making fun of you, Alan,' said Andreana.

'Well, what can I do? That Fili can really tear you apart, and he was really nasty this morning.'

'Oh, Fili is a very funny guy,' said Albert. 'Hey, I didn't know we had plenty of money over here, big bro,' he added rather curiously.

'Yeah,' Fetuao joined in. 'That was news to me too.'

'Oh, that was a bluff,' smiled Solomona. 'Of course, I knew they wouldn't charge Ao for staying in hospital. We are on New Zealand-sponsored scholarships, but if need be, well, Aunt Sili can always rally the clan to donate.'

'And the first person I would call is your father,' chuckled Fiasili.

'Alternatively, we can always sell Alegi,' laughed Albert.

'You guys are picking on Alan again,' said Helen protectively.

'Oh, we're just having some fun, Helen,' said Albert. 'Alegi knows he will get his own back one day.'

'Anyway, I guess it's time for us to go,' declared Solomona. 'Ao, you will just have to be strong and bear with it until the end. We will not make any other plans until Ao comes through this,' he continued, looking at Alan who nodded in agreement. 'No study for you either, sis, this year, but I will keep your mind active until you resume next year, God willing. I will also contact the New Zealand Foreign Affairs Department as well as the Samoan Scholarship Committee.

Forever in Paradise

And I will be the one to inform Mum and Dad, when I know the time is right. There is no need to worry them unnecessarily just yet.'

'Thank you, Mona,' said Fetuao.

'By the way, we are having a barbeque at our flat on Saturday before lectures start. Everyone is welcome,' said Albert as they all got ready to leave, 'and that includes you, Alegi, if you can make it.'

'Yes, please come,' added Andreana.

'Thanks for the invitation,' said Alan. 'I have no plans for Saturday.'

'It's good you could organise something, Pati and Dreana, to kickstart another year,' said Solomona. 'We'll be there, right HR?'

'Yes, we will,' agreed Helen.

'But we must go now,' said Solomona.

'I'll catch up with you guys later,' said Alan.

'You are staying, Legi?' asked Solomona.

'Yes, I'm staying for a while with Ao.'

'Do you have a ride home?' he asked.

'My uncle is picking me up later.'

'Okay then, bye everyone,' said Solomona.

They all said goodbye to each other, leaving Alan and Fetuao to themselves. Alan pushed his chair closer to her bedside.

'I was scared to death the other night,' he admitted. 'I thought Mona was going to kill me.'

'Oh, he's not like that,' Fetuao assured him. 'People are scared of him because he's big and has that fearsome look and voice when he's angry. But when you know him, he's one of the gentlest people you could ever meet.'

'I realise that. Anyway, how are you feeling now?'

'I feel a lot better. Maybe the stress was making my condition worse, but I feel sure I can cope.'

'That's good. I'm here when you need me, and my family has offered its support, too.'

'Thanks. It's nice to hear that. It gives me more strength... That looks like your uncle.'

Alan turned to see his uncle walking towards them.

After saying goodbye to her partner and his uncle, Fetuao sank back, exhausted, into the pillows.

Seven

The sun was setting when Solomona and Helen reached Devonport beach, where Albert and Andreana rented a flat. They parked their car about a block away so that they could enjoy a walk along the beach. The evening air was hot and rather humid.

The beach was still full of people enjoying an evening swim, while seagulls dutifully cleaned up food scraps left behind by beachgoers. Out to sea, container ships passed by, some on their way into Auckland harbour, others to their next port of call. Yachts, speedboats and fishing boats dotted the water. Rangitoto Island looked stunning with the setting sun casting a reddish glow over its luxuriant growth.

'It's a glorious evening, HR,' said Solomona as they strolled along the beach.

'Yes, it is, Mister Tui,' she smiled as she wrapped her arm around his waist.

'You know, this is one of my favourite places,' he said, putting his arm around her shoulder. 'I could sit here all day, watching the boats and the seagulls, and admiring the beauty of Rangitoto.'

'Didn't we stop here the night we celebrated my School Certificate results?'

'It was just a little further down.' As they got closer to the gate at the back entrance to the flat, Solomona stopped and turned to Helen. 'There's something I'd like to tell you before we get to Pati and Andreana's place.'

Helen's face glowed in the light of the setting sun as she gently pushed her hair back.

'What is it, Mister Tui?' she smiled, looking directly into his eyes.

'Well, actually,' he said, smiling, 'there are a couple of things.'

'Tell me what they are,' she urged. Solomona looked out towards Rangitoto Island. He smiled but appeared hesitant.

'Come on, Mister Tui,' she coaxed. 'You're obviously smiling about something, so tell me what it is, please.'

'Okay. The first thing is, I think you look absolutely beautiful tonight.'

'Honestly, Mister Tui?' she smiled as she gently pinched his cheek.

'Honest, HR. Can you see any fluttering of my eyes?'

'Well, thank you for that. You look pretty stunning yourself,' she said smiling broadly.

Solomona laughed softly. 'Thanks. The second thing is, Pati told me that two of our half-sisters and a half-brother will be attending Auckland University this year, and he has invited them along tonight.'

'So?'

'Nothing, but I thought you should know before we get there.'

'Will they be doing undergraduate studies?'

'Yes, they all will. They are the same age as Ao.'

'Hmm, your dad must have been very busy that year.'

Solomona smiled. 'Siring four kids, including three outside the house, in one year? I suppose so,' he said, with a shrug. Grinning broadly, Helen looked up at him.

'What's that smirk for?'

'Nothing!'

'Oh, I know what you're thinking, Miss Jones.'

'Well, you claim to have telepathic power, so tell me what I'm thinking,' she challenged.

'I don't need telepathic power this time, HR. My intuition tells me that you're thinking I have inherited the same potential, right?'

'I guess it's only natural that I should wonder whether the son would follow the father. You have the looks, the body, the brain and personality to charm even the most aloof woman. All you need is the desire,' she continued with a grin.

'Of course, it's only natural to think that way. Mind you, you're not alone. Many are expecting Pati and me to follow in Dad's footsteps. But it's the only aspect of life where Dad has not been a good role model. He has been really great in all other respects. Mind you, many men struggle with the same problem, and in the old days it would have been normal in Samoan society for a man of his standing to have children by different women. But the church has changed that, and though he has struggled, he has been a very good father nevertheless. He was always there to support us in everything we did, even taking time out from Parliament, when he was still a Member, to watch us play sport. I know he sneaked money to my half-siblings, and

I admire that. He has been a great leader, providing stability for the family, village and district, and he has always put the interests of others ahead of his own. But when I was small, the kids at school used to tease me about my dad being a Casanova. So I swore that I would never do what Dad did. When I was at home last month, he told me he was a new person, and he was finally at peace with himself. He certainly looked a different person, and I could see the change in his life.'

'So do you get along well with your half-siblings?'

'I don't see them as half-siblings. They are my brothers and sisters, and I love them as much as I love Pati and Ao. I have six other half-brothers and sisters, but they are older than me, and they are all in Samoa.'

'Your dad was certainly prolific, wasn't he?'

'I suppose you could say that. Come on, let's get going. I don't want them to worry about us.'

Albert and Andreana's flat had a lovely outlook with its large, well-kept back lawn facing Rangitoto Island with access to the beach through a back gate. Albert, Dr Fa'aluma, Alan, Brandon and Owen, Solomona's half-brother, were cooking meat on the barbeque and drinking beer when they arrived. Solomona introduced Helen to Owen. He was tall, but slightly built with the same distinctive reddish hair as Albert and Solomona. The three of them chatted while Brandon ran inside to get some chairs.

'So, Owen,' said Solomona, 'where are Mele and Ula?' inquiring about his half-sisters.

'They're inside, with Andreana, Faye and Sina preparing some salads and nibbles,' he replied.

'Sina? What is she doing here?'

Albert laughed as he turned the meat. 'I think she wants to find out if she still stands a chance.'

Brandon returned with two chairs and a stool. He placed the chairs beside a picnic table and invited Solomona and Helen to sit down. He then went back inside to organise some drinks.

'Sina is a former girlfriend of mine,' Solomona told Helen, 'but we went our separate ways when I left Samoa.'

'Ah, I see,' smiled Helen. 'So maybe Pati is right, eh? But she has no chance, Pati,' she added, reaching out for Solomona's hand and squeezing it. 'Go on, Mona, say she doesn't.'

'Oh, oh, I think you're in trouble, Helen,' chuckled Fili Fa'aluma. 'Sina loves a competition, from what I've heard.'

'She can try, but she has no chance, right, Mona?' Helen insisted.

Solomona smiled as he sipped his drink, 'As Santayana wrote, I remember the past lest I'm condemned to repeat it. I don't live in the past.'

'See what I mean, Fili,' laughed Helen.

Andreana joined them, carrying some bowls of salad. The other women followed, all carrying drinks and food. Solomona and Helen stood up to greet them.

'Helen,' said Solomona, 'I'd like you to meet my naughty sister, Mele, my other naughty sister, Apaula, and this is Sina. Everyone, this is Helen.'

Helen was fascinated at how closely Mele and Apaula resembled Fetuao. Their features, height and mannerisms were so similar, and there was no mistaking the reddish hair. Sina was part-Chinese, part-Samoan and part-German. She was beautiful, slim and quite tall. She had silky, straight black hair worn just below her shoulders.

Solomona slipped away to join the men at the barbeque while Helen took time to get acquainted with Mele, Apaula and Sina. Faye's presence made her feel more at ease.

'Are you at Auckland University, too, Sina?' she asked.

Sina smiled as she sipped her drink.

'No,' she replied, 'I'm doing medicine at Otago. I was home for the holidays and I'm on my way back there. Pati and I were classmates in Samoa, but we haven't seen each other for a while, so I phoned to see if I could drop by on my way. I'll be flying out tomorrow morning. What about you?'

'Oh, my family and I have just returned from England where we spent three years while Dad was working there,' replied Helen. 'I'll be starting varsity this year in Music and English.' She turned to Mele and Apaula. 'I understand you'll both be attending university here too.'

'Yes, we are,' said Apaula. 'Mele will be studying architecture, while I'll be doing medicine.'

'Have you found a place to live yet?'

'We'll be living in the hostel,' replied Mele, 'and I think Owen plans to stay here with Pati.'

'I'm staying in the hostel, too,' Helen smiled. 'Did Mona get you in?'

'No, he didn't,' replied Apaula. 'He didn't even know we were going to stay in the hostel until we checked in this morning. The Foreign Affairs Student Officer arranged everything for us.'

Helen, Faye, Apaula and Mele continued to chat, while Sina wandered over to the barbeque where Andreana was helping the men to finish cooking the meat. Solomona was talking to Dr Fa'aluma when Sina joined them.

'So, Mona,' she smiled, teasingly. 'I see you've got yourself a beautiful white bird.'

'Did I get a white bird this morning, Fili?' asked Solomona, trying to evade the question.

'Did you catch a seagull at the beach?' laughed Dr Fa'aluma.

'Come on, guys,' Sina insisted. 'You know what I mean. Your friend could melt even the toughest of men,' she whispered.

'Oh, you mean Helen?' asked Solomona, trying to look surprised. 'Well, you're right. She certainly melted my heart the first time I met her.'

'I'm glad you are enjoying life here,' said Sina.

'Oh, yes,' he replied. 'We try and enjoy life here. Right, Fili?'

'We certainly do, Sina,' added Dr Fa'aluma. 'That's why I decided to move here. I think King's philosophy of a balanced life based on well-planned priorities works wonderfully. How are things with you guys in the deep south?'

'We also try our best to have some fun,' she said, 'but you know, Fili, it's almost always cold there... So, Mona, you're doing some postgraduate work, I understand.'

'Yes, I'm trying to see if I can carry out a decent research project.'

'Oh, I'm sure that should be a piece of cake for you,' smiled Sina.

'I hope you're right,' he grinned.

'Well, guys,' called Albert, 'I hope you are all hungry. The food should be ready in about five minutes. Dreana, better ask your folks to come out and join us.'

Andreana went inside to find her parents, who were visiting for the weekend.

'Dinner is ready, Mum and Dad,' she said as she walked into the living room.

'You get our food,' said Andreana's father. 'We'll eat inside.'

'Please come and join us outside,' urged Andreana.

'I don't wanna go outside,' replied Mr Smith.

'Why not, Dad?'

'Too many coconuts!'

'Daad!' complained Andreana, 'you don't mean that, do you?'

Her father did not reply. He continued to watch television. Andreana was distressed at her father's attitude.

'Muum!' she urged, 'those are not just any Pacific Islanders. They are Albert's brothers and sisters, a couple of cousins, a few friends of Albert's and the girlfriend of Albert's older brother, who is a *pakeha* like me. They are no ordinary Islanders; they are all university students, plus a doctor... Oh, I'm really disappointed!'

'Sweetheart,' her mother coaxed, 'you can't change the way your dad feels. I know it hurts you, but he's honest. The thing is... just ignore what he says.'

Andreana was upset. She waited until she had calmed down, then went outside and got some food for her parents.

The party outside was in full swing. Dr Fa'aluma was in control of the guitar and the singing, ably assisted by Mele and Apaula. Andreana soon forgot her disappointment with her father and joined the others.

Around 10 pm, Solomona suggested that they all lend a hand to clean up. He then made sure that no one who had been drinking would be driving home.

He offered Apaula, Mele and Dr Fa'aluma a lift back to town and together they wandered along the beach to where the car was parked.

'Don't you think that Sina is stunningly beautiful, Fili?' Helen said glancing at Solomona, who winked at her. 'No wonder someone was smitten, because I don't think many men would have remained unaffected.'

'Well, you know what, Helen,' smiled Dr Fa'aluma, 'they say that beauty is in the eye of the beholder, and I guarantee that King has concluded, having assessed both you and Sina, that you are numero uno.'

Helen smiled, 'You can never disagree with Mona, can you, eh Fili?'

'That's not exactly true,' he tried to object, 'because we do have our disagreements. I suppose the problem is that you're never there when we disagree. So it's just a problem of a biased sample, as King no doubt would tell you,' he laughed.

Eight

Solomona woke at 5.30 am on the second Saturday after lectures had started. It was a cool, but otherwise beautiful autumn morning. From his window he enjoyed the sight of the early morning light filtering across the Coromandel Peninsula at the eastern end of the city and the magnificent gulf beyond.

The beginning of the rugby season was only a few weeks away, and Solomona was still behind in his fitness program. He changed into his jogging gear, then quietly let himself out of the hostel for his early morning run.

Helen woke about 7 am. Solomona had told her the night before that he would be going for a run, and they would have breakfast together when he returned, before heading over to her parents' place later in the day. 'Solomona should be back from his run by now,' she thought. She tidied her room and got ready for breakfast. By 7.30 am, Solomona had not come for her, so she decided to check on him instead. She knocked on his door, but there was no answer.

'Hey, Mister Tui, open the door.' Still, there was no answer, nor any sound from inside. 'Mister Tui,' she called again, 'it's me. Breakfast is almost over.' Still no response. 'Don't tell me he's gone to breakfast already,' she thought aloud. She went back to her room, locked the door and wandered around to the cafeteria.

Only a few people were having breakfast when Helen reached the cafeteria. She went over to the serving area. 'Have you seen Mona this morning?' she asked the cook at the servery.

'No, he hasn't shown up yet. But he likes to come late on Saturdays so he can have a big breakfast.'

'I see. Thank you anyway.'

Helen took her breakfast to a table near the window where she would be able to see Solomona returning. She nibbled at her toast, bacon and scrambled eggs, while keeping watch on the road outside. By the time she finished her breakfast, there was still no sign of Solomona.

'I wonder where he's gone,' she thought. By 9 am when he still hadn't returned, she called Faye, but Solomona was not at the Filemus. She then phoned Albert, but he was not there either.

Helen started to worry. She tried to think about where else he could have gone. Then she remembered Dr Fa'aluma. She looked up his number in the telephone book, and called him. He hadn't seen Solomona either. She was now starting to feel quite anxious. She went to find Mele and Apaula in their rooms, but they had already gone out. She could not think of anyone else to call. So she called her parents.

'Hello, this is the Jones' residence,' her father answered.

'Dad?' Helen ventured in a weak voice.

'Yes, sweetheart,' replied Mr Jones. 'Are you all right?'

'Yes, I am, Dad,' she struggled to hide her anxiety.

'But you don't sound all right, sweetie,' he said, sensing a slight quiver in his daughter's voice.

'I am, Dad, but... I'm worried about Mona.'

'Why?'

'He went for a run this morning, and he hasn't returned. He hasn't called either. He'd normally call the hostel if he knew he was going to be late.'

'Have you checked some of the places he would normally go?'

'I've called his aunt, his brother and some of his friends and he's not with any of them.'

'Hmm, that doesn't sound too good.'

'I know. That's what's worrying me, Dad.'

There was silence. Helen fiddled with the telephone cord while waiting for her father to respond.

'Are you there, Dad?' she asked after a while.

'Yes, I am... Look, I suggest you call the police.'

'Mona doesn't get into trouble with the law, Dad.'

'That's not why I'm suggesting you call the police, sweetheart. It's possible he's been in an accident, and if that's the case, then the police are likely to know. Or, you could try the hospital.'

'I'm scared, Dad.'

'Well, we can only hope for the best.'

'Thanks, Dad. Say hi to Mum and Jos for me.'

'I will. Take care, sweetie, and let us know if you hear anything.'

'All right, Dad. I'd better go now. Bye.'

'Bye, sweetheart.'

Helen felt a shiver down her spine. Her hands were sweating but she felt cold. She tried to reach for the telephone receiver, but drew her hand back. Finally, she plucked up the courage to pick up the telephone and call the police.

'Auckland Police, can I help you?' came a woman's voice at the other end.

'Yes, please,' replied Helen.

'How can I help you, madam?'

'My boyfriend went for a run this morning and he hasn't returned. I wondered whether he might have been hurt in a road accident this morning.'

'Just a moment please,' said the officer as she checked the computer and asked other officers. 'Hello, are you still there?'

'Yes, I am.'

'What is your boyfriend's name?'

'Solomona Tuisamoa, officer.'

'Can you describe him to me please?'

Helen felt nervous. She slowly described Solomona's physical characteristics and his usual jogging gear. There was silence on the line. 'Hello? Are you still there, officer?'

'Yes, ma'am, I am. Where are you calling from?'

'I'm calling from Auckland University hostel. Can you tell me anything?' she asked, sensing something was wrong.

'Yes, in a moment, but first, does your boyfriend have any relatives in Auckland?'

'He has a brother, a sister and other relatives. Why?'

'I want you to listen to me, Miss —'

'My name is Helen.'

'Okay, Helen, listen to me very carefully.'

'Okay.'

'There was a young man who was injured in a hit —'

'Oh, no, no, please!' she cried.

'It's okay, Helen,' soothed the officer. 'He was injured in a hit-and-run accident early this morning and he's at the hospital. He was not carrying any identification, but if your description is correct, it appears that the patient may be your boyfriend.' Helen sobbed. The policewoman tried to calm her. 'Now listen to me, Helen. A police car will be there shortly. They will need to pick up your boyfriend's brother too, and take both of you to the hospital to identify him.'

Helen was still sitting next to the telephone when the police car arrived. A policewoman came into the hostel looking for her. She found Helen sitting staring into space near the telephone, her eyes streaming with tears.

'Helen?'

She looked up, confused, at the sound of her name.

'We're here to take you to the hospital,' the officer said sympathetically.

Helen did not reply; she felt too weak to speak. The policewoman reached out to help her up, then escorted her to the car where another officer was waiting. They drove to Devonport on the North Shore to pick up Albert.

When they arrived at the hospital, they were taken into the intensive care unit, where they found Dr Sherrington, a neurosurgeon, and Dr Fa'aluma by Solomona's bedside.

Solomona was lying very still. His head resembled an Egyptian mummy with bandages almost completely covering it. Only his eyes, nose and parts of his cheeks, which were blue, were uncovered. The room resembled a telecommunication centre with wires and intravenous tubes criss-crossing each other from the life-support machines. He was in a coma.

Helen could not contain herself; she sobbed uncontrollably. She felt very weak, almost too weak to cry. She felt as if her soul had been stripped away. Albert tried to comfort her, but he too could not bear the sight of his brother. He held Helen tight, as he tried to fight off the tears. He felt his throat swelling, and tears ran down his cheeks.

'I'm sorry, sir,' the policewoman said sympathetically to Albert, 'but is that your brother?'

Albert did not answer straight away. His throat felt constricted. He wished he could say no. He looked again at Solomona who remained motionless on the bed. He reached into his pocket for his handkerchief.

'Yes, officer,' he replied as he dried his eyes, still holding Helen and stroking her back, 'that's my brother.'

'Thank you, sir,' she said. 'Doctor Sherrington would like to talk to you. After that, we will need some information from you.'

Dr Fa'aluma approached Albert and Helen slowly with hands in the pockets of his gown. 'We will laugh about this some day,' he thought, sadly, 'but for now... I don't know.' He was unsure whether to offer his sympathy or to try to cheer up Helen and Albert. He put his arms around their shoulders.

'Listen, guys,' he said. 'I'm really sorry about King. But let's try and look on the bright side. At least, he is more than half alive!' Albert tried to smile even as tears rolled down his cheeks, but Helen just continued to cry.

'Thank you, Fili,' Albert struggled. 'How serious is it?'

'He's in a very serious condition, but we are confident he will come out of it. Anyway, here is Dr Sherrington, the Chief Neurosurgeon at the hospital. He'll tell you as much as we know.'

'Yes, Albert and Helen. Mona... is that what you call him?' asked Dr Sherrington.

'Yes, doctor,' replied Albert.

'Okay. Well, Mona's condition, as Dr Fa'aluma just told you, is serious. But I am confident he will fully recover once he regains consciousness.'

'How long do you think it will take him to come out of it?' Albert asked.

'I hope it will not be very long,' the neurosurgeon replied. 'Anyway, he got here just in time for us to drain the blood that was building up inside his skull and exerting pressure on his brain. He suffered serious injury from the impact with the road. Being a tall and big man did not help, but his thick hair probably cushioned some of the shock. Now, when he comes out of the coma, we will need to operate on him because there are blood clots building up in his skull. The amazing thing is that he received no other major injury from the impact with the vehicle. The operation is not urgent, as we'd like Mona to be strong enough to withstand a major operation. But right now, let's pray that he will come out of it all right, and soon.'

'Thank you, doctor,' said Albert.

After Dr Sherrington left, the police officers took some information from Albert, who also wanted to know how his brother was injured.

'Can you tell us how my brother got injured, officer, please?'

'An eyewitness said your brother was hit by a white van as he stepped onto the pedestrian crossing on K Road, between Queen and Symonds Streets.'

'And the van didn't stop?'

'No, it didn't.'

'Have you found the van?'

'No one could give us the registration number. All we know is that it was a white van, but we are continuing our investigations.'

'I see. Well, thank you for everything, officer.'

'It's our job... Would you like a lift back now?'

'Maybe you can drive Helen back to the hostel,' replied Albert. 'I'd like to stay for a while.'

'Thank you, officers,' said Helen as she wiped her eyes. 'I'd like to stay for a while, too.'

Nine

Solomona regained consciousness after three days, but it was much longer before his doctors were confident of the extent of his recovery. During that time, Albert and Helen hardly left his bedside. There was a steady stream of visitors, both friends and family members, every day. Fetuao, however, was not informed of the accident, and neither were Solomona's parents in Samoa. Albert knew that his brother would not want to worry his sister and parents until an outcome was certain. So he pleaded with everyone not to inform them of Solomona's condition. He would let them know at the right time.

Solomona continued to gain strength each day. When he was finally able to recognise everyone, his sense of humour also returned. Although still quite weak, he constantly made jokes about his condition. Occasional jokes from his friend Dr Fa'aluma managed to elicit a smile from him now and then, but he was still experiencing dizziness. He even appeared to enjoy the attention he was receiving from hospital staff, relatives and friends.

Three and a half weeks later, Dr Sherrington pronounced that Solomona was now strong enough to undergo an operation to remove blood clots from his brain, which would also help to ease Solomona's headaches and dizziness.

On the day of the operation, a large group from the Samoan Church came to the hospital to offer prayers for Solomona's recovery. A short service, led by Reverend Tupe, was held by his bedside before he was wheeled into the operating theatre. After the service, Reverend Tupe and his wife, Sene, stayed with Helen and Solomona's family to await news.

Eight hours after the operation began, Dr Sherrington and Dr Fa'aluma appeared, still dressed in their surgical gowns. Dr Fa'aluma winked at Albert and gave him the thumbs-up sign.

'Reverend, relatives and friends of Mona,' Dr Sherrington announced, 'the operation was a success. We are confident he will make a full recovery. He is now in the recovery room and, as soon as he wakes up, he'll be taken to the intensive care unit where we will monitor him for the next couple of days, at least.'

'Thank you very much, doctor, for saving the life of a beloved son to us,' said Reverend Tupe.

'How long will he be in hospital, doctor?' Albert asked.

'At least two months. The back of his skull was fractured and it will need time to heal. It will be a slow recovery and we need to monitor him closely.'

Dr Sherrington excused himself, then left with Dr Fa'aluma.

'Come on everyone,' said Reverend Tupe, 'let us give thanks to God for answering our prayers.'

As Reverend Tupe began to pray, Fiasili looked into her purse. Closing it quickly, she pulled Albert to one side.

'We have to give some money to the pastor and his wife, Pati,' she whispered.

'How much is that prayer worth?' whispered Albert sarcastically, although he came prepared to make a donation.

'Well, it's worth you brother's life,' his aunt replied.

'But it was Dr Sherrington who performed the operation.'

'But God gave the doctor his skills and strength.'

'How much do you need?'

'I have $200 with me, and it would be nice if we could make it $300. I can pay you back when you come to the house.'

Albert took his wallet out of his pocket and handed some money to Fiasili.

'Here is $300. You don't have to pay me back. Mona has done a lot for me, and I don't often get the opportunity to return the favour.'

Helen was curious to know what was going on. She went over to Albert as Fiasili moved back to where Reverend Tupe was praying.

'What's going on, Pati?'

'Oh, nothing much,' Albert replied, with a shrug. 'Aunt Sili and I were just discussing where Mona should stay when he is discharged from hospital.'

'Oh, that's not a problem. I can look after him at the hostel. Mum has also offered to have him at home, but I think it should be okay for him to recuperate in the hostel.'

'That's what I told Aunt Sili,' he replied, deliberately evading the subject of his conversation with Fiasili. 'I lived in the hostel last year and I know they are very good there.'

'Good,' whispered Helen.

Albert moved back to the group as Reverend Tupe said 'Amen'. Fiasili, with $300 in her hand, stepped forward to thank Reverend Tupe and Sene for their prayers and their kind and encouraging words and to make the customary offering of money to the pastor.

'As a small token of our appreciation,' she said, 'here is $300 for your bus fare back to Greylynn.' Helen gasped and looked at Albert in disbelief. He smiled and shrugged.

'Keep the money, Sili,' smiled Reverend Tupe. 'Use it to buy something for Mona.'

Fiasili, still holding out the money, insisted that Reverend Tupe take it, but he continued to decline her offer. She motioned to Faye to give the money to Sene. Faye handed the money to Sene, which she gratefully accepted. A short while later, Reverend Tupe and Sene bade the group farewell.

After the pastor and his wife had left, those remaining decided to go to the cafeteria for a bite to eat while they waited for Solomona to come out of the recovery room. Helen, still trying to understand the exchange she had just witnessed, walked alongside Albert.

'Is that what Sili and you were talking about?' she asked.

'What do you mean?' Albert pretended he didn't quite understand the question.

'The money that was given to the pastor.'

'The money?' he repeated. 'Well... yes, one of the things,' he smiled.

'It looked quite a large sum. How much was it?'

'Aunt Sili said it was $300.'

'Three hundred dollars!' Helen exclaimed in disbelief. 'That's an incredible amount of money.'

'Prayers are expensive nowadays, you know,' he smiled raising an eyebrow. 'Well, actually, life is very precious... especially if it's your brother's. You really can't put a price on it.'

Helen smiled. She was a little confused by Albert's nonchalant attitude, but she also admired it. 'Was the money from you?'

'Some of it,' he smiled. 'In Samoan culture, relatives and friends put their hands in their pockets at times like this. There is a saying that you can give without love, but you cannot love without giving. It's a simple way of saying how I feel for my brother. I don't get too many opportunities to show it.'

'That's a very nice thought, Pati. Mona would no doubt have done the same for you.'

After everyone had eaten, they made their way back to the intensive care unit. Solomona was just being wheeled into his room. Awake, but extremely weak, he looked like an old man with his head shaven and bandaged. He could recognise people and hear them when they talked to him, but he could only move his eyes in response. Helen grasped his hand. He tried weakly to squeeze her hand.

'You behave yourself, Mister Tui,' she whispered, smiling gently. Solomona blinked, acknowledging her presence.

Tears welled in her eyes and rolled slowly down her cheeks. She held fast to his hand as the others queued to wish him a speedy recovery before leaving. Helen and Albert found themselves alone with Solomona, who had lapsed back to sleep. Albert stood near the head of the bed, his hands in his pockets. He tried to imagine what his brother must be going through. His throat felt constricted and tears rolled gently down his cheeks. He took out a handkerchief to wipe his eyes.

'I'll be just outside, Helen,' he said, excusing himself.

Helen nodded at Albert as he closed the door behind him. She looked affectionately at Solomona and his bandaged head and bent to gently kiss his cheek. Her heart felt heavy. The last month had been gruelling, but only now could she allow herself to feel her tiredness. Though sad at the sight of Solomona's pain, the knowledge that he would survive, and hopefully fully recover, had brought some comfort. She slowly lowered her head onto the bed and immediately fell into a deep sleep.

Ten

In the weeks after the operation Solomona made good progress. After two weeks, he could get out of bed and move around. After a month, all tubes were removed and he no longer needed to be fed intravenously. He was able to move around freely and could even take the elevator to visit his sister in the maternity ward. However, he was still closely monitored and was not allowed to move around by himself.

After six weeks, the dizziness was less frequent, and Solomona began to spend time playing his favourite card game, canasta, with his sister, the nurses or Dr Fa'aluma. Helen tried to learn the rudiments of the game, so she could join in when she visited. Dr Fa'aluma joked that Solomona was managing to win all the time.

One Saturday morning, about two months after Solomona's operation, Dr Fa'aluma joined him for a game, with an interested audience of nurses. 'Look at this guy, will you?' Fili said good-naturedly to the nurses and to Helen, who was also watching with interest. 'He's supposed to be sick, but he won't allow me to win a single game.'

The nurses laughed. Helen smiled as she gently massaged Solomona's back. Their laughter greeted Dr Sherrington as he made his daily rounds. The nurses drifted back to their work.

'How do you feel this morning, Mona?' asked Dr Sherrington.

'How does a spring chicken feel?' smiled Solomona.

Dr Sherrington smiled back. 'I can see you're enjoying thrashing my colleague here.'

'Oh, he's just hopeless, doctor.'

'Actually,' protested Dr Fa'aluma, 'I have to let you win — it's hospital policy not to put our patients under too much stress.'

'See what I mean, doctor,' smiled Solomona, 'he's only good for making excuses for his inadequacy.'

Dr Sherrington continued with his examination. 'Well, you are looking good, my friend.'

'So, can I go home soon?' asked Solomona expectantly.

Dr Sherrington smiled, 'Not quite, but —'

'But what, doctor?'

'I guess some fresh air could be in order. Do you have a car, Helen?'

'Yes, I do,' she replied eagerly.

'Maybe you could take Mona for a drive, and bring him back later in the afternoon.'

'Oh, thank you, doctor!' she said excitedly.

After Dr Sherrington left, Helen ran to the telephone and called her mother to see if they could drop by. After packing a few items into a bag, she took the elevator with Solomona to the ground floor. While he waited in the reception area, she went to get the car. Once she had helped Solomona into the car, she turned to look at him.

'Oh, I've been waiting for this day for quite a while, Mister Tui,' she smiled as she brushed his cheek with her fingers.

Solomona smiled back but didn't reply. It felt quite strange for him after spending the last three months or so in hospital.

'Where are we going?' he asked as they drove past Takapuna and on towards the East Coast Road.

'Just relax, Mister Tui, we're going for a drive, and the air of the East Coast bays, the doctor said, will be good for you.'

They drove down the winding road along the beaches of Auckland's North Shore. Solomona had always loved this part of Auckland. It reminded him of the winding, tree-lined road that led to his village in Samoa.

'Ah, I think I know where we're going,' he declared.

Helen smiled. 'Have a guess, Mister Tui.'

'If your parents have moved to Whangaparoa, then it looks like that's where we're heading.'

'You're just too smart, Mister Tui,' she smiled, watching the road ahead. 'Yes, they have. You haven't been formally introduced, except for that brief moment at the airport when we left for England. Remember we were supposed to have dinner with them the day you had the accident.'

'Yes, but being a sick young man, I will be in a very vulnerable position,' he quipped.

'Oh, come on, Mister Tui, no one would harm a gentle giant like you.'

'I certainly hope not.'

'I can guarantee it, Mister Tui. Mum and Dad have been very keen to meet you.'

The Jones house was located on a prominent hill with a beautiful view over the city and the gulf beyond, with its many islands. It was a beautiful two-storey house of contemporary architecture on a magnificently landscaped block. The inside of the house was simply but elegantly furnished. The impressive garden at the front reminded Solomona of his mother's garden at home. As they got out of the car, Helen's parents and her sister, Jocelyn, were there to greet them. Her brother, Alvin, was away at boarding school. Solomona and Helen followed Helen's parents out onto a large balcony overlooking Auckland. The view from the balcony was superb.

The view was filtered through the branches of the many *Pohutukawa* trees in their garden, swaying gently in the sea breeze. Far below lay one of the many beaches on the Whangaparoa Peninsula, its white sand sparkling in the midday sun. Further out, the tip of the Coromandel Peninsula appeared out of the hazy horizon, in contrast to the bright green of the islands in front of it.

'The view from here is breathtaking,' commented Solomona as he leaned on the railing, looking down to the beach.

'It's lovely, isn't it?' Helen's father said as he joined him. 'Anyway, how are you feeling, Mona?'

'I feel good so far, thank you. I just have to take it easy, seeing that this is my first excursion away from hospital. It's good to be out, though,' he replied.

In his late forties, Mr Jones was a fairly big man. He was almost as tall as Solomona but heavier, and his hair was receding.

'Dad spends a lot of his spare time out here,' Jocelyn said as she opened a huge umbrella in the middle of the outdoor table.

Mr Jones, Solomona and Jocelyn sat down around the table in the shade of the umbrella. Solomona was fascinated by how closely Helen and Jocelyn resembled each other. They were like identical twins except that Jocelyn was slightly taller.

'So, Jos,' he said, 'are you happy to be back in New Zealand?'

'Oh, yes,' she replied. 'It's nice to see my friends again. I missed them terribly while we were away.'

'Anything exciting happening at school?'

'Just the usual stuff, you know, assignments, sport...,' she replied, with a shrug.

'Were you able to watch any of the Rugby World Cup games, Mona?' asked Mr Jones.

'No, I didn't. I wasn't well enough unfortunately. Just as well, as I was very disappointed with the organisers for not inviting Samoa to play. I really don't know how they can justify inviting Tonga and Fiji and leaving out Samoa, when we are the current Pacific champion.'

'The politics of these things can be quite vicious,' said Mr Jones. 'I hear it was the New Zealand contingent that argued strongly against inviting Samoa. They are mean-spirited, these people.'

'That's exactly why it was difficult for me to get excited about the All Blacks' win. Like everyone else I was always an All Blacks supporter. There are quite a few Samoans in the team now, but when I heard that New Zealand was instrumental in keeping Samoa out of rugby's first World Cup, I lost all interest in cheering on the All Blacks.'

Helen arrived with a tray of cold drinks. Her mother followed with some snack food.

'Lunch will be ready in about half an hour,' announced Mrs Jones, smiling at Solomona. She was an attractive, youthful-looking woman despite being almost fifty. Solomona marvelled at the resemblance between the girls and their mother. They almost looked like sisters.

'What's Mona drinking?' inquired Mr Jones.

'He's having orange juice,' replied Helen.

'Oh, give the man a beer.'

'He is still recovering from a major operation, darling,' said Mrs Jones.

'And also, he doesn't drink beer, Dad,' added Helen taking a handful of peanuts.

'Who said he doesn't? I haven't come across a student, a rugby player, or a Samoan yet who doesn't drink beer.'

'Well, you just have, Dad. Mona doesn't drink or smoke.'

'Really, Mona?' he asked, surprised. 'That's sound economics.'

Solomona leaned over for a handful of potato chips. 'Well,' he said smiling, 'maybe a glass of red wine with meals now and then.'

'Mona is a good man compared to you, Dad,' joked Jocelyn as she patted her father on the back. 'Do you have any younger brothers, Mona?'

'Yes, he does,' Helen answered with a grin. 'He's a law student, but he has a girlfriend already.'

Jocelyn shrugged and went back to sipping her fruit juice.

'How are you feeling now, Mona?' asked Mrs Jones.

'A lot better, thank you,' he replied. 'Just a bit of dizziness from time to time.'

'It sounded like a terrible accident.'

'I guess it was, but it taught me a valuable lesson, that life's really like a burning candle. One moment it burns brightly; the next moment it flickers and could even go out despite all the potential it may still have.'

'But it's a painful way to learn a lesson.'

'There's a difference between believing and knowing through experience. I guess the important lessons in life have to be experienced... But with no more rugby, I can concentrate on my thesis when I recover.'

'It's good you can be positive about everything.'

'I think it's important to look for the positive in any experience. When you survive an accident like that, you really can't help but wonder why your life was spared.'

'I'm glad that you have such a healthy view of things.'

'I guess it's the most natural thing to do in the circumstances. Otherwise you could remain miserable.'

'So you'll be in hospital for a while yet?'

'Yes, until I've fully recovered. Technically, I have no home and no one to look after me, except the New Zealand Government.'

'Well, you're always welcome to come and stay here. Right, darling?' continued Mrs Jones, looking at her husband.

'Oh yes, Mona, you're most welcome to recuperate here,' Helen's father replied. 'We have a guest room downstairs where you can stay. Alvin's room is the only other room downstairs but he's at boarding school.'

'It's very kind of you, but I think it's better that I stay close to the doctors.'

'Well, think about it,' she said.

Mrs Jones excused herself to check whether lunch was ready. Helen and Jocelyn followed their mother to the kitchen.

They soon returned with food, more drinks, plates and cutlery. Mr Jones blessed the food before they started to eat.

'There's something, Mona, that I've been wanting to talk to you about,' said Mr Jones. Everyone looked at him, wondering what he was going to say. Solomona felt a bit nervous. 'We never had the opportunity to thank you for helping Helen with her School Certificate maths,' he continued. 'It's more than three years, but we haven't forgotten your kindness.'

'Yes, Mona,' added Mrs Jones. 'Helen did very well and she attributed it to the tutorials you gave her and Faye.'

Solomona smiled, 'Oh, don't mention it. I enjoyed lending a hand and, with Helen, I suppose you can say there was an ulterior motive. Mind you, I gained a lot of personal satisfaction from both of them doing so well.'

'But no one gives free lessons anymore,' said Mrs Jones.

Solomona hurriedly swallowed a mouthful of food, then cleared his throat. 'My thinking is that there's no such thing as new knowledge. We build on the achievements of the Egyptians and the Chinese, Socrates and the Greeks, of course, down the ages to the likes of Newton and Descartes, and currently with Erdös. Without them, current and future knowledge wouldn't have been possible. We are still enjoying the music of Mozart and other great composers. Yet, they don't earn money from us. Well, of course, except for Erdös, they don't need it anymore,' he laughed. 'I mean, knowledge really should be for the public good, the international public good. No one should even think about profiting from it. Firms and individuals should be banned from manipulating it for commercial gain. Instead, governments and the international community should compensate any contribution to humanity's knowledge stock, and pay to encourage its further advancement. Everyone should know that we owe most of what we now enjoy to those who have gone before us.'

'It would be nice if all young people shared your attitude, Mona,' commented Mrs Jones.

'Oh, there are plenty of young people who think like me,' Solomona assured her. 'Anyone who takes up teaching, at any level, must have that attitude because teaching is usually the worst-paid profession in virtually every country in the world.'

Over lunch, their discussion ranged across education, politics, history, music, art and sport, among other topics. After coffee, Helen and Solomona prepared to leave.

'Well, thanks everyone,' said Helen, 'but we'd better move along and head back to the hospital.'

'It was very nice that you and Mona could drop by for lunch,' her father said, standing to kiss his daughter goodbye.

'Yes, it was good that you could come, Mona,' added Mrs Jones.

'Listen, Mona,' said Mr Jones, 'if you don't want to recuperate here, you should come and stay for a weekend.'

'Thank you, but it probably won't be for a while yet,' replied Solomona.

'Well, whenever you feel like taking a break, you're most welcome.'

'It would probably be good in late October,' Solomona said, thinking aloud. 'I should be okay by then and perhaps have put some serious work into the thesis, and Helen should have finished lectures by then. She could use a short break before her exams. Let's make it the last weekend of October.'

'Well,' smiled Helen, 'we've got to get going. We don't want the hospital people worrying about where we are. Thanks again, Mum, for the lunch.'

'Yes, thank you very much for the lovely lunch,' added Solomona. 'I really enjoyed the company, and, of course, the view is just awe-inspiring.'

A short drive from her parents' place, Helen stopped the car along the beachfront and together they went for a leisurely stroll. A sea breeze was blowing gently and children were playing football on the beach.

Finding a grassy spot under a *Pohutukawa* tree, Helen spread a blanket in the shade against the base of the tree. Solomona sat down, leaning against the tree trunk, with Helen resting between his legs, her back against his chest. Solomona lowered his chin onto her shoulder so their cheeks touched. He wrapped his arms around her as he gently rubbed his cheek against hers. Helen felt very relaxed, enjoying the warmth of his body.

'I love you, Mister Tui,' she whispered, resting her head on his shoulder, and closing her eyes.

'I love you, too, HR, more than I can possibly say,' he whispered as he kissed her on the cheek. 'Do you realise there was a strong possibility that we may never have been sitting here enjoying each other's company?'

'I know,' she whispered. 'That's why I want to savour every moment we spend together.'

'It's amazing how circumstances can change one's perspective of things and life in general, isn't it? I mean if a person doesn't die from an accident like mine, you have to wonder why.'

She smiled. 'Do you know that my parents are really impressed with you?'

'Are they?'

'Yes, that's why they invited you to recuperate at their place,' she replied, stroking his knee. 'When I first started seeing you, Mum was a bit concerned. She started to like you after meeting you at the airport when we left for England. When I came to exchange cars with Dad, and told them why you wouldn't drive or ride in a Volkswagen car, she really started to believe that you must be someone special. And this afternoon you really impressed her.'

'What did I do?'

'Oh, Mona, you may not realise it, but you always make an impression on people by just being yourself. People love your spontaneity, and the sincerity and profoundness of your thoughts.'

'Do they?'

'What do you think struck me about you the very first time we met?'

Solomona smiled and shrugged. 'My nose?'

Helen smiled back as she gently stroked his temple. 'It's the same things that impress all the others, particularly young women, who have been fortunate enough to meet and get to know you, Mister Tui: good looks, great physique, sexy voice, intelligence, gentleness and a loving heart.'

'Well, thank you for the vote of confidence, HR.'

Solomona was starting to feel sleepy. He suggested they just sleep under the *Pohutukawa* tree, but Helen did not like the idea. Instead they went for a walk, before returning to the hospital.

Solomona would spend another month in the hospital before finally being discharged. His sister, Fetuao, remained in hospital. Her pregnancy was progressing well, and the problems Dr Fox predicted never eventuated. A few months after Solomona was discharged, Fetuao gave birth to a healthy baby boy. Solomona suggested the name Moriah; Fetuao liked Nathan. So the child was named Moriah Nathan Tuisamoa.

Eleven

Helen's lectures finished early on the last day of term in late October. She was keen to return home straight away, but Solomona still had some work to complete on his thesis. Early in the evening, he dropped her at her parents' home, then went back to the university. He had agreed to rejoin her and her family the next day.

After good-natured discussion around the dinner table with her parents and sister, Helen retired to the quiet and comfort of her room to set about organising her study materials for the coming week.

On the normally windy Whangaparoa Peninsula it was a particularly still night. Hardly a sound could be heard outside except for the occasional car passing by. In the early hours of the morning, Helen's mother, on her way to the bathroom, noticed light coming from Helen's room. Expecting that Helen had fallen asleep without turning off her light, she pushed the door open to find Helen propped up in bed reading.

'It's very late, dear.'

'I can't sleep, Mum,' Helen replied, showing no sign of sleepiness.

'What's the matter?'

Helen put down the book. 'Mum, I really don't know,' she said hesitantly.

'Is it Mona?'

'Sort of.'

'Is it something he has done?' her mother sounded concerned. Helen shook her head. 'Is he seeing someone else?' Again, Helen shook her head.

'So what is bothering you, my dear?'

'I really don't know, Mum. I feel so restless and confused. I don't know what to do,' Helen said, absently wringing the corner of her pillowcase.

'Don't know what to do about what?' Mrs Jones sat down on the edge of the bed.

'Well, we've known each other for four years now, since I was in Fifth Form. We still haven't talked about where our relationship is going. In a year or two, he will be returning to Samoa, and I have no idea what his plans for us are.'

'Oh, I see,' her mother sighed. 'Well, we can't solve anything tonight. Why don't you try to get some sleep, and we'll talk about it in the morning?'

Helen felt reassured by the comforting tone of her mother's voice. The feeling of restlessness that had been keeping her awake began to ease.

'Thanks, Mum.'

'Now, get some sleep,' her mother urged before heading back to bed.

Helen woke up early the next morning, after only a few hours' sleep. She felt tired. For some time now, a good night's sleep had eluded her. She was not eating well, and was starting to worry about her final exams in a week's time. Even the thought that Solomona would be coming later that day did not lift her spirits. Time seemed to be moving far too slowly. Finding everything a bit too much to handle, she decided to write Solomona a short note.

'*My dearest Mona,*' she wrote.

'*We spend a lot of time together, but it doesn't seem to be enough. I will be seeing you when you arrive later on today, but somehow that time feels like an eternity away. I guess I just want to be close to you; to be near you, all the time. I feel safe and secure with you. I feel happy and comfortable when you are near.*

Mona, we have known each other and have been going steady now for a long time, but all we have is an understanding. I wonder about your future plans, and whether it sounds too forward to ask if I am part of those plans. It would help me greatly, something that I desperately need as I prepare for my upcoming exams, if you could share your thoughts concerning us with me.

Love you dearly,
Helen'

Helen felt better afterwards. The note was short, but she found writing it rather soothing. After a refreshing shower, she made her way to the kitchen, to find that the rest of the family had finished breakfast.

'Good morning, sweetheart,' her father greeted her over the top of his morning newspaper. 'Take a seat and have some breakfast.'

Mrs Jones went outside to water the garden and Jocelyn had already headed into town on a shopping expedition, so Helen and her father were left alone in the kitchen.

'How are you feeling this morning?'

'Much better than last night, thanks Dad,' Helen replied between mouthfuls of cereal and fruit.

'Yes, your mother was telling me about your sleeplessness early in the morning.'

'Oh, I guess it's a woman thing, Dad. It's just that Mona and I have been very close for a long time, and he may only have, at the most, two years left before he returns to Samoa, but we have not really had a serious talk about where our relationship is taking us. I guess I'm just afraid of losing him.'

'Have you told him that?'

'No, I haven't.'

'Why not?'

'Oh, I don't know, Dad. I suppose I'm uncertain of how he might react. Besides he has been sick, and has been anxious about getting his thesis research underway.'

'What are his plans when he finishes his PhD?'

'He will return to Samoa.'

'And you?'

'I guess that's why I'm feeling so uneasy. I don't know what his plans are; I don't know if I am even part of them.'

'Haven't you two discussed things at all?'

'We do have some kind of understanding, but that's basically all.'

'Well, I'm sure there's no harm in you sharing your thoughts with Mona. After all, he's an extremely intelligent young man, and appears to be very reasonable.'

'I have been wanting to, but —'

'But what?'

'Oh, I don't know, Dad. I just have this fear —'

'Fear of what?'

'Oh, fear of being rejected, fear of being seen to be too forward, I guess. It doesn't seem proper somehow for a girl to appear to be pursuing a man, does it?'

'It all depends,' Mr Jones mused. 'According to Barbra Streisand, a woman in love should do anything to get into her man's world. Honestly, I see nothing wrong with that. Society feels uncomfortable with change, but eventually change is accepted, because it is inevitable; it's what keeps the world going — and exciting. And does society care about how you feel? Of course not. You can never please everyone. But if you make one person happy, the world will be better for it. So make yourself happy, sweetheart, because that would make your mother and me happy.'

'I guess you're right, Dad. We'll probably go for a drive somewhere tomorrow — maybe we'll take the opportunity to have a serious talk about our future.'

'You know, your mother and I have been talking, and I was wondering if Solomona would consider staying in New Zealand if he were offered an attractive job.'

'Oh, I don't know, Dad,' Helen replied, shrugging her shoulders. 'He talks only about returning to Samoa and serving his people — that's why he's here. So I'm always scared to talk to him about staying. He is very principled and stubborn. You know that, of course, but you can try asking him. He might consider it if it comes from you.'

'I talked to his supervisor, Professor Lewis, the other day, and he said Mona is a brilliant student. He reckons Mona is the best Polynesian student ever to have come through Auckland University, and that includes Maoris too.'

'You asked Professor Lewis about Mona?' she asked, somewhat surprised.

'Well, not exactly,' her father replied. 'You see, Bob Lewis and I were at university together. We bumped into each other in town last week. When I told him I have a daughter at university, he said Mona had introduced you to him. That's when he told me about Mona.'

'Yes, I remember meeting him. The Economics Department was having its end-of-year dinner the weekend before last, and Professor Lewis did say that you were at varsity together,' she said. 'Well, as Professor Lewis might have told you, Mona is rare, with an IQ that probably rivals Einstein's. He gets distinctions so easily, and even manages to get 100 per cent in some subjects, particularly Statistics and Mathematics. Remember he helped me pass School Certificate maths with an A after years of failing maths?'

'Of course, I remember. But I'm sure you got an A because of the extra motivation he inspired in you,' smiled Mr Jones.

'Of course, just being with him motivated me. I could never get excited about maths until he tutored Faye and me. He has a tremendous ability to make difficult concepts easy to understand... and the lessons were free.'

'I'm not so sure that the lessons were free,' her father laughed. 'Mona is a good economics student, and one of the first things you learn in economics is that there is no such thing as a "free lunch". I'm sure he knew he would get paid somehow, sometime.'

'Maybe so, but he always says there's no price for the personal satisfaction he receives from helping others. He knows he has a special talent many do not have, and he's always keen to share it. He says sharing is part of the Samoan culture. He makes no fuss about his intelligence — he says it's impossible to be proud of something that he wasn't responsible for creating. He despises those who fall back on their inheritance and don't bother to add to what they have been given.'

'But did you know that he is also from one of Samoa's royal families?'

'Faye told me that a long time ago, but Mona hardly ever talks about it. He just says it's an inheritance. But how did you find out about all this?'

'Oh, the Samoan Consul told me one day.'

'So you *have* been checking up on him.'

'Well, not exactly. The Consul and I knew each other at university — we were on the varsity rugby team together. He invited me for lunch one day, and the conversation, naturally enough, drifted to Mona.'

'What else did the Samoan Consul tell you?'

'Very much what Bob Lewis told me. He said Mona is different and a special student. He has certainly impressed quite a few people.'

Helen smiled as she sipped her orange juice. 'Anything else?'

'No, that was all; we had to eat, you know.'

'Do you think Mona is special, Dad?'

'Well, yes, he's certainly someone special. It's rare to find blue blood and a brilliant mind together,' he smiled, 'and that's why I was wondering if he might be interested in an offer to work in our office. I'm sure you'd like that too.'

'Of course I would, Dad. I hope he'll consider the idea. Ask him this afternoon.'

Helen and her father were still chatting when Mrs Jones came inside to prepare lunch. After a leisurely lunch Helen had the rest of the afternoon to fill, hoping that the time would pass quickly before Solomona's arrival.

She was in the kitchen helping her mother prepare dinner when she heard the car turn into the driveway. Running down to the garage to meet him, she threw her arms around Solomona's neck as he got out of the car.

'Hello, Mister Tui, I've missed you,' she said as she kissed his cheek. 'Come on, I'll show you to your room.'

Solomona grabbed his bag from the rear seat and followed Helen to the guestroom. After a quick hug they made their way upstairs to join the rest of the family.

'Something smells good,' smiled Solomona, winking at Helen.

'Mum's cooking a special dish for you,' she replied.

'Then I'll certainly eat it,' he teased.

'Why? Don't you trust my cooking?' Helen pouted as she punched him in the stomach. She was feeling happy and alive again.

'Ouch! What was that for?'

'Maybe it will help your appetite,' she replied, grinning broadly.

'Appetite? Are you kidding? You know Polynesian men don't need to work up an appetite.'

'Come and talk to Dad while Mum and I get dinner ready,' she said as she walked into the kitchen.

Helen's father greeted him with a warm handshake. 'Can I offer you something to drink?'

'Juice or coke will be fine, please.'

'Are you sure you don't want a beer?'

Solomona smiled, 'No, thank you.'

Mr Jones poured a glass of coke for Solomona and a beer for himself, and motioned Solomona to take a seat. 'How's the thesis coming along?'

'Oh, I've made some good progress. I've almost completed the data analysis. Then I need to write up the results and discuss some of the policy implications.'

'And what's your thesis about?'

'It's about the role of foreign aid in assisting the economies of developing countries, using Pacific Island countries as case studies.'

'Sounds very interesting, Mona.'

'Yes, it is. It's an interesting topic, but also a controversial one.'

'Why's that? Isn't there enough aid, or is the type and form of foreign aid the problem?'

'Well, there are probably as many critics as there are supporters of foreign aid. There is a role for foreign aid, especially in the early stage, but in the long term I don't believe it will help. Low-income countries need market-driven access to the markets of rich countries much more than aid. The critics have argued, quite correctly, that foreign aid had been largely donor-driven, and much has been wasteful. Some donors feel that building water tanks is development, but when they break down, no one can fix them. Some of the policies, like import substitution, have been a complete failure. Some researchers have shown foreign aid to have done more harm than good and, apparently, contributing to further widening the gap between the rich and the poor in developing countries.'

'What do you think is the problem?'

'I think the problem is best summed up by the British economist Lord Bauer. He said that foreign aid is a system of taking money from poor people in rich countries and giving it to rich people in poor countries. And that's another reason why it's such an interesting issue — the politics of foreign aid.'

'So is it a problem of identifying where aid is needed, or is it a problem with monitoring aid programs?'

'The main reasons for giving aid, despite donors' claims, are to expand donor countries' export markets and to make allies for political and strategic reasons. High incomes in poor countries could mean bigger markets for rich countries' exports. Aid is rarely, if ever, given out of altruism.'

'That's very interesting, Mona. Here we are, the taxpayers contributing to New Zealand's foreign aid program, all the while thinking that our government has a genuine desire to develop low-income countries, like our neighbours in the Pacific, but, as you claim, it appears there's an ulterior motive to the whole exercise.'

'That's right. Now, the failure of foreign aid is, in part, due to donors' lack of understanding of the economics of being poor and underdevelopment. Most programs have been driven by the belief that it is the lack of capital, machines and the like that makes poor countries poor. Since they can't afford the investment in capital, they can't make more goods cheaply, so they remain poor — the so-called vicious cycle of poverty. To break the cycle, an injection of capital should provide the remedy. It hasn't been very successful because it causes other problems.'

'Is it a problem of the wrong technology, or is it a case of insufficient spare parts?'

'It's a bit of everything. However, I still believe that the most important resource in any country is the human mind, and aid should concentrate on developing poor countries' human capital. So things like the scholarship program that the New Zealand Government funds, which sponsors people like me, would be more productive in the long term, which is what's needed, provided a mechanism is built into the program to ensure the scholar returns home after his studies. But, in the game of giving aid, ostentation is important. The problem is that the human mind is not easily seen, say, compared to a road or a bridge. The second most important reason for the failure is the lack of markets. It's the main reason why import substitution has failed miserably. The domestic markets in developing countries are usually very small, and the rich donor countries are unwilling to open up their markets to exports from developing countries. There is no point in producing something that no one will buy.'

'And how is foreign aid contributing to the widening of the gap between the rich and the poor in developing countries? Does it give more business to the rich, or is aid money going directly into the pockets of the rich at the expense of the poor?'

'Again, it's a bit of everything, but it's primarily because the policy that governs the provision of foreign aid fails to recognise the relationship between political and economic powers in developing countries. Almost without exception, those who hold political power also control the economies of developing countries. Since aid is channelled through the governments of developing countries, it means that aid funds are also controlled by the rich in those poor countries.'

'So Lord Bauer's analysis, as you said, is right on the mark.'

'Absolutely. In developing countries, things don't trickle down; they bubble up. And if a trickle-down process ever occurs, the trickles dissipate in an instant because they fall into a vast ocean of poverty. Yet, donor countries feel that increasing national incomes is both necessary and sufficient for development. Well, they're wrong. It's necessary, but not sufficient. Without fundamental reforms in the systems that created poverty and underdevelopment in the first place, foreign aid will only exacerbate underdevelopment and poverty in developing countries.'

'So what are you hoping your thesis will contribute to the provision of foreign aid? Are you proposing to stop foreign aid, increase it so that some amounts will trickle down, although you don't believe that it happens, or are you proposing to change the method by which foreign aid is being channelled to developing countries?'

'It's more of the latter. My main goal is to add to the debate and come up with ways to improve the effectiveness of foreign aid. It's important that recipient countries eventually get out of the business of receiving aid, and become able to do things themselves. It's demoralising and dehumanising to depend on aid for a very long time. Aid locks developing countries to rich countries in a new type of colonial relationship. It's important that they are free from such bondage and become masters of their own destinies. Donors must find other channels for aid, like through well-established non-government organisations. They should also recognise the value of education, and, if they are sincere about helping poor countries develop their economies, then they must open up their markets to products from poor countries.'

Just then, Mrs Jones called out that dinner was ready. Still deep in conversation, Mr Jones and Solomona moved into the dining room.

'Hello, Mona,' Jocelyn greeted as she joined them at the table.

'Good to see you again. How's the swimming going?' smiled Solomona.

'Not too bad, thanks,' she replied. 'Listen, guys, what have you two planned for tomorrow?' Jocelyn looked pointedly at her sister.

'We're going for a drive, but you're not invited,' Helen said good-naturedly.

'Why not? I'll behave myself. I promise,' she pleaded.

'Because —' smiled Helen.

'Oh, well, I have school work to do, anyway.'

Later while Mrs Jones served dessert, Mr Jones started to talk about his days at university and about the insurance business in which he worked. He wanted to raise the possibility of Solomona working at his office, but he didn't want to sound too direct.

'By the way, Mona,' he said, 'to change the subject a little, what are your plans when you finish your studies?'

'It's really not so much my plan,' replied Solomona. 'It's very much the Samoan Government's plan for me, as it is with other students under government scholarships.'

'And what is the Samoan Government's plan for you?'

'Well, it's simply to return home and serve the people and the country.'

'You mean work for the government?'

'I guess you can put it that way, although I am always of the belief that, in a democracy, the government serves the people. My attitude is that I will go home to serve the people of Samoa, not necessarily the government, but through the services the government provides. I guess that could change if I feel that what the government does is not in the interests of the Samoan people.'

'And if things don't work out as you expect, what will you do then?'

'I suppose I will have to leave the government service and do something else.'

'Is the Samoan Government doing what the people want at the moment?'

'It's difficult to say while I'm here in New Zealand. There has been some unpleasant news of abuse of power, but I'd like to investigate that for myself. There's a tendency to hear only part of the story from secondhand sources. You know, a little knowledge is a dangerous thing. The worst lies are always the half-truths — a case of information asymmetry, which you would be familiar with in the insurance business.'

'Oh, yes,' Mr Jones agreed. 'It's a real problem in our line of work. But would you consider returning to New Zealand if you find the Samoan public service is not what you expect?'

'The thought has never entered my mind. I always feel that Samoa needs me more than New Zealand does, and I should go where my service is needed most. Why do you ask?'

'Dad could give you a job, right Dad?' interrupted Jocelyn with a big grin.

Mr Jones looked surprised. Solomona stopped eating and glanced at Helen.

'Listen, Mona,' said Mr Jones, gesturing with his spoon. 'Don't get me wrong. I was aiming to put a proposal to you with the hope that you would consider it. I'm convinced that you are someone who can help us. I believe your actuarial and economic skills are just what we need in our office.'

Solomona again glanced enquiringly at Helen.

'Mona, I haven't discussed any of this with Dad,' she insisted.

'It's an honest proposal, Mona. Take some time to think about it,' added Mr Jones.

'It's very generous of you, sir, and I'm obviously flattered by the offer. The selfish part of me wants to accept the offer for obvious reasons, but I have an obligation to the Samoan people, the Samoan Government, my parents and my family that I have to fulfil. Not only that, I have a brother and sister who are also on government scholarships. As the eldest, I feel obligated to set a good example for them, regardless of whether they follow it or not. I hope you understand, sir.'

'Yes, I understand, Mona. You are an honourable young man, and that's why we like and respect you so much. But, aren't there Samoan scholars who have not returned?'

'Oh, sure there are; but I made a pact with myself before I accepted the scholarship that I would return after my studies. It would be a betrayal of that principle and the trust the Samoan Government has placed in me if I were not to return. It would have been better that I never accepted the scholarship in the first place.'

'I think Mona has a valid point, darling,' interjected Mrs Jones. 'Would anyone like a hot drink?' she added.

'Well, Mona, your parents must be very proud of you. You are certainly a very fine young man. It has been a real privilege for us to get to know you.'

'Thank you for your kind words, sir. I hope you understand. I'm sure there must be someone else in the market who can do an even better job than me.'

'Yes, of course I understand, Mona,' smiled Mr Jones. 'However, in case your circumstances change, please keep it in mind.'

'Yes, I will. Thank you.'

They moved to the living room where they continued to chat over drinks before heading off to bed. Helen was elated at how well her father, and her family, got along with Solomona. While disappointed that Solomona had not accepted her father's offer, she was proud of his strong commitment to his principles. She couldn't stop smiling, knowing that her parents were equally impressed with his unwavering integrity. Tomorrow morning they were going to church together, and she couldn't wait to introduce Solomona to her friends there.

Twelve

Helen woke early the next morning, had a quick shower, then went to wake Solomona. She opened the door slowly, had a peek inside, and found him still asleep. Tiptoeing over to the bed, she lifted the sheets and slid in beside him.

'Morning, Mister Tui,' she whispered in his ear.

Solomona struggled to wake up. 'What are you doing here?' he asked, still half-asleep.

'I'm here to wake you up. It's almost time for church. And it's such a lovely day. Perhaps we could go for a drive somewhere after church.'

'What time is it?' He slid up and rested against the bedhead.

'It's almost seven,' she replied as she rolled onto her stomach and looked at him.

Solomona yawned and stretched his arms. 'Man, it feels like I haven't slept in ages.'

'Well, you'd better get up, so we can have breakfast before we go to church.'

'And what are you doing in my bed, Miss Jones?' he feigned shock, as he ran his fingers through her hair.

'I've just had a shower and I'm feeling a bit cold,' she fibbed.

Laughing, he teased, 'Oh, poor baby. I hope you realise I haven't said my prayers yet.'

Helen smiled. 'Don't worry, Mister Tui. I will not lead you into temptation. I've just missed you, that's all.'

'A likely story,' he grinned as he continued to caress her hair. 'But we can't stay here all day — people will become suspicious. Come on, let me get up.'

Solomona had a quick shower while Helen went upstairs to prepare breakfast. When he appeared upstairs, fresh from his shower, Mr and Mrs Jones were already having their breakfast.

'Were you able to get some sleep, Mona?' asked Mr Jones.

'Oh, yes, thank you... until someone woke me up,' Solomona winked at Helen.

After a quick breakfast, they all headed for church just a short drive away. The service lasted less than an hour, and afterwards Helen took the opportunity to proudly introduce Solomona to the priest and her friends. She felt happy, and couldn't hide her smile, as she made sure everyone had the chance to meet him.

'What time are you two leaving today?' asked Mrs Jones, as they headed back home.

'As soon as we're ready, Mum,' replied Helen. She was looking forward to spending as much time as possible alone with Solomona before they had to make their way back to the university.

After friendly conversation over coffee and scones with the Jones family, Helen and Solomona prepared to leave. Her mother had thoughtfully prepared a basket of food for them to take on their drive.

'Well, let's get going, Mister Tui,' Helen urged.

'Thank you very much for a lovely weekend, and for the delicious food.' Solomona shook hands with Helen's parents.

'You're most welcome, Mona,' smiled Mrs Jones. 'We look forward to your next visit.'

Solomona picked up the picnic basket that Mrs Jones had prepared and headed out to the car.

'Well, sweetheart,' whispered Mr Jones to his daughter as they walked downstairs, 'Mona appears to be very principled, but if he loves you, as you said he does, then I think he might consider staying.'

'Thanks, Dad, we'll see,' she smiled as she kissed him on the cheek.

Solomona was leaning against the car when Helen, her parents and Jocelyn walked down the driveway together. They said goodbye, and Helen kissed her parents and sister.

'Drive safely, you two,' Mrs Jones called as they waved goodbye.

'Where are we going?' asked Solomona as they drove off.

'Let's go somewhere quiet away from everyone else,' Helen replied.

'Beach or forest?'

'Let's go to a beach.'

'I think I know just the spot, HR,' he said as they headed for the main highway to North Auckland.

Helen sat deep in thought, as the car passed through wooded hillsides and along grassy valleys. She kept thinking about what her father had said. 'If he truly loves me, then maybe he will stay. On the other hand, why can't I go with him when he returns home,' she thought, almost punching the air in excitement. She was sure now that it was possible for them to be together for the rest of their lives.

'A penny for your thoughts, Miss Jones.'

'Ah, not now, Mister Tuisamoa,' she smiled not taking her eyes from the spectacular scenery. She stole an occasional glance at Solomona, arousing his curiosity. 'It's my little secret — for now at least,' she teased.

After almost an hour of driving, they turned onto an access road that took them along a narrow bumpy track to a beach on the eastern coast not far past Warkworth. Parking the car under a *Pohutukawa* tree they took out the picnic basket and spread a rug on the grass in the shade.

'This is a lovely spot, Mona.'

'I knew you would love it here.'

'Yes, I do, but I'm curious. Who else likes it here?' she probed, looking intently at him.

'Me, of course.' Solomona pretended not to understand her question.

Smiling, Helen knelt on the rug in front of him.

'No, Mister Tui,' she said slowly, but with a big smile. 'I mean, who is the other *girl* who likes it here?'

Solomona took a while to respond. He looked as though he was trying to decide whether or not to answer.

'Who is the other girl?' he repeated, while Helen held both his hands. 'Ah, I remember, but that is *my* little secret,' he laughed.

'Please tell me, Mona,' she begged. 'I won't get angry.'

'Listen, HR, I was only joking. With a beautiful and intelligent girl like you, what else shall a man desireth in life?'

'Liar! I know it when you start spouting Shakespearian language.'

'Honest, HR,' he said, still laughing. 'Ask the *Pohutukawa* trees.' He raised his hands as if preaching. 'They surely would know who had been coming here in the three years you were away, Miss Jones.'

'Yes,' she smiled, as she gently pinched him, 'and the *Pohutukawa* trees certainly have memories.'

'Oh, yes they do, HR. Excellent memories, in fact. For instance, they never forget to cheer us up during Christmas with their lovely red blooms.'

'And they can no doubt recall who Solomona Tuisamoa was picking up shells with here on this beautiful beach,' she mocked.

'Actually, they can recall that there was no one else,' he smiled ruefully.

Helen knew she would never win this argument. She could not recall ever winning an argument with Solomona.

'I believe you, Mister Tui,' she smiled.

'You have to, HR. Actually I know this place because we surveyed it and drew up a map for one of our practical exercises in maths to provide the marine biology people with a contour map showing the sea floor.'

Helen reached into her handbag and pulled out the letter she had written to him the previous day.

'Look, I was going to give this to you earlier, but I decided to wait until we were by ourselves,' she said as she handed it to him.

She lay down on the rug beside him while he read the note. When he finished, he turned and looked at her.

'Oh, Miss Jones, you shouldn't feel so despondent,' he said mockingly. He got up and started to walk slowly backwards away from her, waving the note. 'Life is too great, HR, and time too brief for us to waste.'

'Don't you ever take anything seriously?' she asked as she started to follow him.

'Oh, yes I do; most certainly I do,' he replied, continuing to back away from her. 'But you see, HR, taking life seriously, as my friend Einstein once told me, is relative. What is serious to a beautiful, intelligent and wealthy *pakeha* girl is likely to be very different from what a poor Samoan boy considers to be "serious". A serious life must be a happy life, and a happy life, Miss Jones, should not be a function of circumstances,' he continued, flopping to the sand.

Helen caught up with him, straddled her legs across him and pinned his arms to the sand.

'Now, listen to me, my bright and handsome Samoan boy,' she said, lowering her head close to his face. 'Don't give me that pauper nonsense; you are no pauper. I was serious when I wrote that note.'

'I know you were, HR,' he replied, trying to move his arms, 'and my family may not necessarily be poor, but I am just a poor student.'

'No, you don't think I was serious when I wrote that note, Mister Tui. You don't know how I feel when you're not there.' Helen loosened her grip on his arms and sat back on his stomach.

'I was just trying to cheer you up and buy some time to think about what you said in your note, HR,' he confessed as he reached up with his right hand and touched her face. 'Let's walk to the end of the beach.'

'Do you love me, Mona?'

'You must have asked me that question a thousand times, and I'm very confident that I have replied twice as many times. I fell for you the first time I saw you, HR, and my feelings are still the same.' His tone was suddenly serious, as he reached up to stroke her face. 'But you know what? Go and find the greatest love you can anywhere in New Zealand or, if possible, in the whole world. Bring it back to me, and I tell you —'

'Tell me what?' she interrupted. Just for a moment she had thought Solomona was taking her seriously but now he was mocking her again.

He paused, trying to look solemn, then burst out laughing, 'I can beat that love by 100 per cent!' He gently pushed her to the sand, got up and ran away from her.

Helen was not sure whether to laugh or be angry. He was making fun of her again, but all she had wanted was to tell him how she truly felt. Normally she found his teasing endearing, but now she found it irritating. She turned away, looking far out to sea, as tears rolled slowly down her cheeks.

Solomona realised something was wrong. He expected Helen to chase him as she always did. This time, maybe he had overstepped the mark. He ran back to her, and kneeling in front of her, held her shoulders in both hands. He tried to look at her, but she averted her eyes.

'Oh, I'm sorry, HR. I didn't mean to hurt you. I was just trying to cheer you up. You know I love you. I tell you that at least once whenever we see or talk to each other. You must know that.'

Helen tried to clear her throat. She took the handkerchief he offered her and wiped her eyes. Trying to smile, she shyly met his gaze. Pulling him toward her, she wrapped her arms around him, resting her chin on his shoulder.

'I'm sorry I got upset with you. You know I've always enjoyed your weird Samoan sense of humour. But I was really hoping you would try to understand how I feel, but —'

'Feelings? Oh, feelings are bad!' he interrupted, with a chuckle.

'Can you just listen to me, bloody Coconut!' she said in frustration at his continual teasing.

'Oh, so you are really angry with me?'

Helen paused. She had always found it difficult to discuss serious matters with him.

'Well, not really,' she said slowly, 'but we came here because there are things we need to discuss. You have been making it increasingly difficult for me to share my thoughts with you. Mona, I want to be able to study this week for my exams, but I can't when I feel like this.'

She started to cry. Feeling guilty at upsetting her, Solomona held her tightly and gently caressed her. Picking her up, he carried her to a shady spot where he gently put her down and sat with his arms wrapped around her.

'Now, I'm ready to listen, HR,' he said softly, looking into her eyes. 'Talk to me and unload all your worries, seriously.'

Looking into his eyes, Helen knew that she couldn't stay upset with him for long. She reached out with her right hand and gently stroked his temple.

'I really like this,' she said, savouring his closeness. 'I mean, I really enjoy being with you and holding you — and that is my problem.'

'HR, it doesn't make any sense that you like something that is causing you a problem. Don't you think that sounds rather illogical?'

'Being with you is not the problem.'

'Oh, so what is it?' he inquired.

'Well, let's just say that being *without* you may be a problem.'

'I think I understand now,' he smiled.

Helen paused. She nestled her head against his shoulder. 'You see, I may have just over a year of being with you, then you'll be gone.'

Solomona gently pushed her back until he could look into her eyes.

'If it is any comfort to you, my dear Helen Ruth Jones,' he said seriously, 'no one really knows when my PhD thesis will be completed. I could finish it in a year, or it could take two years. It could take even longer than that. Who knows?'

'I know, but it could also be less than a year, knowing how hard and efficiently you work.'

'It's unlikely that I will finish in less than a year from now,' he tried to console her. 'It's more likely to take another two years.'

'But it's also plausible that you could finish it in a year or less, couldn't you?'

'It's plausible, but highly unlikely.'

'But a year can pass quickly, almost without notice.'

'Come on, it's really unlikely I will finish within a year,' he insisted.

Still, Solomona realised that Helen may have a point. A year could pass quickly for a student engrossed in completing a PhD thesis, he thought, and before he knew it, it would be time to return to Samoa, leaving Helen behind. So far he had avoided thinking about it, but now that reality suddenly confronted him. He remembered how he missed her when she went to England with her family. But then he knew she would return. It was different now. He was not sure he would see her again once he returned home to Samoa. Suddenly, tears started to well in his eyes.

'Are you crying?' Helen asked, surprised.

'I'm sorry,' he apologised, averting his face.

'There's nothing wrong with crying, Mister Tui,' she reassured him.

'I know, but it's not manly to cry.' He tried to smile, 'It's a bit embarrassing, really.'

'Well, sweetheart, it takes a real man to shed tears.' Helen gently wiped away his tears. 'I can't remember seeing you cry before, apart from when you heard about Ao being pregnant.'

'Oh, I did once when a girl at school broke my nose,' he said, trying to smile, 'and when I left home to come to New Zealand for the first time. But now? I guess it shows how much I love you and will miss you when I return to Samoa.'

'Why don't you stay then?' she urged. 'Reconsider Dad's offer. I can help to pay back your bond. I still have lots of money from grandpa's will.'

'It's not the bond, HR. My family can pay it, if need be. It's the principle — I think I've told you this before. It would be a betrayal of that principle, the trust of the Samoan Government and people, as well as of my family. If you do care for me, then please don't burden me this way. And if you want us to be happy, then don't ask me to stay, please,' he pleaded.

'So I guess there is no future for us,' she sighed, feeling despondent.

'What do you mean, no future?'

'I don't want to sound too presumptuous, Mona, but since I first met you, I have always dreamt of having your children. I dream about coming home after work to this bronze-skinned boy with red hair, happily running up to me, with his bronze-skinned sister, with long black hair. In my dreams I see them growing up. The boy becomes the greatest Samoan ever to wear the All Blacks jersey.'

'Greater than the phenomenal B G?' smiled Solomona, referring to B.G. Williams, one of the most talented Samoan footballers to have worn the black jersey of New Zealand's famous rugby team.

'So it could happen?' she asked excitedly.

'Well, anything is possible where there's a will. You know, it's funny, but I've had similar dreams. Why can't we have a great future the way we are? If we were to be married, we might find life rather difficult, but if we keep things as they are, we could remain as happy as we are now. The sort of relationship that Plato suggested.'

Helen wasn't impressed with his apparent change of tone. 'Why does he have to bring up Plato, Socrates, or any other philosopher or religious thinker at a time like this?' she thought.

'But, with your stand of no sex before marriage, there would never be the greatest Samoan All Black.'

'That could create a problem,' he teased, 'but reproductive technology is pretty advanced at —'

'No thank you very much — I'm not some kind of farm animal!' she snapped indignantly. 'Besides, I don't wish to be a single mother. If I have children, I want them to grow up in a natural and normal home with a loving father and an adoring mother.'

'Oh, I'm sorry I upset you, HR.' Solomona regretted his feeble attempt at humour. 'I was just trying to lighten the mood a bit.'

'I'm sorry I got upset so quickly too.'

Helen smiled to herself as she thought of her earlier solution to their predicament.

'What are you smiling about, Miss Jones?'

'Well,' she confessed, 'it's the little secret I referred to while we were driving here.'

'Well, are you going to share it with me?'

'It occurred to me that, if we do get married, we don't have to live in New Zealand. We could live in Samoa; I love you and I could follow you to Samoa rather than ask you to stay in New Zealand. You have a dream, a noble dream that I'd like to share in. I have none — except to be with you and to have your children, in Samoa; in Paradise. I am prepared to follow you wherever you go.' Helen felt excited that she might have, at last, found a way to overcome the final obstacle to sharing a life with her beloved. But Solomona did not show any sign of being excited. He remained deep in thought.

'Well, say something, Mister Tui.'

'Ah yes, it's a nice thought, but—'

'Mona, just tell me the truth. Is there another woman?'

'Helen, you are the only woman in my life!'

'Then why can't we get married and be together?'

'I didn't say we can't get married.'

'Then what's the problem?'

'It's not that easy, HR. There are so many things to consider, and I'm just afraid —'

'Afraid of what?'

'Helen, I'm afraid that if we do get married and live in Samoa, things will certainly not stay as they are now. I'm especially worried that one day I may be forced to make a hard and painful decision. I want to be able to enjoy all the times that I spend with you.'

'What kind of decision?'

'Helen, my greatest fear is losing you,' he confessed, 'and I am scared that if we do get married, one day you might force me to choose between you and my family. And if that were to happen, I would be faced with an unpalatable decision. I don't ever want that to happen. I'd rather be your friend forever than be your husband just until the honeymoon is over.'

'Why couldn't we remain good friends if things don't work out?'

'That's exactly my problem, HR. I don't want my marriage not to work out.'

'Remember you used to say that it's better to try and fail rather than failing to try?'

'Yes, I do remember saying that,' he replied, 'but marriage is, perhaps, the only thing that I wouldn't try on the basis that, if it fails, I could get out of it. It's a holy bonding of two people, and if I estimate the probability of success to be low, then I'd rather not go through with it if the possible source of failure were beyond my control.'

'I promise I will never put you in a position where you have to contemplate such a decision.'

'It's very easy to say that now, HR, but when life becomes miserable and unbearable, and you feel I am not providing you with the support you need, then it's highly likely you will forget any promise you may have made in the past.'

'I promise I will never put you in such a position, Mona,' she repeated. 'So long as you still love me, that's all that matters. And you do love me, don't you?'

'Of course, I do. You are the only woman I have ever really loved.'

'Enough to want to marry me?'

'More than enough.'

'So why can't we get married?'

'My dear, more than enough love may be necessary, but by no means sufficient for a successful marriage, especially when you're married to a Samoan. I'm just trying to be realistic.'

'What is sufficient for a successful marriage between a Samoan man and a foreign woman?'

'When you marry a Samoan,' he explained, 'you don't just marry an individual. You basically marry a family, an extended family, a clan. You will not be able to have much of a life of your own together. What you and your husband have will have to be shared with all the other relatives. Contribution to social and cultural events is a never-ending burden because the power brokers, the *matais*, benefit from those social activities, and no one is game to change the way things are done.'

'If contributing to the family and social activities is the main hurdle, I feel confident I can handle that.'

Solomona smiled. 'It's not that easy, HR. It's a lot more complicated than I could ever hope to explain. I don't think there is a person in this world with enough money to satisfy the so-called cultural obligation, because the more you have, the more is expected of you. I would like to change that, and I also have other goals like developing the local village, where the power of the Tuisamoa title could be of great assistance. I personally don't like having the title because it's a real burden, but I need it in order to accomplish the goals I have set myself. I'm not guaranteed to receive it after Dad — the family makes that decision. My mother told me she is doing her part to ensure Dad puts my name forward, and not any of my half-brothers, but marrying a foreigner is likely to kill any chance I may have. But even if I do get the Tuisamoa title, I wouldn't like to drag you into the dirt of village politics; you are too nice a person for that.'

'I can always wash off the dirt,' she insisted.

Solomona was momentarily stunned by the simplicity of her response to something that to him was a very serious and difficult matter to resolve. He looked at her rather disbelievingly. 'You're an amazing person, Miss Jones. You can see things in black and white. You have courage. I like that.' He paused for a moment. 'Tell you what. When I finish my thesis, you're invited to come with me to Samoa so you can get a feel of what life there is like. Then we'll see what happens. How about that?'

'Promise?' she smiled, as she dusted sand from his shoulder.

'Sure. I promise.'

Helen could hardly contain her happiness. She threw her arms around Solomona, pulled him towards her, and kissed him.

'This is the greatest day of my life!' she exclaimed. She felt like screaming. 'I think I can concentrate on my studies now.'

'You'll have to bring a lot of money because you will need to do a lot of bribing,' he teased.

'Don't worry, Mister Tui. I have enough to buy an island.'

'We shall see. I am yet to see a rich person in Samoa, especially in Lalolagi. Come on, let's go for a walk along the beach before we have lunch.'

Solomona helped Helen to her feet. Hand in hand they went for a stroll along the beach. The tide was starting to come in. Wavelets lapped onto the sand. Seagulls called noisily above their heads over the roar of the Pacific Ocean. Helen held tight to Solomona's hand, feeling like she was riding the crest of the waves as they rolled into the shore.

Thirteen

Solomona worked hard to complete and submit his thesis three years after he started his PhD degree course. Helen received her results, for the third year of her degree program, at about the same time. With passes in all her papers, she faced one more year of studies to complete her Honours degree. She remained undecided about attempting an Honours year, but Solomona urged her to consider it. For now, she was looking forward to a holiday in Samoa with him. Helen had never visited any of the Pacific islands before. She felt excited, and just a little apprehensive. They planned to leave for Samoa three days before New Year.

Virtually all of Solomona's relatives in New Zealand gathered at the airport to see them off — a large group when they were all together. Some of their friends, including members of the church choir and orchestra, and the Joneses were also there to farewell them.

'So many people,' commented Helen in amazement as she surveyed the faces surrounding them.

'There are two events in life that are very important to Samoans: births and deaths,' explained Solomona. 'Arrivals and farewells are viewed in the same way. Every farewell could be your last, and there is always great rejoicing if you make it safely to the end of your journey. Expect the same when we arrive in Samoa.'

Their goodbyes lasted almost 20 minutes. Some of the women and children were crying. The men joked, in Samoan, wondering how a beautiful *palagi* girl like Helen could fall for a Don Juan like Solomona, and laughed among themselves. Solomona smiled and returned their banter as he and Helen moved among them, shaking hands and hugging everyone.

'What are they laughing at?' Helen asked curiously.

'They reckon you are too beautiful, even for a good-looking guy like me,' chuckled Solomona.

'And what did you say?'

'I told them that I agreed, wholeheartedly,' he smiled.

'Ah, you're telling fibs, Mister Tui,' she teased, playfully pinching him. 'That smirk says it all.'

'Well, I told them that nothing beats brains,' he countered.

Helen smiled, 'You're right, Mister Tui. Your brains could easily overwhelm any beautiful girl — that's what worries me.'

Solomona chuckled to himself.

Fetuao and Alan, who had been married shortly after Nathan's birth, were standing to one side. Solomona took Nathan from Alan and held him up. Looking into the child's eyes, he said softly, 'My friend, may you grow up to be as brave and selfless as Nathan the American patriot, and as brilliant as Nathan of the Bible.'

Nathan, who was now an energetic two-year-old, tried to grab at Solomona's glasses. His antics had everyone laughing. Solomona stood nursing him in one arm and cradling his sister with his other arm. Fetuao started to cry as she hugged her brother.

'Now, this is what I was worried about,' whispered Solomona as he tried to placate her. 'Ao, we are not here to mourn anyone's death. Be happy. And make sure your studies and Alan's progress well, and if you find managing Nathan and your studies becomes too difficult, then send him home. I'm sure Mum wouldn't mind looking after him.' He shook Alan's hand warmly. 'Legi, look after Ao and Nathan well.' Alan nodded as he retrieved his son.

Their last goodbyes were to Helen's family, and to Albert and Andreana, who were now also married. 'Look after our sister and her son, Pati,' Solomona urged as he shook hands with his brother.

Finally Solomona and Helen turned to face everyone, waved goodbye, then headed for the departure gate.

Helen was excited to finally be leaving, but was apprehensive about what lay ahead.

It was mid-afternoon when they sighted the Samoan islands. The plane flew over the big island of Savai'i. The sky was clear except for wispy cloud covering the tip of Mount Silisili near the middle of the island. The lushness of the surrounding rainforest glistened in the afternoon sun. Helen marvelled at the rich green of the coastal rainforests and the clear turquoise sea surrounding Savai'i.

'It's so beautiful, Mona. It looks like a paradise.'

'God's creations, like you, HR, are always beautiful,' he murmured, as he leaned across her for a better view.

'The sea is so clear! I can almost see the fish in the water, even in the deep water outside the reefs.'

'It's ironic, isn't it?' he smiled. 'You have a much better view from up here than you do when you are actually on the surface of the water.'

The plane turned eastward and started its approach to Samoa's international airport on the north-west coast of the island of Upolu. Surrounded by coral reefs, pristine waters and white sandy beaches, and dominated by its tree-covered mountains, from the sky Upolu looked like a gigantic flower floating in a huge blue lake.

Helen's first experience of Samoa was a rush of hot, humid air as they disembarked. She reached out to take Solomona's free hand as they reached the tarmac, but he quietly told her that this was not acceptable in Samoa, at least not in public.

'Why not?' she asked.

'Just a different culture,' he explained. 'Modesty, I guess. It's just not done here. Feelings, intimate feelings, are not displayed publicly. There is a Samoan saying that the most intimate and sincere love is given under the cover of darkness. We must be sensitive to our local culture, and sometimes we have to do things, even though we may not like or agree with them, simply because it is the right thing to do.'

Helen felt rather resentful but began to realise that this was one of the things she would have to accept if she wanted to marry Solomona and live in Samoa. She was starting to understand what had concerned him earlier about their differing cultural backgrounds.

As they joined the queue at the immigration desk, Solomona received a warm greeting from the government official. 'Welcome home, Mona.'

'Thank you, Ben. How have you been keeping?'

'Not bad. Home for good?' Ben asked as he stamped Solomona's passport.

'For now, yes.'

'And you have a beautiful lady accompanying you. Is she also staying for good?' The immigration officer flashed a broad smile.

'Oh, I'm sorry,' apologised Solomona. 'Ben, this is Helen, and Helen, this is Ben, a real danger man,' he joked.

'Oh, come on, King, don't give Helen the wrong impression about your old mate. How long do you plan to stay, Helen?' he asked as he stamped her passport.

'Helen is here until the third week of February,' Solomona cut in.

'I gather you two know each other then,' Helen said curiously.

'In Samoa,' Ben replied, 'you tend to know everyone. It's a small place.'

'Ben and I were classmates,' Solomona explained. 'Ben specialised in women studies, and only a handful of the beautiful girls at school at that time escaped unscathed.'

'Ah, I see,' Helen laughed.

'Don't believe any of that, Helen. Mona was the one, not me.'

'I think I believe you, Ben,' she said, nudging Solomona to get him to admit his guilt.

Ben handed them their passports. 'Maybe I'll see you at Tusi tonight.'

'Unfortunately we can't, Ben. We are going straight to Fagaloa, but we'll see you in town sometime soon.' Solomona picked up his cabin bag and gestured to Helen to move through to the luggage collection area.

'Why Fagaloa?' she asked.

'Because Lalolagi is in Fagaloa and most people only know Fagaloa.'

'And what's the Tusi?'

'Tusi is short for Tusitala, the government-owned hotel, and a popular watering hole with students when they come home for the Christmas holidays,' Solomona replied. 'Tusitala is Samoan for writer of tales, and it's the name Samoans gave to Robert Louis Stevenson.'

Loaded down with suitcases and boxes, they moved through to the customs and quarantine areas, where Solomona noticed that two of the officers on duty were friends from boarding school days.

'Welcome home, King, and welcome to your beautiful friend,' one of the officers greeted in English, shaking hands with Solomona.

'Thank you. I'd like both of you to meet Helen,' he said proudly. 'Helen, this is Fa'amaoni, also known as Fa'a,' he continued, pointing to the customs officer, 'and this is Su'esu'e, and we simply call him Su'e,' he added, gesturing towards the quarantine officer.

'Obviously, you guys all know each other well.' Helen was beginning to wonder whether there was anyone in Samoa whom Solomona didn't know.

'We used to wash his clothes at school,' the officers replied, almost in unison.

'Oh, I see. I didn't realise you were so bossy, Mister Tui.'

'The boys' hostel was like a village,' Solomona explained. 'The older boys were the *matais* and they looked after the young ones. In return, the younger boys performed light chores. Some older boys were a bit mean, but that was rare. Fa'a and Su'e arrived during my final year. We all got along pretty well — you certainly couldn't say I was mean, right guys?'

'Oh, no,' said Fa'amaoni. 'King was the best of the older boys, for sure.'

'That's right,' added Su'esu'e. 'He even provided our toothpaste and soap.'

'Anyway, we don't want to hold up the queue,' Solomona interrupted, as he started to open their suitcases for inspection.

'Yes, we'll catch up with you two sometime soon,' replied the officers. 'You can just push your trolley through. We trust you, King.'

As they passed through to the arrivals area, Solomona could see his extended family and friends waiting outside. He waved to them, and asked one of his cousins to take the luggage trolley, then ushered Helen to the VIP lounge where he knew his parents would be waiting.

A police officer, assigned to guard his father, opened the door and showed them into the exquisitely built, air-conditioned *fale*. As they entered, Solomona's mother, Alofa, rose to her feet and rushed forward to greet her son.

She embraced Solomona in a long hug. Looking radiant in her beautiful *tapa* dress, Alofa was a tall woman and seemed much younger than her almost 60 years, which she attributed to an active mind. Tears rolled down her cheeks as she pulled back to look at her son.

Solomona's father, Paramount Chief Tuisamoa, looked on and smiled, patiently waiting for his turn to welcome his son. Almost 80 now, he was an imposing man, six feet tall but a much bigger build than Solomona. He was wearing a black *lavalava* with a white shirt, a tie to match, and a heavy black coat. His closely cropped hair and moustache were all white, indicative of his advancing years.

Solomona walked over to where his father was seated. Tuisamoa raised both his hands to receive his son. Solomona knelt down on one knee and embraced his father. Initially they didn't say anything to each other, but their smiles reflected the warmth and regard between father and son.

'You look good, father,' he said, smiling broadly.

'I haven't been too well lately, Mona,' Tuisamoa replied, 'but, today, I feel a new burst of energy. The anticipation of your arrival with your *palagi* friend has given me renewed strength.'

Standing just inside the door, Helen watched proceedings with a nervous smile. Solomona sensed that she was feeling apprehensive, so he moved to her side and took her hand.

'Mother and father,' he said, 'I'd like you to meet Helen.' Unsure of what was expected of her, Helen smiled and bowed slightly. She hadn't thought to ask Solomona what to do in such situations, and he had not told her. Alofa embraced her warmly. Tuisamoa also rose to greet her. He moved forward slowly. 'You can embrace Dad,' Solomona said softly to Helen, 'this is a private family meeting.'

'Welcome to Samoa, Helen,' said Alofa, smiling. 'You look more beautiful than in the photograph that Mona sent.'

Helen smiled shyly and shrugged as Solomona winked and smiled at her.

'Yes, Helen,' added Tuisamoa. 'You certainly are, but Mona's not a bad-looking guy either.'

Helen smiled; she was starting to feel slightly more at ease.

'Helen is here for the holidays, then she'll be going back to university to complete her Honours degree,' Solomona explained.

'That's very good, but what about your studies, Mona?' his father asked.

'I have submitted my thesis, and I'm hoping that it will be accepted without the need for any corrections or any follow-up work.'

'I'm glad to hear that. But we will have plenty of time to talk. You two must be tired, and it's getting late. Would you tell the boy outside that we want to go now?'

Solomona walked to the door and told the police officer outside that his parents were ready to leave.

After helping his parents into the government car that would take them as far as Apia, Solomona walked with Helen to the car park where his relatives and friends were still waiting.

'It seems like only our people are left,' he said. 'I can't see any strange faces.'

'Don't tell me all those people are here to meet us,' she exclaimed.

'Didn't I warn you before we left Auckland?'

'Oh, look! The bus is covered with beautiful flowers!' Helen couldn't believe the effort that had gone into decorating the vehicles.

'The bus is owned by my cousin who lives not far from here, one of the trucks is owned by another cousin who lives at the eastern end of Upolu, and the other one is ours. The decorations are a sign of respect for a dignified visitor. They're for you, Miss Jones,' Solomona smiled.

'Really?' Helen felt quite overwhelmed and a little anxious about what it all meant. 'I feel rather embarrassed. You're kidding, aren't you, Mister Tui?'

'I'm not kidding, Miss Jones,' he replied. 'It shows that Mum likes you, or rather that she wants to impress you.'

'Well, I am impressed.'

'Well, you are special, you know, HR.' Solomona gave her a wink.

Wanting to speak to everyone, he climbed onto the back of their double-cabin truck and assisted Helen to join him. The relatives and friends gathered around the back of the truck.

'Could I have your attention, everyone,' he began. There was immediate silence. 'This is Helen, and you young boys and not-so-old men...' he said, pointing to some of the men in the crowd, 'you keep clear of her.' There was loud laughter as different names were called out. Not understanding what was being said, Helen looked curiously at Solomona, but he just winked back. She smiled, rather shyly, feeling disconcerted at not understanding what was going on. 'No,' he continued, looking more serious. The relatives and friends became quiet again. 'What I am trying to say is that Helen is very grateful to all of you for coming to meet us, and for all the work that went into decorating the vehicles. But it's time to hit the road; we have to try to catch up with the boss.'

Solomona explained to Helen what he had said. She smiled and bowed her head slightly as she turned to convey her appreciation to everyone. Feeling excited and happy with their welcome, Helen and Solomona settled into the family four-wheel-drive truck and headed for Apia, with the bus and the other truck following close behind.

Fourteen

The main road was clear of traffic as the Tuisamoa family convoy headed out of the airport towards Apia, Samoa's capital, with Solomona's vehicle in the lead.

'Look at the flowers on those trees — they are so beautiful,' Helen gasped, pointing to the flame-coloured blooms of the fire-trees that lined the road from the airport. 'It looks like the road is being protected by walls of fire on both sides.'

'They are absolutely stunning at this time of the year,' Solomona responded, as he concentrated on dodging the pigs and dogs that crossed the road. 'They are Samoa's answer to Aotearoa's *Pohutukawa* trees,' he added, using the name Polynesians preferred when referring to New Zealand.

'I've never seen so many dogs and pigs roaming around before.' Helen was excitedly taking in all the different sights and sounds of Samoan life.

'You will see more as we pass through the villages. In paradise, all living things are supposed to live in harmony. I suppose the pigs, dogs and cats should also have a right to some sort of freedom,' Solomona said as he tried to evade potholes in the road.

'Some of these villages are so clean, and the flower gardens are so beautiful,' she commented, as she waved to the people smiling and waving at them as they passed by.

'Each village has a women's committee,' he explained, 'and one of their tasks is to keep their village looking beautiful.'

'Tell me something, Mister Tui,' Helen said, trying to suppress a smile.

'What's that, Miss Jones?'

'How can people get any privacy in houses with no walls or windows?'

'I'm going to spoil the fun if I tell you. There is nothing like discovering it for yourself. What do you think?'

Helen smiled. 'You can tell me later.' She continued to study the passing villages. 'I've noticed that some of these churches are huge and elaborate, some as large as cathedrals I've seen in Europe, when the villages seem pretty poor and simple.'

'I suppose it reflects the people's values and commitment, or perhaps a demonstration of what they are really capable of if there is a desire and willingness.'

It was late in the afternoon when they reached Apia. The streets were still busy as people were starting to return home after work. At a roundabout in the middle of town, a car that was already on the roundabout stopped to give way to them. All the traffic following it also had to stop. Solomona raised his hand to acknowledge the courtesy as he drove past. The driver of the car smiled, honked his horn, and waved back.

'Do you know him?' Helen asked.

'No,' he smiled. 'This is Samoa. You'll find it's different here.'

'I just saw something interesting on the town clock,' she commented.

'What was that?' he asked as he caught sight of his parents' vehicle, not far ahead.

'The time on the town clock is one o'clock, but the sun is almost setting.'

Solomona smiled and turned towards her. 'It has been one o'clock, oh... for as long as I can remember. It will still be one o'clock the next time you see it. It's paradise, you know.'

The convoy caught up with Solomona's parents and the police officer just before they arrived at the police station. With the police deeming it unnecessary to escort them any further, Tuisamoa and Alofa transferred to Solomona's four-wheel drive. They then continued on, with the bus and the other truck still following behind.

Not far out of Apia, they came to a stretch of road that meandered along the coastline, just a few metres from the sea in many places. The cliffs were sheer granite, making the construction of the roadway any further inland virtually impossible. The villages too clung closely to the shoreline.

'Oh, this is a beautiful drive,' Helen said, admiring the scenery along the way.

'It is a very pleasant drive, isn't it, Helen?' commented Alofa as she glanced at Tuisamoa who had fallen asleep.

The luxuriant vegetation along the roadside was magnificent. The elegant palm trees along the shoreline leaned and swayed in the sea breeze. Waves crashed onto the reefs about 200 metres from the coast. Inside the reefs, wavelets rolled gently to the shore.

There were not many villages on the coast road; mainly vegetation, majestic hills and picturesque peninsulas. Helen fell quiet. She could not take her eyes off the sea and occasionally the hills, as their vehicle wound its way eastward. Alofa had also fallen asleep. More pigs and dogs crossed the road as they passed through small villages. Close to the end of the Anoama'a district, the road turned inland. The majestic hills of the Fagaloa mountain range and the Le Mafa Pass spread before them.

'Oh, look at those mountains, Mona! Aren't they spectacular?'

'Those are the hills of Fagaloa,' he explained, 'and they are even more spectacular if you approach them from the sea.'

As they neared the Falefa Falls, they came across young boys playing cricket on the roadway. Solomona stopped the truck, winked at Helen, and stretched his arms, while the boys cleared their game off the road. A woman, sweeping up fallen leaves and burning them by the roadside, ran to the boys and dragged some of them off the road.

'Hey! Get your stuff off the road,' she instructed sternly. 'Can't you see it's Tui's truck?'

'Would you like to see more spectacular scenery, HR?' he asked as they waited for the boys to move off the road.

'Why do you ask?'

'Because that will determine which route we take. There are two ways of getting to Lalolagi. One is to cross the bridge at the falls, not far from here, and the other is through the Le Mafa Pass in the hills directly ahead of us. They both take about the same time.'

'I would love to see some more spectacular scenery,' she smiled.

'That means we head over the bridge and along the hillside.'

The road after the bridge was very rough. Only four-wheel drives and vehicles with high clearance could negotiate it. In places only the tyre marks gave any indication that it was a road. The sides were overgrown with tall grass and shrubs.

'Why doesn't someone clear the vegetation on this road?' Helen asked.

'There is probably a ban on implements,' Solomona joked, glancing at her.

The truck bounced and lurched along the heavily rutted road. Solomona's parents, who were still fast asleep, did not seem to be bothered by the rough going.

'Why can't the government fix this road?' she inquired, holding on tightly.

'Because the Prime Minister is absolutely mad with Dad.'

'Why is he mad with your father?'

'Because Dad called him a nobody and a useless idiot about three years ago when Dad was still a Member of Parliament. They silenced him by appointing him a member of the Council of Deputy Heads of State.'

'But that was quite a long time ago.'

'Anger, when it's not dealt with straight away, and properly, is like a volcano. It can lie dormant but we know it's still active underneath, and it's almost inevitable that one day it will explode with all its destructive and ugly fury. Look at all the anger in Northern Ireland, the Balkan region, the Middle East, parts of Africa, South Asia, and many other parts of the world. Their anger has run through aeons!'

'Yeah, but —'

'That anger has killed so many people over the years. Our Prime Minister's anger with Dad only means that our road will not be fixed — yet. But I like it that way,' he laughed as he winked at her.

'What do you mean?' Helen couldn't believe that a roadway in such poor condition would be Solomona's preference.

'Well, Fagaloa has the most beautiful scenery in all of Samoa, more beautiful than anything I have seen in beautiful Aotearoa,' he said. 'If the road is improved, Fagaloa will be overrun by tourists and enlightened Samoans. That will surely and quickly ruin God's gift to Samoa. So in my own selfish way, I like the road as it is.'

'You do have a very good point,' she smiled.

In half an hour or so, they had travelled only three kilometres from the bridge. Reaching the steeper cliffs, they could now see the ocean, several hundred metres below. At the tip of a long peninsula, one of many that separated Lalolagi and Fagaloa from the rest of Samoa, Solomona stopped the truck at a lookout and got out to stretch his legs. The bus and the other truck also stopped but no one got out. Helen and Solomona walked to the edge of the lookout. The sun seemed to be suspended above the horizon as if waiting for them to take up their positions. The sea below was fanned by a light breeze while the surrounding vegetation took on a reddish glow from the setting sun. At a distance, they could see smoke from cooking fires rising above the treeline of the Anoama'a district. The hills of Anoama'a rose gently from the sea right up to the tip of Mount Fito. They watched silently as the sun slowly slipped below the horizon.

'It's the most beautiful sunset I've ever seen,' Helen exclaimed as she placed her arm around his shoulder.

'If you want to see a stunning sunset, this is one of a few special places, and I'm glad we got here just in time.'

'Where else?'

'From the top of Mount Lagi, near our village, is another one.'

'Can we go there?'

'It's a pretty tough three-hour climb.'

'I can manage that.'

'But I don't think we can wait until the sun sets.'

'Why not?'

'It's too dangerous coming down in the dark.'

'Even if we have a strong torch?'

'Yes, even with a strong torch. We can climb Mount Lagi, say, Saturday, but we will have to wait for that special sunset until we go to Savai'i.'

They walked back to the truck just as Alofa woke up. Tuisamoa was still snoring.

'Aren't we there yet?' asked Alofa.

'We are still on the big peninsula, Mother,' Solomona replied.

'Hungry, Helen?' she asked.

'No, not at the moment.'

'That's good. There will be plenty of food waiting for us in the village,' Alofa said.

Solomona started the engine and they headed off again. As they rounded the tip of the peninsula, Helen felt as though they were entering a totally different country. There were no houses, and no sign of civilisation nearby. Before them were the lofty mountains that shielded Lalolagi and Fagaloa from the rest of Samoa. They rose majestically from the sea as though to welcome anyone entering the Fagaloa district. There was not much daylight left, but the beauty of the place was not dimmed by lack of light. Mount Lagi towered above them, and sunlight still illuminated its summit. Below, one could see the sea washing up against the rocky peninsulas that continued along the Fagaloa coast.

'This is an awesome place, Mona!' Helen acknowledged. 'Look at the coastline, it's so beautiful. I have never seen anything like this before.'

'You have good taste, HR,' he smiled as he tried to ensure that the truck didn't veer too close to the edge of the road. 'I like that. Most Samoans, though, don't share your view of Fagaloa. That's because they don't have your cultured eyes. But as I said before, there is no scenery like this anywhere else in Samoa. The closest is in Tutuila in American Samoa, but our village's legends say they stole it from Fagaloa.'

'Why wouldn't anyone like a place like this?'

'It's what we call, in economics, revealed preferences,' he explained, smiling. 'In every country, there are urban, suburban, rural and remote areas, where people can choose to live. It appears that, in general, remote areas are the least preferred for a variety of reasons, and Fagaloa is the remotest part of Samoa. A large number of our people who can afford the cost of living there have moved to Apia, many permanently. But the same attributes that people do not like about Fagaloa — its isolation and rugged, but stunningly beautiful, landscapes — are what I like about the place, and why I don't want the road fixed. We all have different preferences, which we reveal by the choices we make.'

'Oh, this is so beautiful,' Helen said as she gazed from the sea to the mountain range.

'I know, it is very beautiful, but you know we can't take any credit for its beauty — God created it. I'm just glad my ancestors chose to settle here. They were certainly more advanced in their perception of beauty.'

'I wonder how beautiful these mountains would look in the afternoon sun.'

'Even better, HR. You can see all that from the top of Mount Lagi.'

It was almost 6.30 pm and was getting dark. The vehicle's headlights illuminated the ruts in the road so that they appeared even deeper. Helen continued to hang on tightly as the truck lurched from side to side. About an hour after they resumed their journey, they took a turn and started to descend.

'That road will take you to the rest of Fagaloa,' said Solomona, pointing back to the main road. 'It's another half a kilometre or so, or about 30 minutes drive.'

'Where are we now?'

'We are now entering Lalolagi's territory.'

'This is a much smoother ride.'

'This is considered to be Lalolagi's private road. The young men of the village maintain it. They get into trouble if the road is not in good condition. The colourful plants on the sides of the road were planted by the women's committee.'

'How far are we from the village?'

'Another five minutes or so.'

'But I can't see any sign of a village. It's pitch black,' Helen said doubtfully as the truck passed under what seemed to be a thick canopy.

'In a minute, you will,' he explained, just before the bright lights of Lalolagi came into view below them.

'Oh, that's beautiful. It almost feels like we are in a plane.'

'It is a beautiful view from up here.'

Two minutes later, they were at sea level.

'What was that we just went through?' she inquired.

'Oh, it's a very thick forest of tall chestnut trees. It runs the whole length of the village, and it completely blocks your view of Lalolagi from the main road. You can see Lalolagi only from the air or from the sea.'

'Yeah, it felt a bit eerie; it's so dark.'

A short while later, they arrived at Lalolagi, Helen with a real sense of anticipation.

Fifteen

Lalolagi was in a festive mood when the Tuisamoa family convoy arrived. Preparations were well underway for a formal welcoming ceremony and a feast to follow. Women and young men were looking busy, and there was lots of giggling, whispering and laughter. The smell of freshly cooked food filled the air, and smoke from the *umu* floated seawards suspended above the water. All the guesthouses surrounding the *malae* were lit, but empty. Virtually everyone in the village had converged on the Tuisamoas' home. The village *matais* and their wives, as well as the pastor and his wife, were already waiting in the large *faleafolau* that served as Tuisamoa's resting and sleeping pavilion. Filled with childlike curiosity, the women preparing food in the kitchen of the *falepalagi* behind the *faleafolau* whispered to each other. The *taulele'a*, or men who do not hold chiefly titles and who serve the chiefs, were talking quietly and smoking cigarettes at the cooking *fale* behind the main buildings.

Solomona parked their vehicle in the carport next to the Tuisamoas' *falepalagi*. After helping everyone out of the truck, he showed Helen inside, where they quickly changed into *lavalavas*, then made their way to the *faleafolau*, which was adorned with flowers, with all the posts entwined with coconut leaves.

'Just follow what I do, HR,' he whispered as they walked to the *faleafolau*.

'Hmm, I can smell the food already,' Helen commented, trying to calm her nerves.

As they climbed the steps to the *faleafolau*, a young woman placed flower *leis* around their necks. They waited outside for Tuisamoa to arrive and take his seat. Solomona took the opportunity to inspect the people inside, outlining to Helen a little about each one. The pastor and his wife were sitting right at the front. The *matais* flanked the pastor and his wife, and their wives were seated at the rear.

When Tuisamoa arrived, he went straight to his designated place at the rounded end of the *faleafolau*. Alofa hurried to the family's *falepalagi* to give instructions to the women serving the food. The pastor, his wife, the village *matais* and their wives offered the usual salutations as Tuisamoa sat down, to which Tuisamoa responded in accordance with custom. Solomona removed his thongs, and slowly entered the *faleafolau* from the rear. Helen did likewise. He walked straight to the middle, with his head slightly bowed, and shook hands with the pastor, then the pastor's wife. He continued along the line of dignitaries until he had shaken hands with all the *matais* and their wives, with Helen following behind him. She could feel everyone's eyes focusing on her, and it was making her very nervous. When they finished shaking hands, Solomona and Helen started to move towards the rear of the *faleafolau*.

'Mona,' called the pastor as they were about to sit down, 'come and sit here between me and Ma'afala,' referring to the *matai* sitting next to him.

Solomona obliged, and Helen followed. As they sat down, the church bell rang, accompanied by the howling of dogs. Almost simultaneously, the sound of the conch shell filled the still evening air. Helen struggled to get her legs in a cross-legged position despite having practised at home in New Zealand. She finally succeeded, much to the amusement of some of the women.

'What were the bell and conch shell for?' she asked as she made herself more comfortable.

'The bell is to signal time for evening devotions, and the conch announces the curfew for devotions,' Solomona answered in a whispered tone.

The pastor announced that they would begin their evening devotions and thanksgiving for the safe arrival of Solomona and Helen.

'What about our stuff, I mean *my* stuff?' Helen whispered.

'Don't worry. Your things are being distributed to all the women as belated Christmas gifts,' he said jokingly.

She reached out discreetly and gently pinched him.

'You're teasing me, Mister Tui.'

Solomona grimaced. 'No, really. They've been taken to your room. We're going to have devotions now, so we need to be quiet.'

Devotions lasted almost an hour. There were two hymns, a Bible reading, a long speech and an equally long prayer by the pastor.

After the service, there was a presentation of *sua* to the pastor and his wife in recognition of their status as the most important guests of Tuisamoa that evening. A large pig, roasted in the *umu*, was the main item of the *sua*. Others included a young coconut with a $50 note covering the opening, a broiled chicken, a fine mat and a package of cooked taro. Outside a young man announced, as loudly as he could, the *sua* and its contents as young men and women paraded to the middle of the *faleafolau* and laid items in front of the pastor and his wife.

The pastor, on behalf of his wife and himself, expressed their gratitude to the Tuisamoa family for the *sua*, after which the meal was served. There were about eight plates of different kinds of food in front of Helen, all to be eaten with taro or boiled rice. She could identify some of them, but was unsure of the others. She remembered Fiasili telling her that there were no potatoes in Samoa. Feeling rather overwhelmed, she was still wondering how she was going to attempt to eat everything in front of her when the pastor announced that he would now bless the food.

'Do I have to eat all of this?' she whispered to Solomona after the pastor had said grace.

About to take a mouthful of his favourite native chicken soup, he smiled. 'I'm afraid that's the rule, right, Nari?'

'What is, Mona?' inquired Tenari, the pastor, as he broke open a taro with his hands.

'Visitors to Lalolagi, especially *palagi* girls, have to finish their food or they sleep with Moso in the forest, isn't that the rule?' he said with a wink, invoking the mythical Samoan giant, who lived, according to local legend, in the forest nearby.

'Oh, yes, that's right, Mona.' Tenari tried to sound serious. 'And Moso is probably very hungry tonight.'

Sekara, Tenari's wife, overheard their teasing and decided to intervene.

'You guys should be ashamed,' she said, as she dipped a piece of taro into the delicious *palusami*. 'Helen probably believes you. You just eat what you can, Helen, they are just teasing you.'

'This guy always does that to me,' Helen laughed as she pinched Solomona.

When they finished the main course, hot drinks, in the form of Samoan *koko*, were served with cake, buttered bread and crackers with jam. Unable to eat any more, Helen just drank the hot *koko*. Solomona advised her to push the rest of the food to the *matai* sitting next to her. The *matai* accepted it gratefully, and gave it to his young grandson, seated behind him, to take home.

Before everyone had finished their hot drinks, Alofa, who was sitting next to Tuisamoa, beckoned to Solomona. Excusing himself, Solomona stepped outside, and walked around the outside of the *faleafolau* to sit behind his mother.

'Yes, Mother?'

'We have to give some money to the pastor and his wife,' she whispered.

'He knows I am just a student, Mother,' he replied. 'I was not working while I was in New Zealand.'

'It doesn't matter. He has been praying for the successful completion of your studies.'

'But I don't have any money with me,' lied Solomona, who didn't like giving money, just like that, to already-rich pastors.

'Well, that's okay. I'll provide the money,' his mother advised.

Solomona returned to his seat. As he sat down, Tuisamoa's talking chief, Lauti, cleared his throat and indicated that he wished to speak. There was a hush in the *faleafolau*.

'The highly respected *Feagaiga* of Lalolagi, Reverend Tenari, and your good lady, Sekara, his Lordship Tuisamoa and his family would like to thank you for your spiritual guidance and the prayers you have offered for their son during his studies. And, as a token of Tuisamoa's appreciation, here is $200 for some chewing gum for your good lady.' Lauti beckoned an untitled man to take the envelope and give it to Sekara. 'Tuisamoa's coffer is rather low and we apologise for the inadequacy of the gift,' he continued, adhering to Samoan tradition of belittling one's offering.

'There is no need for this, your Lordship Tuisamoa,' replied Tenari, in keeping with the custom of not displaying a desire to accept gifts. 'The important thing is that Mona and Helen have arrived safely, and we have all enjoyed a lavish meal. Nevertheless, thank you very much for the money and the *sua*, your Lordship Tuisamoa and your highly respected family. Our children are, indeed, our pride, and the gifts you have provided us tonight are a reflection of your adoration of Lalolagi's favourite son — and it looks like we may also be close to acquiring a *palagi* daughter,' he chuckled, as he winked at Solomona and Helen. Laughter spread around the *faleafolau*. 'So congratulations, Mona. You have made us all very proud, and if there is no space for Helen over here, you can send her to us. We have a large guestroom that is vacant. I can look after her for you,' he continued, his comments again greeted with a ripple of laughter.

Sekara, who was fanning herself with a pandanus fan, playfully hit Tenari on the head with it. 'Poor thing, finish up and let's go. It's already time for my massage.' She grinned and winked at the other women.

The pastor and his wife said goodnight to everyone, then shook hands with Solomona and Helen before leaving.

Solomona explained everything to Helen who had understood little of what had been said. Together they continued to observe the rest of the proceedings.

'Ask another young man to come here,' called Lauti as he looked into an envelope containing more money. A young man with a *tatau* walked in, with his head bowed slightly, and stooped at Lauti's side. 'Here, give each *matai* $20, then come back,' Lauti said as he handed the money to the young man. 'Fathers of our village,' he announced as the money was distributed to the *matais* representing the other eleven families of Lalolagi, 'here is $20 each for your tobacco. Our apologies, again, for the inadequate amount — it's all his Lordship Tuisamoa could afford.'

The *matais* acknowledged the money as each received his share and thanked Tuisamoa. The young man returned to Lauti after distributing the money. 'Okay, give each of the *matais'* wives $10, then come back to me,' he whispered as he handed him more money. Once again Lauti apologised for the inadequacy of the amount. The women also gave their thanks as each received her gift. The young man returned to Lauti's side. 'Okay, now distribute these things to the wives of the *matais*,' he said, handing the young man bundles of candy, soap and biscuits. 'Here is some soap to keep your skin clean and smooth,' he chuckled, addressing the *matais'* wives. 'The young men and women will have their share when they have eaten and completed all their tasks. And that ends what his Lordship Tuisamoa wants to say. May we all have a blessed evening.'

'Thank you very much, your Lordship Tuisamoa,' said Maopo, one of the *matais*, speaking on behalf of everyone. 'You have, once again, demonstrated that we are in very capable hands. You do not need to apologise. You have given us so much tonight, and may God continue to bless you and your family. Mona and ... what's the name of the girl?' he asked. The women, almost simultaneously, reminded him. 'Yes, of course. Mona and Helen, it's good you have arrived safely. But your Lordship Tuisamoa and your highly esteemed family, we will leave now so that you can spend time with your son.'

As Maopo completed his remarks, one by one, everyone filed out. As they left the *faleafolau*, each one chanted the honorifics of Tuisamoa and his family, those of the village, and those of the whole of Samoa. The honorifics included various titles used on formal occasions as well as respectful utterances befitting the rank of the Tuisamoa title. When all the guests had gone, Solomona and Helen moved over and sat between Alofa and Tuisamoa.

'Did you have enough to eat, Helen?' asked Alofa, smiling.

'Oh, I couldn't finish all the food,' she replied, rolling her eyes and patting her stomach.

'How do you like Samoa so far, Helen?' asked Tuisamoa who had not said anything since proceedings began.

'Oh, it's been fantastic so far. The landscape, the people, everything has been wonderful. Personally witnessing your culture tonight has been an eye-opening experience for me. And it's so nice and quiet here.'

'Good,' said Tuisamoa. 'Enjoy your stay and make yourself at home, please. I'm sure Mona has plans for the rest of your stay.'

They continued chatting until Solomona realised it was already 11 pm.

'Well, guys,' he declared, 'it's almost time for the lights to go out.'

'Why is that?' asked Helen.

'Because the power is from the village generator, and it is turned off at 11.30 every night.'

'Oh, I see.'

'Come on, HR, I'll show you to your room.' He pulled Helen to her feet. 'Do you want to have a shower?'

'I'm kind of tired,' she yawned, 'maybe I'll have one tomorrow.'

'Good idea. Me too,' he said, smiling. 'There's no hot water and the water is freezing cold at night.'

The room where Helen was to sleep was beautifully decorated with colourful mats and a floral bouquet on the vanity table by the window. A new mosquito net hung over the double bed, even though mosquito screens covered all the windows and doorways of the house. There were pictures of the Tuisamoa family hanging on the walls. Helen could smell mothballs.

'This is your room, HR, until Sunday,' he said as he sat down on the edge of the bed.

'Why until Sunday?'

'Because on Monday we are moving to Apia where we'll base ourselves while I take you on a tour of Samoa. We will try to see as much of Samoa as possible before I start work.'

'Sounds fantastic, Mister Tui. What's the plan until then?'

'We will get some rest tomorrow, then climb Mount Lagi on Saturday, and Sunday is, of course, God's day — meaning, we mainly eat and rest.'

'You sound pretty well organised.'

'Time is an economic commodity, and organisation assures it is used efficiently. Well, it's time to get some sleep, HR.'

'Where are you sleeping?'

Solomona smiled. 'How about beside your bed?'

'Why not *on* my bed?' she teased as she sat down beside him and rubbed his back.

'Too dangerous, HR. I am sleeping with Mum and Dad at the *fale*,' he said, referring to the *faleafolau* where tonight's welcome had taken place.

'Aren't you too big to still be sleeping with your parents?' she chuckled.

'I'm still a baby, HR,' he smiled. 'In Samoa, one is never too old to be considered a child while ever one's parents are alive.'

'I was just kidding, Mister Tui.'

'I know.' Solomona bounced gently on the bed. 'Mum and Dad have their bed at the northern end of the *fale* — it was covered by a curtain while everyone was there tonight. The girls will have prepared my sleeping mats at the other end, and the middle is left for the spirits of the night. So, shall we say goodnight?'

'Yes, I suppose so, Mister Tui.'

'Oh, before I forget, I had better show you the most important rooms of the house. Come with me, I'll show you where the toilet and bathroom are.'

Helen took her toothbrush from her bag, grabbed her towel from the bed and followed Solomona. From the bathroom window, she noticed another *faleo'o* at the back which was full of people still eating. They had a kerosene lamp in case the power went off.

'Who are they?'

'They're the people who served us tonight,' he explained. 'They have finished washing the dishes, and are only just eating now.'

'Are they all your relatives?'

'A few of them are, but most are Lalolagi villagers.'

Solomona walked with Helen back to her room where they lingered in a long embrace, before saying goodnight. Sitting on the bed after he left, Helen studied the photographs on the walls. Images of her arrival and welcome flashed through her mind as she pondered what a pleasant experience her introduction to Samoan life and culture had been so far and wondered what awaited her during the rest of her stay. She settled into bed with a satisfied smile.

Sixteen

Solomona awoke early on his first morning at home to hear soft, low singing as his parents started their morning devotions, a practice that, unlike evening devotions, is not expected or required of the whole village. He forced himself to join his parents, but slumped back on the pillows and went back to sleep when it was over. When he re-awoke, it was past 8 am. Sunlight was shining across his face and Helen was sitting beside him.

'Breakfast is ready, Mister Tui,' Helen coaxed.

'What time did you wake up?' he asked sleepily.

'The roosters woke me up early. So I found the ladies preparing your Royal Highness's breakfast, and thought I would help them.'

'It must be the first time you have ever been woken by roosters crowing, eh?'

'It is. It sounded like there were hundreds of them.'

'The roosters are our alarm clock,' he said, and then jokingly added, 'The good thing is that if the clock breaks down, you can eat it.'

Solomona got up and was about to put away the bedding when his mother, who had finished breakfast, suggested that he leave everything. Someone else would put it away.

'Let's have some breakfast, HR, then we can go and see if the fish are biting. What do you say?' Solomona was keen to show Helen as much of Samoan life as possible in the short time they had available.

'You're the boss, Mister Tui.'

They found they were alone in the Tuisamoas' *falepalagi* where, after a quick wash, they ate a leisurely breakfast. Everyone else had eaten earlier and had set about their daily chores. By mid-morning Solomona was anxious to try his fishing skills. He found a bush knife and a bamboo fishing rod in the storeroom and, while Helen put on her sandshoes, he packed a couple of *lavalavas* and a towel in a backpack, ready for their outing.

The tide was going out when they reached the beach, so they stopped at the high-water mark underneath some nut-bearing trees. While Helen took in the view, Solomona busied himself with his fishing rod.

'It's so beautiful here, Mona,' she said as she surveyed the bay from the tip of the peninsula opposite Lalolagi, all the way along the shoreline until her view was obscured by a promontory that separated Lalolagi from the next village. Hills rose sharply from the sea, up to several hundred metres, behind the villages along the edge of Fagaloa Bay. Hundreds of small waterfalls gushed out of the side of the mountain range, cascading onto the lush forests below. The falling water left mist in the air that formed a series of rainbows in the sunlight. 'And look at those hills,' she continued, 'they are absolutely fantastic.'

'So you really like it here?'

Helen sat down in the shade, admiring the smooth silvery water before her. Closing her eyes, she took deep breaths of the salty air whipped up by a gentle sea breeze.

'Oh, this is fantastic, Mister Tui. I could just sit here forever and do nothing.' She wanted to savour the warmth of the late-morning sun and the cooling sea breeze. 'This really is paradise, Mona,' she whispered.

The coral reef, which was only about 300 metres from the shore, became visible as the tide continued to recede. There were no human footprints on the sand, only hoofprints and pawprints of pigs and dogs, and the scratchings of chicken and sand crabs. Some pigs were digging in the shallow water close to the shore.

Opening her eyes, Helen turned to have a good look at the village, stretching from the northern end, where the school was located, along to where young boys were playing cricket on a concrete pitch. Lalolagi was about half a kilometre long. Between the school and cricket pitch were houses and the church, with the *malae* extending all the way to the beach. The families' *faleteles*, the church and the Tuisamoa's *faleafolau* formed the front row of buildings. The church was in the middle with the pastor's house behind it. The terrain behind the village rose gently to a thick chestnut forest, which stretched to the ridge running from the tip of Mount Lagi to the tip of the peninsula.

'It's a really delightful place, Mona. Who owns the big *fale* over there near the beach?' Helen pointed to the biggest *faletele*, which stood by itself, directly opposite the church.

'That's ours,' he replied, 'but it's basically Lalolagi's community hall. This isn't the original site of the village. It used to be over the other side of that hill. We'll actually be fishing very close to the original site today.'

'Why was it moved here?'

'When the road reached Fagaloa from Le Mafa Pass, my grandfather decided to move the village here. They wanted to have access to better means of transportation. The road from Falefa now passes above the old village.' Solomona pulled her to her feet. 'Come on, let's go before it gets too hot.'

Picking up his fishing gear, he led her towards the peninsula, passing the school and heading up the hill. By the time they reached the ridge, she was out of breath and thirsty. She sat down on the trunk of a fallen coconut tree while he picked a couple of coconuts from a young tree nearby. He cut a hole in the bottom of one and passed it to her.

'Ooh, this is so refreshing, Mister Tui.'

'It's perhaps the purest drink in the world. It can quickly replenish your energy because it has a lot of glucose. The meat is nice and sweet too... like you,' he smiled.

He opened the other coconut, drank it quickly, then split it open. He cut a scoop from the husk, scraped the meat off the shell, and passed it to Helen.

'That's just a snack for now. We'll see if we can catch some fish for lunch, and we'll take a few bananas from that tree over there to have with the fish.'

'We're helping ourselves to the coconuts and bananas, but are they yours to take?'

'They used to be,' he replied. 'All of Lalolagi's land used to be owned by the Tuisamoa family. My ancestors were the village pioneers. But as new people arrived, they were given *matai* titles. *Matai* titles require land, so my ancestors apportioned the land

and gave a block to each *matai*. There are twelve *aigas* in Lalolagi, including us. Each *aiga* has a *matai* title, all of them orators, or *tulafales*. *Tulafales* are, essentially, the administrators in a Samoan village. The chiefs, or *ali'i*, are the figureheads with little political power. Only our family has three *matais*. The title Tuisamoa is both an orator and High Chief, referred to as the *tulafaleali'i*. Tuisamoa has two *tulafales*. One of them, Lauti, spoke last night on behalf of Dad and the family. The other is Dad's youngest brother, who lives in the United States. In theory, three-quarters of Lalolagi's land should now be with the other *aigas*. The pastor has a small holding, and the rest should still be with us.'

'So who owns this land now?'

'The family near the school.'

'Wouldn't they object or accuse us of helping ourselves to their fruit?'

'In Lalolagi, private ownership is not seriously enforced, and helping yourself like this is okay, provided you keep the place clean. It would be a different story if you were attempting to make a living out of it. Commercialisation has not taken a foothold yet in much of Samoa, including Lalolagi, but it's coming. I would like our people to be ready for it when it arrives. Anyway, I guess we should move on. We need to collect some hermit crabs for bait.'

They walked hand in hand toward the tip of the peninsula, generally known as The Rock because of the extensive lava field at its tip. Just before they reached the bare lava, Solomona veered towards some trees growing on the peninsula close to the water. He squatted, cleared dead leaves from the base of the trees, and picked up half a dozen hermit crabs. He placed them in his fishing bag, before heading out to the tip of the peninsula.

The tip of The Rock was the furthest point out into the sea in the whole Fagaloa region. Solomona and Helen stood and watched the waves washing up on the hard lava rocks, filling a myriad of rock pools as they gently retreated. On the eastern side of The Rock, the waters of Fagaloa Bay sparkled in the midday sun. White terns wheeled overhead. Just for a moment they felt they were the only ones existing in this paradise.

'Come on, HR, let's see if we can catch something for lunch. We'll head back in the direction of the old village.'

Captivated by the beauty of this spot, Helen gazed out to sea a while longer, then turned and followed him. About 500 metres from the tip of The Rock was a large pool. It was almost rectangular in shape, about 10 metres wide and 15 metres long. It looked to be quite deep in the middle, where the tip of a large boulder rose out of the water.

Solomona broke some branches from nearby shrubs and spread them out in the shade, covering them with his towel.

'There's your bed, HR,' he said. 'Take a cat-nap while I try to catch something for lunch.'

'I want to watch what you're doing.'

'Well, please yourself.'

'Is this a natural pool?'

'Apparently. It would be pretty hard for anyone to break the lava to build this.'

'I know, but this pool looks too symmetrical to be natural.'

Solomona smiled. 'I know. Some things look too good to be natural — take your beauty, for instance.'

She blushed and lowered her head. 'You always say things like that. You're full of flattery, Mister Tui.'

'I'm just stating a fact, HR, and if God can create a beautiful person like yourself, there is no reason why He cannot create a pool in steel-hard lava that is almost perfect in shape like this one,' he reasoned as he baited a hook.

Tossing the line into the water, he looked for a comfortable spot to sit down. Before he could do so, he felt a strong pull on his line.

'I think I've caught a fish already!' he shouted, trying to get his footing.

Helen ran over to have a look, as the fish started to pull away. Solomona struggled to reel it in. Finally, he managed to land a reef trout, weighing about 5 kilograms.

'That's a fairly big fish, Mona,' she said admiringly.

'Yes, it is, isn't it?' Solomona studied it proudly. 'Certainly big enough for our lunch. I'll go and get some firewood so we can start cooking it.'

He returned a short while later with a bundle of firewood, a dry coconut frond and some banana leaves. Arranging the firewood into a pile, he started a fire with dry wood, removed some leaves from the dry coconut frond, lit them and placed them beneath the firewood.

Helen could not help but admire his skill and ingenuity in preparing lunch. He prepared the bananas and gutted the fish, then waited for the fire to burn down so that he could cook the food in the hot coals.

When the fish and bananas were cooked, he removed the bananas from the hot coals, peeled off the burnt skin and placed them on a clean banana leaf. Retrieving the fish, he broke it into pieces on the banana leaves, then blessed the food before offering some to Helen.

'Ooh, this is just delicious, Mona.'

'You can't get fish as fresh as this at the market,' he said proudly, 'and if you need salt, well, the sea is right there, next to you.'

'But what are we going to do for drinks?'

'It just so happens the water from that spring over there is the clearest and the most refreshing in the country.'

After they finished eating, Solomona took the *lavalavas* from his backpack, showed Helen how to tie it securely behind her neck, then stretched out on his back on the towel. Helen sat down beside him. He reached out and caressed her cheek. She held his hand and softly kissed his palm.

'Are you having a good time so far, HR?'

'Oh, it's been unreal, Mona,' she said as she rubbed his hand gently against her cheek. 'This is very romantic; almost like being in a movie, you know?'

'Thought you might say that.' He felt he understood her well enough now to be able almost to anticipate her every reaction.

'Don't you think it's a romantic setting?'

'If you say so, HR.'

Helen smiled and looked around her. 'Imagine just you and me in the shade of this beautiful tree. Warm air, calm sea; time seems to stand still, and everything seems so unreal. It's just like a dream!'

'You're getting a bit poetic, HR. So you do like it here?'

'Oh, very much. No wonder people love to holiday here. It's been fantastic, Mister Tui. I'm enjoying it so much. Thank you for inviting me.'

'But it can get boring,' he cautioned.

'Oh, that's a matter of choice. I mean, one can decide to get bored or excited anywhere, don't you think?'

Solomona sat up and looked at her. He motioned to her to sit between his legs where they could both face the sea. Pulling her closer to him, he wrapped his arms around her, locking his fingers around hers. As he rested his chin on her shoulder, Helen could feel the prickles from his unshaven beard.

'I like your attitude, HR,' he murmured.

'You provide a big part of my inspiration, Mister Tui.'

Solomona smiled to himself as he gazed out to sea.

'A dollar for your thoughts, Mister Tui,' she whispered.

'They are a lot more expensive than a dollar, HR.' He gently kissed her ear.

'Well,' she countered, 'name your price, Mister Tui. Are you okay? You seem rather distant, Mona.'

'I was just daydreaming.'

'Are you going to share it with me?'

'Well, it's the thought that always haunts me when I come home.'

'And what's that?' Helen turned to look into his eyes.

'Whenever I'm home, I often wonder why I needed to go to university, and now I wonder what was the point of doing a PhD.'

'But you had good reasons for pursuing an education, didn't you?'

'Of course, I did. I have always thought it's a challenge to reach the pinnacle of any mountain that one chooses to climb. Not only that, knowledge is very important, and a powerful mind is a gift from God. I saw it as my duty to nurture and develop my mind so that I could fulfil whatever purpose He intended for me. Only a good formal education can provide that.'

'So why do you still wonder about the value of getting a good tertiary education?'

'Because an experience like this always teaches me something else about the basics of life.'

'Which is?'

'Well,' he smiled, 'being here has taught me that fundamentally there are only three things that a man really needs in life.'

'Hmm, sounds interesting. I didn't realise we were having a lesson in living.'

'Don't you think that everything that a person does is a lesson in living?'

'I guess so... Well, are you going to tell me the three things a man needs in life?' Smiling, Solomona picked up a twig that was lying next to him. Breaking it into small pieces, he threw them at the waves as they gently washed up on the rocks. 'Come on, Mister Tui. Don't be shy.'

'Well,' he said eventually, 'I have learnt today that all a man really needs is the woman he loves, angelic music and a fishing rod.'

Helen smiled as she gently rubbed his knee. 'And you have all of them here?'

'Yes, I do!' he replied confidently, as he continued to throw bits of twig into the water.

'Can I presume, then, that I am the woman you love?'

'Your face is etched deep inside me, HR, deep inside.' He looked intently at Helen as he reached out and touched her cheek.

Helen blushed. Leaning forward, she kissed him.

'You are also the man I love, Mister Tui, etched deep within my heart too. Well, you have me and you have your fishing rod, but what about the music?'

Solomona smiled. 'Haven't you heard the angelic singing, and the sweet sound of music?'

'They must be performing in your mind, Mister Tui.' Helen never ceased to be amazed by the spirituality that he seemed to possess.

'Not at all, HR, because nothing beats the sounds of nature. To me, it is the best music in the world, much better than the best-produced opera or concert. You know, no other music moves me the way the sounds of nature do — and it's free.'

Stretching, he got up and helped her to her feet. In a swift motion, he lifted her into the air and threw her into the pool, forcing a couple of fish to dart for cover. Caught by surprise, Helen sank to the bottom of the pool, then surfaced spluttering and wiping her face.

'I wasn't ready for that, Mister Tui. You took me by surprise,' she shouted indignantly, as she swam to the side of the pool.

'It appears you have scared all the fish away, Miss Jones,' he laughed, 'but better be careful of the eels!'

'Eels?' she screamed.

'Yep, they are big and they just l-o-v-e *palagi* girls with long dark hair,' he laughed, enjoying her discomfort.

'Get me out of the water now!' Helen's pulse started to race as she reached for the rock ledge.

'Too late, HR, there's a big one right behind you,' he roared as he dived into the pool.

Helen turned, but Solomona was too quick for her. He grabbed her foot and pulled her under the water. Holding her tightly, he helped her swim back to the surface.

'Ah, so you are the big eel, Mister Tui,' she laughed, between gasps.

'You behave yourself, Miss Jones, or the spirits of the pool will get angry with you,' he teased.

'You're just bluffing, Mister Tui.'

They swam to the boulder in the middle of the pool, and lay there side by side, trying to catch their breath.

Helen turned towards him and moved closer until she could feel his warm skin against hers. She gently stroked his chest.

'Tell me, Mister Tui. Is there anything special about this pool?'

'This is the women's pool,' he replied, as he wiped water from her face. She enjoyed his gentle touch on her skin. 'Folklore says that only women are supposed to swim here.'

'And obviously you don't believe in those stories.'

'I did when I was young and ignorant. Now that I'm older and a little wiser, they don't make sense anymore. But I have learnt something very important in that maturing process.'

'What's that?'

'Well, I've come to realise that, for human beings to have a sense of security and comfort, and really just to enjoy life, the cause of or reason for certain phenomena needs to be explained. Every society has its own ways of explaining things. For instance, this rock is supposed to be a young man who disobeyed the taboo, and was turned into a rock by the spirits that look after the pool. We now know that's not possible, but it gave the original inhabitants of Lalolagi peace of mind to know where the rock came from.'

'Greek mythology and stories have that element too.'

'Exactly. The interesting thing is that the ways of explaining existence and phenomena are fundamentally the same across all societies. Only the way the stories are told is different.'

'So you think knowledge is essential for security and comfort?'

'Absolutely! It's the light that illuminates and reveals most, if not all, before us. This allows us to become aware of ourselves and everything around us, as well as our relationships with one another and with our surroundings.'

'Hmm, very interesting. Tell me, is there a men's pool somewhere?'

'Yes, there is. It's on the peninsula at the other end of the old village, almost directly opposite this one.'

'Can women swim there?'

'No one has yet that I know of, but there's no reason why women can't.' Solomona was enjoying Helen's closeness especially in a place that had a special significance for him, but he was concerned that others back at the village may be wondering where they were. 'Come on, we should think about going, before they start worrying about us.'

'Oh, I like it here. I could just lie here forever. With you, of course.'

'God willing, there'll be a next time, Miss Jones.'

Helen did not move. She felt too comfortable. Her *lavalava* had almost dried on the warm rock. Solomona stood up, picked her up and jumped into the water with her in his arms. They swam to the poolside, where he helped her out of the water. They changed into dry clothes, then climbed the hill and headed towards Lalolagi.

Back at the village, Helen had a shower while Solomona helped his cousins cook the *umu* for the evening meal. At precisely 7.30 pm, Tenari rang the bell for evening devotions. Almost simultaneously, the sound of conch shells filled the air, a reminder to the villagers that they should all be inside for evening prayers. Tuisamoa led his family in their prayers, which were followed by their evening meal.

'Did the boys go last week to check if the track up to Lagi is cleared of fallen trees, Mum?' Solomona asked Alofa as, in accordance with custom, the rest of the family sat back and waited for Tuisamoa and Alofa to finish their meal before they could eat.

'Your command, your Lordship, was duly conveyed to your servants and they have complied with your orders, right down to the minutest of details,' replied Alofa wryly.

Tuisamoa, seated in his usual spot at the side of the *faleafolau*, laughed at their banter. Solomona explained to Helen what was being said. She had learnt to appreciate the Samoan sense of humour. She felt happy that her presence did not deter Solomona and his parents from joking in their usual way. All her earlier apprehensions abated as she felt accepted into Solomona's immediate family. The loving and jovial atmosphere within the Tuisamoa family made her feel welcome.

Seventeen

The next day Solomona and Helen woke early. They wanted to start their ascent of Mount Lagi before it got too hot. Alofa was already awake. She, and her nephews' wives, had prepared food and drink for the hikers to take with them. Following a light breakfast, Solomona and Helen packed the things they needed into a backpack, and started out towards the hills.

After a difficult and exhausting climb that took almost four hours, they reached the summit of Mount Lagi. Helen was exhausted and felt dizzy from the long climb and thin air. Solomona quickly pitched a makeshift tent with a *lavalava* and spread another *lavalava* on the ground as a rug, suggesting that Helen take a rest while he had a look around.

It was almost 11 am, with a clear sky and bright sunshine. The magnificent scenery of Fagaloa Bay reminded Solomona why this place was so special to him. The hills Helen had admired the day before were even more spectacular from this vantage point — the cascading waterfalls, the gently flowing rivers, the humid, lush forests and the mosaic of farms beyond. And far below, the sea glistened with silver tints in the sunlight.

In the distance to the east, Solomona could see the smoke from a ferry returning from American Samoa. Further on were the islands of American Samoa. The Aleipata district, with its myriad of islands, at the easternmost tip of Upolu, was clearly visible. To the south were more forest-covered mountains. He could almost see all of Samoa from up here. With no other place visible as far as one could see, it gave one the impression that Samoa was the only place on earth.

Mount Lagi was connected to other peaks by two extremely narrow ridges that fell almost perpendicular to the foot of the mountain range. It was virtually impossible to reach the summit along either of these two ridges. A third ridge ran north to The Rock. This was wider and provided the only safe passage up to the top of Mount Lagi. The three ridges formed the three faces of Mount Lagi — one facing north-east to the Fagaloa Bay, the second facing north-west to old Lalolagi, and the third facing south. All three faces were almost perpendicular to the flat farmland a thousand metres below.

There were no trees on the summit, but very thick bermuda grass provided an immaculate lawn and protection from erosion. Although the sun was bright, they could feel only the cool, light breeze that always blew across the peak.

Solomona walked to the north-east corner of the peak and looked down to Fagaloa Bay, making sure not to venture too close to the edge. He called out to Helen to join him.

'Well, what do you think of the view from the roof of Lalolagi and Fagaloa?'

'It's absolutely beautiful, Mister Tui!' Helen surveyed the magnificent scenery below. 'I have never seen anything quite this beautiful!'

'Well, there is only one Lalolagi and only one Fagaloa Bay.'

'Oh, it's stunning. Do you think it would be possible to build a house up here?'

'Yes, but it would probably need to be rebuilt once a year because of the strong winds during the hurricane season. Do you suppose it's a fitting location for a king's dwelling?'

'Oh, fit for a god, Mister Tui!'

Solomona smiled. 'Funny you should mention that, because this is where the gods, or god, live, or used to live, according to our village legends.'

'Really?'

'Yes, this is where Tagaloalagi, the pre-Christian god of Samoa, and his wife 'Ele'ele live, or used to live. This is heaven, or *lagi* in Samoan. Hell is at the western end of Savai'i, in a place called Pulotu, where the sun sets,' he explained, recounting Samoan and his village's legends of their gods and creation, and occasionally inserting his own interpretation.

'Really? That's interesting.'

'I know,' Solomona replied, looking down at the bay. 'Anyway, Mount Lagi is supposed to have nine levels, each represented by a step-like change in its contour, starting from the sea at the tip of The Rock. And it is here that Tagaloalagi and 'Ele'ele created the first human beings.'

'It sounds very much like the Maori legends, with a God of the same name.'

'That's because the Maoris came from Lalolagi,' he smiled. 'Anyway, apparently Tagaloalagi and 'Ele'ele brought some clay from the eastern river of old Lalolagi, which they used to create the first humans. That river is the only place in all of Samoa where you can find clay suitable for pottery, which is proof, according to our people, that the first person ever created was from Lalolagi.'

'How interesting!'

'Over there, right in the middle of the Mount Lagi's summit, Tagaloalagi made the *umu* that they used to energise their creations while 'Ele'ele moulded the human figures from the clay.'

'Don't you cook food in an *umu*?'

'Yes, we do, but it was initially used by Tagaloalagi and 'Ele'ele in their creation of humans, according to our legends.'

'I see.'

'Apparently, 'Ele'ele moulded two human figures, one male and one female. Their first attempt stayed in the *umu* too long, and the pair were over-cooked. They were darker than Tagaloalagi and 'Ele'ele had wanted, and that was how dark-skinned people came into being.'

Helen was intrigued. She had always had an interest in ancient folklore and mythology and was keen to learn as much as she could about Samoan legends, and especially those of Lalolagi.

'So Tagaloalagi took hold of the pair and tossed them to the south. They landed in Fiji, and that's how we got the Fijians,' he continued.

'That's fascinating.'

'Anyway, Tagaloalagi had a rooster called Moa, which he kept to tell the time. He was a bit upset at Moa's time-keeping performance, so he warned Moa that it would be banished from Lagi if it could not get the time right in future. He prepared another *umu* while 'Ele'ele moulded another pair, one male and one female. Moa, fearful of being banished from Lagi, did not want to make the same mistake. So instead of calling the time too late, he panicked and ended up calling it too early. Although the pair had enough energy to remain alive, they were too soft, not quite cooked and very pale in colour, and that's how white people came about.'

'Like me?'

'Well, that's according to Lalolagi's legends.'

Helen looked suspiciously at Solomona. She could not decide whether he was spinning her a yarn or not. Reaching out, she pinched his side.

'Ouch! Really, Miss Jones, these are Lalolagi's legends. Trust me, HR, I'm not making it up, honest.'

Helen tickled him, 'Yes, you are, Mister Tui. You always enjoy teasing me.'

He laughed, 'Shall I continue?'

'Yes, continue, Mister Tui, but stick to the original script.'

'Well, Tagaloalagi was very angry with Moa, so he banished Moa from Lagi. He took a look at the pale pair in front of him and complained to 'Ele'ele that they were not properly cooked. "I don't want other gods to know about this embarrassment. They would think I can't even tell when an *umu* is cooked. What shall I do?" he asked his trusted and wise wife. He knew 'Ele'ele was the best adviser in the universe and any advice that she gave would be wise advice. "Easy, god Tagaloalagi," replied 'Ele'ele. "No other god lives up here, so you could hide them above those clouds. The clouds will carry them to universes beyond, and no one will ever find out about them." "Ah, brilliant idea, my 'Ele'ele," responded Tagaloalagi. "I knew you would be able to help me."

'While they deliberated on what to do with the uncooked pair, the pair actually grew stronger and started to like Lagi. Tagaloalagi told them what he planned to do, and they begged him to allow them to stay on Lagi or at least be sent down to earth, which was old Lalolagi. "Oh, no way," replied Tagaloalagi. "I have to keep you away from the knowledge of the lesser gods. I will get this right, and once I have done that, I will send that pair to Lalolagi," he continued. The white pair cried, still begging Tagaloalagi to spare them, but he wouldn't listen. He gathered them up, and threw them to the sky to be among the clouds. And that's why we have greyish rain clouds — the rain is the tears of the white-skinned couple.'

'What happened then?'

'Well, Tagaloalagi looked around. There was no Moa to keep time for him. There was also not much clay left. So he consulted 'Ele'ele again. "I will help you keep the time," she offered, though disappointed with his progress so far. "You should think properly about what you do, and not make decisions when you are angry. They are bound to be bad ones, like banishing Moa from Lagi," she continued. "There is more than enough clay for one more pair, but not enough for two. I suggest that we just make them a bit bigger than the first two pairs." So 'Ele'ele moulded two more figures while Tagaloalagi again prepared the *umu*. 'Ele'ele figured that the right length of time should be somewhere between the first two experiments. When she felt it was about the right time, she called out to Tagaloalagi that the *umu* must be cooked. Tagaloalagi removed the cover from the *umu*, and up sprang a man and a woman with big smiles. They were beautiful and strong, with bronze skin like the soil of Lagi. This pleased him greatly, and that's how

Samoans came about. Tagaloalagi was very proud, "I knew I could trust a woman," he boasted. "We really don't need that rooster," he told his wife. "I will send this pair to Lalolagi, and ban roosters from the whole world." He did. He banned chickens from the whole world, which was the whole archipelago, and named the world Samoa, which means chickens are forbidden, as a reminder of that decree. He named the first human male Tuisamoa, and the female Ola, and sent them down to old Lalolagi.'

'That's very interesting, Mona, but I'm curious about the origin of the name Samoa. Some of the Samoan stories are very similar to Greek stories, and there is a Greek island called Samos. Also, Pulotu is very close to Pluto who ruled the underworld in Greek mythology. I find that rather intriguing.'

'Well, you might be interested to know that there is also a Samos in Spain, a Samo in Spain and China, a Samod in India, a Samois in France, and a Samon in Burma. They may also have similar stories. There must be as many candidates for the origin of the name Samoa as there are theories about the origin of the Polynesians, but you won't find a story about great voyages to Samoa as you do in New Zealand Maori legends. To the Samoans, this is where the world began.'

'So what happened to the darker pair?'

'Well, of course, they settled in Fiji. Legend tells us that Fiji was only a swim away, but over time the Fijian islands moved further south as a result of earth movements. So, as you can see, Samoans knew about the plate tectonics concept way before the *palagi* scientists did. Anyway, the Fijian population grew and spread west of the Pacific and to Australia, and all the way to Africa. The Samoan population grew and spread south to Tonga and Aotearoa, north to Hawai'i, east to the Easter Islands, all the way to the Americas and finally to Asia.'

'And what happened to the white pair?'

'Well, they were supposed to have gone to other universes, and the Fijians and Samoans knew they were up there in the clouds, otherwise there would have been no rain. And every time it rained, they felt in touch with their white cousins,' he intoned with a broad grin.

'And why are you smirking?'

'Because I'm coming to another exciting part of Lalolagi's legends,' he replied.

'Go on then,' she urged.

Solomona could hardly contain himself. 'Well,' he continued, 'the people of Lalolagi always thought that the white pair was still living in the clouds crying their tears in rain, until one day a fisherman came home with the first group of Europeans ever to have visited Samoa. The villagers, of course, crowded to the beach to witness their first glimpse of a white person. The Tuisamoa at the time came over, had a look, then concluded, "they must be the nuts from the sky," and that is why white people are referred to as *papalagi*.'

'I have a feeling that the "nut" bit was your twist, Mister Tui, and that's what you're smirking about, isn't it?' Helen gently twisted his ear.

In jerking away from her, Solomona lost his balance and fell onto his back. Helen quickly straddled his stomach and held his hands down. 'I know you too well, Mister Tui,' she insisted, as she bent down and kissed him on the forehead.

'You had better behave yourself, Miss Jones, or Tagaloalagi will send you back to the clouds,' he warned.

'But if he sends me, then you would have to come too, and that would suit me just fine,' she quipped, as she stood up, pulling Solomona to his feet too.

'Actually,' he said, dusting his pants, 'the nut part of the story is true, HR.'

'I believe you, Mister Tui, but thousands wouldn't.'

'But it is true, HR, *pa* in Samoan means burst, as a chestnut would if heated without poking a hole in the casing. *Papa* means many bursting nuts, and *lagi* means sky. So *palagi* means one nut bursting from the sky, and *papalagi* means many nuts bursting from the sky.'

Helen was not completely convinced by his story. She looked out towards Fagaloa Bay, smiling. 'Not a bad story, Mister Tui.'

'But it's true, HR,' Solomona tried to sound convincing.

'I said I believe you, Mister Tui. Anyway, what does the name Tagaloalagi mean?'

'Tagaloalagi is actually made up of three words: *Taga*, which means free; *loa*, which means forever; and *lagi*, which means the sky or heaven.'

'What about 'Ele'ele?'

'It's another word for soil, and a formal word for blood.'

'How interesting. Are there any other interesting legends of Lalolagi and Fagaloa?'

'Have you seen the movie *Ghostbusters?*' he asked.

'Yes I have,' she replied curiously. 'Why?'

'Well,' he grinned, 'I suppose Fagaloa can also lay claim to producing the very first ghostbuster.'

'Really?'

'Yes, his name was Lu Fasiaitu, or simply, Lu the ghost-buster. He was supposed to have lived on those mountains.'

Solomona pointed in the direction of mountains on the eastern side of Fagaloa Bay.

'How interesting.' Helen was still not sure whether he was teasing her again by adding his own version. 'Any more Fagaloa legends?'

'Well,' he smiled, 'the very first fine mat was, apparently, woven near the tip of one of the peninsulas to the east of Old Lalolagi.'

Tiring of storytelling, Solomona suggested they eat some lunch, after which they stretched out for a nap.

It was almost 4 pm when he awoke. It had been a pleasant snooze in the cool air at the top of Mount Lagi. Helen looked very comfortable and showed no sign of waking. He gazed at her for some time. 'She looks even more beautiful in her sleep,' he thought. He leaned over and kissed her forehead, causing her to stir.

'Time to go, HR.'

'Oh, I'm still sleepy, Mona,' she responded resting her head on his lap.

'Come on, HR, we don't want to be stranded up here in the dark.'

She stretched her arms and yawned loudly, but continued to rest her head on his lap a while longer. Eventually, she found the strength to sit up, helped to pack up, then together they began the trek back down to Lalolagi.

'Oh, that was a lovely sleep, especially feeling your warmth beside me,' she said as they set off.

'Glad you enjoyed it. You look even more beautiful in your sleep,' he smiled.

'Thank you for a very pleasant outing, Mister Tui,' she said, taking his hand. 'It was really a lovely day. An exhausting climb, but it was certainly worth it. Having you all to myself again was a real treat, and the scenery is absolutely awe-inspiring.'

Solomona smiled and raised his eyebrows. 'I'm glad you enjoyed it, HR.'

Eighteen

Like other villages in Samoa, Lalolagi observed Sunday as a special day. It was the Holy Day, a Rest Day, and also the Feast Day. By tradition, Sunday meals were cooked in the *umu*. Lalolagi's laws required that all cooking in an *umu* be completed before daylight.

Solomona made sure he was awake early, so that he could help his cousins with the *umu*. Helen was again woken by the crowing of roosters, and wandered over to the cooking *fale* where the men were busy preparing the food. When she arrived, Solomona and his cousins were covering the *umu* with banana leaves.

'It should be ready in about an hour,' commented Siaosimatua, one of three Tuisamoa cousins who lived with their wives in Lalolagi. His real name was Siaosi, but another cousin, who was younger and also lived in Lalolagi, had the same name. To differentiate between the two of them, the word *matua*, which means old, was added to the older Siaosi's name, and *la'iitiiti* was added to the younger one's. Sometimes, people would just use Senior for the older Siaosi and Junior for the younger one. The third cousin was Kaino.

'Morning, HR,' greeted Solomona.

'Good morning Mona, Senior, Junior and master Kaino. Hmm, it smells good already.'

'I suppose the roosters woke you up again,' smiled Solomona.

'Yes they did. I suppose it will take some time to get used to.'

'Let's have something to eat before we get ready for church.'

They headed to the Tuisamoas' *falepalagi*, where they had breakfast, then Solomona's cousins returned to the cooking *fale* to wait for the *umu* to finish cooking. Helen helped the wives of Solomona's cousins in the kitchen while Solomona entertained them with stories.

The morning church service began at 8.30 am. Lalolagi's laws required that all villagers go to church unless very sick. Everyone wore white to the service. Fortunately Helen had come prepared, packing a white dress in her luggage especially for such occasions. At 8 am, a bell rang. A second bell at 8.30 am marked the start of the service.

The church was cross-like in shape, with the head facing east over Fagaloa Bay. The pulpit was at the top of the cross shape facing the congregation. A seating arrangement based on gender and age was strictly adhered to. The school-aged boys sat in the right wing of the church, and directly opposite them were the school-aged girls. Each group had an elderly person to supervise them. The choir sat in the middle of the east wing, the larger part of the church. Virtually all the villagers of adult age were in the choir. The unmarried men who were not members of the choir sat on the right side of the choir while the unmarried women sat on the left. Behind the choir sat married couples and the village elders. A couple of pews at the southern entrance and to the right of the choir were reserved for the Tuisamoa family, with Tuisamoa and Alofa seated at the front.

Helen could feel the eyes of the congregation on her as she entered the church with Solomona, Tuisamoa and Alofa. She looked radiant in white with her beautiful silky black hair loose down her back. Helen sat between Alofa and Tuisamoa, as Solomona was playing the organ and singing with the choir.

Before Tenari arrived, Solomona played some of his favourite music from Bach, Mozart and Rutter. Helen had heard him play some of the pieces at church in New Zealand. As she listened to the music, she closed her eyes and recalled the wonderful times she and Solomona had spent together in the last couple of years. She remembered her devastation at seeing him lying motionless in the hospital. She also recalled some of the crazy and funny things he had done, and a smile crossed her lips. She had been fearful that she would lose Solomona once he had completed his studies and returned to Samoa. She was not afraid anymore. She felt confident that she could live with him in Samoa. Her love for him had grown stronger in the last few days, as she learnt more about his family and the Samoan way of life.

The atmosphere inside the church was solemn. Apart from the beautiful sound of the organ, there was no other noise. Crying babies were quickly carried outside by their carers. Chattering children were quietened by a supervising elder. Helen was brought back from her reverie by a sudden change in the music. Tenari had entered the church and was walking towards the pulpit. Wearing a black coat with a broad tie to match, he faced the congregation, stood with his hands clasped in front of him, and closed his eyes. The congregation rose as the choir sang in beautiful harmony. After a short prayer, everyone resumed their seats.

Tenari welcomed them to the morning service. He extended a special welcome to Solomona and Helen, congratulating Solomona on completing his thesis. With a grin, he expressed his hope that Helen was enjoying her time in Lalolagi, and that one day she would return and become a member of the choir. Helen blushed. Smiling sheepishly, she glanced discreetly at Solomona who winked back at her.

The service lasted almost an hour, with Tenari occasionally making an effort to translate proceedings into English. Helen appreciated his thoughtfulness and felt uplifted by the glorious singing of the choir and the congregation.

'Why do men have to wear those suits in such a hot and humid climate?' she whispered to Solomona, as they queued at the main entrance of the church to meet Tenari after the service.

'I suppose the missionaries must have told our ancestors that God was a *palagi* and he wears a suit,' he smiled.

'But it's so hot and humid.'

'I know. It's absurd, really, if not ridiculously silly.'

'Come and have *to'ona'i* with us,' Tenari greeted, as he shook hands with Solomona and Helen, inviting them to Sunday lunch with the church deacons and their spouses at the parsonage.

Solomona turned and looked at his mother who was following them.

'Is it all right, Mother?' he asked, unsure whether it was appropriate for them to attend the *to'ona'i*, since the deacons were, essentially, all the village *matais*.

'It's the prerogative of the pastor to invite whomever he wants,' she replied.

'It should be a good experience for Helen,' thought Solomona out loud. 'So, Nari, yes we will.' After thanking Tenari warmly for the enjoyable service, he told Helen about the invitation.

'What time is *to'ona'i*?' she asked.

'Oh, when everyone who is expected to attend has arrived,' he smiled as they made their way back to the Tuisamoas' home.

Soon afterwards, children started arriving with *umu*. They each had two baskets, one for Tuisamoa's *sua*, and one for Solomona and Helen. Siaosila'iitiiti accepted the baskets of food on behalf of the family. He described the contents of each basket as he displayed them on coconut leaf trays spread at the rear end of the *faleafolau*.

'Each family in Lalolagi gives a *sua* every Sunday, which is basically food for Tuisamoa,' Solomona explained to Helen. 'This is a very old tradition. I suppose initially it was in appreciation of Tuisamoa's welcoming each family to his village, but it is also in recognition of Tuisamoa's status as Head of Lalolagi. In the old days, this was a daily affair, but now it happens only on Sundays. They also do the same for the pastor. The second *umu* is called an *asiga*, which is offered to visitors or village people who have returned after being away. We normally reciprocate the *asiga*, usually with money.'

'How much money should we give?' Helen asked, intrigued by the amount of money-giving in local customs.

'I would say $5 should be enough, but no one would stop you from giving more.'

Helen took out her purse and gave $10 to each child who brought an *asiga*. Solomona and Helen changed into casual clothes before heading to the pastor's house with Tuisamoa and Alofa, with Solomona carrying their contribution to the *to'ona'i*.

'Come and sit here with us,' Sekara called out to Helen and Solomona, as they and Solomona's parents entered the large, open living quarters of the parsonage.

Solomona looked at his mother who nodded her head. Almost everyone who was expected to be at the *to'ona'i* had arrived and was seated in their designated positions. Tenari was the last to join them. He chanted the formal village salutation, then started the usual pre-*to'ona'i* banter in Samoan. This time, the 'victims' were Solomona and Helen.

'Eh, Tui,' he called, trying to get Tuisamoa's attention.

Tuisamoa didn't hear. Alofa had to nudge him and tell him that the pastor was speaking to him.

'Oh, I'm sorry. I didn't hear you, Nari,' he apologised.

'I was saying that your son did very well,' smiled Tenari. 'He got his PhD, and he must also be close to getting us a *palagi* soprano for our choir.'

Solomona smiled, his head bowed slightly, as he explained to Helen what was going on. Sekara told Helen not to mind old men's talk — it was just Samoan teasing. She assured Sekara that she was quite used to it with her Samoan friends in New Zealand.

'Oh, yes, Nari,' said Tuisamoa, laughing and massaging one knee. 'Well, he is a clever boy like his father.' A ripple of laughter spread around the parsonage. 'And his *palagi* friend, as you can see, is a very beautiful young lady. She is also at university.'

'Mona just has Helen, but I understand you left many *palagi* girls broken-hearted in the... how many years you were in New Zealand? Ten years?'

'That's right, Nari, ten years,' he chuckled. 'And Nari, I tell you there were many of them.'

'Poor thing,' Alofa laughingly addressed the other women, 'he must be wishing that he was still young.' She turned to Tuisamoa and fanned him with her coconut frond fan.

'So how come you didn't bring one of them back with you?' asked Tenari.

'Oh, I just thought at the time they could not fit into our society, Nari,' replied Tuisamoa confidently.

'But wasn't your mother a German and Alofa's grand-mother the daughter of British missionaries?'

'Well, my mother was German, but she was born and raised in Aleipata. Alofa's grandmother was in missionary service, so she was used to living in foreign lands. But the New Zealand girls? Oh, I wasn't so sure of them, Nari, especially at a time when New Zealand was running an apartheid government in our country. My father was very angry at anything that came from New Zealand at the time.'

'Ah, so it is possible for a *palagi* girl to adapt to our way of life?'

'Times have changed, Nari, and I suppose it shouldn't matter whether she's white, red, yellow or pink, should it? If they love each other, that's all that really matters.'

Solomona fidgeted and was beginning to feel uneasy when suddenly the loud voice of a young man at the rear of the parsonage disrupted the frivolity as he announced what each couple had brought for *to'ona'i*, in order of the village hierarchy. In this context, the pastor ranked ahead of Tuisamoa. Helen couldn't believe the amount of food that had been provided. There was even more food than on the night they arrived. After the young man had listed all the food gifts, the baskets of food were taken into the kitchen for serving.

After *to'ona'i*, everyone returned home for an afternoon nap before another church service at 3 pm. Lalolagi looked like a forsaken place on Sunday afternoons. Loud noises were not allowed. Any adult who transgressed this rule was punished by the village council. Noisy children would receive an instant spanking from a *matai*. If not, they would almost certainly receive one from Tenari at their evening devotions with the pastor and his family.

Solomona and Helen decided to go for a walk to the chestnut forest. It was about a kilometre away, but it was a steady climb. The sun was quite hot, and the humidity was almost suffocating. They were both sweating profusely.

There was no one else around. It was quiet except for the humming of cicadas and the odd chirping of birds. It felt as though even the wildlife of Lalolagi had taken a Sunday afternoon nap. The forest was fairly dark even in the bright afternoon light. The coolness of the shade was a welcome respite from the heat. The trees were majestic, with a canopy at least 30 metres overhead, and virtually no undergrowth. They stopped to rest at a huge fallen, worn log next to the pathway.

'This was our playground when we were growing up,' Solomona explained.

'What did you do here?' asked Helen, making herself comfortable on the log.

'Oh, all sorts of things. We played hide and seek, touch, climbing up the small trees, and stuff like that. And up at the higher end of the forest, there were big vines hanging from the treetops. We would cut the vines and use them as swings, like Tarzan.'

'You must have done a bit of damage to the forest then.'

'We did, I'm afraid,' he confessed, 'but that was a time of ignorance. There are no more vines, and I feel really bad about that, but at least the trees are still here. Come on, let's go over the hill and visit the old village site before the afternoon service.'

'I'm feeling a bit tired,' she complained.

'How can you, when you have been resting most of the day?'

'I don't know. Maybe I ate too much.'

'That's possible. In that case I'll piggyback you. Hop on!'

Solomona turned around and Helen jumped onto his back, clinging tightly around his neck.

'Oh, this is lovely, Mister Tui,' she said as she rested her cheek against the back of his head. She leaned forward and kissed him. 'I love you, Mona,' she whispered.

'Don't forget we take turns,' he teased, trying to look serious.

'Take turns?' Helen was aghast.

'Yep. We change over after every hundred metres.'

'Hey! That's not fair!'

'What's not fair? I carry you for 100 metres, and you carry me for 100 metres. What's fairer than that?'

'Oh, but you are much heavier than me,' she groaned. 'I mean, I can't even lift you off the ground, let alone carry you 100 metres?'

'You're giving up already, HR, and you haven't even tried!' Solomona laughed.

'Mona, I don't need to try. I couldn't even roll you over when you are lying down, much less lift you off your feet.'

'Well, I'm sorry, Miss Jones, but that's the deal.' He tried to look serious, as he walked up to the ridge leading to Old Lalolagi.

'Deal? What deal?'

'That we take turns carrying each other for 100 metres.'

'But —' Helen tried to interject.

'There are no buts, Miss Jones,' he chuckled.

'I'm going to bite you if you don't stop teasing me, Mister Tui.'

'I'm serious, Miss Jones.'

'But we didn't make any deal,' she complained.

'Oh, yes, we did. When you accepted my offer to carry you, by happily jumping onto my back, you agreed to the deal. Of course, you accepted it before you checked the small print,' he laughed.

'That makes it even more unfair,' she remonstrated as she pinched his neck.

'I'll show you what's fair.' Solomona continued walking down the hill to Old Lalolagi. A short distance later, he stopped. 'Come on, Miss Jones, it's your turn to carry me now.'

'Mona, I'm not carrying you, not even for one centimetre.'

Helen didn't move, continuing to hold firmly around his neck. Solomona removed his hands from underneath her buttocks.

'Come on, Miss Jones, it's your turn to carry me.'

'Nope!' She shook her head and held on as tightly as she could. 'I'm not carrying you.'

'I promise I'll be a gentleman,' he whispered.

'What do you mean?'

'I'll make your task easy,' he smiled.

'Promise?'

'The trees of the forest are my witnesses.'

Helen slowly slid off his back. As she moved in front of him, he swooped her up from behind, and carried her in both arms.

Helen gasped, 'Mona, you gave me a shock!'

'Why? Don't you like this?'

'Of course, I do, but... you should've, at least, given me some warning.'

'You've had over six years of warning, Miss Jones.'

'Why do you always tease me?'

'It's fun. You look funny when you're being teased.'

Helen locked her hands around his neck. She stretched up and kissed him on the cheek. After a short while, they reached the Tuisamoa family cemetery, on top of flat land about 500 metres above Old Lalolagi. Puffing a little, Solomona put her down.

'Man, you're getting heavy, HR.'

'Is this the village cemetery?' Helen looked at the beautiful garden that surrounded the graveyard.

'No. This is the family cemetery. Every family has its own burial ground. There are no laws here about where you can or cannot bury your dead.'

'It's a beautiful view from up here.' Helen spun around to study the sea below and the hills, including the majestic Mount Lagi, behind them.

'The view from here is fabulous,' he agreed, 'and there's always a breeze blowing.'

'Oh, look, there's even a mausoleum.'

'Yes, but only the Tuisamoas are buried inside it. Other family members have to contend with the elements out here,' he smiled.

'Hmm, that's a bit unfair, isn't it?'

Solomona shrugged as they walked toward the mausoleum.

'And what are those huge boulders for?' Helen pointed to a row of boulders at the eastern end of the cemetery.

'They were put there by one Tuisamoa, quite a while ago, to remind him of the number of wives he had,' replied Solomona. 'Each boulder represents a wife.'

'Really?' Helen was stunned. 'So many of them!' She counted the boulders. 'You mean he had twenty wives?'

'That's nothing compared to one High Chief in Manono.'

'How many wives did he have?'

'Apparently, he had 99. It was not unusual for a High Chief to have 50 wives. Tuisamoa is a Paramount Chief, so 20 wives wouldn't have been many.'

'Ninety-nine wives?' Helen was totally disbelieving. 'Oh, my goodness! How could he manage with 99 wives? He must have been a very strong person,' she chuckled. 'Was he good-looking?'

Solomona smiled. 'I suppose he must have had a decent appearance. However, good looks and strength, I understand, were not necessary. The necessary and sufficient conditions were that he had to be at least a High Chief with some kind of recognition. Someone else got the wives for him, and he had the wives one at a time.'

'What do you mean? He killed one, and then took another one?'

'Oh, no. In the old days, Samoa was very much like old Europe, except that Samoa was way ahead of Europe and Mendel in genetics.'

'What do you mean?'

'Well, in old Europe, they considered they were "improving" the royal blood by marrying with other royals. We now know that eventually leads to inbreeding, and inbreeding causes all sorts of health problems in addition to other inferior characteristics,' he explained.

'Yes, I've heard that.'

'The Samoans, however, considered marrying outside royal lines as a way to improve the bloodline. We now know that cross-breeding leads to hybrid vigour, or simply, it improves the gene, which includes, among other things, brain cells,' he continued, winking at Helen.

'So the Samoans were pretty good scientists?'

'Well, they knew about the movement of continents before modern scientists did. They knew hybrid vigour before Mendel; and their notion that the sun sets in Savai'i was endorsed when the Greenwich system was established in 1884.

As well as that, they knew that plants need light; that the corals spawn seven days after the full moon in October and November; and much more.'

'But why would High Chiefs marry so many wives?'

'Marriages were a source of wealth for the village, particularly for the *tulafales*. High Chiefs would attract a dowry when they got married. On the other hand, low-ranking families were happy to marry their daughters to the High Chiefs because it provided them with the proper connections. Such connections were, and still are, highly valued by Samoans, so families were more than willing to pay the dowry to get them. The *tulafales* were basically responsible for the High Chief's marriages. When they needed wealth, they would look for a family anywhere in Samoa that could bring a large dowry. They would then tell their High Chief that it was time he had a new wife. The High Chief, in general, did not have any choice. The *tulafales* would formally return the current wife to her family, which would be easy if she had already borne a child or was on the way to having a child, then they would make a proposal to the family of the prospective wife. I've not heard of any family that turned down such a proposal. If the *tulafales* wanted more fine mats and other valuables some time later, they simply repeated the process. So it is very easy for a High Chief to have a hundred wives if his *tulafales* are greedy.'

'Hmm, that's very interesting,' Helen mused. 'Now I know why you wanted me to come to Samoa first, Mister Tui.'

'And that is?'

'I think you just want to find out if I could be one of the wives that you would need to break the record of 99 wives.'

'That's possible,' he replied in mock seriousness.

Forever in Paradise

'You're very naughty, Mister Tuisamoa,' she laughed.

Solomona laughed too. 'Come on. Let's get going. It must be getting close to time for the afternoon service.'

They walked back hand in hand until just before the village. The first bell for the afternoon service rang as they arrived home.

Solomona was again due to play the organ. Attire for the afternoon service was fairly casual, especially for the women, young people and children. A large number of the men were still wearing jackets despite the afternoon heat. The pastor was required by etiquette to wear a suit when conducting a service or leading the village in prayer. So despite the coconut frond fan that waved almost non-stop, Tenari was soaked with sweat even before the service started.

After the last hymn, but before Tenari closed with prayer, the church treasurer rose and read out each family's tithe for the pastor and his family for the next fortnight. A total of $1,000 was collected, with Tuisamoa contributing more than 50 per cent.

Before the final prayer, Tenari read out a list of the contributions his family had received from church members during the week, both in kind and in cash. It included the *sua* and money he received the night Solomona and Helen arrived. He thanked the village and church members for all the provisions his family had been given, then he concluded the service with a prayer.

'The clergy are well looked after in Samoa, aren't they?' Helen whispered to Solomona, as they left the church.

'Hasn't anyone told you that God is a Samoan?' he smiled. 'That's what anyone here would tell you, so God's representative has to be looked after very well.'

'You're kidding, Mona,' she laughed.

'No, that's what Samoans believe,' he insisted. 'God may have chosen the Jews to be His voice to the world, but the people of Lalolagi will tell you that God spends His holidays and His Sabbath here — up there on the top of Mount Lagi; it's far too hot and dusty on Mount Sinai.'

'Stop teasing me, Mister Tui.'

'Ah well,' he chuckled, 'yes, I was joking, but the relationship between the clergy and the village is governed by the same principle that governs the relationship between brothers and sisters, the *feagaiga*. As a result, the pastor becomes the most important person in any village, with a sacred status, which is higher than a Paramount Chief or anyone else. So, being a pastor is the best job in Samoa, and even in Samoan communities outside Samoa. Here, they pay no tax, and they always have the best house in the village. In many villages, he may be the only one with a car; and food, money and other things are never a problem.'

As the sun descended behind the hills of Lalolagi, the *malae* filled with young people. Solomona and Helen sat at the front steps of the Tuisamoa's *faleafolau* and watched. Young girls were playing beach volleyball in front of the school, while boys were playing touch rugby nearby. When the rugby ball bounced onto the area where the girls were playing, one of the girls kicked the ball towards the water and asked the boys to go and play on the beach. Quietly, the boys left.

As darkness fell over Lalolagi, everyone went inside to prepare for evening prayers. Children hurried to the parsonage for prayers with Tenari and his family before the bell rang. At 7.30 pm, Tenari rang the bell, the conch shell sounded, and the evening routine in Lalolagi started all over again.

Nineteen

Their few days in Lalolagi passed quickly. Though he relished the time he was spending at home after so long away, Solomona was determined to show Helen as much as possible of the rest of Samoa in the few weeks remaining before she had to return to New Zealand.

After an early breakfast, Solomona and Helen joined his parents in the family four-wheel drive and started the slow trip to Apia. The narrow streets were starting to come alive when they reached the city. Traffic was building up as buses and trucks began arriving from the villages. The police band was rehearsing in front of the police station for the daily flag-raising ceremony at 8 am. It was still too early for Tuisamoa's scheduled check-up at the hospital, so they drove to the family home in the hills overlooking Apia.

The road that crossed the island of Upolu was winding and steep in many places, especially as it moved further away from Apia. After a 20-minute drive through beautiful countryside, they turned onto an access road virtually at the top of the mountain range behind Apia. The road to the house was not sealed but was in good condition. The sides of the road were lined with teak trees, spaced evenly all the way to the house. The fields were lush with growth and still covered with morning dew.

The Tuisamoa family house was about two kilometres from the main road. It was a two-storey *falepalagi* on a single-hectare property. Standing almost in the centre of the property, the house was purpose-built to withstand cyclonic winds. At the rear was a *faleo'o* where Tuisamoa would retreat during the heat of the day. The rear and side boundaries of the property were marked with teak trees, dotted along the fence-line. The front boundary, facing north towards Apia, featured a row of betel-nut trees. A beautiful garden of tropical flowering plants surrounded the immaculate front lawn. Upstairs a north-facing balcony took in the view towards Apia and beyond.

One of Solomona's cousins, Sofia, and her husband, Onosa'i, who worked in the public service, looked after the house. Solomona parked the truck under the carport behind the *faleo'o*. Sofia greeted everyone, then helped to unload the bags and some supplies. Solomona took Helen inside to show her around, finishing the tour at the upstairs balcony.

'Wow!' exclaimed Helen as she took in the landscape spread before them. 'What a beautiful view, Mona.' She could almost imagine the roar of the waves as they broke on the reefs, a few kilometres away. Her attention was distracted by the singing of native birds from an acacia tree at the side of the house.

'It's beautiful from up here, isn't it?' Solomona always loved coming here. The tranquillity and surrounding beauty seemed to give this house an ethereal quality.

'Oh, it really is, Mona.'

'But not as good as the hills and seas of Fagaloa, eh?'

'Of course not, but it's still very beautiful. You can see the whole of Apia, and the sea in the distance. You could even see boats coming into Apia harbour from here.'

'Actually,' Solomona suggested, 'if you had powerful binoculars, you could almost spy on anyone in town from here. And can you see Apia Park with the rugby stadium over there?'

'No!'

'If you look straight to the tip of Mulinu'u, the peninsula at the western end of Apia —'

'Yes, I can see that.'

'Now, Apia Park is almost on a straight line from here to the tip of Mulinu'u. There is a small oval open field —'

'Oh, yes, I can see it now.'

'That's where Manu Samoa plays its matches. And if you had strong enough binoculars, you could sit and watch the games from here.'

'Really? What's that mountain to the left?'

'Oh, that's Mount Vaea, which Samoan legends say was formed when the famous strongman, Vaea, turned into a mountain while watching his sister, Apaula, leaving with Fijians to become the wife of the Tuifiti. On top of Mount Vaea lies the sailor from the seas, Robert Louis Stevenson, or Tusitala, as he was known to Samoans.'

'Oh, that would be an interesting place to visit.'

'Yes. We can visit it before you leave.'

Helen fell quiet. Somehow, the mention of the word 'leave' made her feel uneasy. She was having such a good time in Samoa that she didn't want to think about returning to New Zealand, especially with Solomona remaining behind.

'What's wrong, HR?' Solomona wondered if he had said something to upset her.

He moved behind her and held both her shoulders. When she turned around to face him, there were tears in her eyes. Solomona offered her his handkerchief. After wiping her eyes, Helen wrapped her arms around him and rested her head on his chest.

'I'm sorry, Mona,' she said apologetically. 'I was just getting a little emotional about the thought of going back to New Zealand without you, that's all.'

'Well, it's still about seven weeks away,' he said, trying to cheer her up.

'I know, but it's just when you would like to have more time that time seems to run away from you.'

'Well,' he smiled, 'it's not as if you can't come back. You should be able to afford to visit every semester break.'

'I know,' Helen ventured a smile, 'but it's a long time between university semesters.'

'Oh, you'll be surprised at how fast the time will pass.'

Solomona heard his name being called. Leaning over the balcony railing, he saw Sofia summoning them to breakfast.

During breakfast, a police officer arrived in a government car. Sofia went out and invited him to join them for breakfast. Afterwards, everyone except Sofia went to the hospital, Alofa and Tuisamoa in the government car, and Solomona and Helen in the family's truck.

At the hospital, Solomona and Helen met up with Dr Fa'aluma, who had finished his internship in New Zealand a year ago and was now back in Apia working at the National Hospital.

'Hello, you two!' he greeted them with a broad smile.

'How are you doing, Fili?' asked Helen.

'Hope you're keeping out of trouble, my friend,' grinned Solomona.

Dr Fa'aluma laughed. 'Hey, look who's talking. Do you believe this guy, Helen? I mean, he was almost killed while gawking at some girls instead of paying attention to the traffic, and he's asking me if I have been keeping out of trouble. I mean, come on, King.'

Helen smiled, 'You two love to have a go at each other, don't you?'

'Well, Helen,' Dr Fa'aluma replied, 'you need to find fun in everything you do, or life would be very boring. And it's always safe to laugh at yourself.'

'So how are you finding life back home, my friend?' asked Solomona.

'Let's say it's challenging, but it's very exciting.'

'You mean, very fulfilling?'

'Exactly, King. The pay, as you know, is low, but as you used to say, money isn't everything. I have thought hard about it, and life is certainly worth living — especially here at home.'

'Well, I'm glad you heeded some of my counsel,' smiled Solomona.

Dr Fa'aluma laughed at his friend's modesty.

'Well, Fili, we must be going.'

'Where are you going? I thought you were here with the old man.'

'We're going to Savai'i tomorrow, and we need to go down and book the truck on the ferry. Mum will stay with Dad, and a police officer is looking after both of them. We'll be back before too long.'

'Savai'i, eh?' Dr Fa'aluma gently scratched his chin. 'Well, that should be fun, Helen.'

'I've heard a lot of nice things about Savai'i, so I'm really looking forward to it,' she replied, smiling.

'Oh, I'm sure you'll like it. How long are you going for?'

'We're coming back on either Sunday or Monday,' replied Solomona.

Dr Fa'aluma nodded his head slowly. 'That gives you plenty of time to see the big island. Why don't you go and stay at the resort? I'll ask Mum to give you a good deal.'

'We're already planning to stay at your family's resort,' Solomona assured him. 'Anyway, we must get going. We should return before Mum and Dad are ready to go back to the house.'

Solomona and Helen drove down to the office of the shipping company near the wharf where they booked their passage on the first trip the following day.

When they arrived back at the hospital, Dr Fa'aluma and Solomona's parents were talking in the foyer. After seeing his parents to their car, Solomona and Helen were about to leave when Dr Fa'aluma whispered to Solomona that he wanted to speak with him for a moment. Solomona asked Helen to wait in the truck.

'King, I'm sorry but what I want to tell you is not very pleasant.'

'It's Dad, isn't it?'

Dr Fa'aluma nodded sadly. 'Yes, my friend. I'm sorry, but your old man's prognosis is not promising. The cancer has spread to other parts of his body.'

'How much time does he have?'

'The optimistic forecast is three months, but it's likely to be less.'

Solomona was shocked. His mind raced as he thought about the implications.

'Well,' he replied, his voice wavering, 'at least there's time for us to prepare.'

'Yes,' said Dr Fa'aluma hesitantly. 'Look, I'm really sorry, King. I hate being the bearer of such terrible news.'

'Oh, you don't have to apologise, Fili. It's not your fault, or anyone's, that Dad has cancer. But, have you told Mum and Dad about the prognosis?'

'We have told them in the gentlest possible way — anything to help make it easier for them to deal with your father's situation.'

'Is there anything we can do?'

'Yes. Keep an eye on him, and if the pain becomes too much for him to bear, then he may need to come to the hospital so that he can receive treatment, 24 hours a day.'

'Well, thanks a lot, Fili. I think we'd better be going.'

'I hope you can still enjoy the trip to Savai'i.'

'Yes, we'll try.'

Solomona and Dr Fa'aluma walked to the car park together and shook hands warmly. Dr Fa'aluma walked round to the passenger side to say goodbye to Helen. As they headed back to the house, Solomona's heart felt heavy at the thought that his father's condition was so serious.

Helen sensed something was wrong. 'What did Fili want to talk about?' she asked.

'He said Dad has probably only three months to live,' he replied after a while, still stunned by the news.

'Oh, I'm really sorry to hear that, Mona. Listen, we don't have to go to Savai'i tomorrow. We can always go another time.'

'I was thinking about that, but I know Dad wouldn't want that. He doesn't like people feeling sorry for him, and it's always uplifting for him to see people enjoying life. If we proceed as if nothing is wrong, that should hearten him somewhat and hopefully contribute to his general well-being, but I can't help feeling gutted by the fact that he could go at any time.'

Twenty

Solomona awoke just after 4 am on the morning they were to leave for Savai'i. The first ferry was scheduled to leave at 8 am. It would take an hour to drive the 50 kilometres from their house to the wharf. After waking Helen, he went downstairs to the kitchen and boiled water for coffee. Sofia, whose room was on the ground floor not far from the kitchen, was awakened by muffled sounds coming from the kitchen. She stumbled out of bed and, still half-asleep, shuffled into the kitchen.

'Oh, it's you, Mona,' she said, wiping sleep from her eyes.

'I'm just making coffee for us,' he replied. 'We'd like to leave before 5 am so that we can get in the queue early.'

'Oh, you don't have to be there as early as that.'

'Well, I don't want to be left on the wharf just because I'm late.'

'They're not like that anymore, Mona.'

'Really?'

'Now, once you have your car booked, you are guaranteed a place. They're a lot better than they used to be.'

'In that case, we'll just take our time.'

'Yes. Go and get your things ready while I organise breakfast.'

'Oh, that won't be necessary, Sofi. We're just going to have some toast with jam, a slice of papaya and a cup of coffee.'

'Oh, no, Mona,' she insisted. 'You need a hearty breakfast. Go on, I'll see to things here.'

Solomona quietly walked back upstairs to his room. It seemed that everybody insisted on feeding them since they had arrived from New Zealand. He knocked on Helen's door to see if she was awake. She was changing when he opened her door.

'Oh, I'm sorry, HR,' he apologised, quickly closing the door.

'It's all right, Mister Tui,' Helen assured him. 'Come on in.'
'Are you decent?'

'Does it matter?' she laughed.

'But I haven't said my prayers yet,' he teased.

Helen flung the door open. 'See!' she exclaimed with her hands on her hips. She was dressed in long pants with a white T-shirt. 'So do you think you will still be tempted?'

Solomona smiled, 'You'd be surprised at what runs through a man's mind just by looking at you, HR.'

Helen threw her arms around him. 'When did I ever tempt you enough, eh?' she whispered.

'Only the power of the Holy Spirit has stopped me from being tempted, otherwise the devil would have been dancing with glee. Anyway, have you packed your things yet?'

'Yep.'

'Okay, I'll take your bag while you talk to Sofia, who is getting our breakfast ready.'

Retrieving his own bag from his room, Solomona took their luggage to the truck. Helen followed him downstairs, and found Sofia setting the table. Alofa, who had been woken by all the noise, followed her into the kitchen.

'Did you sleep well, Helen?' asked Alofa.

'Oh, yes, thank you, Alofa,' she replied. 'It's lovely and cool up here — good sleeping weather.'

'It can get really cold in the middle of the year. Please sit down and have some breakfast before you go.'

Sofia placed some toast, fried eggs and canned corned beef on the table. She returned to the bench to get some papaya, a carton of milk and hot water for their coffee.

'Oh, but it's far too early for a big breakfast, Sofi,' Helen protested.

'It's quite a long trip,' Alofa insisted, 'and there are no restaurants along the way. Come on, have something to eat.'

Solomona came into the kitchen after checking that everything was packed ready to go. 'How is Dad, Mum?'

'Oh, he's still asleep,' his mother replied. 'He appears to be all right.'

Solomona sat down at the table. 'Come on, HR, let's get something into our tummies before we hit the road.'

After breakfast, he gave his mother their itinerary, thanked Sofia for organising breakfast so early, then they headed for the harbour. It was still dark when they reached the wharf. It was not yet 6 am, but there was already a long queue of vehicles waiting for the ferry to arrive. Helen, who fell asleep on the way, was still sleeping soundly. Solomona began to worry whether they would be able to get on, despite having booked. Concerned, he got out to check with the driver in the vehicle ahead. Helen woke up as he shut the door. Once the other driver had assured him that the new ferry was much bigger, Solomona returned, relieved, to the truck.

'Where were you, Mister Tui?'

'Just checking to make sure we could get on the ferry,' he replied. 'There are a lot of vehicles ahead of us already.'

'And what did you find out?'

'Apparently, it's a much bigger ferry, and as long as we have our vehicle booked, we should have no problem.'

The ferry arrived just before 8 am. Solomona was very impressed; the new ferry was a vast improvement on the previous one. He woke Helen, who had gone back to sleep while waiting for the ferry to arrive. It didn't take long for all the cargo to be loaded, and for them to be on their way. The 20-kilometre trip to Savai'i took about an hour and a half. Helen relaxed and enjoyed the ride, especially watching the flying fish and the dolphins frolicking in the bow wave of the ferry.

After disembarking at the Salelologa wharf, they drove to a grocery store where they bought packages of mutton. Solomona packed them into three large coolers in the back of the truck.

'What's all that meat for?' asked Helen, curious at the large number of packages.

'We have to visit relatives along the way,' he replied. 'They know the truck, and would be insulted if we didn't stop. And when we visit, we are expected to give what we call an *oso*, which is usually a gift of food. It's always expected from anyone coming from Apia.'

'How many relatives do you have in Savai'i? I mean, you did buy a lot of mutton.'

'Oh, I've lost count,' he quipped. 'At least one family in every village, I guess. And that's why you need a lot of money to live in Samoa.'

'Gee, you must be related to the whole country!'

'We have a saying that a Samoan has more roots than any tree that ever existed. And with all the chiefly marriages in the past to establish connections, it's not difficult to see why Samoans think that way.'

They drove along the north-east coast of Savai'i, stopping off along the way to visit relatives and distribute the mutton. At each stop, they would talk for a while, and usually they were offered something to eat. Each time, Solomona managed to convince his relatives that he and Helen weren't hungry and were in a hurry. By midday, they had reached Sapapali'i, Alofa's village. The *faletele* of Alofa's family was full of women when the truck turned into the driveway.

'It's Alofa's truck,' called Solomona's aunt, Fale, to the women who were sitting weaving mats. 'Oh, look, it's Mona driving,' she added as she got up to have a better look. 'It's Mona with a *palagi* girl. Well, ladies,' announced Fale, 'let's call it a day — we have visitors.'

There was commotion in the *faletele* as the women stumbled to their feet with their unfinished mats in their hands. Solomona stopped the truck behind the *faletele*, and called out for someone to fetch two packages from the coolers in the back of the truck. One container was already empty. Solomona greeted the women and introduced Helen. His mother's relatives all knew him from times when he had spent his holidays in Sapapali'i as a schoolboy. Fale greeted Solomona and Helen warmly and invited them into the family's *falepalagi* behind the *faletele*.

'I'd like you to meet Helen, Aunt Fale. I'm taking her on a tour of Savai'i.'

'You must sleep here tonight,' his aunt said, smiling at Helen. 'She's a beautiful-looking girl, Mona,' she whispered.

'What are you talking about?' inquired Helen, nervous that everyone was looking at her.

'I was telling Mona that you are beautiful,' Fale replied.

Helen blushed. 'Oh, but Mona would say I can't take any credit for that, as I was born that way.'

'It's very kind of you, Aunt Fale, but we'll sleep somewhere on the way. We'd like to keep on going and make sure that Helen sees a lot of Savai'i.'

'Well, it's up to you, but no one sleeps in this house normally,' she replied, gesturing around the family's *falepalagi*. 'But maybe it's better if you don't sleep here, you know?'

'Know what?' inquired Solomona.

'Well, you know the *matais* nowadays. If they find out you're here, they will surely make an *usu* to try to get some money from you. They're just too greedy — they don't know what is proper and what's not anymore. They should be using their time to plant bananas or whatever, but all they do is sit and play cards like vultures waiting to pounce when someone comes around.'

Solomona smiled, 'Is that so, eh?'

'How are your studies going?' his aunt asked.

'Oh, I have finished now. At least I hope I have.'

'That's very good news, Mona. Come on, let's go and have some lunch, then you can leave before the vultures arrive.'

'Where's Papali'i?' Solomona inquired about Fale's son, who was a schoolteacher and the *matai* of the family.

'He's up at the farm with the boys.'

After lunch, Solomona and Helen continued on their way along the north-east coast of Savai'i. They stopped briefly at the memorial to the first Christian missionary in Samoa, Reverend John Williams, opposite the Sapapali'i Church. Continuing on, they passed through many beautiful villages bordering on white sandy beaches. There were more relatives to visit on the way, and they stopped now and then to offer packages of mutton and to meet the relatives. At other times, they stopped and walked along some of the beaches. Helen savoured the opportunity to see such magnificent scenery, enjoying wetting her feet now and then in the warm pristine waters of Savai'i. Leaving the coastline, they passed through rocky fields, rainforests and coconut plantations. In one village, they came across three young boys eating coconut at the side of the road. Solomona stopped the truck and got out.

'Can you get us some young coconuts, boys,' Solomona requested.

'How many do you want, sir?' asked the oldest one.

'Say, enough to fill two of the containers in the back of the truck.'

The boy had a quick look at the containers. 'Okay, you two,' he said to the younger boys, 'you get up there and get all the good ones.'

The two young boys quickly climbed a tree each and pulled down more than a dozen coconuts each. The oldest boy prepared a stick, which he used to skilfully remove the husks. He tossed each husked coconut to Solomona, who placed them in the two empty containers.

'Thank you very much, boys,' said Solomona as he handed them $15.

The boys hesitated. Giggling shyly, they looked at each other.

'It's all right, sir,' smiled the oldest boy, too shy to accept the money.

Solomona left the money on the ground, climbed into the truck, raised his hand to thank the boys again, then drove off.

After an hour, they stopped by the roadside at the western end of lava fields. Drinking from a couple of coconuts, they walked to a depressed area in the lava field, about 20 metres from the road.

'Down there is the grave of a *taupou*,' Solomona told Helen, pointing to the bottom of a pit formed by the lava.

'I can only see a pile of rocks,' she said, looking hard to see if she had missed something.

'That is the *taupou's* grave, and over there is the church,' he added, pointing to limestone walls that were still standing some distance away near the edge of the lava field. 'Both were miraculously spared by the fiery lava, which appeared to encircle them as it flowed down from the volcano. The locals considered it a miracle and attributed it to the power of God.'

They returned to the truck and continued on, passing through more villages and visiting more relatives, where mutton from the third container was distributed. The drive was a bit rough, but the scenery was so beautiful that Helen didn't have time to worry about the bumpy road. It was quite comfortable inside the truck with the air-conditioning on. As they emerged from the western end of an enormous rainforest, they sighted beautiful Asau Bay. Solomona drove slowly to the Vaisigano resort, waving to the children along the roadside who were waving and calling out *'palagi'*. Helen smiled and waved back.

Twenty One

As their truck approached the Vaisigano resort, Helen immediately became enchanted with the place. The resort was in a beautiful cove with a brilliantly white sandy beach. Though close to a village, it was well hidden by a strip of lush rainforest. Except for the roar of the sea and the sound of waves lapping at the shore, the resort was peacefully quiet. A reef encircled the pristine beach about a kilometre off the shoreline. Inside the reef, the water was calm and fairly deep with a water temperature that, she would later learn, was constantly warm.

'Let's get our rooms first, then we can go for a walk on the beach,' Solomona suggested as they pulled into the car park.

As he opened the door to the reception lobby, the shrill voice of the manager and owner, Agalelei Fa'aluma, greeted them. Agalelei was a short stout woman with plump, rosy cheeks, who smiled all the time.

'Hello, Mona dear!' Rushing from behind the counter with short quick steps, she embraced Solomona affectionately. 'Welcome back, my boy,' she smiled. 'And welcome to Samoa, dear,' she added, turning towards Helen.

'Thank you, Aunt Lelei,' replied Solomona, who always referred to his friends' parents as uncles and aunts. 'I'd like you to meet Helen.' Agalelei shook her hand warmly. Helen smiled, feeling slightly embarrassed. 'Helen is here during the university holidays, and I'm showing her around,' he explained.

'I know,' Agalelei replied. 'Fili called last night and told us you were coming. Well, Helen, you must be the luckiest girl in the world — our Mona has to be the most eligible bachelor around.' She raised her eyebrows and nodded as if to emphasise the point.

'I know,' Helen acknowledged, smiling at Solomona.

'Well, congratulations on finishing your thesis, Mona. Fili was very excited about that. Now, am I hearing wedding bells, or am I jumping the gun?'

Helen's cheeks reddened, as she looked hesitantly at Solomona.

'You're probably a little ahead of yourself, Aunt Lelei.' Solomona winked at Helen. 'I'm told that the ship that was bringing the bells got hijacked by pirates near Fiji,' he continued with a laugh.

'Oh, well, let's hope the pirates will release the ship, eh Helen?' she chuckled, nudging Helen gently.

'Anyway, do you want two rooms or one?'

'Two single rooms should be fine, Aunt Lelei.'

'Would you like two single rooms or a double room, Helen?' she asked, with a mischievous glint in her eye. Unsure whether to go against Solomona's wishes, Helen merely shrugged. 'I think she would like a double room, Mona. And why not?'

'Aunt Lelei,' he warned, 'you know what will happen if people find out that Helen and I are sharing a room.'

'Mona,' Agalelei said dismissively, 'even the clergy play around. You are not married yet, but I can see that look on both your faces, and it tells me that one day I shall be receiving a wedding invitation.'

'But, Aunt Lelei, the fact that others do wrong is no excuse for us to share a room.'

'Mona, I know you are a good boy. You always behave yourself, unlike your old man who has been... Hmm, you know,' she lowered her voice conspiratorially, as she winked at Solomona.

'That's exactly my point, Aunt Lelei. Even though Dad has been truly a reformed person for some years now, people remember only his wild days. And because of that, thousands are watching me, waiting for me to stumble, to satisfy the old cliche "like father, like son".'

'I know that, but the difference is I know you and I trust you,' she said with almost parental pride. 'Let them wonder and waste their time; there is nothing you can do about useless gossip and envy. Anyway, I am going to put you in a family unit. It is a large, fully self-contained unit like a motel room, and it has a double bed and two singles. It will be nice to be in the same room, so you can talk as you fall asleep, right Helen?' She winked good-naturedly at Helen.

Helen smiled, and shyly lowered her eyes to the floor.

'But I didn't come prepared to pay for a family unit, Aunt Lelei,' Solomona argued, in a vain attempt to stick to his original plan.

'Don't worry, I can pay for it, Mona,' Helen interrupted.

'See,' Agalelei remonstrated, 'Helen agrees with me — it's women's intuition. Anyway, that's not a problem. The unit will be provided at no cost to either of you. Consider it as our gift: to you, Mona, for finishing your thesis, and to thank Helen for looking after you when you had your accident. Fili kept us up to date on everything that happened in Auckland and at the university.'

Solomona and Helen looked at each other. Speechless, they could only shrug and shake their heads. Solomona tried one last time to plead his case. 'But, aunt —'

'Don't argue with a woman, Mona. You have been a very good example to our young people, and a great companion to Fili and all the Samoan students at university. If the future of this country depends on two people like you, I have no doubt that Samoa will be the best country in the world. This is only a small token of our appreciation for everything you have done. So don't say "but",' she smiled, handing Helen the keys to the unit.

'Well, thank you for your kind words, Aunt Lelei.'

'Mona, they are the sincere words of a mother who has watched you kids grow up to become fine young men,' she replied. 'Now, where is your luggage?'

'Still in the back of the truck. Also, there are *nius* for you in the coolers.'

While Agalelei busied herself organising the collection of their luggage, Solomona pulled a couple of stools up to the counter.

'Let's sit down and have a drink, HR, before we go to the unit. It's so long since I've been here, and there's so much to discuss with Aunt Lelei.'

'What would you like to drink, Helen?'

'A glass of mango juice please, Lelei.'

'You still don't drink beer, Mona?'

'No, Aunt Lelei. I'll have the same as Helen.'

'See?' she smiled. 'You are a good boy; you still haven't picked up any bad habits despite the years you've spent in a place like Auckland.'

'Fili will probably disagree with you there, Aunt Lelei.'

'Oh, he'd be the first one to support me on this, Mona,' she assured him. 'Anyway, enjoy your drinks. Here is the menu for our restaurant and a schedule of this week's activities, if you are interested. By the way, your meals and drinks will be free too. Helen, treat the place as though you are at home rather than in a hotel. Feel free to ask for anything you want at any time... well, any time within reason,' she smiled.

'That's far too much, Aunt Lelei.' Solomona was overwhelmed by her hospitality. 'You are really spoiling us.'

'Oh, well,' she sighed, 'those of us who work hard deserve to be spoiled once in a while, right Helen?'

Solomona and Helen chatted with Agalelei for some time before making their way to the unit, which, they soon discovered, had a wonderful view of the beach and the resort surroundings.

Helen unpacked while Solomona turned on the air-conditioner and opened the curtains to take in the view. Before dinner, they went for a leisurely stroll along the beach. The tide was going out and the sun was setting, behind the rainforests of Falealupo.

'It's so beautiful, isn't it?' commented Helen, kicking up sand with her bare toes.

'The water, the beaches, the people, most things are virtually the same throughout the entire country,' Solomona replied. 'The best beaches tend to be on the southern end of both Upolu and Savai'i, and in some of the calm and secluded coves like this one. But when it comes to scenery, well, you can't go past the hills and coastline of Fagaloa.'

'I know, but this place is special too. It has its own unique magic, just like Fagaloa, Apia and the other places that we've visited. I mean, the whole place really is paradise.' She stooped to pick up a pebble and absently tossed it into the water.

As they walked back towards their unit in fading light, the beach lights of the resort came on.

The resort restaurant was virtually on the beach, the whole structure sitting above it on stilts. Solomona and Helen chose a table outside on the balcony, against the railing right above the beach. Other holidaymakers joined them. It was getting dark, but the moon was already high above the horizon. Agalelei lit candles on the outside tables, giving the outdoor area a magical atmosphere.

A gentle breeze blew across the beach, and the leaves of the trees nearby rustled softly. Solomona and Helen smiled at each other across the table. 'Dinner on the beach, underneath the stars, by the light of the moon and soft candlelight? Whew,' Helen thought to herself. She reached across the table for Solomona's hand.

'You look absolutely beautiful tonight, HR,' he smiled as he gently squeezed her hand.

'I thought this sort of thing happened only in movies, Mona. I'm quite overwhelmed. I mean, the English language doesn't have enough superlatives to describe it all.'

'Then don't even try. Just enjoy it.'

While waiting for their meals, they listened to the resort's band, playing popular Samoan music. The band leader welcomed diners to the resort, extending a special welcome to Solomona and Helen, and wished everyone a pleasant evening, before launching into a favourite Samoan tune. There was applause all around as the band leader bowed to acknowledge the patrons' appreciation of the music.

Just as Solomona and Helen were about to begin their meals, Agalelei pulled a chair up to their table. 'How are things so far, you two?'

'Absolutely amazing, Lelei,' Helen replied, as she spread her serviette on her lap.

'That's great. What about the unit?'

'Well,' Solomona ventured, 'so far there are no problems, but after dinner in a romantic atmosphere like this, and perhaps after a bit of dancing later on, it could become a real concern.'

'Oh, well,' smiled Agalelei, 'what can you do, eh Helen?'

'Mona is very good at fooling people, Lelei,' Helen said confidentially. 'I don't have to tell you how determined he is to maintain his impeccable record.'

'That's why he's such a good boy,' Agalelei laughed. 'Anyway, I'd better let you enjoy your meal. I'll talk to you later.'

Solomona and Helen enjoyed their seafood dinner of lobster, washed down with Samoa's own Talofa wine. In the bright moonlight the white sand of the beach glowed, and the sea looked awash with silver. Mesmerised by the atmosphere and replete with good food and wine, they decided to stay and enjoy the entertainment, pushing their seats together while they listened to the music. Later on, the band started to play some popular music from the 1960s and 1970s.

'Come on. Let's not waste the music, Miss Jones.' Solomona took her hand and led her to the dance floor as the band played the famous Hollies' song *The Air That I Breathe*. Helen rested her head on his chest as they danced. They enjoyed the dancing so much that they stayed until the band finished playing at midnight. Agalelei introduced them to the band members, so they chatted with the band for a while, before retiring for the night.

They slept virtually until lunchtime the next day. After lunch, they spent more time with their host before driving, late in the afternoon, to Falealupo to watch the sunset at Pulotu. The drive through magnificent rainforests was picturesque and peaceful — they seemed to have the road to themselves. Just off the main road, Solomona stopped the truck and led Helen to a rock a few metres away.

'That looks like a human footprint, but it's far too big,' Helen said, pointing to the imprint on the surface of the rock.

'That, according to village stories, is one of the footprints of the mythical giant Moso,' Solomona explained. 'Remember we joked about Moso the night we arrived?' Helen nodded. 'Well, the other footprint is apparently at the very eastern tip of Upolu. That's a distance of over 300 kilometres. There's also supposed to be another in one of the islands of Manu'a in American Samoa, and another in Fiji. Moso was said to be huge, and legend tells us that he was holding up the sky, so it wouldn't collapse on Samoa.'

'Hmm, a Samoan Atlas, eh?'

'Apparently,' he smiled, with a shrug of his shoulders. 'Anyway, we don't want to miss the sunset. Let's get going.'

They continued driving down to the village and stopped at a beach on the western end of Falealupo.

'This place is renowned because of its association with Nafanua, one of Samoa's famous goddesses prior to the arrival of Christianity,' Solomona explained, as they walked to the beach. 'She was born prematurely, but survived, and Samoans used to attribute such cases with divine power. Nafanua apparently grew up in Pulotu, in Fiji. At that time, her people in western Savai'i were being subjected to virtual enslavement by a tyrannical Chief and the people of eastern Savai'i. One day, she heard the moaning of her people's High Chief who was forced to climb a coconut tree upside-down. She jumped into the sea and swam all the way from Fiji to save her people, and this is apparently where she landed, clinging to the root of a *fau* tree as she recovered. According to Samoan legend, she was a brave warrior who defeated everyone she fought. She waged a liberation battle and defeated an army of men from eastern Savai'i. They didn't know that Nafanua was a woman until the wind lifted her battledress. It greatly embarrassed the men, and perhaps Nafanua was embarrassed too at being exposed in public. That particular place was appropriately named *malae o le ma*, or the field of embarrassment, in the village of Fai'a'ai.'

'I've noticed that names seem to be very important in Samoa.'

'To Mister Shakespeare, a name did not seem to be important. But to Samoans, much like the Israelites of old, a name tells a story, and, therefore, can be very important. Remember, I showed you the court that deals with names, albeit *matai* titles. I mean, is there any other country in the world with a court like that?'

'Yes, I remember. It was in Apia,' she replied. 'I can't say I've ever heard of any other country with a Titles Court.'

They left Nafanua's landing place and drove down to the tip of Falealupo. It was getting late, and the sun was dipping towards the horizon. Curious village children crowded around the truck as it stopped. 'Hello, *palagi*,' the children called out as they peered into the vehicle. An old woman appeared and shooed the children away. She was closely followed by an elderly man, who was limping slightly. Solomona greeted them, introducing himself and Helen.

'Tuisamoa?' asked the old man, his voice trembling. 'My goodness, are you the son of Tuisamoa? You shouldn't be standing around in the middle of the village like a person without a home, your Lordship. The whole of Falealupo is your home. Come on, we should go inside.'

Perplexed at not understanding what was being said, Helen looked questioningly at Solomona for a translation of their conversation.

'Thank you for your kind offer, sir,' said Solomona respectfully. 'We just came to see the renowned sunset of Falealupo. We are staying with friends in Asau.'

'Well, I can show you around the place, if you like,' the old man offered.

'That's very kind of you, sir,' Solomona graciously accepted.

Together they walked slowly to the beach, from where they had a good view of Pulotu. The sky took on a reddish glow as the sun slowly slid closer to the horizon.

'That is Pulotu,' the man said, pointing to a huge rock out to sea. 'That's where the lady swam from to save our people,' he continued, referring to Nafanua's epic swim.

Solomona explained to Helen what the old man was saying.

'But I thought you said Pulotu was in Fiji,' she queried.

'If you analyse the Nafanua story, Pulotu can only be near Fiji, or in Fiji,' Solomona replied. 'My theory is that either the people thought that Pulotu looked so far away that it must have been closer to Fiji than Samoa, or there was another Pulotu in Fiji. The next village, Tufutafoe, which has a number of historical sites, also claims to have the real Pulotu. Or it's even possible that Fiji had not moved away from Samoa at the time.'

The enormous rock had an arch in the middle that was clearly visible from the shore. A blowhole in line with the middle of the arch spurted water high into the air as waves rushed in. From their vantage point on the beach, it gave the illusion that the sun was setting right into the blowhole. When a wave spurted water into the air, splashes of colour washed across the sky.

'What an amazing scene, Mona!' Helen gasped.

'When someone died,' the old man explained, with Solomona translating for Helen, 'the spirit would be sent to Lagi if that person was good, and live there forever with Tagaloalagi. However, if the person was bad, the spirit would be transported by a bad-spirit boat to a spot west of Manono. There, it would be dumped into the sea and sucked into a deep tunnel that runs all the way to Pulotu. As the spirit emerged in Pulotu, the waves would come in and crush it and blow it to oblivion. The colours you see when waves come into Pulotu and spurt into the air are the bad spirits being crushed. Some would escape with bruises,' he chuckled, 'and they would torment the living.'

'Do they still believe those stories?' Helen asked.

'I really don't know. But at the time, it offered an explanation about life and the after-life. I think every society has similar stories. However, the striking similarity of the old man's story to the stories of Pluto and Tartarus in Greek mythology, as well as to some of the names — like Pluto and Samos to Pulotu and Samoa — is very intriguing,' Solomona said.

'See! I told you that Samoans, and Polynesians, must have originally come from Greece,' she teased.

He smiled. 'I suppose there must be an explanation, and given the order of things and the principle of causality, if one people came from the other, then your people must originally have come from Samoa, because —'

'No, Mister Tui,' she insisted, laughing, 'it's the other way round.'

The old man stood and smiled, trying to understand the banter between Solomona and Helen.

'See,' said Solomona, 'the old man is smiling because I'm right, HR. As humanity began in Samoa, it makes sense that your people came from Samoa and the Pacific. In addition, Samoans and Polynesians are just a little more beautiful than Greeks, which is consistent with the principle of causality that says the effect cannot be better than the cause,' he continued, winking at Helen. 'You're an exception because you are a product of a gene salad, and your blood has been improved by your Jewish and Welsh blood... see?'

Darkness started to set in, and the smell of freshly cooked food wafted on the air. Walking back to the truck, Solomona thanked the old man for sharing his story with them, and for giving them a guided tour of Falealupo and

Pulotu. He offered the man a $10 note, but it was refused. As their truck started to move away, Solomona threw the $10 note towards him as a gesture of their appreciation.

Back at the resort, they quickly prepared for dinner. Again they were treated to dinner under a starry sky, by candlelight.

'Oh, what a life, Mister Tui!' Helen mused as she sipped her mango juice. 'Imagine this forever: trips through fascinating landscapes and gripping stories by daylight, then dinner under the stars with music and candlelight. It's absolutely unreal.'

'Enjoy it while it lasts, HR, because, as they say, every good thing must come to an end.'

'I know,' she acknowledged, 'but just imagine it: forever in paradise! What a perfect life!'

'Well, savour the moment, Miss Jones.'

The band was again entertaining the guests, but Solomona and Helen didn't stay late. Solomona had planned a longer drive the next day, so they excused themselves after dinner, and retired early.

Next morning, after an early breakfast, they drove south to the village of Tufutafoe where they visited a number of historical and culturally significant sites. They spent most of the day there before returning to Falealupo to inspect a rock that looked like a *fale*. One side of the rock-*fale* was completely covered, but there was a hole near the ridge on the other side.

'So what's the story concerning this rock, Mister Tui,' Helen asked.

'Well, according to legend, Nafanua wanted to build this *fale*. The men offered to look after the whole project, but the women objected, arguing they were just as good. As a compromise, Nafanua agreed that the men would be responsible for one side of the *fale*, and the women would look after the other side. It so happened that the women completed theirs while the men, to this day, as you can see, failed to finish theirs. The *fale* has since turned into rock. That whole event resulted in a Samoan saying, which literally means women are more capable than men.'

'Hmm, that must have been the first battle of the sexes,' she smiled. 'It's very interesting that, in a largely macho society like Samoa, women feature so prominently in many of its legends and stories.'

'I don't think Samoan stories are unique in that regard. If you look at less developed societies, and also those of so-called advanced societies when they were underdeveloped, you would find similar stories.'

'But there must have been a reason for the prominence of women in Samoan legends.'

'Well, if you think about it, life in its most fundamental sense is a struggle against death, isn't it?' he argued. 'And if that is the case, then I suppose that if someone could somehow overcome death, or at least reproduce life, then perhaps that would have been considered powerful. And, of course, only women give birth to new life. So, if power was equated to the ability to reproduce life, in defiance of death, then that might explain why women feature so prominently in Samoan legends and myths. I wouldn't be surprised if the idea of God in the old days was also a feminine figure for the same reason — as the giver of life — and I suspect that may also explain why a sister has a sacred status in her relationship with her brothers in a Samoan family.'

'All these stories are quite interesting, aren't they?' Helen said as they walked back to the truck.

'Oh, they're really fascinating,' Solomona agreed. 'The thing about them is that they all appear to follow a certain line of logic that is not very different from the principles we now adopt in more advanced scientific research.'

They headed back to Vaisigano resort — to another dinner under the stars, by candlelight.

Twenty Two

Solomona's parents had gone home to the village, following Tuisamoa's weekly visit to the hospital, by the time Solomona and Helen returned from Savai'i. Sofia told them that Tuisamoa was looking rather weak, but otherwise he seemed fine. Worried constantly that his father's condition would deteriorate while they were away in Savai'i, Solomona was relieved at the news.

In the following days, Solomona and Helen continued their tour of Samoa with trips to various parts of Upolu, as well as Manono island just off the coast of Upolu. They would drive each day to a place Solomona wanted to show Helen, then return each night to the Tuisamoas' residence in the hills behind Apia. Helen continued to be enchanted by the beautiful and dynamic natural landscape, the pristine blue lagoons, cascading waterfalls and, above all, the happy faces of the Samoan people.

In the evenings, they would have dinner at home, with the chance to enjoy some time with Sofia and Onosa'i. While it was not exactly the Vaisigano resort restaurant, Sofia's Bistro, as Solomona referred to it, was just as delightful, especially when dining on the upstairs balcony overlooking Apia and the nearby countryside. With Solomona's parents at home in Lalolagi, Sofia took the opportunity to spoil her guests, a task she enjoyed as much as they did.

'It appears there's no end to the good life, Mister Tui,' smiled Helen as she sipped her glass of red wine. That day they had visited the island of Manono, where she was fascinated by the monument to the 99 wives of one of Manono's chiefs and by the twelve-pointed star mounted on the highest point of the island, said to be the command post for Manono's High Chief, Tamafaiga, who ruled Samoa prior to Christianity. 'The view is just beautiful and the ambience is so... invigorating!' she added, gazing at the twinkling lights of Apia and coastal villages.

The moon was rising late, but stars were twinkling high above, and candles burnt brightly in the cool, still air. The smell of tropical flowers wafted from the garden below, and with the sound of soft piano music in the background, the setting provided for a very romantic evening.

Sofia had cooked a couple of large lobsters, together with Solomona's favourite, oven-baked octopus in coconut cream, some *palusami* and taro. Solomona sniffed the air appreciatively.

Onosa'i carried the food on serving trays to the upstairs balcony, with Sofia following with jugs of water and fruit juice.

'Ah,' smiled Solomona, 'I thought I could smell something delicious.'

'Hmm,' smiled Sofia, 'Mona always smiles whenever he smells octopus in coconut cream.'

'Okay, Ono,' Solomona said, anxious to begin their meal, 'let's have a quick one; it's dinner time, and it must be very congested upstairs,' he joked, as he asked Onosa'i to bless the food.

Sofia laughed softly. 'Look, he's getting impatient already.'

Onosa'i said grace, then all four of them enjoyed a delicious seafood dinner.

Solomona and Helen's exploration of Upolu and Manono took almost two weeks, ending with a trip to the delightfully beautiful Aleipata district.

'This place is absolutely gorgeous, Mister Tui,' Helen commented as they drove along the white sandy foreshore fronting some of the villages at the south-eastern end of Upolu. 'It doesn't have the majestic hills and picturesque coastline of Fagaloa, but the islands, the clear blue water and magnificent white sandy beaches certainly offer a different, but equally impressive package.'

Solomona waved to children along the roadside who were calling out and waving at them. They rounded the easternmost point of Upolu and drove north to his paternal grandmother's family at Malaela. He had earlier informed them that he would like to take Helen on a tour of the islands off the coast of Aleipata. As their truck stopped under a breadfruit tree, a crowd of children ran toward them, calling out Solomona's name and the word *palagi*, referring to Helen.

'You're a bit early, Mona,' greeted Solomona's aunt, Aiga, tightening her *lavalava* around her. Solomona stooped and embraced his aunt. 'The boys went to get some coconuts for you, but they are not yet back.'

'Oh, that's all right, Aunt Aiga. We have the whole day. Anyway, I'd like you to meet Helen. And Helen, this is Dad and Aunt Fiasili's youngest sister, Aiga.'

'You have a beautiful house, Aiga.' Helen was fascinated by all the family pictures and certificates hanging on the living room walls.

'Thank you, Helen. Of course, it's not as big and grand as the one in Lalolagi, but... it serves us well.'

'Oh, could someone bring in the mutton from the cooler in the back of the truck?' Solomona had almost forgotten the *oso* they had brought with them.

Out of the window he spotted two of his cousins, Pita and Simi, arriving with loads of food and coconuts, and went out to greet them.

'We have everything ready on the boat, Mona,' Pita, the older of the brothers, called out. 'We went to get some coconuts for drinks. So where is your friend, bro?' Just then, Helen stepped outside. 'Oh,' he continued, nodding, 'not bad, man... not bad... better than Sina, I'd say.' Sina had been a classmate of Pita's when Solomona was dating her.

Solomona introduced Helen to his cousins, who were almost as tall as he was, but far more muscular. Helen could feel the roughness of the calluses on their hands as they shook hands. Their fair skin was burnt, and their hair was sun-bleached, typical of those who earned their living outdoors.

'Ready to pull in some yellowfin tuna, Helen?' asked Pita.

'Yes, I am. I've never done it before, so I've been looking forward to it.'

'Okay, let's not waste any time then,' he urged, as he grabbed a basket of coconuts and started walking towards the fishing boat moored at a jetty opposite the house.

Manoeuvring out from the wharf, the boat headed for the closest island. Rounding the western end of the island, they crossed the reef and entered deep water. Pita turned off the motor allowing the boat to drift.

'Upolu looks so beautiful from the sea,' Helen said, as she looked back at the hills of Aleipata, 'and the islands are so green and tropical.'

'Keep the most dangerous and greedy animal — people — away from them, and they will remain green forever,' Solomona suggested.

Simi handed Helen a rod with a baited hook. 'Just let it drop down until it hits the bottom, Helen,' he advised. 'You'll feel it go slack when the line reaches the bottom.'

Simi prepared a rod for himself while Pita and Solomona set about baiting their own.

'Oh!' screamed Helen moments later, 'I think I've got a fish!'

'Already?' Solomona said dismissively. 'It's probably a rock, HR.'

'No, I think it's a fish,' she insisted, 'but I can't reel it in.'

'I'm sure it's a rock, HR.'

Simi put his rod down and took Helen's. Holding the rod with both hands, he turned his head as if trying to hear something. He smiled, 'I think Helen's right, she has got a fish.'

'See, I told you, Mister Tui,' she teased, as Simi reeled in a huge reef trout. 'I caught a fish, I caught a fish,' she sang, feeling very excited and pleased with herself.

'Don't gloat, HR,' smiled Solomona, 'that fish looks like it had a fight with its wife — it's not the best-looking fish I've ever seen.'

'Oh, you're just jealous, Mona,' she chuckled. They all laughed at being upstaged by a female — and a novice at that.

'It's a very good catch, Helen,' Pita assured her, 'and you have beaten the old pros at their game, including someone you know only too well.'

Simi removed the hook and placed the trout in a cooler. Baiting the hook again, he handed the rod back to Helen. They fished for another hour or so, catching more fish from the seabed, before Pita suggested they move on.

'Let's go for a ride, so Helen can see the other islands, and we can try to catch some yellowfins,' Pita suggested.

Solomona and Simi baited their lines and dropped them into the water, hoping to trawl for fish, while Pita guided the boat close to an island with a lighthouse rising above the end of the Aleipata reef. After fishing some more, they headed east until they sighted a large island in the distance.

'That's Tutuila, the main island of American Samoa,' Pita told Helen. 'It's a bit late, otherwise we could have gone there. Maybe some other time, or maybe you and Mona can go and visit the folks in Pago.'

'God willing, we'll go there sometime, HR,' Solomona promised. 'Maybe at the end of the year when you come back.'

Pita turned the boat westward and headed for the islands opposite the easternmost point of Upolu. The coolers were gradually filling up as they reeled in more good-sized fish, including several varieties of tuna. The afternoon sun was beginning to fade, sinking towards the hills of Aleipata, and Pita was conscious that Helen and Solomona had to drive back to Lalolagi that night.

'I think that should be enough for today,' he said, as he wound in his line. As the others stowed their fishing gear, Pita started the motor and turned the boat in the direction of

Malaela. They had been out on the water for about six hours, and had filled two large coolers with their day's catch.

'What are you going to do with all this fish?' Helen asked as Solomona and his cousins emptied the boat back at the village.

'Eat them,' laughed Solomona. 'What else do you do with fish?'

Helen nudged him in the ribs and turned to Pita, 'Keep quiet, mister. I was talking to Pita.'

'Well,' he replied, 'we have to give some to the pastor and the priest; you will take some to Lalolagi; we'll give some to our neighbours and families close by. Whatever is left, we'll sell tomorrow at the market in Apia, together with some fish we already have in the freezer.'

Solomona helped his cousins carry the coolers back to the house.

'Why not spend the weekend here with us, Mona,' his aunt suggested.

'We would love to, Aunt Aiga, but they are expecting us in Lalolagi tonight.'

'Well,' she added, 'maybe next time you and Helen come, you could stay for a whole weekend.'

'Yes,' he nodded, 'we'd love to do that next time we visit.'

After enjoying a mug of hot *koko*, Solomona and Helen prepared to leave. The sun had set, and it was getting dark.

'Thanks so much for showing me around and letting me catch some fish,' Helen hugged Simi and Pita before getting in the truck.

'You're very welcome, Helen,' said Pita. 'We'll do it again next time.'

'We'll see you soon,' Solomona promised as they slowly pulled away, heading for the main road.

'Drive safely, Mona,' Aiga called out as their truck drove out of sight.

Twenty Three

Helen was due to return to New Zealand on the third Saturday of February. Her flight was scheduled to leave at 11 pm, and Solomona and his parents planned a small private family dinner at their house in Apia to farewell her. Only Fili Fa'aluma and Solomona's half-brother, Owen, and half-sisters, Mele and Apaula, who were home for the holidays, were invited.

That afternoon Solomona and Helen drove to Apia to pick up Owen, Mele and Apaula. The five of them were going to help Sofia and Onosa'i prepare the food. Once at the house, Mele, Apaula and Helen helped Sofia in the kitchen, while Solomona and Owen assisted Onosa'i with the *umu*.

'So what did you do during your stay, Helen?' asked Apaula, as she washed some vegetables.

'Oh, lots of exciting things, Ula,' she replied. 'We spent one week in Savai'i — that was unreal, and two weeks touring Upolu. We also managed to visit Manono, and saw the monument to the 99 wives of one of the famous chiefs of Manono and the twelve-pointed star mounted at the top of the island — that was also some experience. In the last week of January, Mona had to go to work. I wanted to do a crash course in Samoan culture, so I braved a three-week stay in Lalolagi while Mona was in Apia, working. This week, I have been in Apia spending some time with Alofa and Tui. Mona says I have now seen virtually the whole of Western Samoa.'

'It seems as though you've had a lot of fun, then,' smiled Mele.

'Oh, absolutely! I mean, if heaven is like the time I have spent in Samoa so far, I certainly look forward to it.'

'What about the three weeks you spent in the village while Mona and the old folks were in Apia? How did that go?' asked Apaula.

'It was a bit difficult without Mona, but fortunately he came home on weekends. It was a good learning experience for me. I attended women's meetings, weaving sessions, a funeral and some other stuff like that. Sekara, the pastor's wife, and Feleni, Lauti's wife, were very helpful. They took time to explain so many things to me and taught me rudimentary Samoan. Tenari, the pastor, was always helpful, particularly with my attempts to learn the language.'

'So what's your overall impression?' asked Mele.

'Samoan culture is certainly a lot more complicated than it looks,' replied Helen. 'Solomona uses the expression of a very bony fish, but I really love it out there in Fagaloa. And to think that it's probably only about 30 kilometres from here. It would not be that far if the road was improved.'

'No, it's not that far at all,' agreed Apaula, 'but I know Mona likes the road as it is. He doesn't like too many people visiting Fagaloa.'

'Yes, he told me that, but I do hope the government changes its mind and does something about it because, as

Mona readily acknowledges, it has the prettiest scenery in all of Samoa. It's really unique.'

'Did he take you out to sample Apia's nightlife this week?' Mele asked.

'I think we must have eaten in virtually every restaurant in Apia, with lunch in one place and dinner in another,' smiled Helen. 'That was really something, and last night I finally had the chance to experience the atmosphere of the celebrated Tusitala Hotel. That was an experience too. Overall, my stay has been really incredible.'

'Hmm, sounds like you've had a great time,' said Mele.

'Yes, I have, and I'm not really looking forward to returning to New Zealand, especially with Mona staying behind.'

'Well,' Apaula reassured her, 'the three of us will be returning next week, so we'll all see you in a few days. Also, Pati and Dreana are there, and so are the others, including Faye.'

With the cooking completed, they sat on the balcony together talking, drinking, listening to music and enjoying the view. Shortly after 6 pm, they moved downstairs to the living room where Tuisamoa and Alofa were waiting for Fili Fa'aluma to arrive.

In his usual jovial mood, Fili announced his arrival just after 6.30 pm with music blaring from his car's sound system. Loudly singing the song he had just been listening to in the car, he made his way to the house.

'Sounds like the comedian has arrived,' smiled Alofa peeking through the curtains. 'He never arrives quietly, does he?'

'Hello, everybody!' Fili greeted them with a broad smile, as he removed his shoes at the door.

'Come on in, your honour, Samoa's Chief Medical Officer,' smiled Solomona.

'Now stop that, King,' Fili challenged his friend. 'Doctor Taulasea hasn't resigned, yet.'

Laughing, Fili made his way around the room and shook everyone's hand, starting with Tuisamoa and Alofa.

Tuisamoa sat quietly, smiling at Fili's antics. Dr Fa'aluma was very much part of the Tuisamoa family, just as Solomona was with the Fa'aluma family. Taking a seat next to Helen, Fili continued with a mock exchange of greetings as if it was a meeting of *matais*, or a host welcoming important guests. Solomona and Onosa'i joined in, much to the amusement of Tuisamoa and Alofa.

'Well, that's enough joking for now,' Tuisamoa said solemnly, as the noise subsided. 'Let's have prayers first. Time is getting away from us.'

Fili leaned over and whispered to Solomona, 'Do you think the prayer will go beyond the ceiling?'

'Shh... keep quiet, you two,' Helen urged.

There was silence as Tuisamoa moved forward a little. He cleared his throat, and asked everyone to prepare their hearts to worship God.

'Is he serious?' Fili again whispered to Solomona.

'Shh! you two,' Helen hissed. Solomona smiled and gestured to Fili that it was time to pay attention.

'Would someone like to start with a hymn?' Tuisamoa asked in a hoarse voice.

Momentarily, Mele, in the most angelic of soprano voices, started singing a popular thanksgiving hymn. Only Helen had a hymn book. No one else needed one. They all knew the hymn by heart, and they all joined in at exactly the same time in perfect harmony as if they had been practising the hymn together for months.

After the singing, Alofa read a few words from the Bible. Then Tuisamoa spoke, wishing Helen a safe flight back to New Zealand and a successful year of university studies, then offered a long prayer.

Afterwards, Tuisamoa and Alofa, being the family elders, were served their meal first, after which they retired to the family room upstairs. The others gathered around the dining table for their dinner amidst much laughter and good-natured ribbing.

Just before 8 pm, Solomona announced that it was time to head to the airport. Everyone was going to the airport to farewell Helen, except his parents.

Helen bade farewell to Tuisamoa and Alofa, while Owen and Onosa'i made sure her luggage was safely packed into the family truck.

'Well, Helen,' said Tuisamoa, in his low confident voice, 'I hope you have had a good time in Samoa.'

'Oh yes, I have, Tui. Thank you very much,' she replied respectfully.

'Well,' he continued, 'this is your home too... yours and Mona's. He's a good boy, you know.'

Helen smiled shyly. She looked at Solomona who winked at her.

'He's not bad, is he?' she smiled.

'Maybe it's better that you marry soon, so people don't talk,' he urged. Helen didn't say anything. She glanced at Solomona who, again, winked. 'But, go... go and finish your studies. There is nothing worse in life than ignorance. All the problems that we have in this world are because of ignorance. Get yourself a good education — that will prepare you to face the challenges ahead.'

Helen looked up, her eyes a little teary. It felt almost like listening to Solomona when he was being serious. 'Thank you for your encouraging words, Tui. I'll try my best.'

Tuisamoa held Helen warmly by the shoulders.

'Helen, may the Lord bless you and keep you, and may His journeying mercies keep you safe on your trip. Please give your parents and family our love.'

Helen was touched by his words. She wrapped her arms around him as she said goodbye. Then she turned to Alofa, standing patiently beside her husband.

'Thank you very much, Alofa,' she whispered, hugging her.

'Take care of yourself, Helen, and give your parents our love.'

'I will,' she replied before she and Solomona headed out to the truck where Sofia and Onosa'i were waiting for them.

As the convoy slowly pulled away from the house, Helen wistfully looked back and waved to Alofa and Tuisamoa standing in the doorway.

An hour later they arrived at the airport. Onosa'i parked the truck while Solomona and Sofia helped Helen with her luggage. The departure lounge was crowded, mostly with travellers returning to New Zealand after the holidays. Among

Forever in Paradise

the crowd, Solomona spotted his boss, Teutupe. Excusing themselves, he and Helen made their way over to where Tuetupe and his family were standing.

Solomona introduced Helen to his boss. Teutupe greeted her warmly, and in turn introduced his family to her and Solomona.

'Ah… the famous Solomona Tuisamoa,' said Amanda, Teutupe's wife, smiling as she shook hands.

'It's a great pleasure to meet you, Amanda,' Solomona said earnestly, 'and these must be the boys your husband is so proud of.' He bent down to speak to the young boys clinging to her hands.

'Yes, they're ours,' she smiled. 'No doubt, your turn will come,' she added. 'I must say that it's nice to finally put a face to the name. Teu has mentioned you often; he has been very impressed with your work.'

'Well, thank you, Amanda,' Solomona said with just a hint of pride.

'And where are you off to, Helen?' Amanda asked.

'Oh, I'm going back to Auckland to finish my studies. I have an Honours thesis to write. Who is leaving from your family?'

'I am,' replied Teutupe. 'I have a meeting in Manila next week with the Asian Development Bank, then I'll be spending a couple of weeks in New Zealand with our daughter who has just started Form Seven at Auckland Girls Grammar.'

'Really?' Helen was surprised to hear the name of her old school. 'That's where I went to school. I was a classmate of Mona's cousin — that's how the two of us met.'

Just then, the public address system announced the arrival of a Polynesian Airline's Boeing 737. Solomona and Helen said goodbye to Teutupe and Amanda, and rejoined the others.

'Well, guys,' Fili said as Solomona and Helen returned, 'crying is permitted, but please, please, no talking.'

Solomona and Helen smiled at Fili's attempts at humour.

'Don't worry, Fili,' Solomona remarked. 'Parting is part of life: we arrive, and we depart; we meet, and we go our separate ways. Parting is, indeed, the only certainty in life. It's what we do when we arrive or when we meet that matters. See?' He placed his arm round his friend's shoulder and patted him good-naturedly.

Helen smiled as she looked at Solomona and Fili. She understood what a special friendship they shared.

'Ah, the words of King Solomon are never shallow,' Fili laughed, 'but I do worry about when Helen leaves. I've had an experience of that before, and believe me, guys, no one could console King during the three years Helen was away in England. If I hadn't held him back, he would have swum all the way to England. And I thought he was a good student of geography,' he continued, his eyes filling with tears from laughing too much.

Solomona smiled. 'You like that story, don't you, my friend? Well, I don't want to be a killjoy, so I'll let you have your fun.'

An announcement advised passengers departing for Auckland to make their way to the departure gate.

Helen started to say her goodbyes. There were whispers of 'Thank you' and 'Safe trip' as she made her way around the group.

Forever in Paradise

'Don't worry about King,' Fili assured her as he and Helen embraced. 'We'll look after him until you return.'

Helen nodded, as she tried to blink back tears.

'Thank you, Fili,' she struggled to get the words out as she wiped her eyes. 'It has been the best and most enjoyable time of my life, that's for sure.'

'Samoa will still be here when you return. It will be here forever, you know!' Fili smiled reassuringly.

The final boarding call came. Solomona picked up Helen's handbag and walked with her to the departure gate. She threw her arms around him, sobbing. Tears coursed down her cheeks. Solomona too struggled to hide his emotions.

'I... I don't want to leave you, Mona,' she mumbled, still holding him tightly.

'Come on now, HR.' He held her at arm's length so he could look into her eyes. 'Don't make things difficult. You will be fine, and before you know it, you will be back here. Come on now... just one more hurdle; give it your all. Okay?'

Helen nodded slowly. An airline officer came out to check whether there were any passengers still straggling.

'Sir,' she asked, 'is either of you on this flight? Passengers are now boarding.'

Solomona and Helen hugged one more time. Helen took her handbag and reluctantly made her way through into the security area. Struggling to hide his feelings, Solomona slowly walked back to where the others were waiting.

Fili patted him on the back. 'I know how you're feeling, King,' he said, 'and... it's okay to cry.'

Solomona ventured a smile. 'I'm fine, Fili,' he assured him. 'Well, guys,' he said turning to the others, 'thanks a million for helping to make Helen's stay such an enjoyable one, especially Sofia and Onosa'i, for the time we were in Apia, and Fili, for the week we spent at the resort.'

Twenty Four

One Wednesday evening, two weeks after Helen returned home to New Zealand, Tuisamoa's health quickly deteriorated. He had been in almost constant pain for a couple of days. At times, the pain was so excruciating that painkillers seemed to be no longer effective. Solomona suggested to his mother that his father should be admitted to hospital. He called his friend, Fili Fa'aluma, who advised him to bring his father to the hospital as soon as possible.

Sofia helped Alofa to pack a few items, while Solomona called an ambulance.

At the hospital Dr Fa'aluma and a palliative care specialist, Dr Tuioti, were waiting when the ambulance arrived. Tuisamoa was wheeled into a large examination room, with Solomona and Alofa at his side. Dr Tuioti, accompanied by Dr Fa'aluma, examined Tuisamoa while Solomona and his mother waited patiently for their verdict.

'I'm afraid his Lordship's condition is not good, *Masiofo* Alofa,' declared Dr Tuioti. 'I don't think he will last a week. All we can do is make him as comfortable as possible.'

Alofa blanched at hearing Tuisamoa's prognosis. Her heart thumped against her chest, and her vision blurred.

'Ooh...' she moaned desperately, 'someone help me please.'

Fili held her tightly as she slumped in his arms. He carefully laid her on a sofa before calling for assistance.

'I think she has only fainted,' he said as he took her pulse and checked her eyes. 'She should be all right, but we need to monitor her to be sure.'

A nurse assisted to carefully lift Alofa onto a trolley so that she could be examined more thoroughly. Tuisamoa had fallen asleep amidst all the commotion with Alofa. The medication Dr Tuioti had given him on arrival had almost instantaneously eased his pain.

'Ah,' sighed Dr Tuioti, 'I'm glad he's asleep. He seems to be very tired.'

'He hasn't had a decent night's sleep for quite a while now,' said Solomona. 'I think the pain has been making it too difficult for him to sleep well.'

'Mona,' said Dr Tuioti, obviously trying to broach a difficult subject, 'Tui's condition will not get any better. As I said, it's unlikely that he will last a week. He is in great pain, and it will only get worse.'

'What are you trying to say, Dr Tuioti?'

'Well, what I'm trying to say, Mona, is that we can end all of Tui's suffering with a single injection which will put him to sleep and give him some peace... You know what I mean. There is no hospital policy on this issue, but it's something that could be considered. I would be willing to help if you and your family so desired. The decision is entirely up to the patient and his family.'

Solomona massaged his chin thoughtfully, then glanced knowingly at Fili, smiling.

'Is there something funny about what I said?' Dr Tuioti asked.

'Oh, no... no, Dr Tuioti,' Solomona assured him. 'It's just that it seems like, every time I am with my good friend, Fili, in a hospital, I'm always being asked to decide on someone else's life. That's all.'

Dr Fa'aluma raised his hands pleading his innocence.

'Well, it was not Fili's idea,' Dr Tuioti insisted.

'Oh, no, Dr Tuioti,' Solomona said reassuringly. 'I'm not saying that this is Fili's idea. It's just that he always seems to be around whenever I am faced with this type of decision, that's all.' He paused for a moment while he considered Dr Tuioti's suggestion. 'To be honest, Dr Tuioti, I'd really like him to be free of pain. However, I am not God. Achieving the goal of ending his suffering by deliberately ending his life is something I can never, under any circumstance, subscribe to. I don't think Dad would approve of it either, despite the pain he must be going through. I really have no idea what God's purpose is, doctor, but I always trust His wisdom.'

'Well, it's something that I thought might be worth considering, Mona,' the specialist said, 'but we respect your wishes, and we'll do the best we can to make sure Tui's final days are as pain-free as possible.'

'Thank you very much, Dr Tuioti. I appreciate your concern, as well as your services in making Dad comfortable in his final days.' Just then a nurse came into the room assisting Alofa who had recovered from her fainting spell.

'I think I would like to sleep here at the hospital,' Alofa said.

'It won't be necessary, mother.' Solomona was concerned for his mother's health and realised she needed to get some rest too. 'You'll only be a bother to the hospital staff. They will take good care of Dad.'

Pacified, Alofa decided to wait for Tuisamoa to wake up before she would agree to go home. A little after midnight, Tuisamoa stirred. His pain had subsided somewhat, thanks to the painkillers the doctors had given him. He asked to be alone with his family. Respecting their patient's privacy, the doctors and hospital staff waited in the corridor.

'I'm feeling a little better,' he said to Alofa and Solomona.

'Well, that's good, dear,' said Alofa, relieved that his suffering seemed to be under control. 'We can't stay now, but we will be back in the morning.'

'I sense that I might go anytime now. I know it's the medicine that is making me feel better, but the disease is not weakening. So, while I am still able, I'd like to see all the *matais* of the family, as soon as possible. Mona, I want you to send a notice to all the *matais* informing them that I want to see them... What day is it today?'

'It's very early Thursday morning, father.'

'Okay. Send a notice over the radio for the *matais* to come here on Friday. And you had better be here too, Mona,' he said, wheezing between breaths.

Solomona stepped outside and indicated to the doctors and hospital staff that they could go back in, and they immediately set about moving Tuisamoa to a private room. Once he was settled for the night, Solomona and Alofa left, relieved that Tuisamoa was finally able to sleep, but anxious and uncertain about his deteriorating condition.

Twenty Five

Solomona's notice was broadcast continually on Thursday until 8.30 that night. With his boss, Teutupe, still overseas, he told the officer in charge that he could not be at work the next day. Early on Friday morning he drove into Apia to meet any relatives arriving in response to the notice. Buses from the outer villages of Upolu and from Savai'i started arriving at the marketplace in the centre of Apia around 6 am. He greeted the *matais* as they arrived and escorted them to his truck. By 7.30 am, eight *matais* had arrived. There were six from Savai'i and two from Upolu, including Lauti from Lalolagi.

'Do you know if there is anyone else still to come, Uncle Maota?' Solomona asked one of the *matais* from Savai'i.

'I think we are all here, Mona,' replied Maota.

'Good. Well, we'll have something to eat here first before we go to see Dad. There's nowhere to eat at the hospital.'

Solomona led the *matais* to an eatery inside the market.

'Did you say Tui is in hospital, Mona?' asked Taua, a *matai* from Aleipata, as they sat down to a breakfast of boiled eggs, buttered bread and *koko*.

'Yes, he is, Uncle Taua. He is very ill. In fact, he doesn't have much time left.'

The *matais* were shocked to learn of the severity of Tuisamoa's condition.

'I wonder what the boss wants to see us about,' pondered Fue, another *matai* from Savai'i.

'I have no idea, Uncle Fue,' Solomona replied, shrugging. 'I simply did what he asked me to do.'

After breakfast, Solomona and the *matais* drove to the hospital. When they arrived, Tuisamoa was awake. The *matais* seated themselves around the room while Solomona placed extra pillows behind his father's head so that he could sit up a little more easily.

'Thank you all for coming,' Tuisamoa said in a weak voice, breathing heavily between words. 'I wanted you to come because I know that my end is quite near.'

There was a light knock at the door and Solomona opened it to find two *matais* from American Samoa, To'oto'o and Pule, standing outside. They had heard the notice on the radio — they said they always tuned their radio to the Apia station during public notice time — and took the first flight to Upolu that morning. They rarely saw the rest of the family except for major family gatherings like funerals, family meetings and weddings.

Tuisamoa cleared his throat. He was trembling slightly. 'Where was I again, Mona?'

'You were saying that you feel your time is near, Father.'

'Oh, yes,' he resumed, 'I feel I don't have much time left. My body is very weak. I could go at any time now. It's only the medication that is keeping me alive.' Respectfully the *matais* paid close attention to what Tuisamoa was saying. 'And, as my final and only wish, I want all of you to promise me that Mona will succeed me to the Tuisamoa title. He is a good boy, and he's clever. He will be good for the family, the village, the district and the country.'

'Your Lordship Tui,' said To'oto'o as he turned to acknowledge the presence of the other *matais*, 'you know very well that this is a serious matter, and we need some time to consider it. Given the circumstances, I suggest that my brothers and I discuss it outside amongst ourselves. Then we'll let you know of our decision.'

Tuisamoa winced from the pain, then urged, 'Yes, of course, To'o, take the boys outside and have a talk.'

To'oto'o led the *matais* outside while Solomona stayed and attended to his father.

'Okay, boys,' To'oto'o addressed the other *matais*, 'this can be quick, or it can be drawn out. Let's try the simple way. We'll put it to a voice vote. All those —' As To'oto'o started to put a motion to the vote, Launiu, a *matai* from Savai'i, intervened.

'I thought you said we needed time to talk, To'o,' said Launiu, 'but you seem to be in some sort of a rush.'

'Well,' To'oto'o replied, 'I have the answer to my question, boys. We cannot get a quick consensus, so we need to sit down and talk it over. We can't really meet here. So, Pule, can you ask Mona to join us please?'

Pule went back inside to fetch Solomona.

'Do you have a vehicle here, Mona?' asked To'oto'o.

'Yes, I do, Uncle To'o.'

'Okay, take us somewhere where we can talk.'

'What about the house up in the hills?'

'No, that's too far away,' said To'oto'o. 'What about a restaurant downtown?'

'Okay,' Solomona replied, 'I'll just tell the nurses that I'm leaving.'

While he ran inside, Pule and To'oto'o had a quick muttered discussion. When he returned, all the *matais* climbed into the back of his truck for the short drive into town.

'Would there be a bar open at the moment, Mona?' whispered To'oto'o, who was sitting in the front with Solomona.

'It's a bit too early, Uncle To'o. It's only 9 am.'

'What about the Tusi?'

'I'm not sure, but we can try. Their restaurant may be open already.'

'Let's go to the Tusi then.'

The Tusitala Hotel was quiet when they arrived. Solomona led his entourage to the hotel's reception area. The *matais* from Upolu and Savai'i looked around them in awe. None of them had ever been to a place like the Tusitala Hotel before.

'Is your bar open, yet?' Pule asked the receptionist.

'Not until midday, sir,' came the cheery reply.

'Is the manager in?' he asked.

'Yes, she is,' she replied and reached for the telephone.

A few minutes later, the manager, in a beautiful *puletasi*, with a large red hibiscus over her right ear, appeared grinning broadly.

'Hello, Mona, darling!' she greeted as she kissed him on both cheeks. 'Looks like you have the Fagaloa rugby team with you!'

'You two know each other?' Pule asked curiously.

'Yes, of course,' she smiled. 'Mona is our most eligible bachelor, but I've just heard on the grapevine that it may not be so for very long.' She winked at Solomona. 'Anyway, we can discuss that later. What can I do for you, Mona?'

'Well, Jenny, these are all my uncles —'

'Gee, you have a big family, don't you?' she chuckled.

'Anyway,' Solomona continued, 'they are the family bosses. They need to hold an urgent meeting, and the contingent from Pago want to accompany the discussion with some body-invigorating liquid. But it appears your bar doesn't open until noon.'

'Oh, that's no problem, Mona,' she smiled. 'We are very flexible here. Our bar time is up to our customers. Given that they need to talk, your uncles can use our meeting room where a waiter can serve them drinks. Wander down to the office when you get a chance, Mona, and we'll have a chat. I haven't seen you in ages.'

'That's very nice of you, Jenny,' said To'oto'o. 'Thanks a lot.'

The receptionist showed the way to the meeting room.

'Well, boys,' said To'oto'o, with a smile, 'looks like we're in business.'

Solomona made sure the *matais* were organised, then followed the receptionist back to the office.

'Ah, the joy of being good-looking and smart like yours truly,' laughed Pule. 'It opens even the most stubborn of doors.'

He drew up a chair next to To'oto'o at the head of the table.

'Well, boys,' Pule suggested, 'let's start this thing properly with the welcoming *'ava*. We are the guests, having travelled from the east, so the rest of you should have brought the *'ava*, but it appears you don't have any.'

'Who would have thought we'd be meeting like this in a place like the Tusitala Hotel, around a boardroom table,' smiled Fue. 'We've never been to a place as posh and sophisticated as this, Pule. But you're the money man, and I'm confident you can also provide the *'ava*, given the unorthodoxy of the setting.'

Just then, the meeting-room door flew open. A waitress carried in a tray with ten bottles of beer.

'Ah, here's the *'ava*,' smiled Pule, signalling to the waitress to bring the tray to him.

Pule removed his shirt and looked at the tray of beer as if it were a stack of *tugase*. Rubbing his hands together, he cleared his throat, then began as though it was a traditional *'ava* ceremony at the beginning of a meeting of guests and hosts during a *malaga*.

'Well, boys,' he smiled, as he eyed the tray of beer, then the other *matais*, 'it's certainly an unusual setting, and we even kicked out the only *taule'ale'a* we had. It is even more unusual that the guest has to provide the *'ava*, and then has to speak about the *'ava*. But provide it I have, and speak I will. I can sense you are dying of thirst, so I won't prolong proceedings any further. There is more than sufficient *'ava* to last the day, I am told, and I shall now exercise my right to distribute it. The first *'ava* will be mine,' he laughed as he took a bottle from the tray. 'Pass it along please, To'o.'

The tray made its way around the table until everyone took a bottle of beer.

'This must be a new *'ava* variety you are growing on Tutuila's hilltop, eh To'o?' joked Satiu, a *matai* from Savai'i, as he sipped his beer.

'Oh, well, Sa, it's just something to break the ice and warm the blood,' To'oto'o said with a chuckle, 'but you guys better make a speech or you won't get any *lafo*.'

The *matais* from Western Samoa laughed and hurriedly got together for a whispered discussion. Then Tofa, a *matai* from Savai'i, delivered a mock welcoming speech. When he had finished, Pule distributed *lafo* of 50 Western Samoan dollars for the speaker, Tofa, and $30 each for the other Western Samoan *matais*.

'I didn't realise you guys had Samoan dollars in the east,' Lauti said, seeing that their *lafo* was not in American dollars.

'We have the same money as you guys,' laughed Pule, who had suggested to To'oto'o at the airport that they get Samoan currency because of the better exchange rate with the American dollar.

'Okay, boys,' said To'oto'o solemnly, as another tray of beer was distributed around the table, 'now that the preliminary matters have been dealt with, it's time to deal with the more serious issue — the main reason for being here. We all know what it is, so let's hear what everyone thinks. Before I hand over to the rest of you, I must declare that I am for Mona being the next *matai* of the family. Even if the old man hadn't expressed his desire to us, I would still have nominated Mona. He is a good kid — I haven't heard a bad word, from anywhere or anyone, about him. He is humble, polite and very smart, something that is critical in this computer age. Does anyone of us know how to operate a computer? No. But he's an expert in them. More importantly, he has a special aura about him — you all saw a clear demonstration of that power just a little while ago. It's unusual to get a place like this for a simple meeting like ours by just walking into the manager and telling her you want a place to talk, but he did. I am confident that the family will, once again, prosper if he is given the chance. Well, I shall end my words there and invite comment from everyone else.'

'We may as well finish off with Tutuila and Manu'a's voice,' said Pule, who was also in a serious mood. 'So I will go next. I am also for Mona, for exactly the same reasons To'o has mentioned. Mona is the right person for this time and age.'

More beer arrived and was distributed around the table, as the *matais* from Western Samoa expressed their opinions. One by one, all, except Launiu, expressed their support for Solomona to be the next Tuisamoa.

'Well, thank you for the opinions expressed on this matter,' said Launiu, feeling somewhat nervous at being at odds with everyone else. 'It appears that, so far, it has been a unanimous vote for Mona. There is no doubting Mona's qualities. But I also harbour ambition to be the next *matai*. I believe I have leadership qualities that will serve the family well. Maybe economically, I —' Launiu was interrupted by To'oto'o.

'Well, Niu, I think I know your concern. You are unhappy with the inadequacy of your *lafo*,' he said as he reached for his wallet. 'Come on, Pule, give this to the boys. Here's another $20 each for everyone.' Pule distributed the money to the Western Samoan *matais*.

'I am also concerned —' Launiu tried to continue when he was again interrupted by To'oto'o.

'You are still not happy, your Lordship Launiu? Okay, here's another $20 to address that concern.' He handed more money to Pule to distribute to the Western Samoan *matais*.

'Thank you very much, To'o,' said Launiu, 'but my concern is genuine because Mona is just a kid and is quite inexperienced. He has not had much experience in dealing with village politics. He has been away most of his life. Also, he is likely to marry a *palagi* girl. If she cannot adapt to our culture and way of life, she is likely to return to New Zealand like others have in the past. Either they will divorce, which will continue to stigmatise the Tuisamoa title, or Solomona could end up going with her, which is not what we want. We need someone who will stay to provide stability, leadership for the family, village, district and country.'

'I see,' said To'oto'o thoughtfully. 'Well, Niu, Mona's inexperience could be one of his strengths — he hasn't been corrupted by village politics yet. Your other concern, though, is a lot more serious. We certainly do not want a continuation of past problems, and I agree with you that the Tuisamoa should reside here, and not overseas. But I trust Solomona's judgement, and I would like to hear from him. You've met the girl anyway, I understand. Is she intelligent and beautiful?'

'Oh, she is the most beautiful thing I've ever seen, To'o,' smiled Fue. 'I've seen many glamorous stars in the movies, but she is more beautiful than any of them. And she's at university too.'

'Ah, well, I am certainly for intelligence and beauty. Now supposing marriage isn't a constraint, would that settle it, boys?' asked To'oto'o. There was a chorus of 'yes'. Launiu did not respond. 'Well, it's good that we have concluded this meeting on a note of agreement. We'll hear from Mona. It's almost lunchtime, so let's have lunch here before we go back to the hospital and tell the boss our decision. To close this meeting, here is another $20 each for you guys from the west,' To'oto'o concluded, as Pule distributed the money to the other *matais*.

To'oto'o went to see if they could be served lunch and found Solomona and the manager in the main office. Clearly preoccupied, Solomona was pacing up and down waiting for the *matais* to conclude their meeting.

'Well, Jenny,' To'oto'o said to the manager, 'we have finished our meeting. We just have a few loose ends to tie up with Mona. We were wondering if we could be served lunch.' Turning to Solomona, he continued, 'Mona, you can come and join us now. We have come to a consensus and we would like to talk to you.'

While the manager organised for a staff member to take the *matais'* lunch orders, Solomona went with To'oto'o. He desperately tried to hide his disappointment and frustration at having to wait even longer. Anxious to return to the hospital, all he could think about was his father lying there, and whether his mother was coping without any support.

Back in the meeting room, Solomona joined the *matais* for lunch.

'Well, Mona,' said To'oto'o as he wiped his mouth, 'we reached a consensus which supports the old man's wishes, so you'll be the next boss. The one small concern that was raised, which is really your personal business, is your *palagi* girlfriend. What's her name?'

'It's Helen, Uncle To'o,' Solomona said as he cleared his throat. He reached for his wallet and took out a passport photograph of Helen and passed it to To'oto'o.

'Hmm, she's a goddess all right,' smiled To'oto'o as he passed the photograph to Pule, 'and did you say she's at university too?'

Solomona nodded.

'Man, I would marry her if I were you, Mona. Forget about these guys,' Pule laughed. 'Women as beautiful as this come along only once in a lifetime.'

'Well, Mona,' said To'oto'o, 'barring any unexpected events, you shall take over from the old man. You will need a wife, and she could be the key to your success as the *matai* of our family. The days of the village *tulafale* making decisions on such matters have long gone. It is now entirely up to the Tuisamoa to take a wife of his choice. Perhaps you can tell us a bit about you and Helen… you know what I mean.'

'Well, To'o and this honourable gathering,' Solomona began, 'I want to thank you first for the confidence you have in me by your positive response to Tui's wishes. I will do my best to uphold and advance the good name of the family. With your support and God's help, I am confident that we will succeed. Now, about Helen and me, Helen has gone back to New Zealand to finish her studies. We have not made any plans or decisions about getting married. But Helen is the only woman I have ever loved, and —'

'What about the part-Chinese girl you brought to Pago before you went to New Zealand the first time?' Pule interrupted.

'Oh, that was Sina, Uncle Pule, but that was a long time ago. Anyway, my priority has always been the family and every good thing that it represents and stands for. My personal desires and self-interests have been suppressed. If Helen and I get married, it would be Helen who would have to make all the sacrifices, and I feel that is not fair on her. Also, I'm not sure if she would be fully accepted into the family. As much as

I would like to marry her, I am not prepared to put her through all of that. I am prepared to sacrifice my personal interests for the family, and that would include not marrying Helen if it might cause problems.'

Silence filled the room as the *matais* listened intently. Looking around at each other when Solomona finished speaking, they nodded as if agreeing to something they had silently discussed in their minds.

'Well, Mona,' said To'oto'o finally, 'I haven't met Helen, but I trust your wisdom. You have a very sharp mind, and Jesus must have left His heart with you when He ascended to Heaven,' he smiled. 'It appears you two love each other very much, and that would overcome any hurdle you might encounter in marriage and living here in Samoa. Helen's an intelligent woman, and that should help her adapt to our culture and way of life. I feel confident she'll make a good wife for a Tuisamoa, if you two decide to get married.' To'oto'o turned to look at the rest of the *matais*, who all nodded in agreement.

'See, my boy,' Pule said as he patted Solomona's back. 'It's all done.'

'Okay, boys,' To'oto'o urged, 'let's get back to the hospital and tell the boss what we have decided.'

Solomona and the *matais* made their way outside to the truck, while Pule went to the office to pay their expenses. Returning to the hospital, the *matais* again conferred with Tuisamoa.

'Your Lordship Tui,' began To'oto'o, as the self-appointed spokesman of the group, 'we have completed our meeting, and have decided to honour your wishes. Mona shall succeed you.'

'Oh, thank you, to all of you, the *matais* of our family,' Tuisamoa said, struggling with each word. 'Mona will be good for the family, and for the village, and the country. Thank you very much. Mona? Take them and give them something to eat before they return home, and make sure each of them has their fare home.'

'Thank you, Tui, but that has already been done,' said To'oto'o. 'We shall leave now so you can get some rest.'

'Are you going back to Pago today, To'o?' asked Tuisamoa, referring to Pagopago, American Samoa's capital.

'No, your Lordship Tui. Pule and I will stay for the weekend at least.'

Solomona drove his uncles back to the bus depot at the market, where he dropped off the *matais* from Upolu. Giving each of them money for their fare and to buy an *oso*, he thanked them again for coming. He then drove to Mulifanua wharf where the *matais* from Savai'i would catch a ferry home. Again he thanked them and gave them money for their fare and for *oso*.

As he drove Pule and To'oto'o back to Apia, Solomona was unusually quiet. Pule and To'oto'o tried to engage him in conversation, but he seemed disinterested, answering their questions mostly with one-word answers. He was totally preoccupied, and unsure of how to react to this morning's events. He felt honoured at being chosen to succeed his father, yet anxious about the enormous responsibility. He should have felt extremely excited at the opportunity to implement at last some of his long-cherished ideas, using the power of a Tuisamoa, but in the circumstances the fear of losing his father dominated his thoughts.

Twenty Six

As he did most days, Solomona woke early. It was Sunday and he planned some quiet time before helping Onosa'i with the Sunday *umu*. Unlike village life, there were no rules at the Apia house regarding *umus* and the other aspects of Sunday life that were commonplace in Lalolagi. In Apia they usually did not have *umus* on Sundays, but his uncles Pule and To'oto'o had requested a hearty meal of *palusami*.

As he sat down at his desk to read and study the scriptures, the house was suddenly illuminated by bright light. Peering through the curtains, he saw a vehicle coming up the driveway. He left his Bible open on the desk and hurried downstairs. 'I wonder who this is,' he thought to himself as he turned on the outside light and opened the front door. His pulse raced at the thought that it could be a vehicle from the hospital with bad news about his father. Apprehensive, he waited for the car to draw up to the front steps. He breathed a sigh of relief as he recognised a Toyota Landcruiser from work. To his surprise, his boss, Tuetupe, was driving.

'We have a surprise for you, Mona,' smiled Teutupe as he got out to open the rear door.

'How was your trip, Teu?' asked Solomona, not paying much attention to what his boss had said.

As Teutupe opened the door, to Solomona's astonishment Helen emerged from the back seat.

'Helen!' he exclaimed. 'You're... oh, never mind.' A host of questions raced through his mind, but they could wait. He was overjoyed. 'Well, this certainly is a surprise. Thanks, Teu, for driving her all the way up here,' he added, as he helped to unload luggage from the car.

'Oh, no problem, Mona, but we'd better get going — I need to get some rest before the morning service. I'll see you tomorrow at the office.'

'Yes, of course, Teu.'

After waving goodbye and watching Teutupe's car disappear into the darkness, Solomona turned to face Helen. Unsure of what to say, she smiled nervously and looked at the ground. Solomona pulled her towards him and held her tight. Neither spoke. In a long embrace they savoured being together again. Dawn was breaking in the east, and roosters crowed from the top of a breadfruit tree in the garden. Morning dew glistened around them.

'Well, my dear,' he grinned, 'you certainly know how to surprise people — I'm absolutely flabbergasted. It's a lovely surprise though.' Helen still didn't know how to broach the subject of her unexpected arrival. She had been thinking about what to say for days before she left New Zealand and during the whole three-and-a-half-hour flight. Happy with her decision to return, she smiled and burrowed her head into Solomona's chest. She felt secure in his strong arms. 'Well, let's go inside,' Solomona suggested. 'It's too damp out here.'

Picking up Helen's luggage, he led her inside. The room she had occupied before she left for New Zealand was still empty. So Solomona dropped her luggage there, then took her to his room. Gently he drew her close to him. Helen snuggled against his chest, assuring herself that they would never again be parted. She smiled to herself and relaxed in his arms. Lowering his head, he kissed her tenderly on the forehead.

'Well, my dear,' he asked softly, 'what has caused your sudden return?' Helen shook her head as though unable to speak. 'I mean, we talked on the phone last night, and there wasn't any hint, either in your voice or in your words, that you were even thinking of returning. You've really got me this time, HR.'

Helen raised her head slightly. 'Sorry, I didn't tell you I was coming,' she said finally. 'I wanted to tell you last night but I was too scared of what you might say. Dad was waiting to drive me to the airport when I called.'

'What do you mean scared of what I might say?'

'Well, I thought you wouldn't like the idea of me returning, instead of staying in Auckland to finish my thesis.'

'Well, of course I would've liked you to do that, because it's what I believe you need to do. But at the end of the day, it's your life, and the decision should be yours. The selfish part of me wants you here, but the selfless part wants you to do what is best for you. In any case, I really have no right to tell you what to do or what not to do. No one knows better what is best for you than you do. And I guess, at the moment, it's being here. Right?' He tenderly stroked her cheek. She smiled and nodded slowly. 'Anyway,' he continued, 'you do have your degree, and the Honours may not make a lot of difference. But tell me what happened. I mean, we talked almost every day on the phone, and it never occurred to me that something was wrong. You would've had a problem getting a lift if Teu had not been on the same flight.'

'I was just feeling so miserable without you, Mona. I mean, I felt absolutely rotten,' she said, then paused. 'I was very tempted to come earlier, but I thought I would wait for Teu, so I wouldn't have to rely on other transport. I thought you probably wouldn't like me to catch a taxi from the airport at that time of the night. I knew when Teu was returning, because we talked about it on our way to New Zealand.'

'Is that all?' he smiled.

'Mona,' she remonstrated, 'you have no idea how I felt sitting on the plane without you, going back to New Zealand on my own. If I had had a return ticket, I would have taken the very next flight back. I just felt really miserable. I struggled to keep my voice under control every time we talked on the phone. Didn't you miss me?'

'Oh, of course I did,' he assured her, 'but I guess not as badly as you missed me. Dad's condition has been deteriorating since you left, and I haven't been able to think of much else. I've had to attend to a lot of family matters as a result.'

'How is he?' Helen's face mirrored her concern.

'Not good, I'm afraid. We'll go and see him before church this morning.' He began to hear noises from the kitchen. 'Sounds like Onosa'i is preparing the *umu*. Listen, you take a nap while I go and help him.'

When Solomona and Onosa'i returned to the house after covering the *umu* and leaving it to cook, they found Sofia, Pule and To'oto'o talking in the kitchen. Solomona whispered to Sofia that Helen was back.

'Ah, there's one girl who will not be going back to New Zealand, Mona,' she chuckled as she spooned fried eggs and canned corned beef onto serving platters.

'That's what I told him,' smiled Onosa'i who was stacking dishes in the sink.

'What was that, Mona?' asked Pule.

'Oh, I was just telling Sofia that Helen's back.'

'Back where?'

'She's back here.'

'You mean she's here in the house?'

'Yes. She's asleep at the moment. She arrived about 5 am. My boss was on the same flight and drove her up here.'

'You mean she didn't tell you she was coming?'

Solomona smiled, 'No. She was afraid that I might tell her to stay there and finish her studies.'

'Well, better go and wake her up.'

'Don't be mean, Pule,' said To'oto'o, 'the poor girl must be tired. Let her have some rest.'

'But I'd like to see her before we leave. I've seen the photo, but I'm a bit of a doubting Thomas. I'll believe it only after I see her with my own eyes.'

'You'll see her when she wakes up. We won't be leaving today.'

'We won't?'

'No. With Tui's condition the way it is, I thought it would be a good idea to stay until we are certain of the outcome. So I called home on Friday, while you were talking to Mona outside, to change our flights to Monday next week.'

'Ah, that's an excellent idea,' smiled Pule. 'I'd like to stay a bit longer in Upolu. It has almost all the trappings of life in Pago now, and more.'

Just then, Helen stumbled out of Solomona's room. She was still rubbing her eyes when she noticed unfamiliar faces in the kitchen.

'Come on in, Helen, and meet my uncles from Pago,' Solomona called.

'Oh, let me wash first, Mona,' she replied as she retreated back to his room.

Moments later, washed and feeling fresher Helen returned to the kitchen. Her soft dark hair shone in the morning light and her smile revealed the exquisite beauty of her strongly Eastern European–Mediterranean features.

'Helen, this is Uncle Pule.' Solomona pointed to a grey-haired man, who was somewhat overweight but as tall as Solomona. 'And this is Uncle To'oto'o.' To'oto'o was slim, about six feet tall and balding.

Helen greeted them in her heavily accented and hesitant Samoan as she shook hands with them.

'Well,' smiled Pule approvingly, 'I can now understand why Mona looks absent-minded most of the time.'

Solomona smiled. Just then, the kitchen door opened, and Alofa, who had been sweeping the yard, came inside.

'Oh, Helen!' exclaimed Alofa. 'Oh, my goodness, you're back! I thought I heard a car pull up first thing this morning.'

'It was Teu's car,' Solomona explained. 'He was on the same flight as Helen, and he drove her up here.'

They chatted about Helen's surprise return over breakfast. Afterwards, everyone got ready for church, except Sofia and Onosa'i who were staying behind to prepare lunch.

Before going to church they drove to the hospital to check on Tuisamoa. When they arrived, Tuisamoa could barely recognise anyone. He was very weak, his voice barely audible. His breathing was rapid and laboured. Dr Tuioti and Dr Fa'aluma were in the room, together with a couple of nurses. The atmosphere was sombre.

'Hey, Helen,' whispered a surprised Dr Fa'aluma, 'when did you get back?'

'This morning, Fili,' she replied as she shook his hand.

'King,' he whispered, 'Doctor Tuioti would like a word with you outside.'

The two doctors and Solomona left the room as Alofa, who sensed that something was wrong, started to weep. Helen held her gently. Pule and To'oto'o looked at each other, not knowing whether to stay or wait outside. The nurses fussed over Tuisamoa, keeping him as comfortable as possible with gentle massaging. Tuisamoa continued to breathe heavily, occasionally gasping for breath, as Alofa watched on helplessly.

'Mona,' said Dr Tuioti, 'we've done all we can, but Tui could go any moment now.' Dr Fa'aluma gently patted Solomona's shoulder and offered his concern.

Solomona, his hands in the pockets of his *lavalava*, looked worriedly away. He tried to steel himself against the news and the inevitable implications of his father's passing.

'Well, Tuioti and Fili,' he said, his throat constricted, 'on behalf of the Tuisamoa family, I would like to thank you two and the hospital staff for all you have done to make Tui's last days as comfortable as they could possibly be.'

His remarks were interrupted by muffled screaming from Tuisamoa's room. They ran inside to find that Tuisamoa had stopped breathing. Dr Tuioti hurriedly attended to him but after a short time, with gentleness and compassion in his voice, acknowledged that Tui had passed away. Alofa wailed as Helen tried to hold onto her. Solomona attempted to comfort his mother, but she was inconsolable. She held tight to Solomona as Dr Fa'aluma led her to a seat.

After ensuring that his mother would be all right, Solomona summoned Pule and To'oto'o outside to discuss funeral arrangements and other matters. The village *matais*, as well as the rest of the Tuisamoa clan, would need to be notified, but they needed to make certain preliminary decisions before informing the family, and the village. Together they decided that four days should be enough time for any overseas family members to make arrangements to return to Samoa for the funeral. So they agreed that the funeral should take place the following Friday.

They also discussed other arrangements including public notification; informing relatives in Samoa and overseas; informing the pastor, the village and the district; the food to feed guests and to be given away as gifts; the mourners; and how to handle any potential difficulties. With immediate concerns settled, they started to go back inside to advise hospital staff of their plans, but Solomona hesitated. He had been thinking about the timing of his title bestowal ceremony. Under the present circumstances, he felt that this was probably the best opportunity to discuss his ideas with To'oto'o and Pule.

'Before we go back inside,' he said to his uncles, 'there's one other matter that I'd like you to consider while we have this opportunity.'

'Go ahead, Mona,' Pule replied.

'I was thinking that it might be a good idea if my title bestowal ceremony took place the day after Tui's funeral, and I'd like to know what you think about it.'

To'oto'o and Pule were taken aback by Solomona's suggestion.

'Well,' To'oto'o replied finally, 'it's not traditional to bestow the Tuisamoa title hurriedly like that — it's never been done that way before. We need to plan it properly. Also, people need time to mourn Tui's passing. Usually, there would be at least a year between the two events. However, nothing is etched in marble, and if your reason is sound, we'll consider it.'

'I know this is a radical idea,' Solomona said, carefully choosing his words, 'and that's why I'm putting it to you for consideration first. I think the idea has some practical merit. First, it provides for continuity of leadership in the family. Second, there are far too many relatives who now live overseas who are likely to want to be here for both events. It could be too expensive for them to come back for the title bestowal ceremony. Third, expenses could be greatly reduced by catering for both events at the same time. Fourth, we can all save time and money by attending two functions in virtually one gathering. But more importantly, having the title bestowal ceremony a day after Tui's funeral should quickly stop people feeling overwhelmed by Tui's death and instead rejoice and celebrate my appointment to the Tuisamoa title. That, of course, assumes that everyone is happy with the decision that I be the next Tuisamoa.'

To'oto'o looked at Pule who nodded approvingly as Solomona discussed his reasons for such a proposal. 'What do you think, Pule?'

'I think Mona has a damn brilliant idea,' he smiled. 'After all, as you alluded earlier, our so-called traditions have changed over the years. Certainly, times and circumstances have changed, and we must learn to adapt instead of being constrained by some obsolete practices. I'll go along with Mona's idea.'

'Come to think about it, Mona,' said To'oto'o seriously, 'you are absolutely right, and there's no reason at all for not doing it your way. The baton is now firmly in your hand, and you must run with it. We would have preferred that you were married first, but that should be all right. Pule and I will inform the family and the village when we all gather in Lalolagi. Consider this one done because he who holds the purse strings calls the shots.'

'Don't worry about the village and the family, Mona,' Pule assured him. 'They are all a bunch of chickens. I'll knock out the teeth of anyone who objects. They won't know it's your idea; they'll probably think it's our Americanised Samoan thinking.'

Twenty Seven

Onosa'i drove Alofa, Pule and To'oto'o to Lalolagi on Sunday evening, then returned to Apia to help with arrangements for family members arriving from overseas. To'oto'o and Pule would inform the village, help Lauti meet guests as they arrived, and make any other needed arrangements. Solomona and Helen stayed in Apia to meet relatives flying in from overseas. They would return to Lalolagi on Wednesday afternoon.

Relatives from American Samoa began arriving on Monday. The first arrivals from New Zealand, the United States and other destinations, including Germany, flew in the next day. Fetuao, Alan, Nathan, Albert, Andreana and the Filemus were among the first to arrive. By Wednesday, Lalolagi's population of around 200 had expanded to over 2,000 people. All of the village's *faleteles*, the school and the pastor's house were filled with guests and relatives. The untitled men, the *aumaga*, had to pitch extra coconut-frond huts to accommodate everyone. Only the Tuisamoas' *faletele* by the beach was empty. Tuisamoa's body would lie in state there when it arrived from Apia.

When Solomona and Helen arrived back at the village, Solomona noticed that the place was much brighter than normal; there was very little shade. It looked like a devastating cyclone had just passed through. Virtually all the trees in the village, and most of the banana trees in the hills nearby, had been hacked down. Solomona felt depressed at what he saw.

'Oh, no,' he sighed as he got out of the truck.

'What is it, Mona?' asked Helen.

'All this destruction of food crops is just madness,' he murmured, shaking his head in disbelief.

'Who would have done this, and why?'

'It's the young men of the village,' he replied, still shaking his head. 'It's an old tradition that I still don't fully understand. I saw it once before when grandpa died, but I was only a small boy then. Perhaps in the old days, the people felt that killing living things could bring their Paramount Chief's life back. I am told that even people could be killed if they got in the way. Any standing or moving object was a target. Now, we will lose all the crops from these trees — it's just madness.'

Early Thursday morning Solomona returned to Apia, with some of the village and family *matais*, to accompany his father's body back to Lalolagi. By midday, the hearse carrying Tuisamoa's coffin arrived in the village, followed by a long convoy of vehicles, led by Solomona and the other family *matais*. The hearse stopped between the church and the Tuisamoas' *faletele*. Tuisamoa's coffin was carried into the church by a team of policemen where a short service was held. The coffin was then taken to the *faletele* where, according to tradition, it was placed with the foot facing north, touching the single main post in the middle of the *faletele*, while the head faced the church entry and the summit of Mount Lagi.

The coffin lay by itself in the middle of the huge room. No one else was allowed inside. Once the coffin was in place, the chanting of mourners began. Bare-chested men in single file, with coconut leaves on their hands, chanted as they circled outside the *faletele*. Different groups of men from different villages throughout the two Samoas took turns. Now and then, a group of women in white dresses and black *lavalavas* would participate, breaking up the continuity of the men's procession.

At the Tuisamoa's *faleafolau*, church choirs from all over the two Samoas, led by their pastors, one by one offered their prayers and words of condolence, and sang hymns. This continued non-stop until the funeral service. Alofa, clad in black, led a contingent of mainly children and women representing the Tuisamoa family. Fiasili, Fetuao, Faye, Helen and Andreana were all there. Solomona, Albert, Alan and all the able men set about ensuring that everyone in Lalolagi was well looked after and that the mausoleum was prepared for Tuisamoa's burial.

When night fell, the chanting and circling of the *faletele* stopped. A specially designated *matai* from Lalolagi, the *taulaitu*, walked slowly to the *faletele*. He carried a small tobacco bag over his shoulder, a basket full of slow-burning firewood in one hand and a broken pot filled with oven ashes in the other. Inside the *faletele*, he placed the pot and the firewood on the floor between two posts, facing the church entry and the summit of Mount Lagi. He lowered all the coconut-frond blinds except the one where he placed the pot and firewood. Then he sat down leaning against one of the posts. He lit a fire inside the broken pot. Taking a few leaves of dried tobacco, he rolled them into a cigar, lit it and started puffing at it. Shortly afterwards, the church bell rang for evening devotions. As the echo of the bell faded, the cool still air was filled with the sound of hymns as Lalolagi began its routine of evening devotions before dinner.

Later that night, Solomona took Helen, Andreana and Faye to the front of the church where, through the lone opening into the family's *faletele*, they could see the *taulaitu* smoking his cigar. The four of them sat on the steps and watched solemnly. Solomona was tired but knew that he would not be able to sleep that night. Helen asked him why the man in the *faletele* was by himself.

'It's one of our pre-Christian rituals that still survives,' he explained. 'According to our village's beliefs, the good spirits come out during the daytime and the bad ones come out at night. The good spirits want to take the body up to Mount Lagi and the bad ones would like to take it to Pulotu. So the duty of the living is to make sure the bad guys don't win. The belief is that there are far too many bad spirits and very few good spirits, so they need the help of the living.'

'I've never heard of that,' said Faye, fascinated.

'That's because you grew up in the land of Maui, the fisherman,' joked Solomona. His heart felt heavy, and he would have loved to just sit quietly with his thoughts, but he had to think about Helen and the others, so he tried his best to lighten the mood.

'That's very interesting. Go on, Mona,' they urged.

'Anyway,' he sighed, 'earlier today, men and women chanted around the house to form a kind of protective barrier so that when the bad spirits come at night, they would be forced to penetrate the many obstacles placed in their way. Hopefully they will be prevented from getting in and stealing Dad's body before daybreak.'

'Why are all the blinds down, except for one?' asked Helen.

'For the same reason — to offer protection for Dad's body. The guy smoking will stay there all night. He cannot leave, he can't go to the toilet, he can't sleep, he'll just smoke all night. The lone opening into the house is the only entry point available to the bad spirits. He is there to guard it, and there is a fire that the bad spirits have to get past. And even if they managed to get in, they would have to come out the same opening, which faces Mount Lagi. Chances are the body would be sucked directly to Mount Lagi by Tagaloalagi's invisible power.'

Intrigued, the girls looked at each other but said nothing. After sitting quietly for some time, Solomona told them that he would like to be alone for a while. Understanding his desire for solitude, they made their way back to the house. The moon was shining brightly, as Solomona sat and watched the *faletele* where his father's body lay in state. He was thinking about his speech the following day, and trying to calm his nerves. At that moment he did not want to contemplate all the responsibilities that would fall on his shoulders after the funeral. He sat there until his mother came to beg him to get some rest to prepare for the following day.

The funeral service for Tuisamoa took place at 10 am on Friday. Solomona had asked, and was granted, that all of Tuisamoa's children, some from his first two marriages and others born outside of marriage, be allowed to attend the funeral. He had made it his business to know and develop a good rapport with all of his half-siblings.

The small church was packed. In attendance were all of Samoa's dignitaries including Heads of State, members of the Council of Deputy Heads of State, Members of Parliament, and members of the Diplomatic Corps. It was very hot inside. Only a light sea breeze offered some respite. There were many speeches including Solomona's on behalf of Tuisamoa's children, which was delivered first in Samoan, then in English.

After acknowledging the presence of the dignitaries, he began. 'My name is Solomona, the eldest child of his Lordship Tuisamoa Lepopoi and *Masiofo* Alofa. On behalf of Tuisamoa's children, I would like to thank all of you for coming today. It is specially hard to bid a final farewell to a beloved father who not only provided well for his family, but who placed the good of others ahead of his own.'

Solomona paused and looked at his mother and his siblings, then at the people in the front pew. 'Dad loved his children. He tried his best to be there for us, always. I remember fondly the times when parliamentary sessions coincided with Pati and me playing rugby at school. Dad would watch our games rather than attend Parliament. To others, it may seem irresponsible, but Dad always thought that there were other MPs who could deliberate on the nation's problems, but we had only one father who could support us.'

Clearing his throat, he tried to calm his wavering voice. He looked at his mother for strength as he reached for the glass of water on the lectern. After taking a sip, he continued, 'He knew that there would always be competing claims on his time, being a public figure and a family man, and when he could not be with us physically, he always tried to make up for it in other ways. When we experienced pain, he comforted us. When we felt low, he lifted us up. When we misbehaved, he disciplined us. Dad, indeed, has so many excellent qualities, but the one quality I admire the most is his honesty. He taught us the value of honesty and the importance of trustworthiness.'

The tears that he had tried so hard to forestall started to well in his eyes. 'Dad never pretended to be a saint. His life was an open book, known by even the lizards and the geckoes. He used to laugh and advise me to leave my cupboard bare, to put less importance on the material things of life. It is simply the best advice I ever received. Dad knew he was a sinner, like all of us. But near the end of his life, he found peace in the knowledge that his sins were forgiven when he humbly submitted himself to the cleansing power of the blood of his Lord and Saviour, Jesus Christ. Yes, ladies and gentlemen, Dad died a free man, indeed! It is for that reason, dear beloved, that we should celebrate his life, rather than mourning his death, for celebration is for the victor whereas mourning is for those who have lost the battle. Dad may have stumbled a number of times, but in the end he triumphed. And that is how I'd like to remember him. Thank you, and may God bless you all.'

As Solomona rejoined his mother, there was a soft muffled rustling throughout the congregation. Some women sobbed quietly while others gently cleared their throats. Alofa was crying openly but calmly. Dr Fa'aluma, sitting behind her, remained ready in case things became too much for her.

After the service, Tuisamoa's coffin was carried to the family cemetery by a team of policemen. Alofa and the rest of the family, as well as Helen and Andreana, followed. A large crowd gathered to witness Tuisamoa Lepopoi's interment. After a short service, his coffin was laid to rest in the mausoleum alongside the remains of other holders of the Tuisamoa title.

With Tuisamoa's body now resting peacefully inside the coolness of the mausoleum, the family, villagers and friends turned their attention to what was always going to be the most important part of a Tuisamoa funeral — the presentation of gifts of money, food, fine mats and clothing to guests from the bereaved family. Solomona, emotionally and physically exhausted, left all the arrangements to the family *matais*. There would be time enough for him to assume the responsibility when he was bestowed with the Tuisamoa title, something that he was both dreading and looking forward to. He decided to join Faye, Helen and Andreana who were watching the proceedings from the comfort of the *faleafolau*.

The presentation of gifts, as usual, was dominated by speeches. The recipients tried to get as much as they could by elevating their claims through status and presumed connections with Tuisamoa. The representative of the Tuisamoa family, in turn, tried to convince the recipient that what had been delivered more than matched their claims. To'oto'o was spokesman for the Tuisamoa family, and he proved to be an extremely competent and persuasive speaker. Fiasili was the main organiser of the gifts. The amount of food, fine mats, money and other goods amazed Faye, Helen and Andreana. Helen had not experienced anything like it before, and looked on in fascination and disbelief.

'The stuff being made available for uncle's funeral must be close to half of Samoa's economy, I reckon,' commented Faye.

'It's amazing where all the goods and money have come from,' said Solomona. 'It has all been contributed by relatives, friends and others.'

'I haven't seen anything like this before,' Andreana added. 'Pati and I have been to some Samoan funerals in Auckland, but they pale in comparison to this.'

'Well,' Solomona explained, 'this one is different because virtually the whole of Samoa, including American Samoa, is involved. For the funeral of one of the Paramount Chiefs, one would expect such a lavish presentation of food and gifts. No family, especially when their Paramount Chief dies, wants to be outdone by others. So, yes, this one has to be one of the biggest funerals, and one of the most expensive too.'

'Why can't it be made simpler, Mona?' asked Helen. 'It seems such a burden to the family of the deceased.'

'I suppose it can be made simpler,' he replied, 'but if you look at it, in theory, it should be what we call in economics a pareto optimal condition. No one should lose out materially, because the bereaved family should return the value of the gifts being received, so it should be like a one-to-one exchange. Thus, in the process, many, if not all, egos should feel a little puffed up at the opportunity to showcase their wares and capabilities.'

'But it doesn't always seem to work that way, does it?' asked Andreana.

'Well, no, because obviously the giver of the gift values the gift differently from the receiver, and that is why the giver often feels he should have received more in return. So a lot of the speeches are, in essence, like a market with agents bargaining for the so-called equilibrium price.'

'But if it's a gift, why should the giver expect anything in return?' asked Faye. 'It's rather an absurd concept of giving a gift.'

'Ah,' grinned Solomona, 'you're very smart, Faye, because that is exactly the point. It would appear that, fundamentally, the process is not a giving of gifts; and it's not motivated by love or real concern. Otherwise, it should satisfy your point, Faye.'

The presentation of gifts continued until late in the afternoon. It was almost dusk when it concluded. Those who travelled from faraway places returned to where they were staying, feeling tired. They were not leaving Lalolagi yet as there was still the title bestowal ceremony the next day. People from nearby villages returned home but they too would return the next day. There was great anticipation among everyone present for the forthcoming ceremony and festivities.

Twenty Eight

The *matais* of the Tuisamoa family, including Solomona's uncle Faigata, who had travelled from California, met after dinner on the night of the funeral to discuss Solomona's accession to the Tuisamoa title the next day. The meeting took place in the large living room of the Tuisamoas' *falepalagi*. Most of the relatives who travelled from other parts of the country and from abroad, including Helmut, a first cousin of Tuisamoa Lepopoi from Germany, were catching up with each other in the family's *faleafolau*. Those who were interested in the *matais'* deliberation were listening from the annex of the *falepalagi* or eavesdropping from the bedrooms. Alofa, though keenly interested, was, by tradition, not permitted to be part of the discussion. Solomona, Helen, Faye and Andreana listened from a bedroom. Even though the subject of the meeting was his accession to the Tuisamoa title, Solomona could not participate, as he was not yet a *matai*. Fiasili was the only woman, and non-*matai*, allowed to participate in her capacity as the oldest female member of the family. Everybody at the meeting was seated on the floor, in customary fashion. As usual, To'oto'o opened proceedings.

'To the highly esteemed members of the Tuisamoa family,' he began, glancing around the room, 'Tui's day went extremely well, and I want to thank you all for the hard work you put in, as well as for your cooperation. That is done now, and we need to focus on the future. There is no better way to do that than to have someone fill the void left by Tui as soon as possible.' He paused momentarily. He was worried that Faigata, known to be a trouble-maker, might object to the decision for Solomona to be the next Tuisamoa. To'oto'o could not shower Faigata with money; Faigata had a successful business in California.

'Faigata,' he continued, then paused, 'it may have surprised you when you arrived to find we had already met and agreed that our nephew, yes, your very own nephew Solomona, should succeed the old man. It may have also come as a surprise that we are proceeding with the ceremony tomorrow. Faigata, we didn't give you the opportunity to express your views on the matter. It is my hope that you will support the unanimous decision of those who live here and serve the family on a daily basis.'

Faigata, a fairly big man with greyish hair and a greying moustache, was smoking a cigarette while listening to To'oto'o. He nodded occasionally and smirked to himself. He squashed what remained of his cigarette in an ashtray as To'oto'o concluded his opening remarks. He sat up straight and looked around the living room.

'To'o, thank you for your remarks. Thank you too for remembering me only *after* you had already made the decision of who would be the next *matai*. So what is the point?' he asked somewhat sarcastically, his voice rising. 'I suppose in your eyes I am nothing, eh? Well, to make sure things are done properly according to the tradition of this family, and the country, I have decided to act. There will be no ceremony tomorrow!' he roared. 'I have here an injunction from the court.' Reaching into the pocket of his shirt, he produced an envelope. 'So proceed with the ceremony at your peril!'

'Damn you, Faigata!' shouted Pule, as the others looked on in shock. 'You've been gallivanting all over the world like a bloody dog in heat and —'

'You shut up, Pule, or I'll stuff this envelope into your mouth.'

'Gentlemen, gentlemen,' implored To'oto'o, as the exchange between Pule and Faigata heated up.

In the bedroom Solomona translated what was going on for Helen, Andreana and Faye. Wanting to reassure him, Helen moved closer to Solomona and put her arm around him.

'So what will happen if the ceremony is cancelled, Mona?' asked Andreana.

'Well, it means it will be postponed,' he explained. 'They will meet again and perhaps make another decision if they decide to revoke the one they promised Dad. If they cannot agree, then there is always the Lands and Titles Court which resolves matters of this nature, although the family will try to avoid going to court — it has never happened before. The Court is a *palagi* institution, and the family doesn't want a *palagi* institution to make the decision for them, especially in matters pertaining to the Tuisamoa title. It is not proper, and it would reflect poorly on the family. It would show a lack of solidarity and unity.'

'What about you, Mona?' asked Andreana.

'I will be as I am, Dreana,' he smiled. 'I trust God's wisdom regardless of what may happen. There is more to life than *matai* titles. The family is very large, as you have seen, and there are many capable people who can become Tuisamoa, including any of those guys in the living room. I'm sure there are a few who have ambitions. Mind you, it's a much easier life not to be a Tuisamoa. The only thing is that if you want to have an influence on life in Samoa, you need to have a *matai* title, or you would never be heard. And with the Tuisamoa title, one can get things done easily because of the absolute power it holds, if one decides to exercise that power.'

'Didn't someone say that absolute power corrupts absolutely?' asked Andreana.

'It was Lord Acton who made that statement,' he replied. 'He's often quoted as such, but that's not exactly what he said, according to the record. He said that power *tends* to corrupt,' he continued, 'and absolute power *tends* to corrupt absolutely. In other words, the outcome depends entirely on the holder of the power.'

The exchange between Pule and Faigata had escalated almost to a fist-fight. Pule challenged Faigata, and Faigata was ready to defend his honour. The other *matais* and Fiasili watched while To'oto'o continued to call for calm between the two. Pule and Faigata belligerently moved toward each other. Finally, Fiasili could not stand it any longer.

'Stop, you two!' she shouted, her eyes open wide with anger. Pule and Faigata froze near the middle of the room. 'Where are your manners? How dare you fight in my presence? You are behaving like animals! You should be ashamed of yourselves. Go back and sit down, immediately!'

Pule walked back to where he had been sitting. Faigata turned to move back to his seat. 'Fai, give me the envelope,' Fiasili ordered, as Faigata was about to sit down. He reluctantly handed it to her. 'Now go and sit down. Where on earth did you get the idea you could defy the will of the family, eh?

Where? Answer me, Fai! Where did you learn this stupidity?' she continued, her voice raised and her gaze fixed on Faigata.

Faye shivered at hearing her mother's anger, as Solomona explained what was going on. Helen and Andreana smiled nervously and looked at Faye, and at each other. They were amazed at how Fiasili stood up to Faigata and Pule when they would not listen to To'oto'o, who was a *matai*.

'Sili can do that?' asked Andreana.

'Oh, yes, she can,' smiled Solomona. 'She can do almost anything she wants — it's the mystique of the *feagaiga*. When Dad was alive, she was the only person who could challenge his authority, or reprimand him, although she would only ever do so in private.'

Faigata did not answer. He hung his head and picked at the mat.

'Fai,' continued Fiasili, 'do you think this family is in Hollywood? You are not in America now. Do you think your court order will change the will of the family? Who was the stupid judge, or whoever, who issued this order, eh? Tell me because I'd like to smash his blooming head in!' In awe of Fiasili's strength, most of the *matais* sat quietly, looking at the floor. 'Someone give me a lighter,' she ordered. Kaino, who was listening from the annex, ran into the room with a cigarette lighter. Fiasili flicked the lighter. 'Now, Fai,' she said as she held the envelope above the flame, 'this is the end of your court order. And if you're not careful, you could end up suffering the same fate. Don't you dare treat this family like something in the movies. This family is sacred, and you shall not take it lightly. Now, tomorrow, all of you,' she continued as she looked around the room at the *matais*, 'need to be on your best behaviour. I will smash the head of anyone who puts a foot out of place.'

Silence filled the *falepalagi* after Fiasili finished speaking. Finally, To'oto'o spoke.

'Sili,' he said, trying to apologise for losing control of the meeting, 'I'm sorry that we behaved badly in your presence. We did not intend any disrespect for you, our sister. This is how the devil operates. He tries to disrupt and set families against each other. Anger is a bad thing, but it's good to vent it so that it can be quickly dispensed with. Fai, our apologies again. It's not that we do not consider you highly. We do, but time didn't allow us to bring you into the deliberations. We wanted our brother to die a happy death. It was the only request he made before he died, and he wanted an answer straight away. Knowing that you love your nephew dearly, and given Mona's qualities, we were confident that you would support our decision. We felt that, in this day and age, a person like Mona is the right choice. We are all old and were educated in the old ways. The world has moved forward and is now in the computer and technological age. Samoa will inevitably become part of the global village, and it's better to have someone who understands all these things. So please reconsider your decision and allow the ceremony to proceed. The whole world is here and expecting the bestowal of the Tuisamoa title to proceed tomorrow.'

Faigata did not reply immediately. He was still trying to come to terms with the humiliating reprimand he had received from Fiasili. Again there was silence apart from occasional coughing. Finally, Faigata spoke, attempting to offer Fiasili an apology for his behaviour.

'Thank you, To'o,' he said slowly, then turned to face his sister. 'Sili, I am sorry for behaving badly tonight. Please forgive me. It is not that I want to defy the will of the family.

I guess it's just that I wanted to be part of the family too, but it's difficult to feel part of it if I can't have a say on matters that are important to all of us. I suppose my action was a spur of the moment reaction. I must admit that I'm in complete support of Mona being the next *matai*. I believe he has all the qualities required of a good leader. So please ignore my earlier outburst. I do apologise. That is all I want to say. May we have a blessed night.'

There were thankyous from all the other *matais*. Pule also apologised for his involvement in the scuffle.

'Well, thank you for your apology and for restoring order and commonsense,' Fiasili said. 'Fai, I'm sorry for the strong words I let fly just now. You all know I say big words, but I don't bite. We should all learn to respect the decision made by those who live in and serve the family, unless the decision is outrageous. We must be able to swallow our pride — that's what clouds our minds — and get on with it. I can't think of anyone better that Mona to be the next *matai*. He may be young, but he is very mature. He is not married yet, but I'm sure he will make a wise decision about that too, when he feels the time is right. Now let us all prepare for tomorrow. It's a great idea to have the *saofa'i* tomorrow, even though a *saofa'i* has never before been held the day after the funeral of a previous holder. But I suppose we have to keep looking for ideas to improve the way we do things rather than being chained to old habits, including bad ones. We should all know what our roles are tomorrow. May God bless Mona and the family. That's all I want to say. May we have a blessed evening.'

After some discussion about the responsibilities of each *matai* during the next day's proceedings, To'oto'o ended the meeting with a prayer. Afterwards, hot *koko* was served with buttered bread. Faigata went to look for Solomona, knowing that he would have heard the deliberations, and wanting to clear up any confusion his outburst may have caused. He found him still explaining what had gone on to Helen, Andreana and Faye.

'Can I have a word with you, Mona, please?' he asked.

'Sure, Uncle Fai.'

Together they walked to the next room where Faigata put his hand on Solomona's shoulder. 'Mona,' he said hesitantly, searching for the right words, 'I hope you didn't misunderstand my intention when I tried to postpone your *saofa'i*. I fully support the decision for you to be the next Tui. It's just that these guys always try to ignore me. I just wanted to flex a bit of muscle, but my sister scared the life out of me,' he chuckled. 'Anyway, I hope you didn't think I would not support you as the next Tui, Mona.'

'That's all right, Uncle Fai. I had a pretty good idea of what was going on,' he replied. 'I knew you didn't really mean what you said. It's all water under the bridge now. But thank you for your support.'

'Well thanks, Mona.' Faigata seemed awkward and hesitant, as though there was something else he needed to say. Finally he blurted out, 'Are you and Helen going to get married, if you don't mind my asking?'

'I'm not sure, Uncle Fai. It's a little difficult right now, especially for her.'

'You should marry her, man,' his uncle urged. 'She's a very beautiful girl. And she's smart — I'm sure she will learn to adjust. If you do decide to get married, don't forget to let me know, okay?'

'We'll certainly do that, Uncle Fai,' smiled Solomona.

Twenty Nine

The night before his *saofa'i* Solomona slept by himself, in the room that he normally used as a study. It was not yet 5 am when he awoke, but already the village was a hive of activity. The young men were preparing *umus* while the young women were cooking a variety of foods for the festivities later that morning, with the ceremony due to start mid-morning.

The village generator had been on all night, so Solomona reached over and turned on his study lamp. Slumping back on the pillows, he contemplated the implications of holding the Tuisamoa title. He felt it was important that he start one of the most important days of his life in a reflective moment with God, as had been his practice over the years.

Opening his well-thumbed Bible to Psalm 23, he read it slowly as he thought about the meaning of each word. He contemplated the message contained in the Psalm, and what he felt the Lord wanted to teach him that day. Closing his eyes in prayer, the words of the Serenity Prayer that once hung on the wall of his room at the university hostel, and were now hanging in his office, came to him and he repeated them out loud, then added:

'Grant also to me Your patience and understanding; fill my heart with Your love and compassion. May Your peace rule in my heart, may all that I do glorify Your name, and may Your will be done in my life, Amen.'

As he finished praying, Helen knocked quietly on his door. It was almost 6 am, and the sun was beginning to appear above the horizon.

'Good morning, Mister Tui,' she greeted cheerfully, as she closed the door behind her.

'Good morning, Miss Jones. Did you sleep well?'

'Yes, I did. I can see you've just finished your morning meditation,' she smiled as she jumped onto the bed. 'Are you ready to face your big day?'

'As we say in Samoa, first things to the Holy Matautu.' Solomona sat down on the floor beside the bed. Helen moved to the edge of the bed, to be closer to him. 'And, yes, I think I'm ready to face whatever challenge the job will throw at me — I have a mighty Ally!'

'I see. Well, I guess you can't be tempted anymore then, eh?' she teased as she caressed his cheek.

'Too late, Miss Jones, too late,' he laughed and immediately launched into a soft and moving rendition of the *Lord's Prayer*. Helen leaned back on the bedhead, and closed her eyes as she listened to Solomona's strong voice. 'See,' he laughed after he finished singing, 'I'm protected by the spirit of the Almighty.'

'That was really nice, Mister Tui,' she said softly. 'Perhaps your next career move should be joining the three tenors to form the tenors' quartet, eh?'

'They've missed their chance, haven't they?' he chuckled. 'Well, that's their loss — I'll just sing for you from now on.' With that, he began to sing, again softly but expressively, the theme song from *Love Story*.

Helen loved listening to him sing, especially when he was in such a reflective mood. She leaned over and kissed him on the forehead.

A sudden knock on the door startled them. Solomona opened it to find his sister Fetuao, with Nathan clutching her dress, holding a breakfast tray.

'Good morning, Nathan,' he greeted as Nathan, sucking his thumb, tried to hide behind his mother. 'Thanks, Ao, but I think I'd rather have breakfast with everyone else.'

'But Uncle Pule and Uncle To'o said to bring it here. They're coming in a moment to talk to you.'

Pule and To'oto'o arrived a moment later followed by two young women carrying their breakfast trays. Fetuao put Solomona's breakfast on his study table, then left with Nathan. Helen got up to leave too.

'You can stay, Helen,' Pule suggested, 'you might like to know what will happen today.' Turning to the young women who brought their breakfasts, he asked, 'Would one of you girls mind getting some breakfast for Helen?'

The young women ran back to the kitchen, and one returned with another breakfast tray. While they ate, To'oto'o and Pule quietly discussed with Solomona the order of proceedings for the *saofa'i*.

Outside, Lalolagi was really coming to life. Instead of the sombre mood of the day before, the village was in a festive mood. It seemed everyone had put behind them their grief at the loss of Tuisamoa Lepopoi. Instead, all they could talk and think about was Solomona's accession to the Tuisamoa title. He was well liked, and there was a strong feeling that his reign could be the best ever, in a line of Tuisamoas that went back to the beginning of humanity.

All around the village there was shouting and hand clapping as, one by one, *'ava* ceremonies were being held in every *faletele*. Smoke from the *umus* hovered overhead. Babies cried, as most were left in the care of older siblings while their parents busied themselves organising for the day's festivities.

Pule and To'oto'o briefed Solomona on the processes, procedures and protocols relating to the ceremony. Helen tried to listen but, with still a very basic grasp of the language, she barely understood a word. Pule and To'oto'o tested Solomona on his knowledge of the required salutation and the proverbial and metaphorical language used by the *matais*. They laughed when he stumbled or made an error.

'Just make sure you don't use a swear word, man,' laughed Pule.

Their laughter prompted a questioning look from Helen, so Solomona explained, with a laugh, 'I'm trying to use the language of orators and these two are afraid I might end up swearing.'

'So the key is,' chuckled Pule, 'don't use any word you are not sure of.'

After their briefing session and a final rehearsal, Solomona had a shower and got ready for the *saofa'i*. Helen too left to change and prepare for the celebrations. According to custom, Pule and To'oto'o helped Solomona put on his costume, bathing his body first in coconut oil.

'By the end of the day I will smell like a dead horse with all this oil,' chuckled Solomona.

'Oh, you can put up with it for a few hours,' said To'oto'o.

As Pule and To'oto'o completed their session with Solomona, Lauti and Faigata arrived. Together with Pule and To'oto'o, they would present Solomona to the village council, as representative *matais* of both the Tuisamoa family and of the village. Alofa and Fiasili arrived soon afterwards. They tearfully hugged and kissed Solomona. Wiping their eyes, they each offered him their best wishes. Fiasili stopped and looked worriedly around her. She was searching for the traditional platform chair that the *aumaga* would have built and which would be used to carry the candidate for the Tuisamoa title to the ceremony.

'Where is the platform chair?'

'I want to walk, Aunt Sili,' replied Solomona, smiling.

Fiasili looked questioningly at Pule and To'oto'o, who smiled and shrugged. Lauti and Faigata shook their heads in disbelief.

'Hmm, another change, eh?' she thought aloud. 'Do you know you will have to walk barefoot?' she asked Solomona.

'Yes, Aunt Sili.'

'You haven't walked barefoot for a very long time. You know that walking on pebbles and stones can hurt your feet, or you could even cut your foot on a sharp object,' she warned.

'Don't worry, Aunt Sili,' he tried to reassure her, 'today is the perfect time for me to try walking barefoot again. I just want to feel the ground beneath my feet, and touch the soil from which my lifeblood and my soul spring.'

'Hmm, you're starting to talk like them already. Just don't behave like them once you become one of them,' she added sternly.

'Hey, Sili,' objected Pule, in mock indignation, 'what do you mean? We are the best-behaved people on earth.'

Everyone laughed as Fiasili scoffed at Pule's defence.

'Well, Mona,' she said, 'we'll leave you now to prepare yourself. May God bless you.' She hugged him and kissed him once more on both cheeks.

Fiasili and the *matais* went to join other family members in the living room, leaving Alofa and Solomona alone together.

'Well, Mother,' he whispered, 'you've been very quiet. Are you all right?'

Alofa looked adoringly at her son, not knowing whether to smile or cry. Though she desperately wanted Solomona to be the next Tuisamoa, and had worked hard to ensure her husband would nominate Solomona, she had had first-hand experience of what life as a Tuisamoa was like. She knew it was a very difficult job. She feared for him, while at the same time feeling happy for him.

'I'm all right, son,' she assured him. 'It's just that it's hard to believe that I'm losing my baby so soon. After the *saofa'i* everyone will look upon you differently. You will have responsibility over everybody in the district, village and family, and their problems will become your problems. Are you ready for that, son?'

While she was happy that the *saofa'i* was proceeding as planned, she could not help but be apprehensive for Solomona. She felt that her son had not had much of a life of his own yet, but here he was, embarking on a life that carried with it such huge responsibilities.

'God is with me, Mother,' he replied, 'otherwise I wouldn't have accepted this responsibility. He is my shepherd; I am not taking this responsibility on my own. You'll also be there to guide and support me as you did with Dad. It was the unanimous decision of the family that I take over from Dad, so I'm counting on support from all of them. I have prepared myself mentally for this. I believe I'm ready to take on the responsibility, Mother.'

'I know, son. I have complete confidence in your ability and your faith in God. I'm just being a worried mother voicing her concern. May God bless you, my boy.' Alofa gave her son a big hug, kissed him on both cheeks, then with tears in her eyes she joined Fiasili in the living room just as Faigata arrived, with Helen, to tell Solomona that it was time to go.

Helen smiled broadly as she opened her arms to embrace him, oblivious of the oil coating his body. Her eyes filled with tears as she realised the solemnity and immensity of the occasion.

'Good luck, Mister Tui,' she whispered.

Leaving him alone, she joined Alofa and Fiasili who were waiting to take her with them to the *faleafolau* where they would watch proceedings with the Tuisamoa family and other invited guests. After a final moment's reflection, Solomona joined the men in the living room, and warmly shook hands with Pule and To'oto'o.

'Thank you very much, both of you. You've been a great help to me.'

'We're very proud of you, Mona,' they replied, almost in unison. 'You'll make an excellent Tui, young man.'

When everyone was ready, Lauti and Faigata stepped out of the *falepalagi* to the blaring sound of gunfire and conch shells, leading the small procession to the *faletele*. Solomona followed, with To'oto'o and Pule immediately behind him. There were loud cheers from the young men of the village, as well as the women and children, all straining to get a last glimpse of Solomona, the young man, before he became Tuisamoa Solomona, their ruler and leader.

Solomona looked regal and imposing. His oiled skin glistened in the sun, exaggerating every muscle. His broad smile charmed the admiring crowd. He wore a magnificent fine mat around his loins, a traditional orator's necklace and a lei of local and foreign currencies around his neck, with elaborately decorated ceremonial headgear, befitting the Paramount Chief status of the Tuisamoa title. He hardly felt the pain of stones and other objects pressing into the delicate soles of his feet, as he walked, with head erect, towards the *faletele*.

Solomona smiled and waved, acknowledging the calls from all around him. The crowd clapped and cheered as the procession approached the *faletele* where all the *matais* and Tenari, the only clergyman in Lalolagi, were assembled. Non-*matai* guests and visitors filled every *faletele* in the village as they watched the procession move towards the Tuisamoa family's *faletele*. Murmurs of respect and admiration were heard among the crowd as Solomona entered the *faletele*.

Inside, the *faletele* was packed with *matais* from throughout the two Samoas and from overseas, all seated in their designated positions, as determined by their rank. At the rear of the *faletele* sat Fetuao, Solomona's sister, dressed in the colourful traditional costume of Tuisamoa's *taupou*. She would be mixing the *'ava* for the *saofa'i*. Flanking her were two senior members of the *aumaga*, one to pour water into the *tanoa* where the *'ava* would be mixed, and the other to administer the distribution of the *'ava*. Outside, at the rear of the *faletele*, members of the *aumaga* sat in the sun, waiting.

On entering the *faletele*, the five men shook hands with the *matais* and Tenari, then sat in their designated positions. A traditional exchange of pleasantries and salutations followed. When the noise died down, Tenari announced that they would begin the *saofa'i* with a prayer. He read from the Bible, then made a short speech reflecting on the importance of the occasion. Kneeling in front of Solomona, he placed his hands on Solomona's head and blessed him. He then excused himself so that the formal part of the *saofa'i* could proceed. Some of the *matais* quickly gathered a few *tugase* and gave them to Tenari as he left.

Once Tenari stepped outside, the formal proceedings of the *saofa'i* began. First, all the *matais* except those from the Tuisamoa family presented the family with the *'ava usu a Samoa*. In reply, the family presented the village, and essentially the whole of Samoa, with the *'ava o le nofo*. One of the *aumaga* pulled a large mat with a stack of *'avas* on it into the middle of the floor until one of village's high-ranked orators signalled him to leave the *'ava* in front of him. The untitled man pushed the mat closer to the orator, then moved respectfully to the rear of the *faletele*. The orator moved forward and spoke about the *'ava* in front of him as he considered how to distribute it. First, he distributed one *tugase* to be powdered and mixed for the *'ava* ceremony, then handed out the rest according to tradition.

Lauti, being the senior *matai* of the Tuisamoa family from Lalolagi, presented Solomona to the village council as the next Tuisamoa. In response, Tula, the highest-ranked *matai* of the village council, accepted him into the village council with a speech that included a blessing. Tuisamoa Solomona responded with his maiden speech, expressing his appreciation for the help and counsel he had received, as well as for the village's blessing. He concluded by expressing his desire to serve the village.

As Tuisamoa Solomona finished speaking, the untitled man who was to administer the distribution of the *'ava* announced the *'ava* ceremony in Tuisamoa Solomona's honour. As the newly inducted member of the village council, Tuisamoa Solomona was the first to be served.

He received the specially prepared coconut shell containing the *'ava*. Holding it in front of him, he made a brief speech. When he finished, he let some of the *'ava* drip onto the floor and said, 'This is for you, God,' then drank the rest. He was now fully accepted into the ranks of the *matais* in Lalolagi, which entitled him to become a member of the village council.

The *'ava* ceremony continued until all the *matais* were served. When the ceremony was completed, *lafos* were given to Tula who spoke on behalf of the village and to the untitled man who administered the distribution of the *'ava*. Solomona removed the lei made of currency from around his neck and handed it to Tula to distribute it to the rest of the *matais*. The proceedings of the *saofa'i* then moved outdoors in front of the *faletele* where the main presentation of food, money and gifts began. An enormous amount of food, fine mats and money was distributed, and To'oto'o was, once more, entrusted with the task of being the spokesman for the Tuisamoa family.

'Where did all this food, fine mats and money come from?' Andreana asked, perplexed by the amount of food provided so soon after the huge distribution of food the day before at the funeral.

'Well,' Albert replied, 'the Tuisamoa family is a very large family, scattered throughout both Samoas and in many countries of the world, and every one of them has made a contribution. It's the only way this could be done, especially in a village like Lalolagi and a district like Fagaloa.'

'What do you mean?' Helen asked, utilising every opportunity to learn as much as she could about Samoan and family customs and traditions.

'Well,' he replied, 'this is the first demonstration of Mona's ability and willingness to serve, as a new *matai*. Food is one of the most important parts of Samoan life. If Mona were to be bestowed with an ordinary title, he would be expected to feed only the village. But because a Tuisamoa is a Paramount Chief, he must demonstrate that he is able to feed the whole district and, in some cases, the entire country.'

'Hmm,' she sighed, 'that's tough, isn't it?'

Albert smiled. 'Yes it is, but it's a family responsibility and, if everyone contributes, it becomes a simple task. That mountain of fish came from Aleipata, the pigs came from Apia, all the cattle came from Savai'i, and the containers of canned food and other processed goods came from New Zealand, Australia, the United States, American Samoa and Germany, and so did most of the money. It's the same with the fine mats, as many of the best are now found outside of Samoa. I don't think our immediate family contributed much except for most of the taro that was consumed yesterday and again today. In the Samoan way of life, we invest in the *aiga*, not in the bank. The bank won't give you a loan for something like this.'

'What happens if the new *matai* can't provide enough food during the *saofa'i*?'

'In many villages,' he explained, 'probably nothing more than a reprimand. However, in Lalolagi, you would have to do it again. They will not recognise the new *matai* here until their stomachs have been filled.'

The distribution of food and gifts continued until late in the afternoon. Guests who had come for the *saofa'i* started leaving once they had received their share of the gifts. As the afternoon light faded, Lalolagi looked more like an abandoned village as the thousands who had flocked there over the last two days departed. Tuisamoa Solomona shook hands with all the *matais*, then walked with Pule, To'oto'o, Lauti and Faigata to the Tuisamoa's *faleafolau* where he was tearfully welcomed by Alofa, Fiasili, Helen and the rest of the family.

Thirty

Tuisamoa Solomona returned to work a few days after his *saofa'i*. He had been able to secure a teaching position in Apia for Helen at Samoa College, the government's top secondary school. So they stayed in Apia during the week, and on weekends returned to the village so that Tuisamoa Solomona could attend to village matters. The council meetings, traditionally held on the first Monday of each month, were moved to the first Saturday of the month to accommodate his work commitments.

Tuisamoa Solomona quickly learned that he had more responsibilities than he had expected. He found that the *matais* looked to him, as the holder of the Tuisamoa title, for guidance and direction concerning most village matters. He also soon realised that, in order to make his ideas and decisions known to the *matais* in the village council without distortion by a *tulafale*, he needed to speak to them himself. The Tuisamoa title was one of few *matai* titles that was both a Paramount Chief and a *Tulafale Sili*, the Highest-Ranked Talking Chief. When Solomona assumed the Tuisamoa title, he exercised his privilege of being a *Tulafale Sili* more frequently than his father did. This gave him the opportunity to question anybody in the council, to make decisions, and to implement his decisions. The *matais* realised after the first council meeting that he could not be swayed by flattery, and that he could get to the bottom of most matters with his astute questioning.

In his early days as a *matai*, Tuisamoa Solomona had been concerned with the state of the school building in the village. Damaged by strong winds two years earlier, it was still in a state of disrepair. During his third council meeting, which coincided with the beginning of school holidays for Helen, he asked why the school building had not been repaired. He knew that financial assistance had been provided by the government and by foreign aid agencies, but there was no sign that any work had commenced. Damage to the front porch of the church had also not been repaired, yet money had been raised for the repair work.

After much finger-pointing and denials, the chairmen of the school and church committees admitted to embezzling the funds. Tuisamoa Solomona was furious, but managed publicly to maintain his composure. Both chairmen apologised for their actions, to which he issued a strong reprimand.

'Such behaviour is unacceptable from leaders of a village who claim to be God-fearing,' he said, his face red with anger. 'I'd like the council to consider a penalty for both committees.'

After a short deliberation, the council decided that the money had to be repaid in full, involving $20,000 for the school and $5,000 for the church. 'To the chairmen of both committees,' he added, 'you have heard the voice of the village. I would like the money to be made available by next Monday, so we can start repair work on the school right away.'

'But your Lordship Tuisamoa,' begged Fui 'Aitupe, the Chairman of the School Committee, 'we no longer have the money. It's a very large amount to provide at short notice.'

'You should have thought about that before you embezzled it,' he replied. 'You will have to be resourceful and find a way to raise the money by Monday.'

The members of the two committees were shocked. There was stunned silence from the *matais* inside as well as from the *aumaga*, who sat outside the council meeting. Finally Tuisamoa Solomona spoke. 'I want both committees to meet with me after we disperse,' he commanded. 'Bring all the committee records and bank books — they will stay with me from now on. Also, from today, I will be a member of both committees.'

'Your Lordship Tui,' Tula argued, as persuasively as he could, 'I realise this matter has upset you, and I cannot blame you, for it is sinful behaviour. But, your Lordship, you should not stain yourself with such misdeeds. Leave the money matters to us. A Tuisamoa should not worry himself about such things, but instead should concentrate on more noble matters. No Tuisamoa, including your late father, has ever bothered with money matters before. So please, trust us; leave money matters to us.'

There was silence as the council waited on a reply.

'Thank you, Tula,' the reply came in a soft, controlled voice. 'I know you're not used to a Tuisamoa being so proactive in a meeting of the village council. I also know that no Tuisamoa before me concerned himself with money matters or with much of the affairs of the village. But I want you to know that I will be a different Tuisamoa. I will be taking an active role in the affairs of the village. The behaviour of these two committees has left me with no other option. I will find it difficult from now on to trust anyone on either of these committees. For your information, Tula, I do think about noble things. I value honesty and trustworthiness, but it's far better if those qualities are put into practice, not just thought about. However, maybe I am moving just a little too fast. So I'll withdraw my suggestion that I join both committees. Nevertheless, from now on, the committees' books and records will remain with me. All records of the village council and concerning church matters need to be kept in one place, so that they are accessible. Hopefully in the future, we will have a specially designated place where we can keep all village papers and records. From now on, I want it known that any decisions to spend village funds must be approved by the council, and financial reports must be provided at every council meeting.'

Silence followed Tuisamoa's words. Even Tula, who would normally debate such matters at length, remained silent. There were no precedents he could invoke and, as he and the others were still wary of Tuisamoa Solomona as a *matai*, they decided to keep their counsel. Afterwards members of the two committees gathered at the Tuisamoas' *falepalagi*.

'I'm sorry, gentlemen, that I needed to say what I did earlier,' Tuisamoa Solomona began, 'but I'm deeply disappointed with your behaviour. It is crucial that you have absolute integrity, and that the village can trust and rely upon all of you. As you seem to have frittered away the funds, I propose to lend you the money. You have three years to repay it, interest-free. You can harvest coconuts from our plantations to help raise the money. The boys will tell you which plantations you can harvest. Now let's make a fresh start, with an emphasis on honesty and transparency.'

He felt quite pleased with his handling of his first real encounter with the village council. He was naturally tense and upset at confronting evidence of corruption, but he felt more confident as the meeting progressed. He sensed he had communicated his intentions well to each *matai* and to the *aumaga* sitting outside, and that he had established a rapport with them in his new role.

The news of his dealings with the school and church committees was eagerly greeted by many in the village, especially the women and the *aumaga*, who were powerless to deal with such corruption. There was a new sense of optimism and enthusiasm in Lalolagi. Finally, they felt they had a Tuisamoa who would not tolerate such behaviour. They had respected and loved Solomona as a young man. He had frequently shown compassion and was always willing to offer his help, including financial assistance, especially when it involved children's school fees. Now that he had demonstrated he was not about to change in his new role, they respected him even more.

As the Tuisamoa family started to gather for devotions that evening, there was commotion outside. Young men were frantically running around and there was a lot of shouting. Tuisamoa Solomona tried to find out what was going on, but no one seemed to know. Normally this time of day was peaceful and quiet as people prepared for evening prayers. Curious, he was about to step outside to investigate the cause of the disturbance when a woman came running into the house, almost knocking him over, and fell to her knees in front of him.

'Oh, your Lordship Tui!' she cried, with hands clasped in front of her, tears rolling down her cheeks. 'Your Lordship Tui... my son is... please help me.'

Everyone in the Tuisamoa household stopped what they were doing, concerned to find out what had happened.

'Calm down, Tina. What about your son?' asked Tuisamoa Solomona anxiously.

'Your Lordship, he's been killed,' struggled the woman.

'Killed?'

A large crowd, mainly women and children who had heard about the incident, was gathering outside. They were eager to hear how their Tuisamoa would deal with the matter. Concerned to avoid a scene, Tuisamoa Solomona told everyone outside to go home. The crowd retreated to the darkness, but no one went home. Back inside, he continued questioning the distraught woman.

'You said your son had been killed?'

'Yes, your Lordship.'

'By whom?'

'By men in the next village, your Lordship.'

He realised immediately that this was an extremely serious and potentially volatile situation. The *aumaga* were probably already in the process of organising a retaliation attack on the assailant's village. He quickly sent for the *pulenu'u* and instructed him to immediately assemble all the men, both *matais* and *aumaga*.

As Siaosila'iitiiti ran out to inform the *pulenu'u*, Tuisamoa Solomona coaxed the woman to join him and the rest of the Tuisamoa family in the living room. She walked, with head bowed, into the living room where she sat down on a mat.

'What was your son doing at the next village?' he asked.

'He went there with some other boys… to play cricket, your Lordship,' she sobbed.

Tuisamoa Solomona walked over to where his mother was sitting and quietly consulted with her. He realised that he must handle such a sensitive matter diplomatically but with firmness, without inflaming the situation any further.

'Well, obviously, you came here because you want me to do something. Is that right, Tina?'

'Yes, your Lordship,' she replied, still sobbing uncontrollably.

'Was there anything in particular that you wanted me to do?'

'I just want… justice for my son, your Lordship,' she said haltingly.

'And what do you consider justice to be in these circumstances?'

'I want one of their boys killed too, your Lordship.'

'Are you sure it is justice, and not revenge, that you want?'

'I… I'm sure, your Lordship.'

'I see,' he said thoughtfully. 'And would you want to do that yourself?'

'Oh no, your Lordship. I want our young men to do it.'

'But why should our young men become involved when the injustice you feel was perpetrated against you, your family and your son?'

'I… I cannot do it myself, your Lordship.'

'Why can't you?'

'I just can't, your Lordship.'

Tuisamoa Solomona paused for a moment before continuing, 'It's not an easy thing to take a life, is it?'

'No, your Lordship.'

'It just doesn't feel right, does it?'

'No, your Lordship.'

The woman fidgeted while everyone sat quietly waiting to see how Tuisamoa Solomona would respond.

'Tell me something, Tina,' he said after a long pause. 'Do you consider yourself a Christian?'

Confused by the question, she did not answer straight away.

'I go to church twice every Sunday, your Lordship,' she replied hesitantly, unsure of what he expected of her, 'and I pray at home every morning and every evening.'

'That's good, Tina, but do you apply Christ's teachings to the way you live your life?'

'I try to, your Lordship.'

'Very well then. I know you are grieving for your son, but do you think you can apply some of those teachings now?'

Tina was even more confused. 'I don't know, your Lordship,' she sobbed. 'It's very difficult. My heart feels weak. I feel gutted. I really don't know if I can forgive so easily.'

'Okay then, Tina, do you want another woman to feel the same feelings that you are right now?'

Tina wiped tears from her eyes with the back of her hand as she thought about Tuisamoa Solomona's question.

'I suppose not, your Lordship,' she replied, starting to feel a little ashamed at her outburst.

'But if we do what you want, then, no doubt, a woman in the next village, whose son would have to die to satisfy your wish, would need to go through the same agony you are. Is that what you want?'

'No, your Lordship. I don't want another woman to feel the pain that I am going through.'

'Shall I take that to mean that you have withdrawn your initial request, then?'

Tina paused, then wiped her eyes dry.

'Yes, your Lordship Tui. Please disregard my request. I'm sorry for putting you through this.'

'Well, that's completely understandable, Tina, but I want to commend you for allowing your Christian values to help you reach such a noble decision. Are you willing to accept any decision that the village council makes on this matter?'

'Yes, of course, your Lordship.'

'All right then, Tina,' he urged, in a soft and concerned tone. 'Leave it to me and to the *matais*. Go and rest now. I will talk to you tomorrow after I meet with the council tonight. We are deeply saddened by the sudden and brutal death of your son, Tina. May the Lord God comfort you and keep you in His loving hands. Please let us know if you need help of any kind.'

As he consoled Tina, Siaosila'iitiiti arrived to inform him that the men had all assembled and were waiting for him. Tuisamoa Solomona asked his cousins' wives to give Tina something to eat. As he left to address the men, he whispered to Helen and Alofa to pray for wisdom.

'What's going to happen?' asked Helen, somewhat shaken by the whole episode.

'With this kind of thing,' Alofa replied, 'only two things can happen. Either war between our two villages or forgiveness. There's no in-between.'

'I see,' said Helen nervously. 'Well, let's hope that the council decides to forgive.'

'It will all depend on Tui. He will need to be strong in the recommendation he proposes.'

The noise from the *faletele* could be heard more than a hundred metres away, as Tuisamoa Solomona walked towards it. The huge conical structure suddenly fell silent as he entered. All eyes were on him, both the *matais* inside, and the *aumaga* outside.

'You all know why we are here tonight,' his voice boomed throughout the *faletele*. 'One of our boys was killed at a cricket game in the next village this afternoon. It is important that we proceed with caution. Reason must prevail. We should not allow our emotions to cloud our vision as we consider what course of action we should take. You must bear in mind the long-term consequences of any decision we make now. Remember that, as the Paramount Chief of the district, I have the power to mete out any punishment you decide upon. So I would like to hear from anyone who has an opinion to offer on this matter. But first, I'd like to hear an eyewitness account of what happened.'

A strongly built young man, who was sitting outside with the *aumaga*, entered the *faletele*. Anxiously he told Tuisamoa Solomona and the assembled *matais* that he had started the fight when he was bowled out. Tina's son had been trying to break it up and had died when someone hit him over the head with a cricket bat. The young man started to leave but Tuisamoa Solomona asked him to stay. He sat down, nervously hanging his head. The *matai* of his family, Misa, was shaken. He knew this spelt trouble for his family. Samoan traditional law dictated that the family of the guilty party be punished rather than the person who actually perpetrated the crime, and punishment by the village council could be swift and severe, depending on the nature of the crime.

'You have all heard the account of the eyewitness, the very person who caused all the trouble,' said Tuisamoa Solomona. 'Now, let's hear from whoever would like to speak on the matter.'

All the *matais*, except Misa who could not participate in the deliberation because it affected his own family, had their say, beginning with Tula and working through to the lowest-ranked m*atai*. There were essentially two issues being discussed: punishment for the family of the young man who started the fight, and the response to the killing of Tina's son. The council, with Tuisamoa yet to express his opinion, was unanimous that Misa's family should be punished to the value of 20 sows and a thousand taros. However, they were divided on the response to the death of Tina's son. The majority wanted retaliation, while a significant number wanted to offer pardon, if the traditional way of seeking forgiveness was employed, in return for 2,000 fine mats, $5,000, 100 sows and 5,000 taros.

When all the *matais* had had their say, Tuisamoa Solomona moved forward to speak.

'I'd like to thank all of you for the opinions you have expressed,' he began. 'I'm particularly pleased that you have all recognised immediately that it was our own man who started the fight that resulted in one of our boys being killed, and that you have dealt with it accordingly. However, since time immemorial, punishments have always been in the form of food. I suggest that, from now on, we alter the form of punishment to something that is more useful and productive than just filling our stomachs. So I propose to change the punishment for Misa and his family to $1,000 to be paid over the next year, and the provision of lunch for council meetings for the rest of this year.'

Everyone in the room and outside listened in hushed silence, waiting anxiously to hear what he proposed concerning their village's response to the killing. He cleared his throat, then continued, 'As for our response to the killing, well, we are all men raised on the principles of the Holy Bible. We were instructed on these principles when we were boys, and we continue to read them now we are older. We all go to church every Sunday, many observe prayers twice a day, and by doing all that, we consider ourselves Christians. Well, men of Lalolagi, unless we apply those principles to our lives, we do not even come close. You see, Christianity is a life that we can all live. It is not something that exists only in our minds, or only on Sundays. Those principles — to love, to be kind, to be patient, to be caring, to forgive, among others — provide a code of conduct that allows us to coexist in peace and harmony here in Lalolagi and with our neighbours. Samoa has a noble tradition, the *ifoga*, which is consistent with those Christian principles. So I say to you tonight, let us wait and see if our neighbours make an apology, according to that noble Samoan tradition. If they do, I propose that we accept it. I have spoken to Tina, the mother of the murdered boy, and this is her wish too. I want to respect her wish, and I ask all of you to do the same. If by sunset on Monday nothing has happened, then we shall consider our next move. We must learn to forgive and to be patient. Violence begets violence, and in the end we all lose — no one wins in war. We have been affronted, but we must learn to rise above the temptation to strike back in like manner. We must let the godliness in all of us rule our hearts, so that we are not consumed by anger. We shall all go home tonight and prepare our hearts for worship tomorrow.'

More speeches followed, all in support of Tuisamoa's wish. Afterwards, everyone quietly made their way home. If there was to be a traditional offering of an apology, an *ifoga*, it would take place on Monday at dawn. Sunday was the Lord's day and nothing else would happen apart from the usual routine of worshipping, eating and sleeping.

It was late when Tuisamoa Solomona returned home. Alofa and Helen were waiting up for him. To everyone's relief, he explained what decisions the council had taken. Helen had been extremely anxious about the outcome of the meeting. Her hope now was that the village where the boy was killed would make an *ifoga*. Feeling tired, she said goodnight, leaving Alofa and Tuisamoa Solomona alone together. Alofa warmed up the *koko* left over from dinner and poured a cup for each of them.

'You're doing well, Tui,' she said encouragingly as she sipped her *koko*.

'Thank you, Mother. It's been a very trying day for me. I feel like I have completely run out of energy. My mind is totally exhausted.'

'Well, you need a wife, son, to give you support,' his mother urged. 'It's not easy being a Tuisamoa without a wife. You must consider taking a wife, whether it's Helen or someone else, and the sooner the better.'

He was taken by surprise by Alofa's comments. He wondered what she was up to.

'Oh, I don't know, Mother,' he smiled, sipping his *koko*. 'I haven't really thought too seriously about it. I guess part of the problem is that I care for Helen so much — she is the one who would have to make all the sacrifices. I know she is more than willing to do that, but I'm not certain whether you, the family and the village will accept her as my wife. That's the problem. I suppose the most important person in the equation is you, Mother.'

Alofa continued to sip her *koko*, as she pondered her response. 'Well,' she said finally, 'I quite like Helen. She is intelligent and polite. She's making a real effort to learn our culture and our language, but more importantly I can see that you love each other. I think she'd be better than some Samoan girls who may be more interested in getting the right connections. You know you can't please everyone. You must do what is best for you first. So, yes, you should marry Helen, if she is the wife you want. The family and the village will have to accept your choice. They did it for Dad's mother, and that was a while ago. I see no reason why they would not accept Helen. But if they don't, well they can all go and jump in the sea.'

Tuisamoa Solomona smiled. He had been trying for some time to discuss the issue with his mother, but didn't know how to raise it. He always found it difficult to read his mother's thoughts, and was afraid that she would not agree to the idea of him and Helen being married. So he was relieved when Alofa raised the subject. More important for him was that his mother was amenable to the idea. The only worry he had now was the question that had bothered him from the start. 'What will happen in the future if things change?' he thought to himself. 'Oh, bugger the future,' he thought. 'Why not just enjoy the present?'

'Well, thank you, Mother, I'll see what Helen has to say. With everything that has happened today, I'm not sure if her feelings will still be the same. I haven't had the opportunity to have a good talk with her for a while.'

Alofa was feeling tired. It was already well past midnight and she was due to attend the dawn service the next morning. Excusing herself, she went off to bed.

Solomona sat alone in the living room for quite a while, sipping *koko* and reflecting on the events of the day. They had been very difficult issues for him to deal with, but he was absolutely confident that God's hand had guided him in resolving them. As was his practice, he tried to see what purpose there was for him and how he could learn from such experiences. Finally, as a smile crept across his face, he realised there had been a reason for what had occurred that day.

Thirty One

Early on Sunday morning, a *matai* from the village where Tina's son was killed, a relative of Tuisamoa's, came to inform him that the village was preparing for an *ifoga* the next day. In accordance with tradition, Tuisamoa Solomona would discreetly inform the *matais* of Lalolagi about this meeting when he met them at church.

In all three church services that day, and at the funeral of Tina's son, the message from Tenari was one of forgiveness. At the *to'ona'i*, Tenari pleaded for compassion and the need to forgive the wrong done by others.

That night, Tuisamoa Solomona stayed up late, preoccupied with concerns about the killing and the *ifoga*. His cousins, the two Siaosis and Kaino, kept him company. Helen, too, was anxious about what might happen the next day.

'You should get some rest, HR,' he suggested, aware of how tired she looked. 'Everything will be all right,' he assured her.

She said goodnight to the cousins and Tuisamoa Solomona walked with her to her room where they hugged each other before saying goodnight.

'Take care, darling,' she whispered as she closed her door.

Tuisamoa Solomona and his cousins stayed up all night, talking and drinking *koko*. Just before dawn, they heard noises from the village *malae*.

'I think they're here,' whispered Siaosila'iitiiti.

'You'd better go and get Tina, Junior,' Tuisamoa Solomona told him, 'and you, Senior,' he turned to Siaosimatua, 'go and get the *pulenu'u* and ask him to assemble all the men in the *faletele*.'

After a short while, Siaosila'iitiiti returned with Tina and the *matai* of her family, Palupe. Kaino served them *koko* and buttered bread. Tuisamoa Solomona once again expressed his sympathy for the tragic death of Tina's son, but indicated that what happened now was completely in her hands, reminding her of the village's decision.

Palupe, on behalf of Tina and his family, thanked Tuisamoa Solomona for helping them get through their grief. 'The wish of the village, your Lordship, will be honoured,' he assured them.

Morning light slowly crept through the village to reveal the men of Lalolagi, both the *matais* and the *aumaga*, gathering at the Tuisamoa family's *faletele*. Outside in the *malae*, in front of Tuisamoa's *faleafolau*, virtually all the adult men from the other village knelt with their heads covered with fine mats, or *ietoga*, a most treasured item in Samoan culture. One man, covered with the biggest and most elaborately decorated fine mat, knelt in front of the rest.

Tuisamoa Solomona deliberated with Tina and Palupe for a while, then sent for Tula, the highest-ranked *matai* of the village council. When he arrived, they discussed together the protocols of an *ifoga*. As already determined, the *ifoga* would be accepted. However, the timing of the acceptance was left to Tina.

'Well, Tina and Palupe, you now need to decide when to accept the *ifoga*,' Tuisamoa Solomona advised.

Tina whispered to Palupe, 'I want to get it over with now, Palu.'

'Your Lordship Tui,' Palupe then informed him, 'we'd like to get it over with now, if your Lordship so desires.'

'Well, Tula, I will leave it to you to guide us now.'

'As you wish, your Lordship.' Tula rose to accompany Tina and Palupe to the *malae*.

Tuisamoa Solomona would not be involved in the ceremony until some time later, so he remained behind.

Meanwhile, Helen had woken up and found Tuisamoa Solomona's cousins in the kitchen, eavesdropping on the deliberations in the next room. The concept of an *ifoga* had been explained to her, but this could possibly be the only time she would ever experience it. She joined Tuisamoa Solomona after the others left, and together they watched proceedings outside from behind the curtains.

'Can you explain to me what's going on, Mona?'

'Sure. As I mentioned last night, we have agreed, as a village, to accept the apology.'

'Yes, I knew that.'

'Now, the rest is merely a formality. As you can see, men from the other village are kneeling with their heads covered with fine mats, called *ietoga*. They can stay there motionless all day until we decide to formally accept the apology. This could be very risky for them if the apology is not accepted. The guy in front is, essentially, the sacrificial lamb. Had we decided not to accept the apology, he would be the first to die. Whatever we do to him indicates to everyone else what the outcome will be. If the apology is not accepted, then war ensues. Acknowledgement of acceptance of the apology is a simple act of removing the *ietoga* from his head; then speeches will follow. They will be invited into the *faletele* where the rest of our village has gathered. More speeches will be made followed by offerings of gifts. But today I will also be handing out some penalties.'

'But how can they defend themselves if all they have are fine mats?'

'Who knows! They probably have Star Wars-type swords and guns,' he grinned. Realising he was teasing her, Helen pinched him gently.

'Well,' he said more seriously, 'they could've come prepared for such eventualities, hiding their weapons not far from here, or underneath their *ietoga*. However, that's not the way things are done now. These days, once an *ifoga* is performed, it is always accepted.'

'Have there ever been cases of apologies not being accepted?'

'Apparently, it was not uncommon in the old days. I'm told that there was one occasion, many years ago, here in our village, where the non-acceptance of an *ifoga* ended in tragedy for our family.'

'What happened?'

'The story goes that when the Tula killed the man kneeling at the front, our village was surprised that members of the other village remained kneeling, instead of defending themselves. When Tula removed the *ietoga* covering the dead man, the village was horrified to see that he was the eldest son of the Tuisamoa at the time. Being tired of all the killings, the young man, realising what would happen, offered himself to be sacrificed. Tuisamoa, the father, was so overcome with grief that he never recovered. He was able to extract a promise from the *matais* of Lalolagi before he died that they would always accept apologies in future. And since then, our village has always accepted apologies. Throughout Samoa, I haven't heard of an apology that hasn't been accepted in a very long time; in fact, since the arrival of Christianity.'

Helen was fascinated. 'It's very interesting, almost like Jesus dying for the sins of the world.'

'Well, Christianity was accepted in Samoa with hardly a problem, I'm told, largely because much of its teachings were consistent with a lot of Samoan culture and customs at the time.'

'But what about the laws of the country in this case?'

'The laws of the country are administered in Apia where the magistrates and the Supreme Courts are located. Here, it's the laws of Lalolagi that apply and, in accordance with Samoan tradition, the word of the *matais* is law. The so-called law of the country is based on British and New Zealand laws. It's the law and justice system of *palagis*. Our government has recognised that justice systems have a cultural dimension. So it has come to accept the fact that the western justice system suits the *palagi*, while the Samoan village justice system works for Samoans. As a result, it has given our traditional system due recognition.'

'Won't the police charge whoever killed the boy?'

'They will if we don't do anything, especially by this process, or if Tina decides to pursue it in court, despite having agreed to accept the *ifoga*. However, that would be tantamount to defying the will of the village, in addition to betraying the village, and the consequences could be very serious for her and her whole *aiga*.'

'So nothing else will happen after this?'

'Well, I've already sent someone to report the matter to the police. I've also notified Teutupe that I will not be at work today and tomorrow. The police should arrive some time today. When they get here, we will feed them. They will write a report of the events and the circumstances surrounding the killing, and the measures we have taken. If we can find the person who actually killed the boy, which we will, then a statement will be taken. They might still want to prosecute the offender, but we'll try to make sure that we handle the matter ourselves to the satisfaction of all concerned.'

'And that's it?'

'Hopefully.'

'You mean the boy will not go to gaol?'

'Gaol? No. Samoan villages have never had gaols. Gaol is a *palagi* institution that is extremely expensive and serves no purpose at all. What's the point of locking a person away for life? What purpose does it serve? It's just a totally ridiculous and very expensive concept. You may as well apply capital punishment to all such cases. The thinking that a person can be locked away for some time and then be expected to be completely rehabilitated when released, as if nothing happened, is totally unrealistic. Our way of dealing with deviant behaviour is cheaper, and more progressive, in that the interests of the victim and his or her family are paramount. The offender is given the opportunity to redeem himself and to remain a productive member of the community. Banishment is the severest way of dealing with serious cases in Samoa, but at least it's cheaper than life imprisonment, and the offender has the chance to redeem himself in another village.'

'But killing a person is not just any deviant behaviour, Mona. It's a very serious act.'

'You're right, HR, but no one is born a murderer, or grows up to be a murderer. It's society that moulds murderers and rapists. We all know that the *palagi* justice system is based on political and economic power. Oliver Goldsmith said it grinds the poor and is ruled by the rich. It's been likened to a cobweb that catches small flies but allows wasps and hornets to break through — according to Jonathan Swift. If you're rich and famous, your chances of winning or escaping justice are almost as certain as the sun rising the next morning, but if you're poor... well, good luck to you. Our system is simple and fair. It's quick, it's cheap and it works. We don't need lawyers to cook up absolutely ridiculous alibis that some judges unashamedly accept.'

Tula, Palupe and Tina arrived at the village *malae*. Tina moved forward and slowly pulled the *ietoga* from the leading appellant's head. Tula then spoke, acknowledging that Tuisamoa and Lalolagi had accepted the *ifoga*. A spokesman for the offending village responded, expressing their shame at killing Tina's son and conveying the collective guilt and contrition of his village. He concluded by thanking Tuisamoa for accepting their apology. The men from the other village were then invited into the *faletele* where the rest of Lalolagi's men were waiting.

Not long afterwards, Tuisamoa Solomona made his way to the *faletele* to join the *matais* from the two villages. As they welcomed him, a member of Lalolagi's *aumaga* interrupted proceedings with the usual exuberant announcement that the *'ava* ceremony was about to begin.

Once everyone had participated in drinking the *'ava*, the real business of the apology took place. Gifts of money, fine mats and food were presented to Tuisamoa Solomona, to the family of the victim and to Lalolagi. As usual, speeches dominated proceedings.

When all the customs and protocols had been observed, Tuisamoa Solomona reprimanded the *matais* of the offending village for the lack of discipline that resulted in the killing of Tina's son. The *matais* listened with heads bowed. He told them that a more serious penalty would be meted out should anything like this ever happen again.

'Is the person who killed Tina's son present?' he asked, his voice reverberating around the *faletele*.

'He is, your Lordship,' replied the spokesman for the offending village, and he called for the offender to come forward.

A young man, perhaps not even 20, entered the *faletele* and sat at the rear where the *aumaga* conducted the *'ava* ceremony.

'Which family are you from?' Tuisamoa Solomona asked.

'I am from the Mitamita family, your Lordship,' the young man replied hesitantly.

'Mita,' Tuisamoa Solomona turned to face Chief Mitamita, 'I will leave decisions concerning the punishment of your family to your council. However, you must take full responsibility for the actions of members of your family, and I urge your council to deal with this matter appropriately. Your son has taken away someone precious to Tina, someone who would have provided for her in the future and especially when she is old. To compensate for that loss, your son must provide food for Tina every Sunday for the rest of his life, or until such time as Tina determines. In addition, he must ensure that he never hurts anyone again.'

Mitamita hung his head and willingly accepted responsibility for the action of the young man from his family.

A police vehicle arrived as Tuisamoa Solomona finished speaking. The police officers were invited into the *faletele*, where they spoke to witnesses and wrote their report. After eating refreshments offered by Lalolagi's *aumaga* and satisfying themselves that all evidence had been taken and that appropriate punishment had been meted out, they left with gifts of food in coconut baskets.

There were more speeches after which the *matais* of both villages shook hands and bade farewell to each other. The two *aumaga* groups outside did likewise.

Alofa and Helen were relieved that the matter, despite its serious nature, was resolved peacefully.

Thirty Two

It was past midday when all the activities associated with the *ifoga* were completed. Tuisamoa Solomona was weary from stress and lack of sleep. Needing a break, he suggested to Helen that they go fishing off the peninsula, west of Old Lalolagi. She had not been there yet and, keen to see the men's pool, she readily agreed.

It took more than half an hour to reach the pool, which was close to the tip of the peninsula. The pool, in the middle of a flat lava shelf, was about a quarter the size of a football field, and dropped straight down into the sea. It was a perfect oval shape, oriented north to south, about 25 metres long and 15 metres wide. Near the centre, it was quite deep. Behind the pool, a 30-metre cliff rose sharply up a thickly forested slope. A natural tunnel through the rock provided access to the pool from the track.

When they reached the pool, Tuisamoa Solomona spread a *lavalava* over a layer of coconut fronds near the base of the cliff. Exhausted from events over the last 24 hours, he lay down and had a nap in the shade of overhanging trees. Helen rested her head on his chest and read a book. Waking around mid-afternoon, Tuisamoa Solomona decided to try his luck at fishing. While Helen continued to read, he fished for almost an hour, without a nibble.

'It appears you've scared the fish away, HR. Not one bite.'

Helen looked up from her book. 'That's probably because it's too late for their lunch,' she smiled.

'This is not good. We must catch a fish or we can't go home.'

'Why?'

'It's just the rules of fishing here,' he explained.

'Traditional rules or your rules?'

'Well, mostly traditional.'

Helen smiled to herself, wondering whether he was teasing her again.

'Can you do me a favour please, HR?'

'Sure, what do you want?' She slowly closed her book and stood up.

'I need you to come and sit with me. I have a feeling that any fish down there must be male fish — a few female pheromones might help to attract them.'

Helen walked over and knelt down behind him, leaning close to him and resting her chin on his shoulder.

'Is it the marine fish that need the female pheromone, Mister Tui, or is it the big terrestrial fish?'

Tuisamoa Solomona just smiled. Helen wrapped her arms around his chest and gave him a gentle squeeze. He jerked, pretending it had hurt.

'Gee, you're very strong, Miss Jones.'

'You're telling fibs, Mister Tui,' she smiled.

'Okay, assuming I am telling fibs, let me suggest something.'

Forever in Paradise

'Go ahead,' she replied curiously.

'If, after the next five minutes, I still can't catch a fish, we may need to perform a small fish-catching ceremony.'

'What sort of ceremony is that?'

'Oh, I'll explain it all to you if we need to perform it.'

'You're not going to sacrifice me to the fish, are you?'

Tuisamoa Solomona laughed. 'No, no, of course not. I wouldn't do anything like that, but I will need your cooperation.'

Five minutes elapsed, and still no fish were caught.

'Well, Miss Jones, looks like we'll have to see if the ceremony can yield us a fish.'

'Explain the ceremony to me first.' Helen was dubious, and still not sure if she was the butt of one of his jokes.

'Okay. See the cement chair over there at the end of the pool?'

'Yes,' she replied slowly, looking in the direction he was pointing.

'Well, you need to go and sit there while I go into the tunnel and prepare the bait.'

'And what do I need to do?'

'Nothing. Just sit there, look at the tip of Mount Lagi and wait until I give you instructions.'

She walked over to the cement chair and sat down, looking at Mount Lagi as instructed. Meanwhile, Tuisamoa Solomona ran through the tunnel, and picked a flower from a creeper vine growing on the other side. From inside the tunnel, he called out to her, 'Are you looking straight at the tip of Mount Lagi, HR?'

'Yes, I am.'

'Okay. Now, I want you to close your eyes. Make sure you can't see anything, or it won't work.'

'Okay, my eyes are closed.'

'Are you sure?'

'Come on. Hurry up, you twit. Of course, I'm sure.'

Tuisamoa Solomona quickly tiptoed over and dropped to one knee in front of her.

'Now, you can open your eyes, HR,' he whispered.

Helen opened her eyes slowly. She stifled the urge to burst out laughing at the sight of Tuisamoa Solomona kneeling in front of her offering her a flower.

'Marry me, Helen Ruth Jones!' he smiled, holding out the flower to her.

She froze momentarily. She was stunned, but excited, unable to speak. Regaining her composure, she took the flower.

'Of course, I'll marry you, Paramount Chief Tuisamoa Solomona,' she said softly.

Fumbling in the pocket of his shorts, he pulled out a ring and gently slid it onto her finger. Standing up, he lifted Helen and stood her on the cement chair.

'See,' he smiled as he held both her hands, 'I managed to catch a fish, or is it a mermaid? So the ceremony really works.'

Helen pulled him towards her and embraced him. Entwined in each other's arms, neither spoke. Then Tuisamoa Solomona pulled away, feeling a wet patch on his shoulder.

'You're crying, HR. Are you okay?'

'Oh, I'm sorry, honey. I'm just overwhelmed. The tears are for so many feelings, but mainly joy.' She tried to smile. 'But you're a damned hard coconut to crack,' she continued with a sudden change of mood. He smiled and held her tight, caressing her hair. 'For a very long time,' she whispered, 'I wondered if I would ever hear those words from you.'

'Oh, ye woman of little faith,' he grinned and kissed her gently.

'With a man like you, I think any woman would need more than faith,' she laughed.

'Well, as I said when we discussed this once before, I would've had no hesitation in popping the question a long time ago if it concerned just the two of us. But you've seen how complicated it can be. So now, it's all systems go, provided you pass the virginity test,' he teased, knowing that the practice had been abandoned more than a hundred years ago.

'Virginity test?' Helen was aghast. 'Stop teasing me, Mister Tui. This is one of your mean jokes, right?'

'No, it's not a joke, HR,' he insisted, struggling to look serious. 'The bride of the Paramount Chief must be a virgin.'

'And if she is not?'

'Then there will be no wedding.'

'Hmm, how interesting. And why is that?'

'It's the law. It's our culture.'

'Well, you know I am. Isn't that enough?'

'It's not me, HR, it's the people. They need to know you're a virgin.'

'Well, you can just tell them that I am. They believe and trust you.'

'Oh, that's not sufficient, HR. It must be publicly demonstrated.'

'Publicly demonstrated? Oh, no!'

'That's right. It's part of our culture.'

'And who will conduct the test?'

'A talking chief. Well, actually the highest-ranked talking chief.'

'Oh, yuk! How embarrassing!'

'Will that change your mind, Miss Jones? Will you still become my wife?'

'I'd like to marry the Paramount Chief without the virginity test,' she said firmly.

Tuisamoa Solomona smiled, 'Oh, but that's not possible, HR.'

'I'm beginning to get a sneaking suspicion you're teasing me again, Mister Tui.'

'Me? No, HR,' he insisted, smiling.

'Yes, you are. I can see that smirk of yours, Mister Tui. Come on, admit it.'

He could hardly contain his mirth. Helen tried again to get him to admit it was another one of his jokes.

'Well,' he said finally, in between bursts of laughter, 'I thought you would've remembered that I'm the highest-ranked talking chief.'

'See,' Helen tickled him. 'I knew it, I knew it.'

Laughing heartily, he lost his balance as he tried to avoid her tickling. Grabbing hold of her, they both fell into the pool. Gasping for air, they swam to the side of the pool. Tuisamoa Solomona held on to the side of the pool while Helen locked her legs around him and tried to stay afloat.

'I was laughing because I get the honour of performing the test,' he grinned.

'In that case, I wouldn't mind it,' she said as she tried to catch her breath, 'although I don't like the public part of it.'

'Well, we can decide to do away with that part if you want to.'

'They don't really do those things anymore, do they?' she insisted.

'Of course not, but that's how it used to be before the arrival of Christianity. I thought I'd throw it in for a bit of fun — and just look at the reaction I got. You are even swimming here in the men's pool when, in the past, it was absolutely off-limits to any women. Anyway, to change the subject, have the events of the past few days affected your view of life in Lalolagi, and maybe of Samoa generally?'

'Not really, although I must admit to feeling quite sad about it all. It's hard to believe that a place that looks so innocent and tranquil like Fagaloa, and that people as fun-loving as Samoans are, can still produce men with the capacity to embezzle public money or to take another person's life.'

'That's something that Miss Mead must have missed when she did her research in the late 1920s. But wherever there are human beings, one has to expect trouble — even in paradise. Of course, we can minimise the occurrence of such unpleasant events by developing communities that are inclusive, that emphasise responsibility rather than rights, forgiveness rather than revenge; communities with a simple system of justice that recognises cultural diversity, where the emphasis is on the victim, but not at the expense of the offender. Above all, good governance is vital. This means, appointing your most competent and honest people to run the affairs of the community. It doesn't matter what system of government you have; it's the people who run it that matter. And that's the problem, because it's extremely difficult to find competent people who are honest, or honest people who are also competent. Often, it's the dishonest and greedy people that gravitate to politics.'

'Well, I must say I was very impressed with the application of the concept of forgiveness through the —'

'*Ifoga?*'

'Yes, through the *ifoga*. If that had occurred in a western country, the victim's family would have asked for the death penalty, or a life sentence. But as you said, what purpose does that serve?'

'The great Mahatma Gandhi once said that an eye for an eye will leave all of us blind. Imagine such a life, eh? But the *ifoga* was part of Samoan culture before Christianity, so it points to something that is absolutely fundamental to the nature of human beings. Our ancestors knew the importance of forgiveness in order for people to coexist, and Christianity reinforces it because the central message of the Gospel is also forgiveness. Where pardon was not guaranteed before, now it is unthinkable that such would not be the case when an *ifoga* is performed. It shows that Christianity is not just a faith. It's a way of life that, without a doubt, is possible to live, and it's a way of life that is absolutely worth living. More important, it's also a lot of fun. The feeling of blessedness inside when you realise you have overcome a temptation of any kind, which for me has been a constant companion for years now whenever we're together,' he smiled, 'is absolutely divine. And because it's a conscious effort of the mind and will, it feels as though you're forever in a state of heavenly bliss, where circumstances become irrelevant. It must be how it feels to be in heaven, you know.'

Helen wiped drops of water from his face and moved closer to kiss the droplets from his lips.

'Well, honey, you've demonstrated that it's possible to live such a life, and I must say that I really respect and admire you for that.'

'Do you think you can stand the pressure of having to live and basically serve a people who are still struggling to improve their economic and living conditions?'

'Well, my feeling is that I can handle anything with you by my side. I thought a lot about what you used to say in the early days of our relationship, about having a dream and striving to make it a reality.'

'And what did you decide?'

'Well, I couldn't come up with a dream more noble and meaningful than yours. I mean, is there a life more meaningful than a life dedicated to the service of a people so that their lot can be improved and their happiness enhanced?'

'So?'

'So I thought I may as well follow the dreamer of noble dreams and make his dreams mine. And I'm sure that the more I immerse myself in the culture and way of life in the village, the more satisfaction I will get from even the little things. I suppose we all have that void within us that needs to be filled. I guess different people fill it in different ways. The thrill of facing and meeting a challenge excites most people. But this is probably the greatest challenge of all, and I have no doubt that it should also provide the greatest satisfaction that anyone could ever hope for.'

Tuisamoa Solomona smiled. 'Well, you must be very brave, because the price of following that dream could be very, very high.'

'Oh, it's not bravery, but love, my dear, that I believe will see me through. I know you don't believe that love is sufficient for a successful marriage, but from my viewpoint it is. I found out, in the three years I was in England, that I really love you, and I'm confident my love for you can overcome the most trying circumstances.'

'Hmm, you must've done a lot of thinking about this, HR. I must say I'm impressed. I have no doubt we'll make an excellent team with, hopefully, any little ones that may come along. But I hope you realise that serving the people of Lalolagi, and Samoa, was not exactly my dream.'

'Yes, I know that.'

'Good, because my dream, as I've told you before, is to discover God's purpose for me, and to fulfil that purpose. If I can do that, then I shall have no fear of death. For me, it's the only life worth living.'

'Well, I thought a lot about the future when I went back to New Zealand. I remembered reading one of Leon Uris' books where he wrote that it's one thing to poke your nose into others' business, and it's quite another thing to put your heart into other people's problems. Women are known more for the former, but I'd like to be known for the latter.' Helen paused and looked searchingly into his eyes. 'There is one thing, though, that I think I would need in order to survive life in Samoa.'

'And what's that, HR?' he asked curiously.

She didn't reply immediately, but thought carefully about how to express her request. 'I enjoy living here, as well as the company of the people, but I think at times I would like to have some privacy, some space where I can escape and refresh myself, you know?' Helen worried that raising such an issue might jeopardise his marriage proposal.

Tuisamoa Solomona was taken aback. He thought hard about her request, as it would not be easy to fulfil. 'Oh, I don't know, HR,' he replied pensively. 'There are many things to consider. We need money —'

'I still have plenty of money from grandpa's will,' she interrupted.

'Okay, but we have to consider our role as the *matai* of the family and the village leader. Would we be more effective that way, because what you're suggesting is building a house somewhere outside the village? Let's wait a while and see how things progress. We have plenty of time, and if we decide it's a good idea, then we'll do it.'

Helen could only agree to his suggestion. Though she would have liked an immediate answer, she understood his dilemma, and was happy to wait.

Thirty Three

Tuisamoa Solomona and Helen were married on New Year's Day, one year after Helen's first visit to Samoa. It was a clear sunny Saturday morning. *Umus* had been prepared from early light and smoke from them was gradually dissipating out to sea. The white sand on the beach and in the village *malae* glistened with morning dew. A cool sea breeze blew gently across Lalolagi.

The village was once again inundated with people from all parts of Samoa and with relatives and friends from overseas. The Joneses — Helen's parents, her sister Jocelyn and brother Alvin — were there, of course. They had been offered accommodation with the pastor and his family. The Filemus had all travelled from New Zealand. To'oto'o, Pule and many relatives arrived from American Samoa, Faigata and his new American wife, Theresa, came from California, as did Helmut from Germany. Albert, who had finished his law degree and was preparing for his admission to the Bar, had come home with his partner, Andreana. Fetuao, who had just finished the second year of her commerce degree, arrived with Alan and Nathan. Tuisamoa Solomona's good friend, Dr Fili Fa'aluma, and his family were also invited guests. The staff of Treasury were in Lalolagi en masse, as were some of Tuisamoa Solomona's friends from university who now lived in Apia. Also attending the wedding were dignitaries and members of the Diplomatic Corps.

The ceremony was held in the newly renovated church, which quickly filled with guests. Many more stood outside and listened to proceedings. The service lasted less than an hour. After photographs of the bridal party, taken in Lalolagi and in the hills overlooking Fagaloa Bay, Pita and Simi took the newly married couple and the wedding entourage for a tour of Fagaloa Bay in their newly acquired 30-metre fishing boat. Not yet used for a fishing trip, it still smelt brand new. Fagaloa Bay was calm, as usual, with barely a ripple. Without waves breaking over it, pinpointing the location of the reef was difficult, but with Simi keeping a lookout, they were soon cutting through the glistening water.

'Next time you come to Aleipata, we'll go fishing in this, Helen,' Pita said. 'It has very comfortable sleeping quarters down below, and will easily get us to Pago.'

'This is fantastic, guys,' Helen said, as she surveyed the fittings of the elegant new boat.

'It will also be our tour boat,' Tuisamoa Solomona grinned, 'so it will have to visit us on a regular basis.'

'Well,' Pita shrugged, 'what can I say, eh Helen? He's now the boss, and we have to obey his commands. We almost panicked that the boat would not be ready in time for the wedding.'

'Oh, don't worry, Pita,' she assured him, 'I'll see to it he doesn't become too mean. But the boat must have cost a fortune.'

'It *was* expensive, but when someone is prepared to defray much of the cost, then it's not a problem.'

'Oh, I see,' she said, looking questioningly at Tuisamoa Solomona.

'Don't look at me, HR. It wasn't me,' he confessed, 'but I do know who bought it.'

'Uncle Faigata paid for virtually the whole thing,' admitted Pita. 'When he came for Uncle Tui's funeral, we told him that we wanted a big boat, a real boat. He asked us how much money we had. We didn't have much, and of course such a big boat was always going to be fairly expensive. So he bought it on condition that it would also be used for Lalolagi until such time as the road is improved.'

Pita took the wedding party to every village lining Fagaloa Bay, where well-wishers cheered and waved to them. They waved back in acknowledgement. The tour took more than an hour, after which they returned to a lavish reception under a huge shelter that the village *aumaga* had erected on the *malae*. Entertainment at the reception was provided by the band from the Vaisigano resort. Memories of their trip to Savai'i and their stay at the resort came flooding back to Helen on hearing them play again. Other entertainment was provided by groups from various villages and, in true Samoan tradition, each group tried to outdo the others. After the entertainment, gifts of food, money and fine mats were presented to the pastor and his wife, and to the invited guests. As usual, the gift-giving was dominated by speeches. The amount of food, fine mats and money given away almost rivalled the excesses of Tuisamoa's funeral.

That night, the whole village, led by Tenari and Sekara, gathered at the Tuisamoas' *falepalagi* for evening devotions and dinner, followed by *fiafia* that lasted late into the night. After most guests had left, the Tuisamoa and Jones families gathered together in the living room to watch the opening of wedding gifts.

As Helen finished opening the gifts piled on a table, various members of the two families began handing more gifts and envelopes to her. The first came from the Joneses. Alvin, on behalf of the family, handed Helen an envelope and made a short speech expressing their love for the newlyweds and their good wishes for their future happiness.

'Thank you, Lord!' she exclaimed as she opened the envelope. 'It's a car key, Mona!' Excitedly she showed off the keys for a brand new double-cabin truck. 'Thank you, Mum, Dad, Al and Jos. This is a fantastic gift.'

There were hand claps, thankyous and congratulations from the onlookers.

'Whew!' exclaimed Tuisamoa Solomona. 'Thank you, Mum and Dad, Jos and Al. Hey, that's right, I can call you Mum and Dad now. That will take some getting used to.'

'It's our pleasure, son,' Mr Jones replied. 'That will also take some getting used to, but we are very proud to have you as a son, Tui. I'm not quite sure how to feel about having a Paramount Chief as a son-in-law, though. Anyway, Helen said a truck would be more practical here, so we've ordered one for you. It's at the Nissan dealers in Apia, and it's ready to be driven away.'

'Okay, Tui and your *Masiofo*, the lovely Helen,' smiled To'oto'o, as Pule handed Helen an envelope, 'here is the gift from Tutuila and Manu'a. We hope you'll have time to use it.'

Helen slowly opened the envelope. 'It's a couple of airline tickets, honey! Oh, and there's money too!' She quickly counted the money. 'Oh, my God, there's US$20,000!' Tuisamoa Solomona smiled and shrugged. 'Thank you so much, To'o and Pule, and all you guys from the east.' Studying the ticket, she added, 'The plane ticket is to Saua. Where's that?'

'Ah,' smiled Pule, 'his Lordship has been telling you that Lalolagi is the centre of the world. Well, Saua, in Manu'a, is where the world began. His Lordship's ancestral roots are also in Manu'a, but he has never even set foot there. So there is no excuse now. You two must come and visit.'

'Thank you very much, Manu'a and Tutuila,' Tuisamoa Solomona acknowledged all his relatives from American Samoa, 'but I'm a bit scared to visit Manu'a now, you know.'

'But why, honey?' Helen asked.

'Well, it's not like going to the Vaisigano resort, HR. Going to Manu'a as a Tuisamoa is a *malaga* — it's a lot more involved than an official visit by the Head of State of another country to Aotearoa, you know. We can't go there just by ourselves. We have to take a whole group of people with us, a *matai* or two, some untitled men, and some unmarried young women too. The *oso* will not be lamb chops, but fine mats and a lot of other stuff. It's just a bit more complicated.'

'Oh, I see,' she said quietly.

'Yes, but we'll certainly come to Manu'a and Tutuila,' he continued. 'We'll plan it properly and we'll let you know. Thank you again.'

'Lest you think Uncle Sam came unprepared,' chuckled Faigata, 'we also have something for the new couple.' Theresa handed Helen an envelope.

'Mona, it's another set of plane tickets!' she exclaimed, peering into the envelope. 'They're first-class tickets to LA! Oh, thank you very much, Theresa and Fai.'

'You're very welcome, Helen,' Theresa replied.

'We're flying out together next weekend,' Faigata explained, 'so you'll need to get organised as soon as you can. The rest of Uncle Sam's present will be given to you over there.'

'Well,' smiled Tuisamoa Solomona, 'that will be easy. It's only LA, the movie town, so we don't need to prepare as we would for a meeting with a Samoan village, like Saua in Manu'a. We'll be able to fly out next week, Uncle Fai, and thank you, Aunt Theresa, for the tickets.'

'Aren't you working next week, Tui?' asked Alofa.

'I'll tell you about that later, Mother.'

'What about Aleipata, guys?' Aiga asked her sons, Pita and Simi. 'Don't we have a gift for the newlyweds?'

Nodding, Pita handed an envelope to Simi who passed it to Helen. She smiled as she read the card inside.

'It's a three-day fishing trip on... *Queen Helen*? What's that?'

'That's the name of our new boat,' Pita explained. 'We've been wondering what to call her. It's the most beautiful boat we've ever had, thanks to Uncle Fai and Aunt Theresa, and now that you are the *Masiofo* of Tui, and such a beautiful *Masiofo*,' he smiled, 'I thought that we'd call her *Queen Helen*, or *Kuini Eleni* in Samoan. Sorry, guys,' he shrugged and laughed apologetically to his mother and Simi, 'but that's its name now.'

'That's really nice of you, Pita, and the rest of Aleipata. I think that deserves a kiss from the bride.' So saying, Helen gave Pita, Simi and Aiga each a kiss.

'That's not fair,' came a chorus from all the others.

'Oh, okay,' she smiled, 'I'll give everyone a kiss then.' She proceeded to give everyone in the room a kiss, except the groom.

'You forgot the most important person, Mrs Tui,' he chuckled.

'Remember, specials are always last,' she smiled, winking at her husband. 'That's why yours will come later, honey.'

'That's all right then. Thank you to the people of Aleipata. There is one problem, though — three days is not nearly long enough. We will have to renegotiate the terms and conditions of that gift, especially now that you've used my wife's name on your fishing boat, without my permission,' he chuckled.

'What about the big island, guys?' Fale asked her children.

'We have a small box here for the new couple,' smiled Papali'i as he handed Helen a gift-wrapped box, 'and we are also inviting them for a guided tour of ancient Savai'i and its famous rainforests.'

Unwrapping the box, Helen removed a leather case, which she unzipped to reveal a gold-edged Samoan Bible and hymn book. Both had leather covers with their names engraved in gold lettering.

'Thank you very much, Savai'i.' Helen passed the Bible and hymn book to her husband. 'This is very special.'

'It's our pleasure, Helen,' smiled Papali'i. 'It's just a small reminder to his Lordship that it was Sapapali'i where the first missionary landed in Samoa.'

'Mother always reminds me about that, but it was up there in those hills that the first human, the first Samoan, was created,' he chuckled, gesturing in the direction of Mount Lagi. Everyone laughed as Papali'i and Tuisamoa Solomona engaged in a spirited debate about whether Sapapali'i or Lalolagi held greater significance in Samoan history.

'Anyway,' Papali'i concluded, 'we thought that since you are now the priest and priestess of the family, you'd need the tools of the trade.'

'Thanks, brother,' Tuisamoa Solomona acknowledged, 'Savai'i has probably given us the most important gifts one can receive.'

'Is there a present from Apia, Sofi?' Alofa asked.

'Oh, sure there is,' smiled Sofia as she handed Onosa'i an envelope to give to Helen.

'It's a dinner for two at Sofia's Bistro, honey,' she said as she read the card inside. 'Thanks very much, Sofi and Ono.'

'A dinner?' Tuisamoa Solomona asked, his voice hinting at some confusion. 'We will also need to renegotiate the terms and conditions of Apia's present. It should read: endless dinners, not just one dinner.'

'I hope the Kiwis have something for the new couple,' Fiasili said as the laughter died down.

'We certainly do,' Brandon replied, 'and they'd better like it because, if they don't, then they'll get Mum instead.' He struggled forward with a fairly large frame wrapped in brown paper.

'Brandon loves picking on me at family gatherings,' Fiasili whispered to Alofa and Mrs Jones as everyone laughed at Brandon's remarks.

There was a note attached to the frame. Helen read it out aloud, 'Lest you forget'. Curiously, she slowly removed the wrapping from the frame. 'Oh, my!' she exclaimed, 'it's a photograph of our special place, Mona.' She showed everyone a large framed photograph of Albert Garden's flower-clock at Auckland University with the Old Arts building in the background. 'This will have to go in our room,' she smiled, winking at Tuisamoa Solomona.

'Wait a minute,' he said, sounding puzzled. Once he had everyone's attention, he continued in mock seriousness, 'I'm not sure I know that place.'

Helen pinched him. 'The Paramount Chief is lying to his family,' she chuckled. 'For your information, everyone, our love story began on that very bench near the flower-clock.'

Helmut then presented the newlyweds with a cheque for $20,000 in Samoan currency.

'Well,' smiled Lauti, 'I suppose it's now Lalolagi's turn, eh? Well, guys, what do we have?'

'It's coming,' called someone from the kitchen as a stream of people emerged carrying trays of hot *koko* and cakes.

'Well, ladies, Junior, Senior and Kaino,' Helen said to Tuisamoa Solomona's cousins and their wives, 'we cannot thank you enough for everything you've done for us since I set foot in Samoa, and especially during the wedding. So thank you very much.'

As everyone settled down to their late-night snack, Tuisamoa Solomona banged on the coffee table to get their attention.

'Please continue with your supper while you listen,' he began. 'I'd like to take this opportunity to thank Helen's family and my family for making our day such a memorable one. But we do have a couple of announcements, which I believe will be of interest to everyone. Faye wants to say something, so, in keeping with the spirit of the *feagaiga*, I'll let her go first.'

Faye smiled and looked uneasily around the room. 'Thanks, Tui, I just want to let everyone know that I'm not returning to New Zealand. I've decided to stay and look for a job here.'

Stunned silence followed her announcement.

'Faye has been dying to move to Samoa ever since Helen returned,' Fiasili whispered to Alofa and Mrs Jones.

'A very interesting decision, Faye,' said Tuisamoa Solomona. 'Many village people would find it rather bizarre though, but that's because they have a different perspective from yours. So, why, if you don't mind my asking?'

'Oh, many reasons, Tui,' she replied, 'but I guess the key one is that I'm sick and tired of people asking me where I'm from, when I was born and bred in New Zealand. I suppose coloured people can never really be fully accepted into white-dominated societies.'

'That's terrible, Faye,' Mrs Jones was shocked to hear of such intolerance in her own country.

'It's the media, I tell you,' Helen's father went on, 'because the journos are virtually all *pakehas* and they look for the sensational and the ridiculous. They're not interested in the many good Islanders; they only look for the few trouble-makers, and they use them as the yardstick to judge everyone else by.'

'You've made the right decision, Faye,' smiled Helen. 'This is the place to be to avoid all the racism and hypocrisy of New Zealand. Tui will get you a job. He just called the Director of Education and I was offered a teaching job at Samoa College straight away. Imagine that? So, there should be no problem.'

'That's right, Faye,' Tuisamoa Solomona assured her, adopting a pompous tone, 'I own Samoa's Public Service.' He chuckled as Helen pinched him.

'Anyway,' Faye said, 'since it's now certain that Helen is staying, it has made my decision easy.'

'Well, Faye,' Tuisamoa Solomona laughed, 'don't be so sure, because I can still ask for a deportation order if she can't carry 50 coconuts down the hill.' Everyone laughed as Helen pinched and nudged him. 'Sorry, Mrs Tuisamoa.' He bowed in an exaggerated fashion towards Helen before continuing in a more serious tone, 'It's a free world, Faye, and that's why it's important that we develop the village and our country, because you never know what might happen. A nation must always have a home, despite the likelihood of a blurring in racial and ethnic lines in the future. You'll have no problem finding work here. We're desperately short of teachers. You'll enjoy it here too; life is a party in Samoa. Now it's my turn to make an announcement. Well, it's a small announcement with huge implications. I have decided to resign from Treasury, and Helen will no longer be teaching at Samoa College. That is the long and short of it.'

No one spoke after Tuisamoa Solomona dropped his bombshell. Alofa was devastated. She had always wanted one of her children to teach at Samoa College, but she was equally proud that Helen was teaching at the government's top school. She had also hoped that Tuisamoa Solomona would one day be the Head of Treasury. All her dreams and aspirations appeared to have vanished before her eyes.

'It appears you two have been planning this for some time,' Helen's father remarked, in an attempt to break the silence.

'Helen and I have been talking about it since we decided to get married, Dad. So, yes, we have given it a lot of thought, and prayed about it, before arriving at our decision.'

'I'm sure you have great prospects at Treasury, so why have you decided to leave now, at virtually the beginning of a promising career?' asked Mr Jones.

'There's no question about the promising future I could have at Treasury, Dad, but for a number of reasons, I feel it is better that I leave.'

'Is there something wrong with the Treasury, Tui?' Helmut queried.

'The Treasury is fine, Uncle Helmut, and the people are fantastic. It's just that I was hoping that they could differentiate between life in the office and life outside the office. I guess that was a naive wish on my part. It's been very difficult for the staff to relate to me as they would to any other staff member. The reality is, I am Tuisamoa, a Paramount Chief, regardless of the context or circumstance, and they are very conscious of that. It has also been difficult for my boss to deal with the fact that he is the superior of a Paramount Chief. It has affected both his management style and his decision making. All these matters can be redressed if I quit.'

'It's certainly a noble decision, Tui, but Samoa could use your knowledge, skills and expertise in its Treasury Department,' said Mr Jones. 'So, what are you two going to do now?'

'Fishing should be good,' chuckled Alvin. 'Let me know if that's your plan, guys; I'll quit varsity and come and join you. Right, Dad?'

'Yeah, that would be fun,' added Jocelyn. 'I'll come too. I think living here would be cool.'

'You can do whatever you want... after university,' Mr Jones said firmly.

'Well,' Tuisamoa Solomona continued, 'there are a lot of options available. Professor Lewis tried to convince me to join the World Bank even before I finished my degree, but I guess that is now extremely remote. I could always take up politics. All I have to do is inform the village and district, and the job would be mine. But Plato reckons politics is not for decent people, even though Aristotle said you pay the price of being ruled by small-minded people if you stay out of it. But I think Plato was probably right. Another option is the position in the Council of Deputies that Dad held, but that is really for people who want to be seen and not heard. We feel that working to be a good Paramount Chief should be our first priority. We'd like to do something here in the village. Hopefully that could extend to the whole of Fagaloa, and perhaps the rest of the country. Ever since I saw Auckland from the air for the first time, I always dreamt of how wonderful Fagaloa would be if it were half as prosperous as Auckland.'

'It's always nice to dream big, Tui,' Helmut said approvingly.

'I agree, Uncle Helmut. Those who refuse to dream condemn themselves to a boring and miserable life. In any case, dreams are free… that is, until you want them to become a reality.'

'And you think you can achieve your dreams by quitting Treasury and with Helen quitting teaching?' asked Mr Jones.

'The wealth of nations, Dad, as so eloquently put by Adam Smith, is not the result of the work of governments, but the efforts of private individuals who enthusiastically do their best with what they have. I don't think the government could implement my dreams — politicians are interested only in their own agenda, which tends to be short-term and aimed only at personal gain and political longevity. That's why I've decided to quit. I want to see Samoa develop economically, socially and spiritually, but it has to start somewhere, sometime, and someone has to take responsibility for it. We've decided to do our part — this is where we'd like to start, and we want to do it now, our way.'

'Oh, you'll just be wasting your time, and perhaps our money, Tui,' advised Faigata. 'These people don't deserve your dreams. They're too proud and lazy. They won't appreciate anything you do for them. It's like casting pearls before swine.'

'Many have the same impression you do of those who choose to stay in villages, Uncle Fai,' Tuisamoa Solomona said earnestly, 'but I think it's only a veneer. When you really get to know them, and get underneath that cover, you'll find that they also want a decent standard of living, something that we tend to take for granted. Many have developed a dependent mentality, forever asking relatives overseas for just about everything they need. Some are developing the habit of asking me for money to pay for things like school fees, requests I find very difficult to deny because it's for the good of the children. That cycle needs to be broken, because a dependent life is a life full of despair and devoid of human dignity. I think we should encourage people to change.'

'I suppose you must've developed some plans already, then?' asked Helmut.

'Yes, we have made some plans, Uncle Helmut. And, Al and Jos, you might be surprised to hear that fishing is part of the development plan for Lalolagi. So, yes, if you still want to, you can certainly join us, but — '

Forever in Paradise

'Oh, cool!' exclaimed Jocelyn. 'Can I, Dad?'

'But… we will hire only expats with university degrees,' continued Tuisamoa Solomona.

'Man, you're almost as difficult as Dad, Tui,' complained Jocelyn, jokingly.

Everyone laughed. Even Alofa managed to smile. Mrs Jones whispered to Alofa and Fiasili that it was nice to see the young ones having fun talking about such serious issues. Meanwhile Kaino went around the room, refilling cups and mugs with hot *koko*.

'However,' smiled Tuisamoa Solomona, 'being my one and only sister-in-law, exemptions may be considered. But it will be good to finish your degree first, Jos. When do you start?'

'This year.'

'Well, we haven't even started yet. In three years' time, you should be finished if you work hard. By then, we should be up and running. You can spend your Christmas holidays here, getting used to what we are doing, and if you're still interested after varsity, then you can join us. The same with you, Al, although you must be close to finishing by now.'

'If I keep passing all my exams, I should finish my engineering degree in a couple of years,' he replied.

'What Tui is suggesting is a good idea, you two,' Mr Jones agreed. 'So what are your plans, Tui?'

'Well, the first thing we would like to do is move the village back to its original site.'

'Hey, that's a great idea, Tui,' said Pule enthusiastically. 'The old site is much more beautiful and spacious. But after 30 or so years here, it's going to be difficult to achieve. How do you plan to do it?'

'Well, Uncle Pule, I don't know yet. I hope God will give me an answer. I know it will be very costly for everyone. But we shall see.'

'We can help you with the cost of a new house, Tui,' offered Helmut. 'Just let us know when you decide to proceed. You can easily contact me through Fai and Theresa.'

'Thank you, Uncle Helmut. We'll let you know.'

'You can always use your power as Tuisamoa and order the village to move,' suggested To'oto'o.

'Wouldn't people object?' wondered Mr Jones.

'No one can question an order by a Tuisamoa,' replied Faigata.

Tuisamoa Solomona smiled, 'Samoa operates on the Aristotelian principle, Dad, that liberty and individualism are quite different things. To cultivate —'

'Ah!' Helen interrupted, 'that's a Greek idea. I told you, didn't I?'

'No, Mrs Tui,' he grinned, 'it's a Samoan idea popularised by a Greek.'

'I've been telling him, Mum, that Samoans and Polynesians must have originated from Greece because there are so many similarities, but he doesn't believe me.'

'No-o-o, Helen!' came a chorus from the Tuisamoa family amidst much laughter.

'Come on, guys,' she continued, 'what I say is true — you just need to look at the evidence.'

Again a chorus of 'no' resounded around the room.

'Didn't Tui tell you that the world began here in this village, Helen? Well, in the old village?' asked To'oto'o, smiling.

'To'o, he told me all sorts of things, including his own version, I believe, of human creation. And yes, he did tell me it began here, but I'm not convinced.'

'Anyway,' interjected Tuisamoa Solomona, 'we can always come back to that. Just let me finish the point that I was trying to make before someone rudely interrupted me. I was trying to say that Samoans believe, as Aristotle did, that to cultivate individualism in the name of liberty is inviting chaos. Samoa is a lot more orderly than places like the United States and elsewhere. Freedom is not going against the community or breaking away from the community, because people are not islands. Humans are spiritual, social beings who need one another. Freedom is knowing what role one can play in the community and making the effort to fulfil that role. And that includes introducing new ideas and being able to demonstrate their value to the community.'

'Don't you want to include some people from the village in the development of the plan?' asked Mr Jones.

'I've spent a long time living among them and talking to them, and I know what their aspirations are. We've developed a plan to meet those aspirations, given the resources of the village and whatever aid programs can offer. We won't use any family resources, including money. It's a village project. Everyone has to own it — it's the only way to accomplish anything at the village level in Samoa, at least in the beginning. Samoan villages are natural kibbutzim that operate a little like a moshav. We have to harness that collective spirit in a productive way for all. So the village will become like a modern kibbutz. And if, in the future, some feel they can do better on an individual basis, then we shall make room for that kind of enterprise too, so long as it serves the common good. We can't have a one-size-fits-all policy forever, but we can in the early stages when everyone is virtually at the same level. If we need funds, the village will have to borrow them.'

'So far so good, Tui,' chuckled Faigata nervously, a little concerned that he might be asked to make a sizeable contribution.

'Don't worry, Uncle Fai,' Tuisamoa Solomona reassured him, 'Uncle Sam, American Samoa, Aotearoa, Australia and Germany will be our last resort.'

'Oh, no!' Faigata teased.

'Anyway, the development plan has immediate, medium and long-term objectives. The immediate objective is to get some funding from aid agencies to finance projects that have the potential to earn money quickly. The land here is fertile but prone to soil erosion because of its hilly contours. So fishing is going to be the main income-earning activity, at least in the early stages. I've prepared a proposal that I plan to submit to aid agencies to fund and equip four fishing craft. I'm hoping that Pita and Simi will agree to run some training courses.'

'I didn't know we were part of your plans, Tui,' Pita interrupted.

'Sorry, I should have consulted both of you first, but now you know,' Tuisamoa Solomona smiled. 'You'll be paid; you won't be expected to work for nothing.'

'That's okay, Tui,' Pita assured him, 'I was just kidding. I'm sure we can offer our services free, provided your men don't annoy me.'

'You can bring some of the fish to Pago, and we can sell them for you,' suggested To'oto'o.

'Actually, that's part of the plan too, Uncle To'o. I was just coming to that, but I'm glad you could see where I was heading.'

'That will be our contribution,' offered Pule.

'So far,' Tuisamoa Solomona continued, 'that's the only contribution I have planned for American Samoa, but it's a very important one. Anyway, we will also be selling produce in Apia, initially at the fish market. Eventually, we plan to have a store in Apia. California, Aunt Theresa, will be considered some time in the future. Because of pollution considerations, we can export only frozen fish. We have no intention of major processing here.'

'Sounds very good, Tui,' said Mr Jones. 'We might be able to help too. Give us a yell if you need some financial help.'

'Thank you, Dad. I hope we don't have to resort to that, but if we do, it will be a loan arrangement. We have money in the bank we can lend to the village initially.'

'So you won't be doing any farming, Tui?' asked To'oto'o.

'Yes, we will,' he replied. 'Given the risk of soil erosion, crops will be limited to tree crops. We will grow fruit trees like mangoes, and cash crops like cocoa and *'ava*. Staple foods will be for village consumption only. We also plan to replant the forest with native hardwood trees. The rivers at the old site have slowed to a trickle because people have been clearing trees near riverbanks and catchment areas, so that will be a priority area for tree planting. We also propose to raise some livestock, mainly pigs and poultry because of their cultural value in Samoa.'

'You've certainly planned well, Tui.' Helen's mother was impressed by the comprehensiveness of their plan.

'We think we have, Mum,' he replied. 'Anyway, once these projects are well established, we then want to go into tourism, but in a small way. There is a beautiful cove just over the hill on the western peninsula of Old Lalolagi. We would like to build a small resort there, away from the village. Our people are skilled at producing first-class Samoan handicrafts, and we propose building a store there to sell such items. The idea is to mobilise everyone, including the *matais*, young and old, able and not so able. The *matais* may not like the idea at first, but it will be difficult for them not to get involved if I take a leading role.'

'I suppose they must enjoy just being waited on,' Mr Jones suggested.

'That's right, Dad, they do. They feel they have done their share of serving, and now it should be their turn to be served, which is the usual order of things in Samoa. But my intention is that they will take a leadership role in all this. Anyway, the cornerstone of our development plan is education, because all economies in the future will be driven by knowledge and new ideas. But it's not enough to just be knowledgeable; we must also be able to use knowledge productively. So it's important that our people are taught to think creatively. Adults will be taught skills by Samoan and overseas experts, and we have included that in our proposals. Helen and I will devote our time to educating the village children by assisting the teachers the government provides. Faye may like to consider that, once it's up and running and we've reached a level where students can sit for external examinations. I will be seeing the Director of Education, before we take up our American relatives' holiday offer, to discuss our plans for education here in Lalolagi, and eventually for the whole of Fagaloa.'

'And what is your plan for children's education?' Helen's father asked.

'Samoan children spend a lot of time doing too much housework, including cooking, cleaning and farming, and not enough on learning and having some fun,' he replied. 'So we plan to have children attending school for much of the day so they can learn, play and develop.'

'Excellent stuff, Mona,' Mrs Jones said approvingly. 'And if you need a babysitter, I'll be available.'

'Thank you, Mum,' he smiled, winking at Helen. 'We'll consider taking you up on that offer if the coconut tree bears fruit.' Ripples of laughter echoed around the living room. 'But yes, we are excited about the future here. We're very confident that, within three years, Lalolagi will be a prosperous village.'

Thirty Four

Relatives from overseas and from American Samoa started heading home within a week of the wedding. Only Faigata and Theresa remained, and they flew out a few days later together with the newlyweds, leaving for their honeymoon. Helen and Tuisamoa Solomona intended to stay at least a month in America, but they were in California only a week when Samoa was hit by a devastating cyclone, causing widespread damage. They immediately cut short their holiday and, after hurriedly organising shipments of relief supplies, returned home as soon as Samoa's international airport had reopened.

As their plane flew over the Samoan islands, they were shocked at the extent of the devastation. The islands looked like dead beasts picked clean of their flesh by vultures; rocks littered the forest floor of once densely covered mountains. Fields were parched and dry like a drought-stricken Australian outback. The once lush rainforests resembled Vietnam's jungles after being sprayed with chemicals during the Vietnam War. Without foliage, the trees stood like tall, twisted crosses in a gigantic graveyard. Many more lay on the ground, criss-crossing one another, fallen soldiers on a battlefield. It was a very sad sight. Helen could not control her tears. She leaned onto Tuisamoa Solomona's shoulder and sobbed. Holding her tightly, he worried about what state Lalolagi would be in.

The drive from the airport was unlike any they had experienced before. The fire-trees had lost not only their flaming blooms, but also their beautiful green leaves. There were plenty of dogs, pigs and chickens still scavenging by the roadside, but there were no cricket games to be seen now. Whole villages were reduced to piles of rubble. In Apia, crews of workmen tried to patch damaged roadways and buildings. Even the beautiful coastal drive was replaced by scenes of despair, with bare hills and naked or fallen trees replacing the lush green vegetation. The beautiful rows of palm trees that previously lined the shore now stood like giant fingers sticking out of the sand, their crowns hacked off by the force of the wind.

The drive after Falefa Falls was no different. The once-beautiful green hills were now scorched brown fields. The coastline of Fagaloa was still majestic with the sea washing over lava rocks, but Mount Lagi stood like a tired, worn-out peak in a desert. It still towered above everything else, but with its dense vegetation either burnt by salt-laden wind or ripped from its face by the ferocity of the wind, it looked vulnerable, as if conscious that its secrets had finally been uncovered. The turn-off into Lalolagi felt like a totally unfamiliar place. The village was completely exposed to view as the cover that the mighty chestnut forest once provided was gone, the trees defoliated, many uprooted.

Nothing, it appeared, had been spared. The sight of the village was depressing. It looked like an out-of-control

Forever in Paradise

bulldozer had raced through the whole place. Virtually every structure had been levelled to the ground. Only the Tuisamoas' *falepalagi* and the church still stood, but the scars of their battle with the cyclone were clearly visible. The windows of the church were all shattered and had been replaced temporarily by mats. Much of the corrugated-iron roof was gone, no one knew where. The front porch of the church was also gone; some said it had been dumped in Fagaloa Bay. What was left of the church did not look safe. The Tuisamoas' *falepalagi* hadn't fared any better. Windows were smashed and some of the roofing material destroyed. The whole structure was leaning — it had been propped up to provide shelter for the Tuisamoas and for Tenari and his family. The village women and children occupied the church after the men braced it with logs. The men had then erected makeshift huts for themselves at the rear of the village.

Tuisamoa Solomona called a meeting of the whole village, men and women alike, the evening they arrived back in Lalolagi. The meeting was held at the church after dinner. After a short prayer, led by Tenari, he rose to address his people.

'It is not in the best of circumstances that we meet tonight,' Tuisamoa Solomona struggled to control his emotions. 'First, I'd like to thank you all for your courage during the cyclone. Fortunately, no one was killed or seriously injured. As you know, we find ourselves in dire circumstances. Our village is decimated, and everything that we invested money and time on has disappeared. But the Bible says God speaks to us through wind, fire, earthquake and the other natural events that test our faith and resolve. There is no doubt that God wanted to communicate something to us. We cannot let the cyclone defeat us. We have to rebuild the village. This church will surely fall if we remove those props. So now I have a proposal that I'd like to put to you for your consideration.'

After Tuisamoa Solomona outlined his idea of moving the village back to its original site, Tula moved forward to comment on his proposal.

'Your Lordship Tui,' he began, 'you know this village will do whatever your Lordship suggests. We have been on this site for quite a long time now, and we have had so many problems over the years here. Yes, this site has made it easier for us to get to Apia, but it seems that it has also been a curse. We never had such problems in the old village. It is well protected from strong winds, but here we are exposed to the blustery easterly winds. I'd like to suggest to everyone that we support his Lordship's proposal. We have nothing left here.'

After Tula had spoken, all the other *matais* spoke in favour of the proposal. Tenari thanked and praised the village *matais* for their quick decision to support Tuisamoa's proposal and for their commitment to rebuilding the village on its old site.

'Thank you all for supporting my proposal,' Tuisamoa Solomona continued. 'But I also want to let you know that I'm no longer working for the government. I've decided to work for our village instead. I have prepared some development plans, which I would now like to discuss with you. These will be village projects, and will involve all of us, working together to raise the living standard of every individual in the village.' He went on to discuss details of the plan that he had already outlined to his family after the wedding.

'Well, your Lordship Tui,' Tula responded, 'your word, as always, is our command. The wind that destroyed Samoa and our village must have been sent by God to give us a new beginning. For never in the life of this village has a Tuisamoa taken such a lead. It never seemed proper before for a Tuisamoa to do so. But from your lofty position, you have decided to join us, to motivate us for the good of everyone. I suppose times have changed. I'd like to ask the whole village to support the proposal his Lordship has presented to us. Perhaps you could now discuss the details of how we should organise ourselves.'

The other *matais*, as expected, expressed their approval. The women whispered their support from the rear of the church. As the noise died down, Tuisamoa Solomona discussed further details of his development plans and how he wanted the village to participate.

'Again,' he said, 'I'd like to thank all of you for your support. This project will benefit all of us. Now, initially, our main task will be the rebuilding of our village. I have organised for food and building supplies from the United States, New Zealand and Australia, and there will be some from Germany as well. So food should not be a problem for a while, but we need to replant banana and breadfruit trees and some of our other staple crops right away. We will pool our lands together so that we can properly plan the planting of crops. Each family will provide one *taule'ale'a* for that task, while the rest of us will work on rebuilding the village. Now, the first thing we need to rebuild will be our church and the parsonage. I have been in touch with the government, and I was told that we would have builders coming from New Zealand and America for this purpose, but we need labour. I suggest that —'

'What about building materials for the church, your Lordship?' interrupted Maopo, who at 80 was one of the oldest *matais* in Lalolagi.

'I will check with aid agencies to see whether they can provide some.'

'We went to see them last Wednesday, your Lordship,' said Maopo, 'but they said they can't help us, because the church doesn't have any economic value.'

Tuisamoa Solomona smiled. 'I will have a chat with them next week, Opo. With these things, it's a matter of knowing how to get them to understand our point of view. I can easily demonstrate the economic contribution the church makes to a Samoan village in the long term, especially the education our own Reverend Tenari and Sekara provide. But leave that to me.'

'Can we build something like the old church?' asked Maopo. 'It felt holier than this chicken shed. This one feels more like a nightclub.'

Everyone laughed, wondering when Maopo had been inside a nightclub.

'If we have enough money, your Lordship Opo,' smiled Tuisamoa Solomona, 'your wish shall be granted. That type of church is very expensive to build nowadays because it was massive and, from what I have seen in old photographs, much more elaborate. As you are no doubt aware, we will all need to make some contributions, but I suggest that we base those contributions on capacity to pay, and not on the usual per-family basis. We should also receive donations from village members living overseas. I contacted many of them while I was in America, and they are already organising monetary assistance, as well as food supplies. With regard to our need for labour, I suggest one *taule'ale'a* per family, especially to help get us started.

'After the church and the parsonage, the next buildings will be the school and the teachers' residence. Helen and I plan to work with the teachers assigned by the government. We need to ensure that we get good teachers and that they stay a full five days each week, instead of four, as has been the case until now. We hope to educate our children here until they complete their secondary education. Children need the security that the family provides, and they need to be mature when they leave the village for further schooling. Faye, Fiasili's daughter, is staying, and she is trained to teach up to that level, and so are Helen and I.

'Now, aid agencies will have no problem providing us with building materials as well as funds, but we need to provide most of the labour. I have already checked with Treasury, and officials have advised me that aid money can be used for this purpose, and there will be some available for residential buildings as well. It seems like the only thing now unaccounted for is rebuilding the *faleteles*. As far as I can see, there is enough timber on the ground to build at least twelve *faleteles*, so that should not be a problem. We will all need to work together to get all the structures in place as soon as we can, so we can get some normality back into our lives. Are there any questions?'

'Sounds very good, Tui,' Tenari offered.

'What about tools and that sort of thing, Tui?' asked the leader of the *aumaga*.

'The village doesn't have any tools, but each family has tools of some sort, including the ever-reliable bush knives,' he responded. 'I suggest that we bring what we have. That way, we can pool our resources. We have a couple of chainsaws that the village can use to cut timber. Our family's truck can also be used where needed. Now, are there any more questions?'

'What about the women, your Lordship? Do you have tasks planned for us?' asked Sekara.

Tuisamoa Solomona smiled. 'Ah, the ladies. Well, they'll do whatever job they feel comfortable with. Mother told me not to order the women around. I have to comply with that, or I'll get myself into trouble.'

Everyone laughed loudly, especially the women.

'Are there any other questions? No? Okay then. May I suggest, Nari, that we have a short service at the old village site, before sunrise on Monday, to consecrate the land and to bless our new beginning?'

'Yes, of course, your Lordship,' replied Tenari. 'Did everyone hear that?' There was a resounding 'yes'. 'Okay then, on Monday before sunrise, we will meet at the old village site.'

'Thanks, Nari,' Tuisamoa Solomona concluded. 'After the service, we can begin to clear the site and start work. I will be going to Apia after that, with Nari, to see government officials, aid agencies and suppliers. On that note, I declare this meeting closed.'

Thirty Five

The whole of Lalolagi, adults and children alike, gathered near the beach at the old village site on Monday morning before sunrise. The young men lit a huge fire on the beach. As daylight was breaking, Tenari moved forward to speak. Everyone gathered together in complete silence. The only sound was from the waves breaking on the reef and lapping onto the shore a few metres away.

'Let us begin with a reading from God's holy word,' Tenari announced as he opened his Bible. Using a torch, he read from Psalm 127. 'Dearly beloved,' he continued, 'we are gathered here at the dawn of this new day and new week to forge a new beginning for our village. We have decided, as the prophet Nehemiah once did when he returned to rebuild the Walls of Jerusalem, to start anew by rebuilding on the old village site. The task before us is enormous and challenging, but it is also exciting and hope-restoring. However, unless the Lord builds the house, as the Psalmist says in our reading this morning, and in our case, our village, our labour shall be in vain. I was very moved when his Lordship Tui requested that we have this dawn service to bless this new beginning. It indicated to me that his Lordship clearly wants the Lord's help in this endeavour. In his short reign as head of this village, he has shown the wisdom and leadership that many communities are crying out for. I suppose much of this must be the result of his good partnership with his beautiful *Masiofo*, Helen. May the good Lord look kindly upon you both, your Lordship Tui and Helen, and may God bless the whole of Lalolagi. To conclude, may we always remember that unless the Lord builds our village, we shall labour in vain. Let us sing a hymn, then I will close this service with a prayer.'

After the service, Tuisamoa Solomona lit a bundle of dry coconut leaves. Holding up the burning leaves, he shouted, 'To a new beginning,' then used the burning leaves to start a fire under dry vegetation. The place burst into flame, smoke billowing into the air, as everyone retreated to the beach. A light breeze fanned the fire slowly inland.

After breakfast back at the destroyed village, Tuisamoa Solomona, Tenari, Helen and Sekara left for Apia. The rest of the village returned to the newly consecrated site where the fire had completely burnt off the dry vegetation to reveal the foundations of many structures in the old village. The *matais* organised the women and children to clean up the place, while the young men went up into the mountains to cut timber for use in building the *fales*.

The aid-seeking party returned around sunset. While in Apia, Tuisamoa Solomona and Helen collected the truck the Joneses had bought them as a wedding gift.

As darkness descended over Lalolagi, Tenari rang the bell for evening devotions, and the night-time routine in the village began once more. It sounded different this time, though, with everyone so enthusiastic about the project they had just begun together.

After dinner, Tuisamoa Solomona, Helen, Tenari, Sekara, Alofa, Faye and Tuisamoa Solomona's cousins and their wives sat around drinking *koko* and chatting about the outcome of the trip to Apia.

'So how was your trip, Nari?' asked Alofa.

Tenari smiled, 'I think it went extremely well, don't you, Tui?'

'Oh, yes, it was beyond my expectations. The different aid agencies appear to be coordinating relief measures very well. They will provide building materials for the school and for the teachers' houses, and some for the church, but not enough for the one Maopo, Tenari and I have in mind. But we should be able to provide the balance, eh Nari?'

'I think another hundred or so grand should provide whatever our hearts desire, Tui,' he smiled. 'At least, we have the cement and much of the timber we need. So it's the small items like wiring that we have to cover, as well as the pews and the stained glass.'

'That's right,' Tuisamoa Solomona confirmed. 'The aid agencies will also provide enough materials for thirteen houses, the same size as this one. That's a house per family including the parsonage. The houses, of course, will have no walls. It will be up to each family to put up the walls. There won't be enough funds, though, to build a house like this one or a parsonage like the one that was destroyed. But, like the church, we should be able to provide the balance, especially for the parsonage. They will also be sending builders. The government has organised heavy machinery to arrive tomorrow to start earthworks and to construct a roadway from the main road down to the old site, and to help with the whole construction program. There will be volunteers from abroad for some of the construction work. So we are pretty well set for a major construction, or should I say reconstruction, project?'

'That's fantastic,' said Alofa. 'We did a lot of cleaning today. The boys have been sawing timber all day, and sliding the logs down from the hills.'

Once Tenari and Sekara had excused themselves and gone to their room, Tuisamoa Solomona moved closer to his mother to convey further details of the day's outing.

'There was also some good news in my bank account today, Mother,' he smiled.

Alofa looked surprised. 'Why? Don't tell me the pledges from your fundraising drive have arrived already?'

'Yep, the Germans have deposited almost half a million dollars into my account. When we were in California, they learnt about the cyclone, then called Uncle Fai to ask if he was organising relief supplies. I was able to speak to Uncle Helmut and give him my account details. He said he would deposit some money into it, but I had no idea it would be that much. I think Uncle Fai was able to collect about US $100,000, and I'm still expecting pledges from the Kiwis and the Aussies to arrive. If we can get all that money, we should be able to build a house that's even bigger than this one. We have to, so that when guests visit, we can house everyone. We can give the material intended for us to help with the parsonage.'

'Hmm, you did very well, Tui.' Alofa was relieved that so much had been achieved in such a short time.

'Tui is becoming a very good global beggar, isn't he, Mum?' chuckled Helen.

'Well,' Tuisamoa Solomona added, 'one doesn't need to be a genius when fundraising in these kinds of circumstances. Mother, there's something else I want to mention, and I'd like to hear your opinion. Helen and I would like to build a private house on the western peninsula of Old Lalolagi.'

He had thought hard about Helen's request to have a private residence away from the village. While it was difficult for him to entertain the idea of living outside the village, he had come to realise that such a house was very important to her. He also saw the value of having some space for himself. Before returning from California, he had accepted Helen's idea and they had agreed that a spot close to the men's pool would be an ideal location.

Alofa was stunned by her son's suggestion but felt she had to accede to his wishes. 'Oh, I don't really know, Mona — no other Tui has ever done it before. I suppose it would be all right. But there's no road, and assuming we get the generator running again, it would be difficult to get power down there.'

'That's why I'm asking, Mother, because the machinery will be here tomorrow to start the earthworks and build a road to the village. I could ask them to continue the road further on to the peninsula. It's barely a kilometre and a half from the main road.'

'Do you have the money to build another house?'

'Yes, we do, Mother. Well, it's mostly Helen's money.'

'And who will live in the house in the village?'

'You and everyone else will live in the village, while Faye, Helen and I will live at the peninsula. Those guys in New Zealand, Pati and Andreana, Ao, Legi and Nathan, should all be returning at the end of the year. That's a lot of people, and your stepchildren might also want to join us here. Well, at least Owen, Mele and Ula. They all have to complete their studies and any practical requirements this year, although Ula will have to return for her internship. I will need a bit of space, and we'd like to be able to entertain friends when they visit without bothering the rest of the village. And I think not having to live together is good for a happy family too.'

'What about our evening devotions? You realise that, as a *matai*, you also become the family priest.'

'That's no problem, Mother,' he replied with a grin, 'I'll designate Junior as the priest in charge in my absence.'

Everyone laughed, but Tuisamoa Solomona's joke did not amuse his mother.

'Yes,' she responded, rather sarcastically, 'it's Junior this, and Junior that —'

'I was just kidding, Mother,' he tried to reassure her.

'Well,' Alofa replied sternly, 'you have to start learning to be serious, not just in public, but at home as well, at least some of the time.'

'What I have in mind, Mother,' he went on, 'is that the new house in the village will be the official residence of the Tuisamoa, and the new house on the peninsula will be the private residence. You know? Like a Head of State. We all meet in the village as a family for evening devotions and dinner, and then Faye, Helen and I will retire to the peninsula.'

Her concern assuaged, Alofa smiled. 'Of course, you can do whatever you like, Tui. There's a nice pool over there too.'

'That's one of the main reasons for selecting that spot. We'll build the house on the ridge above the pool. We should be able to use solar and maybe wind power, so hopefully we won't need power from the village generator. The wind blows non-stop out there.'

'But you'll need water too,' Alofa reminded him.

'We'll have to investigate getting connected to the water source that the aid agencies plan to build,' he replied.

'In that case, I suppose it should be okay,' his mother responded.

Worn out by all the activities that day, she excused herself and went off to bed. Tuisamoa Solomona and the others continued to discuss the building projects late into the night. There was laughter and much excitement as they tried to imagine how the new village would look when completed, and as they discussed the expected prosperity that would follow if their projects succeeded.

Thirty Six

Earthmoving and road-building machinery and trucks arrived early the next day. Work on a road linking the old village site to the main road began immediately. It was just over a kilometre long and, by day's end, trucks carrying supplies were able to negotiate the still-rough route.

The following day, builders and labourers from overseas, provided through aid programs, some of them military personnel, arrived, and the massive construction work began. They initially worked on village structures approved by the government: the school, the teachers' living quarters, houses for the families, the parsonage, the Tuisamoas' *falepalagi*, a water reservoir and reticulation system, toilets, landscaping, and other work as needed. A contractor specialising in old-style churches also arrived with his workers to start building the village church. The people of Lalolagi were specialists in building *faleteles* and *faleafolaus*, and they concentrated on building guest *fales* and the Tuisamoa's *faleafolau*. Virtually every able-bodied person was working, in construction, transportation, cooking, or in the preparation of building materials for the *fales*. Six men were assigned to replant trees, including banana trees and other staple commodities. The start of the new school year was delayed until classrooms were available and residences for the teachers were completed. School students were quick to offer whatever assistance they could. A few women stayed behind in the destroyed village to look after babies, the younger children and the elderly while everyone else assisted at the new site.

Many buildings and structures went up almost overnight. The sound of trucks, saws, drills, falling timber, hammering, and other construction noises was constant throughout daylight hours. Everyone worked almost non-stop from before sunrise until an hour or so before evening devotions. The site looked like a United Nations training camp for peace-keeping forces. About a hundred foreign service personnel, each wearing their country's military uniform, lived in tents along the beach. The dwellings approved by the government went up quickly, due to their simple design. The first one was completed in only one week, and all the houses, eleven in all, were built in less than a month. The church, the school, the teachers' houses, the *fales* and the Tuisamoas' *falepalagi* took much longer because of their size and complex designs. Except for the pastor and his family and the Tuisamoas, the people of Lalolagi moved into their new residences as soon as they were completed.

The road to the village was slowly being improved. When it was completed a month later, Tuisamoa Solomona asked the roadbuilders to extend a road along the ridge to the tip of the peninsula where they had decided to build their home. It was a much easier road to construct because it sloped gently all the way, without a lot of rock or shale to be excavated. It was completed in less than three weeks, just before shipments of prefabricated building materials for the house arrived from New Zealand, all organised by Helen's father. Work on the private residence began at once. Tuisamoa Solomona also took the opportunity to improve the road from Falefa Falls to the village, which he now realised would be needed as the village embarked on its long-term economic development program.

As soon as teachers' residences were completed, Tuisamoa Solomona decided to start the school year using some of the village houses as classrooms. Education in Lalolagi was set to take a major step forward. The secondary school program that Tuisamoa Solomona requested was approved, and he began implementing it immediately. The secondary school initially had twelve students, with Faye, Helen and Tuisamoa Solomona, all paid by the government, as the only teachers. The principal of the primary school retained overall administration of both schools. The daily presence of Tuisamoa Solomona at the school boosted confidence and morale of both staff and students.

The twelve-classroom school was completed eight months after construction began, and the school was able to move into its new facilities at the start of the final term for the year. The parsonage was completed a few weeks after the school opened, followed by the Tuisamoas' *falepalagi* another month later. Both the water system and generator were already operating, and Lalolagi's rebuilding program on its original site was approaching completion. Only the church, the *faleteles* and the Tuisamoa's *faleafolau* were not yet completed, as well as the landscaping of the village. These final items were all expected to be completed in time for the inauguration of the new village, including the church, on the first anniversary of the cyclone.

The private residence on the peninsula was completed about the same time as the family's *falepalagi* in the village. It was an impressive mansion with seven bedrooms, a typically large Samoan-type living room, family room, games room and a library. The house was oriented east to west, built along the ridge with the front facing north. A garage, large enough for four cars, was erected behind the house. Many of the trees on the site were left standing, and landscaping was designed to incorporate the natural environment. Tall trees provided shade around the house, and the constant sea breeze kept the place cool. A garden of tropical plants brightened the outside of the house. On the eastern side of the house, a spacious paved courtyard overlooked the pool, some 30 metres below. A steel fence was installed to prevent anyone from falling over the edge, and benches, ideal for relaxation and soaking up the beautiful scenery of Fagaloa's coastline and majestic Mount Lagi, were erected along the fenceline. Cement steps provided access to the pool below. Electricity was generated by solar and wind power, and the house was connected to the village's water supply.

When all the fittings were completed and the utilities connected, Tuisamoa Solomona, Helen and Faye moved into their new home. A few weeks later Helen's parents timed a visit from New Zealand to coincide with the expected birth of their first grandchild, and to attend the inauguration of the village and the church.

'The place looks and feels so different, Tui,' Helen's father said as they drove towards the house on the peninsula.

'Yes, Dad, it does, doesn't it? The lights you can see down there are from the village and the bay is just over that hill. It's a very different place from the one you saw when you were here for our wedding. I'll take you for a tour of the village tomorrow.'

They arrived at the house a couple of minutes later. 'Wow!' exclaimed Jocelyn. 'This is cool, Mum. Come and have a look at it.'

'It's certainly a lovely house, Tui,' smiled Mrs Jones.

'Well, we have to thank Helen's grandpa for his generosity, Dad for organising the materials and shipping them over here, the architect for a very attractive tropical design, and the builders for their attention to detail.'

'Which room is mine, Helen?' Alvin asked, as he carried his travel bag into the living room. 'I'd like one with a view.'

'All the bedrooms have excellent views, Al,' laughed Helen. 'This isn't like our house in Whangaparoa where the views are limited to the front rooms. Your room is at the end of the hallway.'

Helen showed Jocelyn and her parents to their rooms, then joined Faye in the kitchen to organise a quick dinner of pasta. After dinner, they talked late into the night until exhaustion forced them all to bed.

Next morning, Helen and Tuisamoa Solomona took the Joneses on a tour of the new village. They stopped at a lookout at the western end of the village.

'It looks absolutely magnificent, Tui,' commented Mr Jones as he surveyed the extent of work completed in the village. 'How did you manage all that construction work in such a short time?'

'It *is* beautiful, isn't it? It's a bit hard to believe the total irony of it all.'

'What do you mean, Tui?' asked Mrs Jones.

'Well, this is virtually what I had dreamed of. I had hoped one day to stand here and see the shining corrugated-iron roofs, not just of the parsonage and our family's house, but of the whole village. I wanted people to find it difficult to identify the Tuisamoas' residence from up here. I was looking at no less than ten years, but realistically up to fifteen years, of hard work on village projects to earn enough money to achieve this. You may recall the uncertainty I was facing of how to move the village back here.'

'Yes, I do remember that.'

'Well,' he continued, 'I didn't have to do a thing. The irony of it all is that the cyclone literally obliterated the former village. According to official sources, ours was the worst-affected village in the whole country. It was because of that same cyclone that we have all this. The building materials, the equipment, the engineers, the builders and virtually everything else have all been provided by the government and by the international community, except for our family's house and some materials for the church and the parsonage and the *fales*. The roofing materials and cement for the village's *faleteles* and the *faleo'os* were provided by village members living overseas, and so were some of the materials we used for the church and the parsonage. We also had something like an international military camp set up here after the cyclone — that was the main reason for everything being completed in such a short time. The Lord certainly works in mysterious ways,' he smiled. 'Now, all we have to do is concentrate on our village projects, most of which have already started.'

Lalolagi at its original site, with a little modification to the original layout by Tuisamoa Solomona, was indeed an impressive sight from the lookout. Unlike the village destroyed by the cyclone, which faced the sea, the new village faced north, oriented along an east–west axis. All the buildings were constructed along semi-circular arcs patterned on the horseshoe shape of the mountains surrounding the village. The first row of structures comprised the village's *faleteles*, with the church at the centre, the Tuisamoa's *faleafolau* next door, the school at one end, and a cricket pitch at the other end. The next row of structures included the dwellings built by aid agencies and the government, the parsonage behind the church, and the Tuisamoas' *falepalagi* next to the parsonage. Then there was a row of *faleo'os*, showers and toilets, and finally the cooking *fales* to the rear. Directly opposite the church, and not far from the beach, was the Tuisamoas' *faletele*. It was the only structure on the beach side of the village, just as in the destroyed village. The *malae*, about the size of two football fields, was grass-covered, unlike in the destroyed village where it was bare earth and sand. Lalolagi was built in a perfect semicircle with the church, the parsonage and the Tuisamoas' *faletele* as the centrepiece.

'Did you say that the place was parched brown after the cyclone?' asked Alvin.

'Yes, it was, Al,' Helen replied. 'You could see the rocks and bare soil on the mountains. Mount Lagi was the worst. The whole place looked as if it had been defoliated with herbicide. But look, it's all so beautiful and green again now, as if nothing happened. Even Mount Lagi is almost restored to its former beauty. Only the coconut trees have not recovered yet.'

From the lookout they drove down into the village. The Joneses met Alofa, Tuisamoa Solomona's siblings and other family members who had returned a week earlier, their university studies finished for the year. Albert and Alan had just been successfully admitted to the New Zealand Bar. Only Apaula would be returning to New Zealand the following year to complete her medical internship.

'This is a beautiful house, Alofa,' commented Mrs Jones as she looked around the enormous living room.

'It's all Tui's idea,' smiled Alofa. 'With just the three boys and their wives and children, I felt lost in the place until the others arrived from New Zealand last week.'

'Well,' said Tuisamoa Solomona, 'it's a family house. Everyone living overseas provided funds, and I made sure the money was put towards the house. In the tropics, if you build a house with rooms and walls, you need a wide verandah where you can relax, and which provides airflow through the whole house. That's why we have floor-to-ceiling louvres in all rooms.' He proudly led his in-laws on a tour of the ten-bedroom *falepalagi*.

'How are you feeling, Helen?' asked Apaula, 'Any sign of the baby coming yet?'

'Oh, I don't really know what to look for, Ula,' smiled Helen.

'It won't be long now,' Apaula advised.

'Come on, HR,' Tuisamoa Solomona called after her, 'let's get going.'

'Where are you off to?' his mother asked.

'We're just taking these guys for a tour of the village before it gets too hot,' he replied.

Tuisamoa Solomona and Helen took Helen's parents to the new church. Not yet completed, there were still a lot of people working on the site, busily adding the finishing touches.

'This is going to be a very impressive church, Tui,' said Mr Jones as Helen took her mother inside.

'Yes, it is, Dad,' Tuisamoa Solomona replied. 'It's built on the foundations of the original church, although this one is just a bit bigger.'

'What's the capacity of the church?'

'It should seat about 300 in comfort, which is actually more than the population of our village.'

'Why do you need a church bigger than the village's population?'

Tuisamoa Solomona smiled. 'In Samoa, when you prepare dinner, you don't cook just for your own family; you cook more in case you have unexpected visitors. We've decided to apply the same principle to the church.'

'It's very beautiful inside, Tui,' commented Mrs Jones, 'and the stained glass is fabulous.'

'Let's hope it will have a positive influence on the behaviour of the village,' he smiled as he stepped off the concrete path outside the church and set off across the village *malae*.

Helen and her parents followed him to the Tuisamoas' *faletele*, not far away. Workmen were still completing the interior of the structure, with some starting to put wooden shingles on the roof. Tuisamoa Solomona and his entourage stood outside and looked at the immense structure.

'It's certainly very impressive, Tui,' Mr Jones said. 'I've always been impressed by the skills of the people who build these *fales*.'

'Yes, it is a big *faletele*. Like just about everything else that has been built so far, this has been erected on its original foundations. But we'll be using cement for the floor this time, instead of pebbles. It's the only *faletele* being built in the traditional way without any nails, except for the floor and roofing materials, and with all the internal carvings. That's why it has taken longer to finish, although one year is still fairly quick, but then we've had lots of volunteer labour. All the other *faleteles* have simple internal structures. But then this is, fundamentally, a *faletele* for the whole village, so we want to make sure it looks as traditional as possible.'

They walked down to the beach, about 20 metres away. Standing at the high-tide mark, Helen's parents surveyed the beautiful shoreline.

'Can you see our house at the peninsula from here, Mum?' Helen helped her mother locate the house near the tip of the peninsula.

'Oh, yes, I see it. You've picked a lovely spot, haven't you? Look out there. What's that big rock out to sea, Tui?' she asked.

'Well, that solitary rock is leading a very lonely existence out there,' he chuckled.

'There's a local legend about that rock, Mum, but Mona won't tell me what it is,' Helen said.

He smiled, 'Because it will only add fuel to her theory about the origin of Samoans and Polynesians.'

'Come on, honey,' Helen coaxed, 'there are more of us here now to enjoy your story. Won't you tell us?'

Tuisamoa Solomona laughed, 'Well, that rock was supposed to be a woman called Fa'avauvau. The story is similar to the Greek legend of Niobe, and that's why I didn't want Helen to hear it.'

'Really?' smiled Mrs Jones, winking at Helen.

'Yes,' he continued. 'The stories have similar elements. Fa'avauvau was chasing a whale that had swallowed her son while the boy was swimming near the shore. She realised she wouldn't catch the whale, so she stood and cried. As she did, she turned into a rock. Her tears formed a stream that sprang from underneath the rock, which killed the reef and corals, forming a passage in the reef that boats use to enter the open sea. But she didn't become a mountain like Vaea and Niobe, as in the Greek legend.'

Helen smiled, 'See, Mum, and he wouldn't believe me that Polynesians could have come from the Middle East and Asia Minor.'

'That's very interesting,' Mrs Jones said. 'It's certainly very similar to the legend of Niobe but, as you said, Tui, Fa'avauvau didn't turn into a mountain.'

'Meaning,' he looked teasingly at Helen, 'it's not the same, Mrs Tuisamoa.'

Their tour continued in the direction of the school at the other end of the village.

'This looks like a big school, Tui,' Helen's father commented as they strolled into the school compound.

'Yes, it is. We took the opportunity of building it bigger than we needed, in anticipation of all the children of Fagaloa coming here instead of going to Apia, assuming that our secondary program succeeds. I'm quietly confident that we will succeed. There are too many university-educated people in the family who have now returned, and who are willing to help, for the program to fail.'

Together they started to head towards the teachers' living quarters, which nestled below a rejuvenated rainforest at the foot of the hill behind the school. They had gone only a short way when Helen let out a yelp.

'What is it, Helen?' her mother asked in concern.

'Oh, my God!' moaned Helen. 'My back hurts. I think my contractions are starting.'

Shocked, the group quickly rushed Helen back to the Tuisamoas' *falepalagi*. Excitement and mild panic followed. The hospital was too far away, and it was obvious that the birth was imminent. Alofa quickly curtained off one end of the living room, while Apaula prepared some of the equipment she would need, equipment she had brought with her in case of emergencies. Alofa called Albert to fetch the village's traditional midwife.

'Ula should be able to deliver the baby, Mother, unless there are complications,' Tuisamoa Solomona said, as he helped Helen onto a makeshift bed. 'I could even do it myself, if necessary,' he smiled, winking at Helen in an attempt to cheer her up.

'Okay then, all men out. The three of us will stay to assist Helen,' Alofa ordered, as she shepherded her son and Mr Jones out of the curtained area.

Tuisamoa Solomona rushed home to fetch some of the baby things that Helen had packed in readiness for the birth. When he returned, he heard a baby's cry coming from inside.

'Gee, that was quick, Mrs Tui,' he called out as he walked into the living room.

'It's a girl, Tui,' smiled Mr Jones. 'She was born not long after you left. She certainly didn't want to muck around.'

'Well,' he murmured thoughtfully, 'that means Helen and the Jones family will name the baby. I suppose you would like a Welsh name, eh Dad?'

'Is that a Samoan tradition?'

'Oh, no. It was an agreement Helen and I made between us — if the baby was a girl, she would name the child, and the right would be mine if the baby was a boy. The one who doesn't have naming rights still has a veto, though.'

'In that case, yes, it would be nice to have a Welsh name. But let's see whether Helen already has a name in mind.'

As the men chatted in the living room, Faye, Fetuao, Andreana and Jocelyn busied themselves cleaning and tidying the house, while Alofa and Helen's mother helped Apaula wash and dress the baby and tend to the new mother. When Helen was finally breastfeeding the baby, Alofa beckoned Tuisamoa Solomona to go in and be with his wife and baby.

'Hello, honey,' she smiled as he tiptoed in. 'Come and look at her,' she said proudly, as she gently brushed back some hair from the baby's forehead.

Tuisamoa Solomona sat down at his wife's side, gently kissed her and stroked her back. His smile stretched from ear to ear. He couldn't quite believe this little bundle was really theirs.

'This is so exciting, HR,' he whispered. 'I really can't describe how I feel, but it's amazingly uplifting.'

Helen smiled. 'The feeling is exactly what I expected: happy, fulfilled, joyful — everything one could expect in paradise, I suppose.'

'You two look lovely together,' he marvelled. 'So have you decided on a name for her yet?'

'I think I like Anwen Anthea. It's a Welsh–Greek name that aptly portrays her heritage on my side. Did you remember our agreement?'

'Of course,' he smiled, 'but I also remember I have a veto... but I think I like Anwen Anthea too.'

'So what needs to happen now, honey?'

'Well, we can't go back to the peninsula today. Everyone in the village, and Tenari and Sekara, will be here tonight for the official village visitation, to bless and welcome little Anwen Anthea. We'll need to stay here, maybe for a couple of days. Faye and your family can still stay at our place though.'

Anwen Anthea fell asleep after her feed. Helen carefully put her down on the bed beside her while Tuisamoa Solomona lifted the curtain so everyone could take a peek at the baby. He could not wipe the smile from his face. Helen looked at Anwen lying peacefully by her side, oblivious to the attention she was receiving from her parents' families. She felt exhausted and sore from the delivery, but it could not erase the ecstatic feeling of giving birth to her first child. 'This really is paradise,' she thought to herself, as she gently lay back and fanned herself.

Thirty Seven

The new village, albeit at its old site, and the new church were inaugurated, as scheduled, on the first anniversary of the cyclone. There was still work to be done on both the church and the Tuisamoas' *faletele*, but it was minor and would soon be completed. Representatives of aid agencies and government officials were special guests at the celebrations. Also present were village members who were home for the Christmas holidays, as well as relatives from throughout the two Samoas. It was the first major event in the 'new' Lalolagi, and the village was filled to capacity.

The inauguration ceremony began in the morning with a church service, followed by a tour of the village and inspection of all completed facilities, then a ceremonial feast at the new parsonage. During the feast, there was a presentation of *sua*, traditional gifts and fine mats to aid agencies, government officials and *matais* who were guests of the village.

Although the new village was the featured attraction, the focus of attention for many guests was the youngest member of the Tuisamoa family, who was now just over one month old. Even representatives from aid agencies and government officials could not resist having a peek at baby Anwen during the gift presentation, as she lay peacefully in her bassinette at the feet of her proud parents. When Agalelei picked her up and planted a kiss on her cheek, it started what seemed like a ritual involving newborns in an all-women's church. The child was passed around among the women, with each woman planting a kiss on her soft rosy cheeks, occasionally unsettling her. Everyone laughed and pointed at her each time she let out a startled whimper.

The day after the inauguration, a village meeting was called by the *pulenu'u* at Tula's *faletele*, instead of the Tuisamoas' yet-to-be-completed *faletele*. After the usual *'ava* ceremony, there was a final collection of gifts of money received from guests the previous day. The money would be used to pay back all loans the village had taken out to purchase extra materials for the church and the parsonage. Before the meeting dispersed, Tuisamoa Solomona addressed his people.

'Chiefs and orators of Lalolagi, I want to take this opportunity to thank all of you for your cooperation and hard work. This time last year, we were literally blown from the surface of the earth. We didn't point fingers and ask whose sin it was that brought the wrath of God to our village, given that we were the most severely affected in the whole country. Instead, we trusted His wisdom and carried on. Today, we stand witness to what God can achieve. Now that the task of rebuilding our village is almost complete, from here on we shall focus our attention on our development projects, which are now underway and starting to provide for our needs. More important for our future, however, is our school. This year will be the second year of our secondary program. We hope we will have our first batch of students sitting for the School Certificate

Forever in Paradise

examination next year. If we are successful, that is, if enough students pass and qualify for the Pacific Higher School Certificate examination, then the government will make more resources available and all students in Fagaloa will begin attending our school. So we need your full cooperation, especially those with children who will be sitting for the School Certificate next year. The preparation must start now, not next year. May God bless us from this day forth.'

The development projects did extremely well in the second year, with fishing, poultry, a piggery and taro crops bringing in increased revenue for the village. Fishing was particularly successful, earning large sums in US currency from American Samoa. The increase in revenue allowed wages to be paid in cash, with a surplus remaining in the bank. The commercial tree crops and *'ava* plants were also growing well, with some trees close to bearing fruit. Skills training in fishing, crop and animal husbandry, administration and office management were conducted throughout that year. The secondary school program also progressed well. There were still only three teachers — Tuisamoa Solomona, Faye and Helen — who also participated in other village projects in their spare time.

It was also an exciting year for the Tuisamoas. Their second child, a son, whom they named Tavita, was born not long after Christmas, a few months after Anwen's first birthday. The Joneses again timed a visit to Samoa to coincide with the birth. Apaula, who delivered Tavita at home on the peninsula, had fortunately returned home during a break from her internship. Mrs Jones, as she did when Anwen was born, stayed for three months after the birth to help look after Tavita. As before, Alofa took over when Helen's mother returned to New

Zealand, so that Helen could continue teaching and attending to her other commitments, including the Women's Committee and the church choir. Helen's grasp of the Samoan language was now good enough for everyday conversation, and together with her husband she directed the choir, introducing new music, and often playing her oboe.

The third year of Lalolagi's development program was, according to Tuisamoa Solomona, critical, particularly for its education program. It was the first time that students at the school would sit for the Samoa School Certificate examinations. To ensure that those preparing for external examinations would spend as much time as possible on their school work, a dormitory housing 50 students was built next to the teachers' residences. All twelve students sitting for the School Certificate that year lived in the dormitory.

Alvin had successfully completed his engineering degree and decided to stay and participate in some of the village projects. His arrival in the village provided a much-needed boost to the teaching staff. He shared the teaching of Mathematics and Science with Tuisamoa Solomona. Helen continued to teach English, while Faye shared the teaching of Economics with Tuisamoa Solomona and also taught Geography. They were the only subjects offered in the secondary program due to a lack of facilities and staff, with all students studying the same subjects. Other members of the Tuisamoa family provided tutorials when they were home for weekends from their public service employment.

The revenue-earning projects continued to make excellent progress, and Tuisamoa Solomona finally registered the whole program as a business enterprise, owned by the village.

The Inland Revenue Department had been trying to get him to register it as such, but he simply told them that he would do so when he felt the time was right.

The success of the projects prompted Tuisamoa Solomona to consider establishing the store and office in Apia, as proposed in the original plan. Moreover, the higher level of village income enabled him to persuade the church elders, who were also the village *matais*, to set aside 10 per cent in order to run the church and all church-related activities, including an allowance to supplement the pastor's income. This freed the village from extra contributions, apart from a fortnightly tithe for the pastor and his family's upkeep. Tenari's wife, Sekara, was also paid a wage for her work both at the church and in the village. In addition, all members of the village of working age unable to work due to physical or other disabilities were put on the payroll, with Tuisamoa Solomona arguing that their role still contributed to the good of the village. The number of people in that category was quite small, as only the very elderly and one person who was severely handicapped could not play an active role in the work of the village.

During the Christmas holidays, the Joneses returned to Lalolagi for their holidays after Jocelyn completed her degree in accounting. Apaula also returned, having completed her training as a gynaecologist. Tuisamoa Solomona and Helen held a party at their house on the peninsula on Christmas Eve to celebrate Anwen's second birthday and Tavita's forthcoming first birthday, as well as the success of Apaula and Jocelyn in their studies. It was largely a family affair, with the only friends invited being Fili Fa'aluma, Tenari and Sekara.

'How do you think our students fared in the School Certificate exams, Tui?' asked Tenari.

'I'm fairly confident they did well, Nari,' he replied as he bounced Anwen on his knee. 'I think we should get at least one full pass. I'll be happy if 50 per cent of our students qualify to sit the Pacific Higher School Certificate next year.'

Tavita, who was already walking and overly energetic for his age, broke away from Alofa's grasp and scampered across the room, bumping into his mother.

'Vita!' grimaced Helen as she tried to grab hold of him. But he was too quick for her and toddled back to Alofa.

'He takes after his father, doesn't he?' laughed Fili. 'He loves a bit of rough and tumble.'

'Oh, I don't know, Fili,' confessed Helen with a grin. 'He won't sit still for more than a minute. He doesn't want to be carried, and he just loves jumping onto people — and I seem to be his favourite target.'

By now Tavita had made his way over to Alvin who was sitting at the back of the living room. Unable to stay still for long, he broke free of Alvin's grasp and ran from one person to another, keeping everyone amused with his antics. Meanwhile, Anwen sat quietly on her father's lap.

'Dinner's ready, everyone,' Fetuao announced. 'We'll start with the holy ones, the elderly, and they'll be followed by the beautiful ones.'

'Ah!' Dr Fa'aluma laughed, 'in that case, I should be in the first batch — I don't really qualify for the last group.'

'We can all eat at the same time,' suggested Tuisamoa Solomona. 'The others can get their food and eat in the living room. Nari, Sekara, Mum and Dad, Mother, Fili and Faye, all of you come and eat at the table with Helen and me.'

Before starting their meal, they gathered around the dinner table and bowed their heads as Tenari blessed the food.

Thirty Eight

The fourth year of Lalolagi's development began with the kind of news that Tuisamoa Solomona had been praying for. Of the twelve students who sat the School Certificate examinations, nine qualified to study for the Pacific Higher School Certificate. Now he could approach the Department of Education for more teachers and resources.

He successfully negotiated an arrangement whereby Lalolagi would recruit its own teachers. The department would pay their regular salaries, and Lalolagi would provide an additional allowance to each one. Out-of-town teachers were offered free food and housing, and were invited to participate in village activities in their spare time. With such inducements, Lalolagi attracted some of the best teachers in the country. A young US Peace Corps volunteer, Karl Dawkins, arrived in the village to teach Science and Biology. With the quality of the teaching staff now greatly improved, Tuisamoa Solomona withdrew from teaching, limiting his involvement to being the Chairman of the Education Committee.

The new school year started well. However, by late February, some parents were alarmed to learn that Karl

Dawkins was teaching their children that humans had evolved from monkeys. Tenari was unhappy too, but he and Tuisamoa Solomona determined that commonsense should prevail. They agreed on a compromise, and called a parents' meeting so that Tuisamoa Solomona could address their concerns.

The meeting was held at the parsonage one Friday evening after dinner. Karl had not been invited to attend. Tuisamoa Solomona hoped to avert any potential problems without involving him.

'I'd like to thank everyone for coming tonight,' he addressed the worried parents. 'We are all tired, and, like many of you, I would rather be at home right now. However, we have a very important matter to discuss. I realise you're all upset about Karl teaching something that is totally inimical to your beliefs and Christian values. Let me assure you that it is not his fault. The material is in the syllabus, so it must be taught, or our children will find it difficult to pass their exams. What Karl is teaching is simply the scientific explanation of how human beings may have been created. Now, to resolve this issue, Nari and I have decided that we will also offer religious studies in the school syllabus, in which the biblical explanation of creation will be taught. I plan to discuss this with Karl after this meeting concludes. I also feel that, perhaps, we should have more parent meetings where we can discuss ideas and issues. Nari can talk about the history of the church and other church-related subjects. I can talk about economics and science, or any other topic of interest, including romance, if you like,' he chuckled. The men shouted their approval amidst great mirth. Some of the women made light-hearted comments to each other that it was all most men thought about. 'Seriously, we can always do with a little more understanding and knowledge,' he concluded.

As usual, no one asked any questions or objected to the resolution of the issue offered by Tuisamoa Solomona and Tenari.

Afterwards, Tuisamoa Solomona went to see Karl in his quarters.

'Please have a seat, Doc.' The enthusiastic young teacher had taken to calling him 'Doc' as a mark of respect and affection, a name Tuisamoa Solomona quite liked.

Karl was a little nervous. While the two of them had often enjoyed stimulating conversation together, Karl realised that Tuisamoa Solomona would not be calling on him at this time of night unless there was something wrong.

'Would you like a cup of coffee, Doc?'

'That would be nice, thank you, Karl,' he replied. 'White and no sugar, please.'

As Karl disappeared into the kitchen, Tuisamoa Solomona looked around the sparse living room with its cane furniture and woven mats — all supplied by the village.

'So, are you settling in okay, Karl?'

'Oh, very well, thank you, Doc, very well.'

'Are you finding life in Lalolagi a little too isolated?'

'Oh no, I love it here, Doc,' Karl replied. 'This place is a real paradise. It has most of the trappings of modern-day life, yet the pace of life is slow. I just love it.'

'I'm pleased to hear it, Karl. What about the teaching?'

'It's been a challenge, but it has also been fun. Why do you ask? Is there a problem?'

'Well...' Tuisamoa Solomona was hesitant. He did not want to offend such a gentle, intelligent and enthusiastic young man. 'I don't really know how to put it, Karl. Let's just say that there's a slight problem.'

'Oh, I see.' Karl began to feel rather anxious. He had loved this new posting and wanted to stay as long as possible. He hoped he hadn't offended anyone unintentionally.

'Yes,' continued Tuisamoa Solomona as he sipped his coffee. 'Some of the parents are upset that you're teaching their children that human beings evolved from monkeys.'

'We're doing a unit on evolution, Doc,' Karl said matter-of-factly.

'Yes, I know, Karl.' Tuisamoa Solomona tried to sound reassuring. 'That is exactly what I told the parents tonight.'

'You mean you've had a meeting with the parents tonight?'

'I've just come from there. I felt that I had to nip the problem in the bud before it gets out of control, which could land both of us in an awkward situation.'

'I see. Were the parents very upset?'

'Well, some probably were, but it's a little difficult to tell. You realise that Samoa embraces a mixture of traditional beliefs and Christianity. People here believe that God created everything in the manner set out in the Bible. There are no monkeys in Samoa, and humanity, as some will tell you, started right here in this village. Most people of Lalolagi have no other knowledge, so we are dealing here with a potentially problematic situation.'

'So, should I stop teaching evolution then?'

'Well, no, but perhaps the manner of teaching it may need to be modified.'

'What do you mean, Doc?'

'It's my impression that you're teaching evolution as a fact. I know many scientists struggle to separate theories from facts, but your students should know that evolution is only a hypothesis, a scientific explanation of how things might have happened. It's when you start referring to monkeys as our ancestors that you upset people, because you are then presenting evolution as fact rather than theory.'

'I see. I'm sorry, Doc. I was just trying to make it a bit more interesting. I didn't realise I was upsetting everyone.'

'I know that, Karl, and I commend you for your efforts. While it may be fine to say such things in New York, they won't impress anyone in Lalolagi, I'm afraid.'

Karl nodded slowly. 'I'll take note of that, Doc.'

'Anyway, we resolved at our meeting tonight to also offer religious studies, where Tenari will teach topics such as creation, to provide the needed balance.'

'Won't that confuse the students?'

'It shouldn't if the teachers are good, and I believe both you and Tenari are excellent teachers. The secret is to remain objective. Let the students decide for themselves. They'll be able to do that once they have the skills to analyse and understand the available information. Our short-term goal is for them to pass their examinations.'

'I'll try to teach it that way, Doc. I think I've made the mistake of being overly enthusiastic at the start of my teaching career.'

'That's not a bad way to be, Karl,' he smiled. 'But, tell me, do you really believe in evolution?'

'Well, as you said, Doc, it's a scientific explanation. It seems fairly logical to me, but I guess I don't really know.

Sometimes I have my doubts. There are bits that don't make sense to me. What about you, Doc? What do you believe?'

Sipping his coffee, Tuisamoa Solomona smiled. Karl was starting to relax as the conversation became a little more esoteric.

'Well, you know I'm an economist, Karl, and an economist's answer to questions like that is: it depends.'

'Come on, Doc. You must have a view on these things. You've read widely and studied many subjects seriously, including science.'

'Well, let's say that I believe in both. Will that satisfy you?'

'But how can you believe in two ideas that seem to oppose one another?'

'Well, they don't really. But before I get to that, let me say that Darwin was not the first person to propose that humans could have evolved from another species. The legends of many peoples trace their ancestors to animals, trees, birds, fish and other such things. In Samoa, we have the story of an octopus with a famous human son, but I think the most famous story of all is Sumeria's Gilgamesh epic. It tells the tale of a man-like ape named Enkidu becoming human while having sexual intercourse with a certain Shamat for six days and seven nights —'

'They had sex for six days and seven nights?' Karl laughed incredulously.

'So the story goes. Enkidu was certainly not human!' They both burst out laughing before Tuisamoa Solomona could continue. 'Anyway, those legends show that the idea of evolution must be as old as the first humans, and that's probably where Darwin initially got his idea. Coming back to your question, the so-called creation–evolution debate should not have occurred at all.'

'Why not?'

'Well, for a start, the theory of evolution is not a scientific theory at all. It has been masquerading as such, but it's simply a philosophy of biodiversity, or of biology if you like. Creation is a fundamental truth. Now and then, science provides a bit of detail on how it might have occurred, but science cannot dispute the fact that it did occur, or nothing would exist now. In the case of living things, the only debate is whether they were created as described in the Bible or as explained by the theory of evolution.'

'I'm sorry, Doc, but I'm a little confused.'

'Well, Darwin's theory is about the origin of each species, not the origin of life. In essence, he simply suggested that maybe we were not created as explained in the Bible, but through a long evolutionary process. The origin of life is beyond evolution. It's the atheistic evolutionists who don't like God in life's equation who are causing all the confusion. First, they jump at Arrhenius's suggestion that life may have come from other planets, without asking how that life came into being in the first place. Then they make the bizarre suggestion that non-living matter may have randomly combined to form highly complex living organisms. Not only is that bad science, but it's also utter nonsense. It makes the theory of spontaneous generation look absolutely brilliant. Lifeless matter suddenly developing self-consciousness? That's how silly some scientists have become. You'd have a better chance of reeling in a shark in your bathtub! You'd need power and intelligence we cannot even fathom to transform freely existing non-living elements into living cells, let alone complex living creatures.'

'That's one of the things I have difficulty accepting. Sorry for interrupting you, Doc. Please go on.'

'I was just going to say that you can't exclude God from the process of evolution that eventually led to the existence of human beings, if that indeed is what happened.'

'What do you mean?'

'Well, the principle of causality says there is no effect without a cause, and the effect cannot be greater than its cause. Thus, it's inconceivable that a single-celled animal can will itself to change, as some evolutionists have suggested, over millions of years, to become complex beings like elephants, or complex and self-conscious beings like humans, unless a far superior cause was involved.'

'What about the environment in which the organism lives? Nature, if you like?'

'Ah, now you're talking like a scientist, Karl. You see, science can't bring itself to using the word God, so it refers to Mother Nature instead. But you have to ask yourself, what causes the environment and all the other elements?'

'I suppose that's a fair suggestion. Anyway, in terms of our existence, which concept do you support? The biblical or the Darwinian concept?'

'One thing we can be sure of, Karl, is that we will never be able to correctly answer that question. Both ideas are highly plausible, but unfortunately neither can be experimentally verified. So they will forever remain in the realm of conjecture. The Darwinian concept has some appeal, but there are questions that I've been unable to answer satisfactorily.'

'For instance?'

'Well, why didn't all monkeys become human at the point when the theory of evolution says the change occurred? Also, as evolution is largely a function of time according to the theory, we should still be observing new species emerging. However, this is not the case. No monkey has become human recently, no fish has emerged from a coconut tree, or anything like that. Only evolution within a species seems to be continuing. Why? It doesn't make sense, but science doesn't offer a satisfactory answer.'

'So you support the biblical version of events, do you, Doc?'

'I'm happy with the biblical version of the creation of living things, Karl. It's not impossible that different species were created as described in the Bible, then evolved as dictated by their environment and the limitations imposed by their respective genetic make-up. We can use the concept of creative evolution, which the French philosopher Henri Bergson proposed, to describe it. Creative, because the process of creation continues, or there would be no new life. Evolution, because each species continues to change. The Darwinian suggestion that one species evolved to form another species is purely speculative.'

'But don't you think the information from embryology, anatomy, palaeontology, genetics, molecular biology and other sciences supports Darwin's theory?'

'It also supports the biblical version. The same data point to a common architect and builder, given the similarity in design, material and structure of living things.'

'But there's a time frame in Darwin's theory, Doc, which says humans were the last to have evolved.'

'Ah, the time frame... Well, once again, Karl, that same data also support the biblical version. In case you've forgotten, the Bible's account also has a time frame, albeit of one week. The sequence of events in that week is almost exactly the same as in the theory of evolution, where humans were also the last to develop. The one-week time frame no doubt indicates the power of God, but it could very well have been a very long period, as the palaeontologic data seem to suggest.'

Karl started to say something, then paused. 'Is it possible that the Bible and Darwin could've been talking about the same process?'

Tuisamoa Solomona smiled at the probing question. 'As I said, Karl, they differ only in the details.'

Karl nodded pensively. 'Yes, yes, your exposition is very sound, Doc. But if God created, say, the universe and everything in it, then who created God?'

'Ah, you're in pretty good company now, Karl, because Bertrand Russell, and I'm not saying your morality and sexuality are anything like his,' he laughed, 'was also troubled by that question as he pondered Saint Thomas Aquinas's answer to it almost 800 years ago.'

'And what was Thomas Aquinas's answer?'

'Well, essentially that it was not possible for God to be created if He were the First Efficient Cause. Russell argued that the First Cause must itself have a cause. It sounds logical, but he was too preoccupied with fighting the church, so his mind was probably prejudiced. He might have thought otherwise had he used Kant's principle of pure reason, or his abundant mathematical skills. If you think about it, Karl, ultimately there must have been a beginning, an ultimate efficient first cause as

Saint Thomas Aquinas called it. Science will not find it because the truth is beyond its realm, but there has to be, Karl, there has to be, or there'd be no *pisupo*, my friend!'

Karl nodded slowly. 'There's so much we still don't know, eh Doc?'

'There is, Karl, and much will remain unknown, no matter what the state of our scientific knowledge and technology may be, because to know all would be to know God's mind. And trying to achieve that would be like Saint Augustine's little boy on the beach trying to scoop the ocean into his small puddle on the seashore — it can't be done. Those who have dared have found themselves being wasted away, if not driven mad. It'd be like looking at the sun unaided — it would blind you. Anyway, it's getting late, and Helen is probably wondering where I am, so I'd better get going.'

'Well, Doc, it's been a very interesting conversation. I'll try to be more aware in future of local sensitivities and beliefs in the way I teach.'

'Thanks, Karl. And thanks for the coffee too — it was great. No wonder my friend Erdös says the purpose of mathematics is to count coffee beans,' he smiled.

Opening the door to leave, Tuisamoa Solomona turned to face Karl. 'Just for the sake of curiosity, Karl, suppose our friend Darwin was right after all. Who would have been the first to develop? A man, or a woman?'

Karl laughed. 'I really couldn't say, Doc.'

'Ah, you see, Karl,' he chuckled, 'the biblical version is again superior because it offers an unambiguous answer to that question. In fact, it has two. One is the macho version with Eve being created from Adam's rib. I think the evolutionists would like that one. The other is the same as our village's story of creation by God Tagaloalagi and his wife, 'Ele'ele — I think that's the more sensible one.'

'Don't you think that God doesn't always seem to make sense, Doc?'

'Oh, yes, He does, Karl, always,' he smiled. 'It's the limited and confused human mind that doesn't make sense of it most of the time.'

Tuisamoa Solomona said goodnight and walked to his car in a pensive mood. He had thoroughly enjoyed his conversation with Karl. He realised that, in the last few years, there had been limited opportunities for such stimulating discussions about his special areas of interest. He sighed. Looking up, he silently gave thanks for the goodness and generosity of those he was privileged to be amongst.

Thirty Nine

The village produce store in Apia opened at the end of June in the fourth year of Lalolagi's development program. As originally planned, Helen managed the store until they could train someone to take over from her. She was initially assisted by three young women and three young men from the village. Jocelyn was employed as a bookkeeper–accountant for all the operations in Lalolagi. Her office, in the same building, became the main office for the village's development program. The Tuisamoa children stayed in Apia with Helen, so Alofa accompanied them to provide babysitting assistance. They stayed at the Tuisamoas' residence together with Albert, Andreana, Fetuao and Alan, who were all employed in the public service. On weekends, they would all return to Lalolagi, leaving Onosa'i and Sofia at the house in Apia.

On New Year's Eve, six months after the store opened, close friends and relatives gathered in Lalolagi to celebrate Helen and Tuisamoa Solomona's fourth wedding anniversary. Their third child was due any day.

All the members of the Tuisamoa family who worked in Apia had gone home the day before, as had Jocelyn, Alofa and the children. Helen and her assistants had to wait until they closed the shop that afternoon. She knew she would not have to worry about preparations for the party. Relatives and friends were seeing to that. It was not going to be a lavish affair, just a casual get-together.

In Lalolagi, friends and family members had arrived for the holidays. Tuisamoa's half-brothers and half-sisters arrived early the previous day. They were all staying at the house on the peninsula. Only Fili Fa'aluma had yet to arrive. He was on duty, and would not join them until New Year's Day. Everyone was in a party mood. They talked, reminisced, laughed and played games. The swimming pool was a popular focal point for the visitors.

Helen and her assistants were expected back in the village around 4.30 pm, but by 5.30, there was still no sign of them. Tuisamoa Solomona started to worry. A short while later, while he was playing with the children in the garden, he heard his name being called. He saw two boys running towards the house, waving.

Sensing something was wrong, he sent the children inside and hurried to meet the boys. 'What is it, boys?' he inquired anxiously.

'It's Helen, your Lordship,' they panted, trying to catch their breath.

'Helen? What about her?'

'She's had an accident... near the second river, your Lordship.'

'Oh, my God, no!'

Panicking momentarily, Tuisamoa's mind went blank. The colour drained from his face and he felt close to fainting.

Quickly regaining his composure, he rushed into the house and mobilised family and friends to help.

'Ula,' he ordered Apaula, 'get the first-aid kit and come with me. Pati, Legi and Al, we might need you to help, too. It's getting dark, so bring some lamps. Get the bus, get some more help, and follow me.'

When they arrived at the scene of the accident, they found the village truck, which Helen used for the store, perched precariously against a huge chestnut tree, almost 20 metres below the roadway. It was only a short distance from the edge of a waterfall with a vertical drop of another 20 metres to boulders below. Helen's three male assistants had been thrown from the back of the truck and did not seem to have suffered any serious injuries. They had been able to clamber back up the slope and were sitting, dazed, by the roadside. Helen and the three female assistants were still trapped inside the cabin of the truck.

Apaula attended to the injured men while Tuisamoa Solomona and the others desperately tried to free Helen and the other women. They realised that they had to be extremely careful. If they rocked the truck too hard, it could slide past the chestnut tree and plunge to the rocks below. They knew they could not get anyone out until the truck was on more solid ground. So they determined to move the truck onto the flat river bed just to the left of where it was perched.

Soon afterwards, a bus arrived, filled with men from the village, some carrying gas lamps. Alvin followed in one of the village trucks with some heavy tools that he thought might be useful.

The men worked quickly to build a bridge from the truck to the river bed near the top of the waterfall. Using ropes, they slowly slid the truck to the safety of the river bed. The doors were jammed, so Alvin used his equipment to hack them off. Finally, they were able to remove Helen and the other women from the wreck. They had all sustained major injuries, with Helen being the most seriously affected. She had lost a lot of blood and was unconscious. Apaula did the best she could with the limited resources of the first-aid kit.

While trying to stabilise her condition, she noticed Helen had regained consciousness, but seemed not to recognise her. 'What's happened?' she asked in a weak voice.

'You've had an accident. Your truck ran off the road. How are you feeling?' Apaula tried desperately to keep her awake. In her weakened state Helen was mouthing words that were barely audible.

'What is it, Helen?' she asked, bending down to place her ear close to Helen's face.

'Are the others all right?' she whispered.

Tuisamoa Solomona, who was now kneeling beside her, asked hurriedly: 'What did she say?'

'She's asking if the others are all right,' Apaula replied.

'They're fine, sweetheart,' he said, gently squeezing her hand. Helen didn't respond. 'Ula, I think we need to get her to hospital, right away,' he continued urgently, motioning to Alvin, Alan, Albert and some other men to help him lift Helen into the bus.

The other three women were already seated inside Tuisamoa Solomona's truck, ready for the trip to hospital. Helen opened her eyes and tried to smile.

'You're here, honey,' she whispered weakly.

'Don't try to speak, sweetheart. Try to conserve your energy.'

Settling Helen on blankets in the aisle of the bus, Tuisamoa Solomona asked Albert to drive while he and Apaula saw to their patient.

Albert drove as fast and as carefully as he could, trying not to jar the bus unnecessarily. Alvin followed close behind in Tuisamoa Solomona's truck, with Alan driving the family truck. Both trucks were filled with anxious villagers. Tuisamoa couldn't help noticing how ghostly pale Helen had become. He knew that Apaula had done all she could, and it was now a matter of getting Helen to the hospital as quickly as possible.

'I'm so cold,' Helen whispered weakly. 'Are you there, honey?'

'Yes, I'm here, sweetheart,' he replied covering her with more *lavalavas*. Apaula encouraged him to keep talking to Helen to try to ensure she stayed awake. 'Just hang in there, darling,' he urged. The progress of the bus seemed to be far too slow, but he knew that Albert was doing his best. 'I wish we could go faster!' he whispered, feeling completely helpless.

Helen looked at him intently. 'Am I that bad?' she asked anxiously.

'You'll be all right, sweetheart,' he desperately tried to sound convincing.

'I love you, honey,' she whispered softly.

'I love you, too, sweetheart.'

By the time they arrived at the hospital, Helen's condition was extremely serious. They had been unable to stop her from lapsing into unconsciousness towards the end of the trip. Helen was rushed into the Emergency Unit with Tuisamoa Solomona by her side, urging her to hold on. Medical staff worked feverishly to stabilise her condition. By now, Helen seemed to be oblivious to her husband's presence.

Dr Fa'aluma, who was working in the Paediatric Unit, heard about Helen's accident and quickly came to offer help. He led Tuisamoa Solomona into the waiting room and tried to comfort his friend. Despite the best efforts of the medical staff, Helen's condition deteriorated.

At 10.30 that night, the senior surgeon came into the waiting room. The look on his face was not encouraging.

'How's she doing, doctor?' asked Tuisamoa Solomona, his voice cracking.

The surgeon hesitated. 'I think we are losing her, your Lordship. We've done everything we can, but she'd lost too much blood by the time she got here, and her injuries, especially to her vital organs, are very severe.' Tuisamoa Solomona stood motionless, staring at the floor. He did not speak. Dr Fa'aluma placed his hand on his friend's shoulder, consoling him. 'We need to make some difficult decisions, your Lordship,' the surgeon continued tentatively. 'Perhaps we should at least try to save the child.'

Tuisamoa Solomona stood in stunned silence. Fili tried unsuccessfully to get him to respond. A nurse came out to fetch the surgeon. Helen was slipping away, she whispered. The surgeon rushed away, leaving a bewildered Tuisamoa Solomona and Fili in the waiting room.

Just before midnight, Helen passed away. Doctors quickly operated on her and delivered a baby girl by caesarean section. In the waiting room Tuisamoa Solomona knew instinctively that he had lost his sweetheart before the surgeon appeared, bringing the devastating news.

'Your Lordship,' the surgeon said in a trembling voice, 'I'm sorry that we could not save your wife, but, look, you have a beautiful baby girl.'

Numb with grief, Tuisamoa Solomona placed his hands over his face. Insistent crying forced him to glance up at the nurse holding his baby daughter, still streaked with blood, in her arms. He tried to smile, remembering how it felt when his first two children were born, but he couldn't. He felt gutted, his throat constricted. His vision blurred as tears welled in his eyes and rolled down his cheeks. He dropped wearily to his knees, struggling for breath. For a fleeting moment, he wished he too could die, but then he thought about his children and the grand plans he and Helen had for them.

Helping him back to his feet, Fili held his friend, trying to console him. Tuisamoa Solomona pulled Fili to him and wept. After a while, a calmness seemed to descend on him. He straightened the sleeves of his shirt, then asked Dr Fa'aluma to accompany him to inform those from the village who were waiting outside.

When news of Helen's death reached Lalolagi, it was greeted with complete disbelief. Grief quickly spread; wailing women tried to come to terms with their loss. Though a foreigner, Helen had become one of their own; she had given so much to the people and their village. Even Tenari and Sekara struggled to retain their composure. They knew they had to remain strong in the face of such tragedy, but they too were fully tested. In public, they managed somehow. In private, it was almost impossible.

Helen's funeral was delayed for ten days to allow her parents time to return from Britain, where they had gone on a business trip. It also gave friends and relatives from overseas the opportunity to join in farewelling her. The village was filled to capacity, as people from throughout Samoa and elsewhere came to pay tribute to her.

Among the friends who came from overseas were twelve members of the Methodist Church Choir from Auckland, four members of the church orchestra they had played with when they were at university, and Helen's oboe instructor, Dr Davids.

The village church, despite its large capacity, was packed. Many were not able to fit inside, but were forced to stand outside listening to proceedings. Alvin, realising that the church would not accommodate everyone, wired speakers to the sound system and hung them in the trees, so that those outside could follow the service.

Despite the sea of people, the silence was incredible. The only sound was the soft melodies Albert played while everyone waited for the arrival of the Tuisamoa and Jones families. Tuisamoa Solomona had asked Albert to play some of Helen's favourite music.

The bereaved families finally arrived and took their seats at the front of the church where the coffin stood solemnly, covered and surrounded by flowers. Tuisamoa Solomona, flanked by his mother and Mrs Jones, sat in the front pew. They were joined by Mr Jones, Faye and Jocelyn, who were looking after Anwen and Tavita. Alvin, Fili Fa'aluma and members of the Tuisamoa family filled the other pews.

As Tenari began the service, Tuisamoa Solomona struggled to contain his emotions. His mother and mother-in-law each held his hand. It was especially difficult for him during the singing, when the New Zealand choir sang Rutter's heart-rending requiem *The Lord is My Shepherd*, with Dr Davids accompanying them on the oboe, and Fauré's *Cantique de Racine*. Both pieces had been among Helen's favourites. The sound of the oboe felt so heavy in his heart — it was like listening to Helen play. He could not control himself and broke down. Music had always been such an important part of their lives.

He began to fret that he would not cope sufficiently to be able to speak. Just writing the speech had been difficult enough. He fought hard to remain composed, but the pain of his loss overwhelmed him. His mother and Mrs Jones tried to comfort him.

As the service progressed, he seemed to find an inner strength and calm. When Tenari called on him to give the eulogy, he strode confidently to the lectern. Turning towards the congregation, he saw so many loving and sympathetic faces. He kept reminding himself to stay strong. Tavita, who had been trying to break free of Faye's grip, ran up to his father. Faye made an attempt to retrieve the child.

'It's all right, Faye,' Tuisamoa Solomona said, with a smile. 'He doesn't know what he is getting himself into. Now, he will be the one to give the speech.'

The congregation laughed half-heartedly, but silence quickly resumed.

Tavita grabbed his father's hand and looked up at him with a grin. Tuisamoa Solomona raised his finger to his lips and signalled to him to be quiet. He then picked him up and sat him behind the lectern. He whispered to the child to stay still and keep quiet because he was going to say something important to everyone. Tavita slumped back into the chair. Tuisamoa Solomona thanked him for behaving himself, then returned to the lectern.

He began by acknowledging and thanking the dignitaries, the same ones who had attended his father's funeral, and everyone else who had come. He briefly recalled his wedding day. 'Just over four years ago, many of you were in the smaller church at the previous village site to celebrate our wedding. And here you are again, in this new and marvellous church, because death has tragically ended our marriage. Dearly beloved, Helen is no longer with us. Her body is in the coffin before us, but she is now with God. I have no doubt about that, and we should rejoice for her. It is where she would want to be. Before I conclude, dearly beloved, allow me to pay tribute to the woman who has meant everything to me.'

Tuisamoa Solomona struggled to fight back tears. He reached for a handkerchief and wiped his eyes, then continued haltingly, 'Helen was an extraordinary person, and a loving and wonderful wife. She had all the qualities that King Solomon worshipped in a woman. She was beautiful, both physically and within her heart. She was highly intelligent, full of compassion, and very understanding. She was a loving and caring mother to our children, and I am sure my parents-in-law will tell you that she has also been a wonderful daughter. But the one quality that I admired most in her was her selflessness, her generosity. She gave her time, her talents, her money, and anything she had so others may know that God lives. As if to prove a point, even death did not stop her from giving. Her last gift for me,' he added, his voice cracking, 'was a beautiful little daughter, delivered after life had departed from her. Anastasia Victoria is still in the hospital. She doesn't know anything yet. But when she grows up, I will see to it that she knows why she lives. Thank you for your love and support for our children, our two families and myself. May God bless you and keep you all. In Christ Jesus, I thank you.'

As Tuisamoa Solomona picked up Tavita, who had fallen asleep, and returned to his seat, a group of three young men from the village, with twelve-string guitars, played and sang a Samoan song, *Blessed are Those Who Die in the Lord*. Tuisamoa Solomona wept as he listened to the young men's stirring music and the sweet harmony of their voices. But when, after the benediction, he heard the sound of the trumpet, as the New Zealand orchestra played *Going Home*, from Dvorak's *New World Symphony*, he completely broke down and sobbed uncontrollably. His mother and Helen's mother tried their best to comfort him.

After the service, twelve young men from the village choir carried the coffin in a long procession to the Tuisamoa family cemetery where Helen was buried near the mausoleum. A shelter would later be erected over the grave.

After the interment, Tuisamoa Solomona, with Alofa on one side and Helen's mother on the other, turned and slowly walked back to the village. He looked towards the summit of Mount Lagi, but momentarily his vision was blurred by tears. Family members tried to cheer him up. They were all grief-stricken, but it seemed as though Tuisamoa Solomona was shouldering all their sorrow.

Forty

It was a glorious Saturday morning with brilliant sunshine. A light breeze was blowing from the sea, causing the palm trees along the shoreline to sway gracefully. Waves soundlessly washed up on the rocks below the Tuisamoas' house on the peninsula.

It was about a month since Helen had died. Tuisamoa Solomona had not slept well in all that time. The emotional strain had taken its toll on his usually abundant physical energy. He struggled to do virtually anything. He seemed distant and withdrawn, and had lost a lot of weight. He felt like crying most of the time, but it seemed that his tears were flowing internally, constantly clogging up his throat. Self-pity was overwhelming him. He knew he had to break out of it, but he did not know how. He realised that his children needed him, as did his people, but he was finding it extremely hard to carry on.

The arrival home of his baby daughter, Anastasia Victoria, from hospital earlier in the week seemed to have had a positive impact on him. He started to smile again. He was more talkative. He seemed less pent-up, more relaxed. In the last few weeks, he had been waking before 5 am each morning. But on this morning, he slept soundly, as if he had not slept in ages. It was already 7 am. Sunlight was shining through the windows brightening up the whole house, except for Tuisamoa Solomona and Helen's room where the blinds were still drawn and the room in darkness.

Mrs Jones had prepared breakfast, and was listening to classical music on the radio. She looked anxiously at the clock. Past 7 am, and still no sign of her son-in-law. Helen's father was outside in the garden with young Anwen. Faye was also outside occupying the ever-energetic Tavita.

'Jos,' Mrs Jones asked her daughter, who was playing with the baby in the living room, 'would you please check to see if Tui is up yet?'

'Sure, Mum,' she replied, picking up Anastasia and heading for her brother-in-law's room. Tavita came dashing past them and flung the bedroom door open, diving head-first onto the bed.

'Oh, my goodness,' Tuisamoa Solomona was startled awake by the rush of bright sunlight from the open door. 'What time is it?' he asked, as he sleepily rubbed his eyes.

'Come on, Vita,' called Faye, as Tavita buried his head underneath the sheets. 'Your Dad is still resting.'

'It's okay, Faye,' Tuisamoa assured her. 'He can stay. I'm getting up now, anyway.'

Tavita slowly lifted his head to see if Faye was still there. Smiling at Tuisamoa, he jumped at him, wrapping his arms around his father's neck.

'Hey, take it easy, young man. You could hurt someone.'

Tavita smiled, then clumsily kissed his father on the forehead.

'Hey, mate, I told you to take it easy. Why are you so aggressive this morning?'

The exuberant child just smiled at his father. Grabbing one end of the sheet, he lifted it up and looked around underneath it.

'What are you looking for, Vita?'

'Mmm... Mmm... looking for Mahmmy,' he grinned.

Tuisamoa Solomona sat up. 'Oh, I see. You're looking for your Mummy?'

'Uwhere's Mahmmy, Dahddy?'

'Well, remember I told you that Mummy has gone on a very long trip, son?'

'I... I... I wanna my mamma,' the toddler cried. 'When's Mahmmy coming back?'

'Well, Mummy won't be coming back, Vita, but one day we will all go to be with Mummy.'

'I... I... I wanna go naow.'

'You want to go now? Well, I'm afraid that's not possible.'

'U... uwhere deed Mahmmy go?'

'Mummy's gone to be with God, son.'

'Gone uwhere?'

'Mummy has gone to be with God, Vita. Remember the other day, Mummy was in a black rocket?' Tavita nodded. 'Well, Mummy flew in that rocket to where God is.'

'Ba... but... I wanna my mamma here.'

'Well, it's just not possible, son.'

'Ba... but uwhy, Dahddy?'

'Because God's country is very far away in the sky, and the rocket that Mummy took can't come back.'

'You mean far away like Staar Durek, Dahddy?'

'Well, kind of.'

'Me and Mahmmy uwatch Staar Durek a lot, and I know haow to get there. You jast say, bi... bi... bim me up Skottee, and you there. See? Let's go naow to Mahmmy. You hold Ven and Ana's hands, and I clime on yoa bahk, the... then say, bim me up Skottee, and we'll be there with Mahmmy. C'mon, Dahddy, let's go naow to Mahmmy.'

'I'm afraid it's not that easy, son,' he laughed.

'But uwhy... uwhy, Dahddy?'

'Because God is much, much farther away than Scotty, son.'

'You mean, far, far ahway, Dahddy?'

'Yeah, far, far away.'

'But, Mahmmy said Skottee can bim enuwhere.'

'Maybe anywhere except where God lives, Vita.'

'Ooh, I wanna my mamma back.'

'Me, too. I would dearly love to have Mummy back.'

'Den let's go n get Mahmmy.'

'But we can't, Vita.'

'But uwhy?'

'I've already told you why.'

'Ooh, I don' like dog; very bad dog.'

'No, no, son, it's not dog. It's God, and God is good. Anyway, come on, we'd better go and have some breakfast. Everyone must be wondering where we are.'

Tuisamoa Solomona washed and changed quickly, then carried Tavita into the kitchen.

'So how are you feeling this morning, Tui?' asked Mrs Jones.

'Oh, much better, Mum... much better, thank you,' he replied, smiling. 'It's been really hard. But Ana's arrival this week has certainly given me back some energy. And Vita... well, he said some really funny things just now.'

'He is so full of energy, aren't you, young man?' Mr Jones patted Tavita's head. 'He's a typical two-year-old; always on a high.'

Tavita grinned and looked around at everyone.

'It was really funny,' Tuisamoa Solomona smiled. 'He said that we can go to his Mummy by just asking Scotty in *Star Trek* to beam us up.' He laughed, but just as quickly tears filled his eyes.

The others didn't know what to say. They knew that his pain was still raw, and were unsure of how to deal with it.

'Ba... but I saw it, Dahddy,' protested Tavita.

'You've been watching too much television in Apia, young man,' his father said sternly, then laughed.

'I have a suggestion to make,' declared Mr Jones. 'Why don't you and the children come with us for a short break to New Zealand? What do you say, Tui?'

The suggestion caught Tuisamoa Solomona by surprise. He immediately thought about his responsibilities in the village. Looking around the room, his gaze was attracted by light reflecting off glass covering a poem titled *Don't Quit*. 'Rest if you must...' he recited to himself words from the poem. 'Yeah, it would be nice to have a short break, but who would look after things while I'm away?' he wondered to himself.

'Well, I hadn't thought about it before, Dad, but it's probably not a bad idea,' he replied. 'I'll go and talk to some people after breakfast, and see if I can take a couple of weeks off.'

After eating, Tuisamoa Solomona went to the village and consulted Tenari and some of the *matais*. He felt that it might also be a good opportunity to give others the chance to run the business side of the village's development projects. Tenari agreed he would take charge with the assistance of the *matais*.

Tuisamoa Solomona returned home and excitedly told his parents-in-law that he could take three weeks off.

Forty One

After a relaxing stay in New Zealand, Tuisamoa Solomona and the children arrived back in the village late one Friday afternoon. Helen's mother did not return with them to look after the baby, as she had with the other two children. Tuisamoa Solomona assured her that Alofa would be able to care for the children, but that she should visit whenever she wanted to see her grandchildren. There was never a shortage of babysitters, with so many women in the village more than willing to look after the children. The first thing he did when he arrived back was to visit Helen's grave.

That night, there was the usual welcoming celebration in the Tuisamoa's *faleafolau*. It was attended by the whole village as well as the Tuisamoa family. As usual, the evening routine started with devotions, led by Tenari, then dinner followed. Afterwards Tuisamoa Solomona presented some gifts of material and clothing he had brought from New Zealand to thank the village for their prayers while he was away. He also presented *lafos* to Tenari and his wife, the *matais*, their wives, the *aumaga* and the *aualuma*. After the distribution of gifts and *lafo*, the gathering dispersed.

'What's the program for tomorrow, Nari?' asked Tuisamoa Solomona as he and Tenari walked to his truck.

'We're having a village cricket game instead of going to Apia,' replied Tenari. 'It's West versus East. You will lead East, and I will captain West.'

'And the prize?' smiled Tuisamoa as he handed the baby to Alofa who was waiting in the truck with Faye and Jocelyn.

'Refreshments for next Saturday's game.'

'I suppose you've prepared for that already, haven't you?' he asked, as he slid into the driver's seat.

'We shall see, Tui,' Tenari replied. 'Game time is 9 am. See you tomorrow at the pitch.'

As Tuisamoa Solomona started the engine, Albert and the rest of the Tuisamoa family came out to say goodnight.

'Are you going anywhere tomorrow morning before the game, Tui?' Albert asked his brother.

'No, I don't think so. Why?'

'Oh, nothing really,' Albert replied. 'We'll see you tomorrow then. Don't forget to bring your *palagi* cricket bat, Alvin.'

Everyone shouted and waved goodnight as the truck pulled away heading for the peninsula.

When they arrived home, Alofa excused herself and went straight to her room with the baby. Alvin boiled some water for coffee while Faye put Anwen to bed.

'You can put Vita on my bed, Jos,' Tuisamoa Solomona called to his sister-in-law. 'He'll be sleeping with me.'

'I think I'll pass on the coffee tonight, Al, if you don't mind,' he continued. 'I'm a bit tired, and I'd like to get an early night. But can I see you all tomorrow morning, say, before sunrise? Maybe we can have a sort of sunrise service outside in the courtyard.'

Unsure of what he had in mind, or why, Alvin, Faye and Jocelyn agreed anyway.

'Sure, Tui. Sounds good,' Alvin responded.

Next morning Tuisamoa Solomona woke early. It was still dark. The morning star was shining brightly low in the sky, and rays of light were just starting to appear over the horizon. He could hear the faint echo of roosters crowing in the village. He gently got out of bed and covered Tavita, who was still fast asleep. After washing his face and dressing quickly, he picked up his Bible, classical guitar, some song sheets, a torch and a blanket, then went outside into the courtyard. It was a cool morning, with a light breeze blowing across the peninsula. It was quiet except for the rumbling of the open sea and the waves washing up on the rocks below. He sat down and set about tuning his guitar. Strumming quietly, he started to softly sing some favourite songs. Shortly afterwards, Alvin stumbled out of the house, wrapped in a sheet.

'Morning, Tui,' he greeted, rubbing his eyes.

The two of them continued to sing as the sun began to rise. A while later, Faye and Jocelyn joined them. They sat together singing for about half an hour. Then Tuisamoa Solomona opened his Bible and gave a short reading. He looked as though he wanted to share something with the other three.

'There are a few things I want to talk to you about,' he began, 'and I thought a sunrise service on my first morning back would be a good time to share my thoughts with you. First, though, thank you for getting up so early. I also want to thank you for helping Tenari and the *matais* to keep things going while I was away. More importantly, though, I want to discuss the future.' Looking pensive, he paused for a moment. 'I've been thinking while I was away that, with Helen gone...,' he struggled to fight off tears, as a wave of grief overtook him.

'I'm sorry, guys,' he apologised, wiping his eyes, 'sadness just rushes back every time I think or talk about her. Anyway, with Helen no longer here, I suppose the bond that has held us together is no longer there, or at least is not as strong as it used to be. What I'm trying to say is that I don't want you to feel obligated to stay. This will always be your home, but you have your own lives to pursue, and your future is still ahead of you. The village projects are progressing well, people have learnt the necessary skills, and we should now be able to be more self-sufficient. Everyone who was studying overseas is now back, including Ula, Owen and Mele. Even though they are all employed in the public service in Apia, I can always call on them in their spare time. Mum will look after the children; she is more than happy to do that. So I'd like you three to feel free to do whatever you like. If you feel you want to stay, by all means do so. If you feel you want to move on, then please do. I really enjoy having you around but, as I said, you have your own lives to live.'

Alvin looked at the others. They seemed uncertain as to who should respond first. Finally, Faye spoke.

'Thank you, Tui, for sharing your thoughts with us,' she said. 'We've been discussing this while you were in New Zealand. Helen may have gone, but life must go on. Memories of her will always be with us; her presence is all around us. We want you to know that we have all decided to stay here. The decision has been easy for me because this is home, but Al and Jos also want to stay. The children will need their aunt and uncle from their mother's side. And we think we can all live happily together here.'

'Yes, Tui,' Alvin added, 'people are predicting the end of the world soon — it was supposed to happen at the end of the millennium. It would be nice to be close to heaven when it does come,' he smiled, looking towards Mount Lagi. They all laughed.

'Tui, Helen's sudden death was a huge blow to all of us,' admitted Jocelyn, 'but life here hasn't changed. I want to stay on here too. There is so much still to do — I want to see the projects we have started bring self-sufficiency and prosperity to Lalolagi.'

'Well, thank you very much, guys,' he smiled. 'That will certainly make life a lot easier for me, and I'm sure for the children too. Anyway, Al, Nostradamus did predict that some catastrophic events would occur around the end of the millennium. But so far that hasn't happened. Given the success he has had with predicting future events, and the signs the Bible says would signify Jesus' promised return and the end of the world, maybe that time is just around the corner. Who knows? But yes, it would be nice to be close to heaven when it does happen. But it's even better to be in heaven already, and that's one of the promises in the Bible, in John 3:16. It's true, and anyone can experience it. Come on, let's sing a few songs, then we can end with a prayer. Anyone who wants to pray should do so.'

Tuisamoa Solomona started strumming his guitar. They sang *Morning has Broken; You'll Never Walk Alone; No Man is an*

Island and then ended with *To Dream the Impossible Dream*. After singing together and ending with a prayer, they all embraced one another.

'I'll get breakfast organised, while you guys get ready for the cricket match, if you like,' Tuisamoa Solomona offered.

'Oh no, Tui. We'll do that,' Faye insisted.

'In that case,' he replied, 'I'll just go over to visit Helen's grave. I'll be back as soon as I can.'

As the four of them started to go inside, they heard singing coming from the direction of the village. Curious as to where the noise was coming from, they strained to see who it could be. Albert's truck came into view, heading towards the house. With him were Andreana, Fetuao, Mele and Apaula, with Alan, Nathan and Owen sitting in the back. Still singing, they stopped close to the house, waking Alofa and the children. Tuisamoa Solomona and the others walked over to greet the visitors.

'So what's all the noise about, you guys, so early in the morning?' Tuisamoa Solomona asked, as Alofa stumbled outside, with Tavita and Anwen following close behind.

'Well,' said Albert, smiling, 'we are here, your Lordship, to tell you that all of us, except for Ula, have resigned from the public service to set ourselves up in private practice. Only poor Ula can't do that yet because she has just started to pay back her bond. We felt that, by being self-employed, it would make it easier to help with the village projects. Those who can work in the village will do so. Owen has agreed to build the wharf you wanted at the bay. We have also all agreed to contribute to a scholarship fund in Helen's name at our alma mater. So that's why we are being so noisy at this hour of the morning.'

'That's a lovely surprise, Pati,' smiled Tuisamoa Solomona. 'Thank you everyone for your thoughtfulness. Look, Faye and Jos were just about to prepare breakfast. Maybe you would all like to join them. I'll be back shortly, and we'll talk some more then before we go to the game.'

'I wanna come with you, Daddy,' Anwen whined.

'Me too, Dahddy,' cried Tavita.

Tuisamoa Solomona smiled as he patted Anwen's cheek and ruffled Tavita's hair. He looked questioningly at his mother who nodded for him to take the children.

'Okay, you two, ask grandma to put on your shoes and some warm clothes.'

Everyone went inside. The women piled into the kitchen and helped to prepare breakfast, while the men sat around the living room, playing the guitar and singing traditional songs. Hearing Anastasia crying upstairs, Tuisamoa Solomona went to check on her while Alofa changed the other two children. He found his daughter fascinated by the mobile hanging above her cot.

'Good morning, Ana,' he smiled tenderly at her, as he reached down and pinched her rosy cheeks. She kicked excitedly as her father picked her up. 'Do you want to come with Daddy too?'

He changed her, then carried her into the living room. The other two children were dressed, ready to go.

'Are you taking Ana as well?' his mother asked.

'Yes, I guess she doesn't want to miss out. She could do with a little fresh air. Anyway we won't be away long.'

Tuisamoa Solomona fastened the children into their seats in the truck, then drove to the village. He put Anastasia into a baby harness, then, holding the other two children by the hand, walked up the hill to the Tuisamoa family cemetery.

While the older children played, Tuisamoa Solomona picked a flower from the cemetery garden and gently placed it on Helen's grave. Her photograph smiled back at him from the headstone. He held Anastasia so she could face her mother's photograph.

'Well, Ana,' he whispered, 'say hi to your mummy.'

Looking at Helen's smiling face brought tears to his eyes. Wiping them away with his sleeve, he smiled and gently stroked his daughter.

'Well, HR,' he whispered softly, 'you sleep well, my love. 'Til we meet again, forever in paradise.'

Tuisamoa Solomona touched his fingers to his lips, then gently touched Helen's photograph. He rose to his feet, and turned to where Anwen and Tavita were playing.

'Come on, you two,' he called out, 'let's go home now. Ana is hungry, and grandma will be waiting with breakfast ready.'

They ran to their father, shouting and giggling. Tavita held on to his father's leg while Anwen grabbed his right hand. Together they walked back to the truck singing songs the children had learnt at Sunday School.

Glossary

aiga	1: family, either nuclear or extended; 2: related; 3: home
ali'i	1: chief; 2: lord; 3: gentleman; 4: polite word for man or boy
ali'isili	high chief
Aotearoa	the pre-European name of New Zealand, preferred by Polynesians
asiga	1: gift of food given to visitors; 2: a visit
aualuma	young women, or daughters, of a village who have normally finished school
aumaga	group of untitled men in a village
'ava	1: shrubby pepper (*Piper methysticum*); 2: a beverage made by mixing water and crushed roots of the *'ava*
'ava o le nofo	collection of sun-dried *'ava* that the family of a candidate for a *matai* title gives to invited *matais* during the installation ceremony
'ava usu a Samoa	collection of sun-dried *'ava* that *matais* invited to a *matai* title installation ceremony give to the family of the *matai* candidate
fale	house
faleafolau	a large oval-shaped house, usually used as the dwelling of a *matai*
faleo'o	a small oval-shaped house, usually used as the dwelling of other members of a family
falepalagi	a western-style house

faletele	a large circular-shaped house with a conical roof, used mainly as a guest house
fau	hibiscus tree
feagaiga	1: covenant; 2: pastor; 3: minister
fiafia	1: entertainment; 2: joy; 3: enjoy; 4: be happy
ietoga	a fine mat made from narrow strips of pandanus leaves, a treasured commodity in Samoan culture
ifoga	formal or public apology
koko	hot beverage made from cocoa beans
lafo	gift of money or fine mats
lagi	1: sky; 2: heaven
lavalava	1: wrap-around; 2: clothes
malae	1: open space in the middle of a village; 2: village green
malaga	1: ceremonial visit; 2: journey; 3: trip; 4: travel
masiofo	1: wife of the paramount chief; 2: queen
matai	1: titled family head; 2: chief
niu	1: green coconut; 2: coconut tree.
oso	1: travellers' gift to host; 2: provision for a journey; 3: jump; 4: dash; 5: hop; 6: rush
pa	1: explode; 2: burst
pakeha	New Zealand Maori word for white person
palagi	1: white person; 2: thing pertaining to western culture
palusami	polite word for a Samoan delicacy *lu'au*, made from taro leaves and salted coconut cream
papalagi	plural for white person
pisupo	canned corned beef

Glossary

Pohutukawa	a New Zealand tree that blooms, with vivid red colour, at Christmas time
pulenu'u	village mayor
puletasi	woman's two-piece attire consisting of a top and a *lavalava*, both of the same material
saofa'i	installation ceremony of a *matai* title
sua	1: chief's daily meal; 2: presentation of a special gift of food
tanoa	bowl
tapa	1: cloth made from bark of paper mulberry, usually decorated with geometric patterns; 2: clothes with such geometric patterns
taro	starchy tuber *Colocasia esculenta*, which forms the staple of the Samoan people's diet
tatau	1: male tattoo from knee area to waistline; 2: proper
taulaitu	1: spirit medium; 2: spirit priest
taule'ale'a	an untitled man
taulele'a	men who do not hold chiefly titles and who serve the chiefs or *matais*
taupou	daughter of the high chief
to'ona'i	Sunday lunch
tugase	dried *'ava* root with stem intact
tulafale	orator
tulafaleali'i	a *matai* whose title is both an orator and a chief
tulafalesili	highest-ranked orator in a village
umu	1: stone oven; 2: food cooked in stone oven; 3: a structure that houses the stone oven.
usu	a formal call to important visitors to a village